OUT OF
TUPELO

OUT OF TUPELO

MARK GILLEO

PRESS

ALSO BY MARK GILLEO

- Terminal Secret
- Favors and Lies
- Love Thy Neighbor
- Sweat

2020 Press, LLC.

Copyright © 2018 by Mark Gilleo

Visit the author's website at www.markgilleo.com

ISBN: 978-0-9990472-2-4

ISBN: 978-0-9990472-3-1 (ebook)

First trade edition: September 2018

10 9 8 7 6 5 4 3 2

Cover photograph provided by Michael Mees @ www.michael-mees.photography

ACKNOWLEDGEMENTS

I WOULD LIKE to thank the following people for their input and/or editing assistance: Dave Allen, Chris (Coach) Barker, Tim Davis, David Dutil, Emma Edmunds, Diana Ellis, Sue Fine, Scott Forrest, Joel Frost, Michele Gates, Jeffrey B. Krieg, Carroll Reed and Sheridan Snedden. Without your help, I wouldn't have gotten this one out the door. I would also like to extend gratitude to my editor, Nora Tamada.

Last but not least, I would like to thank my wife, Ivette, for all of her support.

CHAPTER 1

THE DREAMS ALWAYS ended the same. The only variation was the delivery of the pain. Hot flames licking the edge of the bed, singeing his skin. Fire lapping at the windows and doors, preventing escape. In the last month alone, he had found himself trapped in a burning theatre and baked in a subway car engulfed in searing heat.

Tonight, fire had rained from the sky in a hailstorm of torches, burning through his clothes as he ran, searching for shelter. A choking breath snapped Edward back to consciousness as he sat up in bed and his eyes thrust open. He gasped. Perspiration covered his body. His hand searched for the switch on his bedside table and light stretched across his side of the room. He checked the time on the small clock next to the light, the digital display hidden behind a jar of skin moisturizer and a bottle of water.

Edward's wife, Holly, rolled over, her hand landing gently on his sweaty arm.

"Are you all right?" she asked, her words slurred in a tired mumble.

"I will be."

Her hand moved to his abdomen and drifted towards his waist. "You want me to help put you back to sleep?" she asked, eyes still shut.

"It's late."

"Your loss," she said, removing her hand and rolling over. "Just remember I offered."

Edward took a sip of water from the bottle on the bedside table and turned off the light. He stared at the ceiling in the darkness as the minutes stretched to nearly an hour. He fought the urge to get out of bed, not wanting to wake his wife a second time.

The mobile phone buzzing on the bedside table was less considerate.

"This is Edward," he whispered into the phone as Holly rolled over and opened one eye.

"Good evening, Mr. Winston. This is the North Mississippi Medical Center. We have a couple that just arrived who need a translator. You were on the list of volunteers. Sorry to call so late."

"I was awake," Edward replied, putting his feet on the floor.

"Does that mean you're available?"

"I am."

"If you can come to the labor and delivery entrance, we would be grateful."

"I'll be there in a half hour."

*

Situated at the crossroads of intersecting highways, truck traffic near Tupelo never completely died. Even at two in the morning, a steady hum of tires rumbled across the terrain surrounding the largest city in northern Mississippi.

From Saltillo, Edward pulled onto Route 45, falling in behind a trio of eighteen-wheelers headed south, Walmart emblazoned on the side of each trailer. Fifteen minutes later Edward's eyes scanned the horizon, searching for a glimpse of the Bancorp South building. At eighty-four feet, the bank's headquarters was the tallest structure for a hundred miles in any direction. A slew of gas station signs vied for second place on the list. The lack of man-made height, and the flat-as-a-pancake geography known as Dixie Alley, made the city of Tupelo almost invisible from the highway. It wasn't until Edward headed down the exit ramp that the small downtown peeked into view.

A half mile from the highway, Edward pulled his Toyota Camry through the front entrance of the North Mississippi Medical Center. A short walk through the darkened parking lot led him to the bright lights of the hospital lobby.

The coffee stand near the entrance was closed, but the full-length mirror on the wall next to the caffeine vendor was open for business. Edward grimaced at his appearance as he passed. He had splashed water on his face and run a brush through his hair on the way out of the house. Neither hid the fact he had just rolled out of bed.

Edward approached two women in identical purple scrubs sitting at the small reception desk. Smiling, he introduced himself to the salt-and-pepper-haired woman on the left who was the first to look up at him.

"My name is Edward Winston. I was called to help translate."

"Which language?"

"Japanese."

The woman's face turned suspicious and she eyeballed Edward from head to toe, devouring the details of his thin five foot eight frame draped in rumpled clothes.

"*You* speak Japanese?" the woman asked.

"I do. Though it may not look like it."

"Well, then. Come on back," she said, standing from her chair.

Edward followed the woman through two sets of swinging doors and his escort motioned for him to grab a seat in a chair near the end of the hall. The woman disappeared around the corner and reemerged several minutes later from the opposite direction with a doctor in tow, a medical mask pulled down below his chin.

"I hear you're my translator," the doctor said, approaching Edward. A stethoscope clung perilously to the large pocket on his white coat. A name embroidered on the breast pocket indicated the doctor was an OB-GYN. The wrinkles on his forehead suggested the doctor had been delivering babies in the middle of the night for decades.

"I am."

"Japanese?" the doctor asked.

"That's right."

"How did that happen?"

"Studied there. Lived there. Worked there."

"And now?"

"I'm an engineer at the Fujita Automotive plant in White Springs. We manufacture a lot of the parts used by Toyota for their cars made here in Mississippi."

"Fujita Automotive?"

"Yes."

"Well, then you may know the patient you're going to be translating for. Her husband also works for Fujita Automotive."

"I'm not surprised. Quite a few Japanese nationals work at the plant. There's also a regular rotation of employees visiting from headquarters in Japan. A lot of engineers. A lot of programmers."

"Do any of them speak English?"

"A few."

"Well, the husband who's here speaks very little English. More relevant to me is that his wife doesn't speak any at all. I need a few specific medical questions answered and only the wife can answer them. She's the pregnant one. She's the one who knows how she feels."

"Is she injured?"

"No. She's experiencing premature labor contractions, but I'm hoping to keep the baby in the oven a little while longer." The doctor paused and then asked, "Have you ever done this before?"

"Translated?"

"Yes."

"I translate between engineers all the time. I've never translated in a medical environment, but I took the required training to qualify as a translator for the hospital. There may be a few medical terms I don't know, but I can get my point across. I should be fine."

The doctor started walking down the hall and Edward followed. The doctor spoke over his shoulder as his pace quickened.

"The husband of the patient had a contact number for the company's liaison. Some kind of translator. We called. No one answered. You were next and last on the volunteer translator list."

"I heard the company's liaison officer is in Japan. Some kind of family emergency."

"Then I'm glad you were available. If you hadn't answered your phone, we were going to call a professor of Japanese literature in Memphis and see if he would be willing to drive down."

*

Edward was resting on the sofa in the waiting area as the sun first peeked through the large glass window behind him. With his eyes shut, Edward flipped his business card through his fingers, making it disappear and reappear on alternating sides. Edward didn't hear the doctor approach and was startled when the OB-GYN cleared his throat and spoke.

"Nice magic skills."

Edward opened his eyes. "Thanks. It's a bit of a habit. Self-entertainment. Been doing magic tricks since I was a kid. My wife is my only real audience."

Edward sat up and handed his business card to the doctor. The doctor took the card and his eyes briefly fell to the thick scars on Edward's left hand. Edward noticed the doctor's attention and raised his arm slightly. "A car accident a few years ago. Second and third degree burns on my hand, arm, shoulder. Some on my back and neck."

"I imagine summer here in Tupelo is uncomfortable."

"It's not the best. But I try to look at the bright side. Everything still works." Edward wiggled his fingers as if it to provide proof.

The doctor nodded and changed the subject. "For what it's worth, after tonight, you can add delivering a premature baby to your résumé."

"I'll try to squeeze it in somewhere. You never know."

"Thanks again for coming out in the middle of the night."

"I was already up. Glad I could help." Edward motioned towards the business card in the doctor's hand. "My phone number is on the card. Call me if you have problems with the couple upstairs. I have to work today, but I can translate for you over the phone in a pinch."

"That may work."

The doctor started to turn away and then asked a final question. "Out of curiosity, how did you even know to volunteer as a medical translator? It's not something that occurs to most people."

"My mom was an emergency room nurse when I was growing up. She used to tell me how the hospital always needed translators. And when I lived in Japan, a lot of people helped me out. I was trying to return the favor."

"Karma. What goes around comes around."

Chapter 2

EDWARD ENTERED THE bedroom, turned on the light in the small closet, and perused his clothing options for work.

"How was the hospital?" Holly asked, still in bed. Her brown hair was tussled. A pink T-shirt hung from her shoulders. She ran several strands of hair behind her ear and pushed herself up, back against the headboard.

"Okay, I think. A wife of one of the engineers from work went into premature labor. She delivered at four thirty this morning."

"Uh-oh. Did everything come out all right?"

"It did, but they're moving the baby and mother to Jackson. From what I gathered, the doctor seemed to think everything will be fine."

"So you didn't get any sleep?"

"Not much. Slept for an hour or so on a sofa in one of the waiting areas."

"Are you going into work?"

"Meetings all morning. A couple of guys from headquarters are coming into town to talk about plant expansion. Looks like I'll be busy for another year."

"You'll always be busy."

Edward shrugged his shoulders. "Work is work. We can't really complain. What's on your schedule today?"

"The contractors are coming. I think they're putting in the rest of the windows out back and finishing the tile in the new bathroom."

"A new bathroom will be nice. We won't have to elbow each other when we're brushing our teeth."

"Who says you'll be using the new bathroom?" Holly asked, flashing a near-perfect smile.

"I meant to say the new bathroom will be nice for you. I'll take the old bathroom."

"Smart man."

"Sometimes."

"I also have a yoga class this afternoon, but I should be back in time to make dinner. If you're planning on being home to eat."

"We'll see how the day goes."

*

Edward entered the fifty-man office on the front side of the massive Fujita Automotive facility. The unassuming square office building sat adjacent to a manufacturing floor large enough to serve as a hangar for a half-dozen jumbo jets.

Edward nodded at the American receptionist and the de facto first layer of security at the plant. The woman replied with a robotic "Good Morning," barely glancing up from her position at the desk near the front door.

Edward stopped for a coffee and weaved his way to his office on the second floor. A large window on the south side of his office offered a view of flat cotton fields as far as the eye could see.

He admired the scenery for a moment, then sat down behind his desk. He logged in to his computer as his boss cast a shadow over the threshold of his office.

"What are you doing here this morning?"

"Working."

"I heard you were up all night at the hospital delivering a baby. Take the day off."

"I was up all night anyway. The hospital was just a distraction."

"That's not what Mr. Watanabe thinks. He's very grateful for your assistance. Very grateful."

"That's nice, but I really don't think they wanted to have the baby here. The wife was planning on flying back to Japan next week."

"Maybe, but the Watanabes were glad you were around. And for your help, take the day off."

"I can't. We have meetings this morning that have been rescheduled twice already. And we have a large team staying up late in Tokyo to conference in."

"If you're going to be stubborn, then stay. But I'm letting you know you can go home any time."

"Thanks for the offer."

*

Edward's early morning translation heroics were rewarded by a steady stream of interruptions as coworkers stopped by to show their appreciation for his assistance with their colleague and his pregnant wife. Ninety minutes into the procession, Edward closed his door on the parade of graciousness. He grabbed his notepad and ever-present water bottle from the small bag he religiously carried to and from work. He took a swig of water, paused, and followed his first swallow with three large gulps. He set his bag on the corner of his desk and noticed a sheet of paper peeking up at him from inside the bag.

He reached down and plucked the note from the backpack.

You're my hero, and tonight I'll show you how I treat my heroes. Love, Holly.

Edward folded the note and noticed a pair of red lace underwear protruding from the inner pocket of his bag. He removed his wife's favorite tantalizing undergarment and smiled before stuffing the lingerie back into his bag and closing the zipper.

CHAPTER 3

THE WINSTON RESIDENCE was a one-story brick home halfway down a street that ended in a narrow cul-de-sac. With fifteen hundred square feet of living space, the house was more than large enough for a young couple without kids. The ongoing construction of an additional eight hundred feet on the back of the house would ensure enough room for guests and a baby.

Edward's headlights flashed across the front of his wife's car as he pulled into the empty driveway. Seconds later, Edward pushed the front door open and announced his arrival. He noticed his wife's purse on the sofa as he took off his shoes. The smell of dinner hung in the air. From the front door he could see the lights in the kitchen were off. He passed through the small dining room and flicked the light switch in the kitchen. A pot of chili sat on the stove and Edward removed the lid and inhaled. He glanced into the kitchen sink and eyed a single dirty bowl. A drinking glass with a faint lipstick mark stood on the counter next to the sink.

He called for his wife again and received no response. He walked back through the dining and living room and headed down the short hall to the two bedrooms and the small bath. After two additional tours of the house, he left a message on his wife's voicemail and sent three texts. As the minutes passed without a response, Edward felt panic starting to creep in. He took his search outside and poked around his yard before speed walking through his neighborhood with his head on a swivel, his fingers punching numbers into his cell phone. Sweating, Edward came back through his front door an hour after returning home from work. Fingers trembling, he called 911.

*

A lone Lee County Sheriff patrol car with its lights off arrived a little before eleven p.m.. Officer John Gooden got out of the car, his large frame towering over his vehicle. Discerning eyes noted the car in the driveway and the second vehicle parked on the street. He turned his attention to the front of the house and observed the shadow of a person pass through the room. A moment later the same silhouette appeared in the same window, heading in the other direction.

Officer Gooden ambled up the four short stairs to the front porch and knocked, his thick knuckles rapping wood.

*

Edward pulled on the doorknob and pushed the screen door open. Officer Gooden stuck his hand out. "Officer John Gooden. Lee County Sheriff's Department."

"Edward Winston. Come in."

Stepping inside, Officer Gooden's eyes slowly tracked to each corner of the room. From the front door he could see half of the house, from the living room, through the dining room, to the edge of the kitchen.

"I understand you want to file a missing person report on your wife," the officer said, removing a small notepad and pen from his pocket.

"That's right."

"How long has your wife been missing?"

"I don't know."

"You don't know?"

"I came home from work. She wasn't here. So a couple of hours."

"Where do you work?"

"At Fujita Automotive over in White Springs."

"What do you do there?"

"I'm an IT engineer."

"What time did you get home this evening?"

"After nine. Almost nine thirty."

"When was the last time you saw your wife?"

"This morning, before I left for work."

"And the last time you spoke with her?"

"I called her this afternoon to let her know I would be late for dinner."

"Was she home at that time?"

"She was. At least she said she was."

"Any reason not to believe her?"

"No."

"Are you sure she's missing? Maybe she just took a drive. Went to the store."

"Her car is parked in front of the house. Her purse was here when I got home. Same for her keys and wallet. They were all on the sofa. I moved them to the dining room table. The only thing missing is her cell phone."

"She has that with her?"

"I haven't found it. It's an iPhone with a red case. It has a decal of someone doing yoga on the back."

"What about friends? Any friends she could be out with?"

"She has some friends from the yoga studio."

"What yoga studio is that?"

"Tupelo Honey Yoga and Meditation."

"Downtown?"

"That's right."

"How long has she been taking classes there?"

"She started taking classes when we moved here. Two years ago. She began teaching classes this past winter."

"So she's a teacher?"

"Part-time."

Officer Gooden nodded.

"Have you called the yoga school?"

"I did. It's closed for the night."

"How about her friends?"

"I called all the ones I have numbers for."

"Do you have an alarm system on your house, Mr. Winston?"

"I don't. But Holly mentioned that she wanted to get one," Edward replied, his voice cracking.

Officer Gooden looked at Edward with a piercing gaze. Edward was perspiring, his eyes open, his expression frantic. The officer's attention dipped to Edward's khaki pants and then to his buttoned oxford. Sweat had turned the light blue shirt several shades darker. Officer Gooden seemed to notice the scars covering the back of Edward's hand.

"You mind if I take a look around?"

"No. Go ahead. But don't you want to call it in first? Issue an APB or a BOLO."

"Let's take a quick look around, first. Make sure your wife isn't taking a nap somewhere."

"A nap?"

"Sounds strange, I know. But I had a husband call about a missing wife earlier this year. Found her alive and well on the far side of the bed. Asleep on the floor."

"Seriously?"

"One hundred percent true. Turns out the wife had been hiding a drinking problem. But she most definitely wasn't missing. The husband never walked around to the other side of the bed when he was looking for her."

"I checked the far side of the bed. And under it too," Edward replied.

"A quick tour, Mr. Winston. That's all."

Edward waved the officer deeper into the house.

With Edward as his escort, the large uniformed officer performed a thorough, systematic search of each room, opening closet doors, checking behind curtains, and peeking into the shower. The pantry in the kitchen was probed and the cabinets under the sink inspected.

Finished with the original footprint of the house, Officer Gooden stopped in front of the large plastic tarp covering the entranceway to the construction site on the back of the house, just beyond the kitchen.

"What's through here?" Gooden asked.

"We're having an addition put in. A master bedroom, bathroom, and a small family room."

"And were the workers here today?"

"Yes. I called the contractor already. He said his crew left at five."

Officer Gooden pushed the tarp to the side and stepped through the large doorway into the room.

Edward provided a quick briefing of the project's progress. "We still need floors in the main room, lights, and a ton of paint. But it's starting to take shape. They just installed the windows and doors. The air-conditioning is up and running."

"Hard to get through a Mississippi summer without AC," Officer Gooden responded without taking his eyes off his surroundings. He poked his head into the new bedroom and bathroom. Without closet doors and furniture, options for hiding in the new addition were limited.

The officer rattled the handles of the newly installed French doors and then tugged on each window in turn. The window on the side nearest the garage slid open and Office Gooden looked over at Edward.

"Should this be locked?"

"Probably. But you know how it is with work crews. Not everyone is doing what they should."

Officer Gooden dropped his gaze downward in the direction of the wooden surface of the subfloor. "Did you check these windows when you came home?"

"No. I was looking for my wife. Besides, the windows are new. I'm not in the habit of checking them yet."

"Fair enough," the officer said, pausing for another few seconds.

"Can we step into the yard?" the officer asked. "I want to see the perimeter of the house."

"Sure."

Twenty minutes later, Officer Gooden completed his search of the property.

"That open window in the back of your addition bothers me a little. It's only a couple of steps from that back window to the garage and driveway. It's a convenient egress and regress for a vehicle parked in the driveway."

"Holly and I have been parking in the street so the work trucks can park in the driveway."

"Can I see inside your vehicles?"

"Of course."

Officer Gooden opened the doors of both Edward's and his wife's cars and shined his flashlight across the interiors and then the trunk.

With the resounding thud of the closing trunk interrupting the chorus of crickets, Officer Gooden sighed. "Well, it doesn't appear your wife is on the premises."

"I already knew that."

"Just doing my job. Let me make a few calls and get a description of your wife out to local law enforcement. I need a recent photograph if you have one. We have some paperwork to fill out, but it won't take long."

Tears welled up in Edward's eyes. He nodded.

At the small dining room table, Officer Gooden slid the completed missing person report to Edward, who scribbled his name on the bottom line and added the date and time.

Officer Gooden stood from the table. "I don't want to sound any warning bells, but if your wife is indeed missing, you may need some emotional support. Do you have any friends or family in the area? Anyone who you can lean on? Anyone you can call?"

"A few coworkers."

"That's good. What about family?"

"I have a brother in California. We don't see each other much."

"How about your wife's family?"

"My mother-in-law passed away a few years back from a stroke. My wife's father was never around. I've never met him. I think our lack of family was something that drew us together. If that makes sense."

"It does. It does. I'm not sure how you do it, but I'd try to surround myself with some support. It's important."

Edward nodded. "What's the immediate plan?"

"First, I'll call in the bloodhounds and see if there's any indication your wife took a walk. There's a lot of rural land not too far from here. Maybe she took a walk, fell, and injured herself. It's dark tonight, but that doesn't bother the dogs much. They should be here within the hour. My business card is on the table. You can give me a call if you need me. After the canine unit gets here, I'm going to run down to the station and get the wheels turning on the missing person report."

"Okay. What else can I do?"

"If you can get me a list of all of your wife's friends, that would help. Also a list of the people who have been working at the house."

"I'll get you a list in ten minutes."

Officer Gooden looked over at the tarp in the kitchen. "Who's your contractor?"

"Hechinger Homes."

"Good old Ted Hechinger. He's been around these parts forever."

"Seems like a good guy. What about organizing a search party for my wife?"

"Let's wait till morning and see what we have. The dogs will search the neighborhood tonight. But we need daylight for a proper search party. Humans don't have the best night vision. We might miss something, despite our best intentions."

"What am I supposed to do? Just sit around and wait?"

"Call everyone you know. Have them call everyone they can think of. Get the word out."

Officer Gooden began to stand and then offered Edward a dose of reality. "Mr. Winston, just so you're aware, statistically speaking, it's likely your wife is out with a friend or friends. She may not be missing any more than she wants to be missing. And I understand that's not something you particularly want to hear. I know. But it is a possibility."

Edward's face turned red at the officer's attempt to discuss the probability of his wife cheating on him. Little imagination was needed to read between the lines.

"Holly is not having an affair."

"How have things been on the home front recently?"

"My wife is not having an affair," Edward reiterated.

"I just wanted to prepare you for the possibility of any eventuality. I'll be outside walking the neighborhood. Don't be surprised when the dogs arrive. They can make a racket."

*

Edward sat on the steps of his front porch with his cell phone in his lap. He listened to the bloodhounds in the distance, their sharp barks piercing the air. He tried to call his wife again and hung up when it went to voicemail for the twentieth time. For the next hour he sat on the stoop, listening to the fading barks of bloodhounds as tears trickled down his cheeks.

CHAPTER 4

OFFICER GOODEN SAT in Sheriff Blazer's office as the elected official at the top of the law enforcement food chain slipped on his reading glasses. Tall and lanky with gray hair, Sheriff Blazer leaned back in his chair and lifted the missing person report off his desk. He reached the end of the document and set the paper back down. His sharp blue eyes looked across his desk at Officer Gooden.

"Did you get any sleep last night?" the sheriff asked.

"Not much."

"What does your gut tell you about our missing yoga instructor?"

"My gut says it doesn't look good."

"No chance it's a case of a bored housewife? Maybe someone with a boyfriend on the side?"

"That's always possible, but I don't see it."

"What about the husband?"

"An engineer. Works out at the Fujita plant. Seems like a decent man. Seems real worried about his wife."

"Any leads?"

"The couple is having an addition put on the back of their house. A lot of workers coming and going. That's where I'd start."

Officer Gooden handed the long list of contractors to Sheriff Blazer. The sheriff perused the list and then whistled.

"Like I said, a lot of folks coming and going. Ted Hechinger's crew is doing most of the work. He's got his own plumber and electrician. He subs out floors, windows, and doors. Palmetto Windows is on site. Hot Tin Roofs is installing a new roof. Probably a few illegals in the mix, but primarily all the companies use local employees."

"And we ran the bloodhounds, right?"

"We did. They didn't pick up on anything."

"All right. Let me assign a detective and you can get him up to speed."

Sheriff Blazer stood from his seat and both men headed out the door.

*

Detective Will Rafferty's dark blue sedan crawled down the warming morning asphalt. A sea of parked vehicles lined both sides of the street. He pulled the car into the last available spot, near the end of the cul-de-sac where the small subdivision met a large field.

Detective Rafferty exited his car, his red hair and pale skin reflecting in the morning sun. He took a moment to observe the neighborhood before shutting the door and walking up the street. His head moved slowly from left to right as he strolled, his eyes taking in the details of the houses. A minute later he joined a group of people gathered in the front yard of the address he'd been given. Fifty men and women, many of them Asian, were seemingly organizing themselves into small groups on the lawn. Hats, walking sticks, backpacks, and water bottles littered the grass.

Detective Rafferty nodded to a woman who was doling out instructions to others, and the woman broke away from her duties.

"I'm looking for Edward Winston," Detective Rafferty said.

"He's inside."

"What's everyone doing here?"

"We're going to search for Holly."

"And how do you know the missing woman?"

"Holly and I work at the yoga studio together in town."

Detective Rafferty turned his head. "Are all of these people from the yoga studio?"

"Not all of them. Some are from the yoga studio. Some are from the plant. Some are from the neighborhood."

"Are you working with anyone from the Lee County Sheriff's Department?"

"No. Should we be?"

"It could be helpful."

"I think you need to talk to Edward. He's organizing this."

*

Detective Will Rafferty held the screen door open for a stream of volunteers in hiking pants and hats leaving the house to join the larger group on the lawn. From his position at the dining room table, Edward noticed the man in the suit at his front door. Crossing his living room in a few short steps, Edward came forward and introduced himself.

"Edward Winston."

"Detective Will Rafferty, Lee County Sheriff's Department. I'm taking over your wife's investigation."

"What happened to Officer Gooden?"

"Officer Gooden is a patrol officer. Your wife's case has been assigned a detective."

"And that's you."

"Yes."

"Nice to meet you. Have you spoken with Officer Gooden?"

"I met with him at length prior to heading here. And Officer Gooden is available if we need him."

"I'll take all the help I can get."

Detective Rafferty nodded out the window overlooking the front yard.

"It looks like you have a lot of help. I don't know if I've ever seen someone organize a search party so fast."

"I got lucky. I have helpful coworkers and my wife is well-liked."

"I understand you want to keep things moving, but I have a favor to ask."

"What's that?"

"Is there any way you can hold back on your search party? Just until I can get a couple of officers out here to accompany them. To oversee the search. To make sure any evidence is protected."

"The dogs already searched last night and they didn't find anything. I didn't think there was any harm in us going out again in the daylight."

"That's fine. But let's do it right. Let's make sure everyone knows not to touch any evidence. Let's make sure everyone understands the chain of custody. We all want to avoid corrupting a crime scene, if one is found."

"How long will it take to have officers out here?"

"I can have people here within the hour."

"That's fine by me."

"All I'm asking for is a little coordination."

"I understand. And in the spirit of openness, you should know I also called the *Daily Journal* and the *Lee County Courier*. Both of them are sending out reporters. WTVA is dispatching news cameras. Hopefully both papers will run stories tomorrow. The TV crew said they will have something on the six o'clock news tonight."

"You move fast, Mr. Winston."

"I'm from Chicago. We move faster up North," Edward said, not realizing the insult until it had escaped his lips. Then he added, "All statistics say that the first forty-eight hours are the most important in a missing person investigation. The clock is ticking."

CHAPTER 5

EDWARD WALKED PAST the old pickup truck parked on the left side of the driveway. A For Sale sign rested on the dash, its location unchanged for the last month. Edward climbed the front steps to his neighbor's door and rapped on the doorframe. His knock was met by enthusiastic barks from a yappy Yorkshire terrier through the closed door. Edward paused and then knocked again, the guard-dog-on-duty repeating his unwavering response. Seconds later the door opened, revealing both his neighbor and the dog.

"Good afternoon, Mr. Poole," Edward said.

Mr. Poole, a veteran local car mechanic renowned as much for his automotive wizardry as for his spectacular comb-over, forced a smile.

"Hi, Edward. Sorry to hear about Holly. Any word?"

"Nothing yet."

"How are you holding up?"

"Not too well."

"I'm sorry I missed out on the search party. I was down in Yazoo City picking up a Chevelle. I didn't even know there was a search until I got back."

"Don't worry about it. You got a minute?"

"Sure," Mr. Poole responded. "Just let me put Tarzan in his room," he added, motioning towards the dog at his feet.

Moments later, Edward was on a plush burgundy sofa in Mr. Poole's living room. Old photos hung on the wall. Stale air filled the room.

Mr. Poole came back without his dog and Edward spoke. "I stopped by because I've been talking to everyone in the neighborhood and was wondering if I could ask you a couple of questions?"

"Of course."

"Did you see anything suspicious last night? Sometime between four and nine thirty or so? Any chance you saw Holly leaving the house? Taking a walk? Did a friend pick her up?"

"No, I didn't see Holly."

"You see anyone suspicious lurking around?"

"I didn't see anyone suspicious. Nothing out of the usual. The construction crew working on your house was here most of the day, but that's pretty much how it's been for the last month or so. Your wife parked her car on the street, probably so the workers could park their trucks in the driveway, closer to the house. But she's been doing that for a while."

"You pay attention, Mr. Poole."

"What's not to pay attention to? Neighbors pay attention. Besides, when I'm working in the garage, I can see straight across to your house from the windows in the door."

"Did you see which of the contractors was the last to leave?"

"Sure did. By the time I had dinner the only truck left was for the window guys. Red truck. Palmetto Windows."

"You sure about that?"

"I'm sure. Saw it leave. After the red truck left, the driveway was empty."

"What time was this?"

"After I ran to the store. Which was after dinner. Which was after the early news, so probably around six or so."

Edward could imagine his wife prattling around the kitchen, putting the finishing touches on dinner. Maybe adding another dash of Tabasco to the chili.

"Did you see who was driving the window truck?"

"Guy with a ponytail. Had a big chew in his mouth."

Edward cranked his neck and looked out the front window, his gaze measuring the distance across the yard to the street. "You saw the man's chew from your house?"

"No. I wasn't in my house when I saw him. I was getting my mail from the mailbox. Not but fifteen feet from there to the middle of the street. Got a real good look at him."

"How old was he?"

"Thirty or so. Hard to guess people's age these days. Kids look older. Older people trying hard to look younger."

"Did the driver say anything as he passed? Give you a wave?"

"He never even looked over."

"Did you think that was odd?"

"A little unfriendly, maybe. Then again, maybe he just had something on his mind. You ever drive and not remember driving when you get to where you're going? Don't remember stopping at any lights or stop signs and wonder if you did?"

"Sure."

"Then you know what I mean."

Edward paused to ponder his neighbor's point and then continued his inquisition. "Was there anybody else in the truck?"

"Not that I saw. Just the driver. But those window company trucks are a little different. They look like a standard pickup, but they have racks for windows on the back and places to stash equipment."

"What are you saying?"

"I'm saying there was only one person in the cab of the truck. I can't speak to the rest of the vehicle."

"Would you recognize the driver if you saw him again?"

"If he didn't clean himself up, I probably would. Now, if he cut his hair, shaved, wore a suit, and smiled ... well, there'd be no guarantees."

"Would you mind if I had the detective come by to talk to you?"

"I already talked to him."

"You did?"

"Yes. This afternoon."

"Detective Rafferty?"

"That sounds right. I have his card around here somewhere."

*

Edward crossed the street, and by the time he reached his air-conditioned living room, sweat glistened on his forehead. A moment later he plucked a business card off the dining room table and punched the numbers for Detective Rafferty. On the third ring, the detective answered and Edward pounced on him with the information his neighbor had just provided.

"My neighbor says you talked to him this afternoon about my wife."

"I talked to all of your neighbors. All of the ones who answered their doors. The ones we haven't spoken to yet will be interviewed as soon as we can reach them. We're crosschecking all statements that were made. All leads. We're running down multiple possibilities."

"I'm specifically referring to a red truck from Palmetto Windows. A red truck my neighbor says was the last vehicle to leave my house. The neighbor's name is Mr. Poole. I don't know his first name. He is an older gentleman who lives across the street. He's a semi-retired mechanic. Right now there's an old pickup truck for sale in the driveway."

Detective Rafferty cleared his throat. "I'm aware of the lead. And I probably shouldn't be telling you this, but one of the trucks from Palmetto Windows was reported stolen late this morning."

Edward's voice rose with excitement. "That sounds promising. Find the driver. Talk to him. Find the truck. Go to his house. Get a search warrant. My wife could be tied up in a basement somewhere."

"We've spoken to Palmetto Windows. And we're still waiting for information regarding the driver of the truck that went missing. It's on my short list. We're preparing to question the employee once he's identified, and serve a search warrant, if necessary."

"That's it?"

"The company has a dozen trucks. We're working on identifying the exact truck that was out at your house and confirm it was the same vehicle that has gone missing."

"I thought my neighbor gave you a description of the driver? A guy with a ponytail. Get his name and number."

"I'm waiting for that information."

"You'll have to excuse my ignorance, but how hard could that be? What could be more important than talking to the person who was last seen with my wife?"

"Like I said, Mr. Winston, it's on my short list. Let's not start jumping to conclusions."

"Jumping to conclusions? An eyewitness account of the last person to see my wife?"

"Who exactly saw this person *with* your wife? I don't remember hearing that particular eyewitness account. Did your neighbor say he saw your wife?"

"No."

"Well, then it's possible your wife may have been gone by the time this window truck left for the night."

"She wasn't gone."

"Were you there?"

"No."

"Let us do our job, Mr. Winston. I know you're upset, but let us do our job."

"Who are you looking into at this very moment?"

"We're going through the list of yoga students at the studio where your wife worked."

"And...?"

"Actually, there are several people of interest we are chasing down. Did you know your wife had two different men blacklisted from the yoga studio for inappropriate, sexually suggestive comments?"

"I didn't," Edward replied, bothered by his wife's secrecy.

"Well, that's motive."

"I think you should still start with the window guy."

"Okay, Mr. Winston. I'm going to let you have a few moments to calm down. Once you're thinking more clearly, give me a call back. In the meantime, let me do the detective work and I'll keep you informed."

Edward was about to respond when the call ended.

He looked at the phone, cursed, and then grabbed his keys off the counter.

CHAPTER 6

PALMETTO WINDOWS WAS located a block past the railroad tracks heading east out of town. The front of a long warehouse served as the office and showroom. The rest of the space, a vast cavern towards the rear, was inventory. For a company that made its money selling windows, the large building had exactly one: a sheet of plate glass facing the parking lot.

Edward pulled his car into one of the six spots marked as customer parking in front of the building. He felt the sun hit the back of his neck as he stood from his car. It was almost six in the evening, but the large concrete slab and the lack of shade baked the parking lot as if it were in an oven set on broil.

Edward pulled the front door open and was greeted by a cool blast from the air-conditioning and an older woman sitting at the desk near the entrance.

"Good evening," the woman said. Edward put her age somewhere north of sixty. Probably a window installer's mother or aunt. The nameplate on the desk read "Darlene."

"Good evening, Darlene," Edward replied. "I was looking for a worker here, but I can't remember his name. He has a ponytail. Maybe somewhere in his late twenties or early thirties."

"Sounds like Pervis."

"Does he have a last name?"

"Wade."

"Is he around?"

"Did he steal something?"

"No."

"Break something?"

"No, ma'am. He was installing windows on my house and we were talking about an old truck one of my neighbors was thinking about selling. I was just passing by and thought I'd mention that my neighbor may be willing to negotiate on the price." Edward surprised himself with the ease of his spit-balled response.

"Well, all of the boys are done for the day. One of the gang is celebrating his birthday. They're all down at the Brew Ha. 'Course, they're down there most nights anyway."

"Where is that?"

"The Brew Ha Bar and Grill, though the only thing they grill is burgers. Straight down Main Street for two blocks and hang a right on Briar Ridge. It's not too far down the road."

"Thank you so much."

"What did you say your name was?"

"Thank you," Edward repeated as he stepped back outside.

*

The exterior of the Brew Ha sported the same half-barrel warehouse design that Palmetto Windows did. The difference from the exterior was that the Brew Ha had chosen the side of the warehouse for its front entrance, giving the windowless hole-in-the-wall more width and less depth. A collection of vehicles, largely pickup trucks and SUVs, filled the gravel lot.

Edward yanked on the heavily tinted front doors and stepped into the bar. As the doors shut behind him, sunlight from the outside world vanished, casting the room back into dimmer light.

Edward remained near the door as his eyes adjusted. A waitress with a tray of beers looked over before returning her attention to a burly customer in dirty jeans who playfully slapped her ass.

Edward noted the bar at the back of the room and headed in that direction, surveying his surroundings as he went. A group of men were playing pool on a table to the right. To his left, a team of men in matching red shirts sat around two tables pushed end to end. Edward perused the company name on the shirts as he headed for the neon Budweiser sign behind the bar. Country music played from a jukebox along the wall. At the bar, he slipped into one of the half-dozen empty stools.

The bartender, a man in his fifties with a tattoo for each year of life, uncrossed his burgeoning forearms.

"What're ya drinkin'?" the man asked ambivalently.

"Budweiser in a bottle," Edward said. He hadn't come to drink, but he'd seen enough movies with dive bars to know it was better to have a glass bottle in hand, just in case.

A door slammed to Edward's left, a heavy thud coming from a dark hallway. A rusted sign on the wall indicated the restrooms were located somewhere in the proximity of the noise.

Seconds later, a black-haired man with deep forehead wrinkles stumbled from the bathroom hall. At the doorway to the main room, the man adjusted his overalls. Then he reached into the depth of his crotch and adjusted himself. He paused and stared across the expanse of floor between his position and the bar, as if considering whether he could make it to his seat without falling. Then he took a deep breath and walked straight to his empty chair and sat down, two stools away from Edward.

The bartender delivered Edward his beer and the black-haired man tapped the bar one time with a single finger to order his drink. The bartender poured a draft for the man and placed it in front of the regular. Fox News played on the small TV behind the bar.

Edward's eyes moved from the TV and focused on the mirror behind the bar. Peering through a smattering of liquor bottles, Edward could see the room behind him in a piecemeal reflection. He spent several minutes silently watching the team from Palmetto Windows. He counted fifteen window installers in total, subconsciously nodding his head as he moved from one man to the next. He noted that two of the men had long hair. Only one sported a distinctive ponytail.

Edward took a sip of his drink and watched as the man he assumed was Pervis Wade threw back his beer and poured another from a pitcher on the table. A collection of beer bottles stood among the pitchers and mugs.

The adrenaline that had propelled Edward to the Brew Ha was suddenly taking a back seat to nausea. He took a larger swallow of his beer to calm his nerves and reminded himself he had just come to talk. Friendly questions from a worried husband looking for answers to his wife's disappearance. As an IT engineer who spent most of his days behind a computer or in meetings, the Brew Ha was a firsthand glimpse into a world Edward had only heard existed. Slowly spinning in his chair, he took his first direct look at the group of men in their matching Palmetto Windows shirts.

As he considered the appropriate segue for questioning a complete stranger about his missing wife, the front doors of the Brew Ha opened and light again flashed through the bar. Edward squinted.

As his eyes adjusted to the blast of sun and the door shut, Edward watched Darlene, the secretary from Palmetto Windows, approach her coworkers. She patted one of the men on the shoulder and unceremoniously placed a gift-wrapped birthday present on the table. The man stood and gave the receptionist a hug. Then Darlene's eyes met Edward's.

Edward nodded, slowly turned away, and focused his glance back to the mirror behind the bar. He watched in the reflection as Darlene disengaged from the celebratory embrace and stepped towards the man with the ponytail. She whispered into his ear and the man nodded.

A moment later, with another flash of light from the doorway, Darlene left the bar.

Edward could feel the heavy stare of the man with the ponytail on his backside. Through the mirror, he watched as the subject of his curiosity reached into his pocket and removed a tin of snuff. Then the man swiped an empty bottle off the table and spit into its long neck.

Edward's pulse increased and he felt sweat drip from his right armpit. He took his eyes off the mirror and didn't see Pervis Wade approach until the man was standing next to him at the bar.

"Darlene says you were looking for me. She said you stopped by the office and wanted to talk to me about a truck for sale."

Edward tried to smile. "I think we both know that's not true."

"I knew it wasn't true. But there are a lot of crazy people in the world these days. *You* might've thought it was true."

"I didn't. Sorry for the lie."

"Do you want to tell me why you're really coming to my work? Stalking me at my favorite bar?"

"I'm not stalking you. I just wanted to ask you a few questions. I also felt like a cold beer. It's been a long day."

Pervis Wade again spit into the bottle he was holding.

"My name is Edward Winston. I live up in Saltillo. Not far from the old golf course. Your company has been installing windows at my house. You replaced all the old ones on the front and installed new ones on the addition we're putting on the back. Tom Hechinger is doing most of the work. Your company was subcontracted for the windows. You've been out there off and on over the last week or so."

Edward stuck out his hand and the man with the ponytail switched his spittoon to his other hand.

"Pervis Wade."

"Nice to meet you, Pervis."

"You say you live up in Saltillo?"

"Yes. Just outside the city limits."

"You sure you're looking for me? I spent most of this week in West Tupelo. Maybe one of the other guys was out at your house."

"One of my neighbors gave a description that made me think it could have been you."

"Then maybe it was me," Pervis replied with a devilish grin. "We do a lot of houses. Hard to keep them all straight."

"I'm asking about last night."

"Going to have to think about that for a minute."

"Please do," Edward replied, swallowing hard.

"The reason I'm asking is because my wife, Holly, went missing yesterday evening. About the same time she went missing, a Palmetto Windows company truck was seen driving out of my neighborhood by one of my neighbors."

"And you say we're putting in windows at your house?"

"That's right."

"Well, then I guess seeing a red company truck in the neighborhood at the end of the day wouldn't be unusual, now would it?"

Edward noted the venom in Pervis's voice.

"It wouldn't be unusual unless it was the last vehicle on the scene before my wife disappeared. Not to mention, according to the sheriff's department, one of the Palmetto Windows trucks went missing this morning. I'm just trying to connect the dots."

"You heard about the missing truck?"

"I did."

Pervis spit into the bottle. "I'd like to help, but I'm not sure a neighbor seeing a truck for a company that was doing work at your house has anything to do with a missing person. Or a missing work truck that was stolen miles away, on the other side of town. Seems like a flimsy reason to hunt someone down during their free time."

"I wasn't hunting you down. And my wife is missing, so maybe you could show a little common courtesy."

Pervis's eyes seemed to darken. "I'll tell you what. I'll mosey back over to my friends and see if any of them recall seeing anything out your way yesterday. Maybe one of them saw something."

The stare between Pervis and Edward lasted several long, uncomfortable seconds.

"That would be helpful," Edward conceded.

"Give me a minute."

*

Edward watched Pervis stroll back to the table as the man seemed to follow through on his promise.

"Careful with that one," the black-haired man seated at the barstool said in Edward's direction. The man never averted his eyes from the small TV behind the bar.

"Are you talking to me?"

"Who the hell do you think I'm talking to?"

Edward turned his head one hundred and eighty degrees. The bartender was no longer tending bar. The black-haired man in overalls, Edward, the TV, and full shelves of liquor were the lone occupants of the entire bar area.

"Why do you say that?"

"Because Pervis Wade is trouble. Been trouble his whole adult life. Be trouble the rest of his life."

"What kind of trouble?"

"The kind that gets you a good seat in hell."

"Do you know him, or are we just spreading rumors?"

"Ain't a rumor. Half the town knows."

Edward leaned forward and peered down the counter. The man stared straight ahead. Edward could see the man was older, his black hair obviously procured from a box in the men's beauty section of Walgreens.

Edward switched tactics and turned on his barstool. From his new perspective, he located the man's reflection in the mirror behind the liquor bottles. Between the gin and vodka, Edward's eyes met the man's, pupil to pupil.

"What're you trying to tell me?"

"I ain't *trying* to tell you nothing. I'm telling you straight out. If you think Pervis Wade is going to do anything to help you, or tell you the truth about anything you wanna know, you got another thing coming."

"Right now, he's the only lead I have on my wife. He was driving the last vehicle seen at my house before she went missing."

"If Pervis Wade was the last person to see your wife, then I'm truly sorry."

"Why's that?"

"Because there ain't no happy ending to that story."

The old man slugged his beer, got up from his seat, and headed in the direction of the bathroom. Halfway down the hall, the man pushed his way out a back exit and disappeared into the waning sunlight on the rear of the building.

Edward considered going after the man when Pervis Wade tapped him on the shoulder.

"None of the fellas remember being at your house yesterday."

"We both know that's impossible. Your company installed the windows. Each window has a sticker on it with your company's name. You are a subcontractor for Ted Hechinger. There is a paper trail."

Pervis Wade raised his hands.

"Easy. Easy. You got me. You got me. I thought about it and I do remember working out in Saltillo this week. I believe I was working at your house yesterday."

"You were?"

"I was. I was. A rambler on Village Trail?"

"That's right."

"I was there. Solid brick house. Big yard."

"Did you see my wife?"

"I saw her every day I was there. A real beauty. You did real good for yourself."

"Did you see her yesterday? Before you left?"

"I did. She was cooking something. Smelled like chili."

"Did you see her or smell her?"

Pervis exhaled and his breath made Edward's stomach turn. He fought the urge to gag from the mix of beer, chewing tobacco, and, likely, a few rotten teeth.

"Did you go to college, Edward?" Pervis asked.

"I did."

"Did you study hard?"

"I studied."

"You must have, because you seem smart. Real smart."

Edward shrugged his shoulders.

"Have you ever heard the expression: 'Never be the smartest person in the room'?"

"No," Edward answered. "I haven't heard that one. Why?"

"Just curious. Tell me, Eddie, are you the smartest person in this room?"

Edward looked around. "I doubt it."

Pervis Wade inhaled deeply and again spit into his twelve-ounce spittoon.

"You never answered my question, Pervis. Did you see my wife or just smell her cooking before you left for the evening?"

"Which would bother your more, Eddie. Me seeing her or smelling her?"

Pervis smiled, black flecks of tobacco peppered his lower lip.

Edward's grip tightened on the neck of his beer bottle and the veins in the back of his hand bulged.

"I get the feeling this conversation is over," Edward managed to say.

"See, you are the smartest guy in the room."

CHAPTER 7

EDWARD HEARD A knock on the front door and yelled, "come in" without bothering to see who it was. The last thirty-six hours had seen dozens of visitors wearing a path from the front door to the kitchen. The wives of several coworkers, who had come to the house as a show of support, were currently bustling around the stove. Food was stuffed into every crevice of the refrigerator. Frozen meals stood shoulder to shoulder in the freezer. Sandwich platters littered the dining room table.

Edward headed towards the front door as it opened. Detective Rafferty stepped into the living room and poked his nose around the corner. Eyeing the quartet of women swarming the kitchen, Detective Rafferty flicked his head in the direction of the privacy offered by the front porch. Edward followed the detective out of the house.

"We need to talk," Rafferty said, slipping a piece a chewing gum into his mouth.

"I left you a voicemail last night. I've been waiting for you to call me back."

"I got your message. And I'm hoping you have a good reason for going to Palmetto Windows last evening and accusing one of their employees of being involved in your wife's disappearance."

"I didn't accuse anyone of anything at Palmetto Windows. I was at some shitty bar a few blocks away. And before you tell me I shouldn't have been there, you should know I met the driver of the truck who was seen leaving my house the night Holly disappeared. A real classy individual by the name of Pervis Wade. We had a civil conversation like two grown adults. He admitted to me he had been at my house."

"Why did you go and do that?"

"Because I'm looking for my wife."

"How much detective experience do you have?"

"Enough to know the last person to see someone alive is usually the prime suspect."

"Edward, I like you. I get it. You're grieving. But you can't run around taking the law into your own hands."

"I just asked the man a few questions."

"Well, it may have backfired on you."

"Why's that?"

"Because we went to Palmetto Windows this morning to start searching their trucks."

"That's good news. But I thought the truck you needed to search was missing."

"Maybe and maybe not. Palmetto Windows has a dozen trucks. According to their office help, Darlene, the keys to the trucks are on a pegboard in the warehouse. It's first come, first serve. Take a key. Take a truck. Apparently, some trucks are better than others. Some have better AC. Some have better radios."

"Meaning?"

"Meaning that in order to be thorough, we needed to search all the trucks. Which means I had to coordinate some help. Searching a dozen trucks isn't a one-man job."

"Then it's a good thing the Lee County Sheriff's Department has more than one officer."

Detective Rafferty's face turned a shade of red. "As I said, we executed the search warrant first thing this morning. Unfortunately, the search of the vehicles turned up no evidence related to your wife's case.

Edward could feel his pulse rate quicken. "Well, that leaves one vehicle left to search. The missing one. It's a big red truck with the company name down the side. It shouldn't be hard to find."

"It's already been found. Burned out near a cotton field just south of town. Torched. There's not much left."

"When?"

"Found it this morning. It was discovered in an isolated plot. No real neighbors to speak of. No one called the fire department. No one recalled seeing flames."

Edward stifled the nausea welling inside his gut. The urge to purge passed and he stood straight, eyes watering.

"Was a body found in the vehicle?"

"No. The vehicle appeared to be empty."

"So the guy I confronted yesterday at the bar kidnapped my wife, stole a company truck, and then destroyed the evidence."

"We may never know."

CHAPTER 8

THE OLD MAN with the dyed black hair was at the same barstool, again dressed in overalls and a white T-shirt. Edward pulled out a stool near the entrance to the hall, putting himself in position to block the path to the bathroom and the rear exit, just in case the man decided on another hasty retreat out the back. The PBR clock on the wall behind the bar read 3:05 p.m.

"I thought I might find you here."

"Why's that?" the man responded.

"Because yesterday when I was here, you didn't tell the bartender what you wanted. You just tapped your finger on the counter and he served you a beer. That tells me you're a regular. It was also pretty early yesterday when I stopped by. And not to be rude, but it seemed like you'd already had a few by the time I arrived. So between the bartender knowing your drink order without you saying anything and the fact you seemed to have started drinking early, I figured you might be a regular."

"Not a lot of drinking spots on the east side of town. I don't live but a couple of minutes away. Stumbling distance."

"Can I buy you a drink?"

"Not if you're thinking you got a shot at taking me home."

The bartender appeared and Edward ordered a beer. The black-haired man with deep forehead wrinkles added, "I'll take a shot of Johnny Walker. Blue if you have it."

"I have to get that from the back," the bartender said, disappearing into a wood-paneled room just off the end of the bar.

"Expensive taste for a dive bar," Edward said.

"You ever had Johnny Walker Blue?"

"Once. I'm not much of a whiskey drinker, but the person I was with when I had it seemed to like it. And he knew his liquor."

The bartender's thick forearm delivered Edward's beer and then placed an empty shot glass on the bar. He took a few seconds to carefully pour a full shot, right up to the rim.

"Holler if you need me. I'm going to be out back unloading kegs," the bartender said before disappearing.

"My name is Edward Winston," Edward said, lifting his beer.

The old man raised his shot glass and nodded his head.

"Jim Bartlett. But most of my friends just call me Bartlett. Been that way since I was in grade school. Some people just call me Bar, for obvious reasons."

"Nice to meet you, Mr. Bartlett."

"Just Bartlett. You can drop the 'mister.'"

"Okay then. Bartlett."

The man nodded again, touched his mouth to the top of the shot glass, and smacked his lips. He carefully placed the glass back on the bar. His eyes dropped to Edward's left hand and then slowly ran up his arm.

"Does that arm give you trouble?"

"What?"

"Your arm. Your hand. I noticed yesterday. Got a better look at it just now."

Edward lifted his hand and the light from the neon sign behind the bar gave the scarred flesh an odd hue.

"Burned ten years ago," Edward admitted, surprised the stranger broached a subject most people tried hard to ignore. Stares were common. Unsolicited questions about his scars were rare.

"How did it happen? If you don't mind me asking."

"Car accident."

"Damn. But given that you're sitting there on that stool means you made it out alive. I reckon that's all that matters."

"I guess so."

"Tough rehab?"

"Half a year in the hospital. Basic rehab for another year. Skin grafts. A few surgeries. Second and third degree burns. Back of the hand. Most of the arm. Some of the shoulder. Side of neck. A little on the back."

"Make you thirsty?"

"I try to stay hydrated but it's not easy here in Mississippi. I try to keep in mind that there are a lot of people worse off than I am. I was only burned on fifteen percent of my body."

"Just fifteen?"

Edward flashed a quick smile. "It's an inside joke. I always thought it was interesting the doctors were so specific about the percentage."

"You go through a lot of skin moisturizer?"

Edward put his beer on the counter and stared into the man's eyes with deeper curiosity. "Yeah. I use a few moisturizers. There's a good one from Japan you can get online."

"I ain't ever been online."

"Never?"

"Nope."

"Probably better off. Except I wouldn't have a job without a computer."

"What do you do?"

"I work at Fujita Automotive in White Springs. We make parts and glass for the Toyota plant down the road."

"Good job?"

"It pays the bills."

"You're probably too young to realize, but most folks my age have a hard time understanding how the Japanese ended up creating manufacturing jobs in this country. For decades we sent those jobs to all corners of the world. Now the Japs bring them back."

"I think they call it a win-win. The company sells their cars here, and these days most of them are built here. Give people jobs so they can use their money to buy their product. It was a logical step."

Bartlett took another taste of his liquor and then tilted the glass back. A quarter of the whiskey disappeared.

"I was hoping to continue our conversation from yesterday," Edward said.

"It wasn't a conversation. It was a warning."

"Okay. A warning. Anything else to warn me about?"

Bartlett looked around the watering hole.

"Who are you looking for?" Edward asked.

"Eyes. Ears."

"It's just you and me. And the bartender in back."

"The bartender don't like Pervis Wade any more than you do. He just puts up with him because the boys from the window company drop a thousand dollars a week in this place. Sometimes more. Hell, I've seen them drop a grand in a single night when things get rowdy."

"Can't blame the bartender for ignoring trouble from the goose that lays the golden egg. You do what you have to do."

"Yes, indeedy. We all do what we have to do."

"And that's why I'm here," Edward said. "Doing what I have to do. And I was hoping you would help."

"With what?"

"I want to know everything you know about Pervis Wade."

"I told you enough."

"Things changed."

"Since when?"

Edward explained the stolen Palmetto Windows truck subsequently found burned out in a cotton field south of town.

"Classic Pervis Wade," Bartlett, said. He moved his hand to his beer, leaving his shot glass unattended.

"What do you mean?" Edward asked.

"I mean Pervis Wade should probably be in jail for any number of things he's done."

"Like what?"

"Name it."

Bartlett's gaze seemed to melt into the bottles on the bar and he was quiet for a moment before he spoke.

"It's a fairly well-known fact that Pervis Wade beat a man to death with his bare hands. Over a parking space. The case was ruled self-defense because the dead man had a tire iron in his possession. Or so the story goes. The curious part was the man had another tire iron in the trunk of the vehicle. I'm no mechanic, but I don't think too many people carry around an extra tire iron."

"My wife carries a AAA card in case she gets a flat."

"Exactly. And if you believe the rumors, the tire iron the dead guy had only fit lug nuts for a commercial vehicle, not a passenger car."

"So Pervis wrestled the tire iron away from the guy and then beat him to death with his bare hands?"

"More likely that Pervis beat the man to death and then placed the tire iron at the scene and made up the whole story."

"Jesus."

"I tried to warn you."

"What else has he done?"

"Robbery."

"What did he steal?"

"A fishing boat. A big one. Nothing ever came of it. He returned the boat to the owner and everyone shook hands."

"Theft and murder. Nice guy."

"Last year he had his third DUI dismissed on a technicality."

"A thief, a drunk, and a murderer," Edward said.

"Sounds like the beginning of a joke. A thief, a drunk, and a murderer walk into a bar. Just need to come up with a punch line," Bartlett replied.

"I don't think I want to hear one."

"Pervis is evil. And I know from watching you guys talk yesterday that he enjoyed toying with you. I think he gets off on it. Like a cat with a mouse. And you were the mouse, in case you didn't figure that out yourself. No offense."

"I think he's still toying with me."

Bartlett moved his hand back to his shot glass. "Do you think Pervis took this work truck and burned it?"

"I do," said Edward.

"And the police believe Pervis may be involved with your wife and her disappearance?"

"I don't see how they can't. The last man seen leaving my house before my wife went missing was driving a truck that was stolen and later torched."

"Sounds awfully suspicious."

"Yes it does."

"But I'm sure whoever Pervis hires as a lawyer will be quick to point out that cars do get stolen here in Tupelo every day. Work trucks, too."

"The timing is just a little too convenient for me."

Bartlett shrugged his shoulders.

"What would you do if you were me?" Edward asked.

Bartlett thought about the question, grunting as he considered his response.

"Not sure. Go back to the police. Put the pressure on. Maybe hire a private detective."

"Why a private detective?"

"Because if Pervis Wade is one step ahead of the police, you need to be one step ahead of both of them."

"Hiring a private detective is something I've only seen in the movies."

"Private detectives can do things real police can't do. Things that local politics and even the Constitution don't necessarily allow, if you get my drift."

"Anyone in town you can recommend?"

"There are a couple of places around. You shouldn't have any trouble finding them."

Edward checked the time on the PBR clock.

"But before you go kicking this hornet's nest any harder, you may want to find out more about Pervis Wade. Just so you know what you're getting into. Check out some of the court records. Get a copy of his criminal history. It's all public information."

"Why would I do that? You already warned me what kind of person he is."

"Seeing is believing. Some things need to be seen with your own eyes. You say your wife is missing. You say Pervis Wade was seen at your house. You came to his bar asking questions. A truck was torched. You need to open your eyes and stare directly at the devil you're dealing with."

A long silence fell on the two men before Edward downed the rest of his beer and pushed his empty mug away from his seat.

Bartlett finished his shot and stood from his stool.

"You heading out?" Edward asked, also standing.

"Just draining the lizard. If you're not here when I get back, good luck with your wife."

"Thanks."

Bartlett took a step, stopped, and turned. "I've got a favor to ask you."

"What's that?"

"Don't keep coming around here. It's not safe for you, and I don't need trouble at the only bar near my house."

"You really think it's dangerous to come here?"

"I do."

"And why isn't it dangerous for you?"

"Because I'm not you. I'm only in danger if you go running off at the mouth, telling people we've been talking. So don't."

Edward pushed his stool back towards the bar. "If you think Pervis Wade is so dangerous, why did you help me?"

Bartlett placed one of his hands on a barstool and started undoing the clasps on his overalls. Before Edward could protest, Bartlett's old denim overalls hit the floor, balling up near the man's ankles.

Edward took one look at Bartlett below the waist and understood. Heavily scarred skin covered both legs, stretching from the overalls around his ankles to his upper thighs where his tighty-whities hung.

Bartlett looked down at his own legs and then up at Edward.

"Fifteen years ago I fell through unsecured scaffolding at work. Spent a little too long in a vat of hot water."

"Ouch. Where do you work?"

"I spent twenty years at Mississippi Steel down in Columbus. After the accident, I was forced to retire. Took a settlement and disability. Second and third degree burns over twenty percent of my body. Fortunately, my balls and pecker were spared. Still got problems walking. And I can't eat crabs or crawfish no more. The sound of those suckers scratching the side of the metal pot as they get cooked alive is too much for me."

"Sorry."

"You don't have to be sorry."

"I still feel bad."

"Life goes on, as you know. But now life goes on in baggy overalls."

Edward again looked down at his arm and then at Bartlett's legs.

The older man bent down, pulled up his overalls, and fixed one side over his shoulder.

Bartlett stared into Edward's eyes and added, "So you asked why I helped you. My answer is simple: some brotherhoods are thicker than either blood or water."

CHAPTER 9

EDWARD PARKED AND shoved two quarters into the meter on West Jefferson Street. He crossed two lanes of asphalt and headed for the door of the Lee County Justice Center, a white four-story building with soaring columns that gave the structure a sense of judicial authority.

Edward placed his belongings in a blue plastic basket and passed through the metal detector. He noted the dozen or so law enforcement officers crisscrossing the lobby. A second group jawed with one another near the elevators.

The third floor of the building housed Taxes, Real Estate Assessments, and Records. Edward followed the small sign hanging from the ceiling and arrived at an alcove with a counter window. A woman in her twenties with a diamond stud in her nose stood from a nearby desk and smiled.

"What can I help you with?"

"I'm looking for copies of official records."

The woman handed him a laminated piece of paper. "That's the list of available records. The cost of each record is on the right. I'll need to see an ID."

Edward read through the records list, ranging from marriage licenses to death certificates.

"Which one of these covers criminal records?"

"Criminal and arrest records both fall under court records."

"How long will it take?"

"Depends on how much information we have. I have to make copies.

But just so we're clear, we only handle records for Lee County. If you want a background check on an individual that covers other jurisdictions, we don't do that. You wouldn't believe how many people show up here asking us to run background checks on their new boyfriend or girlfriend."

"No background checks. Got it. And you only cover Lee County, which includes Tupelo and the surrounding areas."

"Wow. Someone who actually pays attention to what is being said. Now, what's the name of the person you're inquiring about?"

"Pervis Wade."

"Can you spell that for me?" the clerk asked, grabbing a pen and a stack of Post-it Notes.

Edward spelled and the woman jotted. "Take a seat. Let me see what I have."

Edward took the laminated list of records to a chair against the wall, directly across from the records alcove. Twenty minutes passed and the clerk reappeared with several folders. Edward rose from his chair and approached the counter.

"Here's all the information I could find. A few arrest records with the associated court proceeding documents. He doesn't have a criminal record."

"I know he's had trouble with the law. I assumed he had one."

"You only get a criminal record if you've been convicted. This person has no adult conviction record."

"Does that mean he has a juvenile record?"

"He may. I was just differentiating because, well, there's a difference."

Edward placed the laminated records menu on the counter and put his finger on the middle of the page. "I wanted to ask for one more set of records, if I could."

"We don't close for another half hour. You can request anything you want."

Edward kept his finger on the lamented sheet and said, "I want any search warrant records for Pervis Wade and Palmetto Windows."

"The window company over near the train tracks?"

"That's correct. Pervis Wade works there. The search warrant I'm looking for was served this morning."

The clerk paused and tilted her head to the side.

"Okay. That should be easy. We only process a couple of search warrants a week. Let me see what we have."

Edward waited another ten minutes, foregoing the chair for pacing up and down the hall.

"Excuse me," the clerk said as Edward appeared and disappeared out of view. He stopped pacing and moved back to the counter.

"We don't have a record of any search warrants for Pervis Wade or for Palmetto Windows."

"You don't?"

"No."

"Are you sure?"

"Yes. I was actually pretty sure when you asked, but needed to double-check. I didn't remember seeing either one of those names on any search warrants this week."

Edward felt the hair on his right arm stand on end.

"Any chance it's just stuck in the wheels of bureaucracy somehow? Like I said, the warrant was supposed to have been served this morning."

"I checked. We have no record of any search warrant to be executed today. "

"Is it possible it just hasn't been filed yet?"

"I guess. But it would be very unusual not to have a record in the system. They typically need to be filed before they're executed."

Edward took a deep breath and stared into the depths of the records office behind the woman at the counter.

"You have to be kidding me," he whispered almost inaudibly.

"Excuse me?"

"How much do I owe for the arrest records?" he asked in a louder voice.

The clerk grabbed the calculator on the corner of the counter and quickly tapped on the numeric keys. She turned the calculator so Edward could see the total and said, "We take cash, check, or credit."

CHAPTER 10

EDWARD TOOK A cursory pass by Palmetto Windows without stopping. From the road he could see Darlene at her desk through the front window. He drove for another block, turned around, and then pulled down the gravel road that led to the rear of the building.

He kicked up dust until he reached the back of the warehouse where a chain-link fence topped with barbed wire enclosed a large parking lot. Edward pulled through the open gate to the lot and came to a halt. A single red truck was backed up to the warehouse loading dock. As Edward exited his car, a man wearing the standard Palmetto Windows company shirt appeared from inside.

"No customers allowed back here," the man said, apologetically.

"Okay. No problem. I was just hoping to ask a couple of quick questions."

The man had a goatee and moustache that met at the sides of his mouth. Gray hairs were in the first stages of their assault.

"Are you the same guy from the bar last night?" the man asked.

"I am."

"Well, your friend Pervis ain't around."

"I'm not looking for Pervis. And he isn't a friend."

"How can I help you?"

"What time did you get to work this morning, if you don't mind me asking?"

"Not sure how that's any of your business."

"I'd probably feel the same way if a stranger ambushed me at work and starting asking questions. But my wife's been missing for two days now and I'm running out of time and patience."

The man seemed to squint in a moment of suspicion. "Well, I sure as hell don't know how your wife disappearing has anything to do with what time I got to work this morning. But from one married guy to another, I'll tell you just the same. I got here a couple of minutes after seven. Earlier than everyone except Darlene out front."

"Are you usually here that early?"

"Yeah. I got little kids so I'm up early anyway. I clocked in if you want to see my timesheet."

"No, I believe you. What about everyone else?"

"Most of the boys ran a little behind this morning. I understand they stayed out late on account of the birthday party at the Brew Ha. I was on my first job of the day before any of the other installers even showed up to get their truck and inventory."

Edward considered his next question before asking it. "Did you hear about the stolen work truck yesterday?"

"I did."

"Does that happen much?"

"A stolen truck?"

"Yes."

"Not since I've been working here. We have tools stolen off the back of the trucks on occasion. Even a window now and then. But the whole truck? No."

"Did you notice the truck was missing when you arrived?"

"Nope. But it's not my job to count the trucks. I'm only responsible for my truck."

"Your truck?"

"Yep. Number nine." The man motioned towards the yellow sticker on the window on the back of the cab indicating the number.

"I thought you guys took whatever truck you wanted. First come, first serve."

"Who told you that?"

"I'm not sure I want to say."

"Well, it ain't true. Each employee has a truck assigned to them. Every once in a while someone will quit the company and there's a bit of shuffling for a better vehicle. But for the most part, everyone keeps his own truck. Easier to keep a handle on maintenance. Drive the same truck every day and you know when the brakes are getting soft. When the tires feel low. When the truck starts pulling to one side."

"Makes sense."

"Some of the guys take their trucks home at night. I don't because I have two kids with two car seats. Some afternoons I have to pick my kids up from school. The truck doesn't do me any good. Two car seats won't fit."

Edward looked around the lot. "So if you have truck number nine, what number truck does Pervis drive?"

"Number four."

"Are you sure?"

The man nodded. "Yes, I'm sure."

"And is number four the truck that went missing?"

"That's right."

"Is this lot secured at night?"

"It is. Big padlock on a big chain on the gate. All employees have a key." The man nodded in the direction of the fence.

"Was the gate locked when you arrived yesterday?"

"It was. I open it most mornings."

"So someone stole the truck without cutting the lock?"

"That's what I heard. But like I said, sometimes the guys take their trucks home at night."

"What about Pervis?"

"He usually drives his own car."

Edward's attention faded for a moment, then he asked, "Were you here this morning when the police served their search warrant?"

"I don't know anything about a search warrant."

"This morning. A search warrant should have been served this morning by the Lee County Sheriff's Department."

"Not as far as I know."

"So the police didn't talk to you? Your truck wasn't searched?"

"Nope."

"And you didn't hear anything about the police coming out here? Nothing about them searching any of the other vehicles."

"Just what I've heard from you."

Edward stood in silence, trying to process what he had learned.

"You got me curious now. What were the police looking for?" the man asked.

Edward started to answer but stopped after spitting out the first few words. "So, no run-ins with the police at all?"

"That's right."

The man climbed down from the loading dock and headed towards the driver's side of the truck. Looking over at Edward the man asked, "You feeling okay?"

"Not really, why?" Edward said, his face pale, his gaze disconnected.

"Well, don't take this the wrong way, but you seem to be talking a bit of nonsense. I have a cousin who's as normal as can be until he forgets to take his meds. You're kind of acting like him."

"I'll be all right," Edward lied. "Thanks for your time."

CHAPTER 11

EDWARD PARKED HIS car in the visitor's row of the parking lot for the Lee County Sheriff's Department, a non-descript silver box of a building under the landing path for the airport. He could feel his heart pounding, the blood coursing through his carotids. His pulled open the front door to the building with trembling hands. An officer at a platform desk sat behind a small Plexiglas divider.

"Good evening. How can I help you?"

"My name is Edward Winston. My wife, Holly, went missing earlier this week. I'm here to speak to the man-in-charge."

"The man-in-charge?"

"That's right. The man-in-charge. I'm sure you've heard the expression, even in Tupelo."

"And what did you say your name was?"

"Edward Winston."

"Have a seat. I'll be right back." The officer did as promised and said, "You're lucky Sheriff Blazer is available to see you. He's a busy man and it's getting late."

"And he's the highest ranking person at this location, correct?"

"That's right, *the* alpha dog. The top banana. Where the buck stops. The man-in-charge, as you say. All of the above."

Edward nodded. "Lead the way."

"I suggest you simply address the sheriff as 'Sheriff Blazer,'" the officer said before ushering Edward through the small metal detector.

"Follow me."

The walk through Lee County Sheriff's Department was as dull as a stroll through Fujita Automotive. Most of the employees were partitioned behind cubicle walls, only the top of their heads visible as Edward followed the officer through the labyrinth of the office floor.

A minute later Edward was standing at the threshold to Sheriff Blazer's office as the man-in-charge was finishing a phone call. The officer who had escorted Edward across the work floor made eye contact with the sheriff and received a nod in return. The officer disappeared and the sheriff motioned for Edward to sit down on one of the two leather chairs facing the large desk. Edward moved to sit as the top banana hung up the phone, stood, and extended his hand. Sheriff Blazer pulled at the cuffs on his shirt as his lanky frame returned to his seat. He ran his fingers through his perfectly combed gray hair and donned a serious expression.

"Mr. Winston. I'm sorry to meet you under these circumstances. I'm also very sorry to hear about your wife. Rest assured we're doing everything we can to locate her."

"That's why I'm here, Sheriff Blazer. I want to make sure everything is being done."

"I assure you we handle all our missing person cases with the same level of energy and conviction."

I hope not, Edward thought, stifling the remark before it escaped into the open.

"I had some concerns about the investigation. Something quite troubling actually. And fair warning, it may be something you'll find quite troubling as well."

"Should we call the detective on your case into the office? Maybe it's something he needs to hear as well."

Edward stood from his seat and motioned towards the door. "Do you mind if I close this?"

"If you think it's necessary."

"I would prefer it," Edward replied, shutting the door and returning to his leather chair.

"I have reason to believe that the detective on my case, Will Rafferty, is not performing his duties in good faith."

Sheriff Blazer scowled. "Those are serious accusations."

"Yes, they are. Which is why I warned you what I'm about to say may be troubling."

"Go on."

"Are you aware of the details of my wife's disappearance?"

"I have a pretty good handle on it. I'm updated on every unsolved felony and missing person case on a daily basis. I understand a search warrant has been issued for a commercial work vehicle at Palmetto Windows. It has also come to my attention that one of the vehicles we wanted to search has been found destroyed in South Tupelo."

"That's correct."

"I'm sure from your perspective that probably seems like a real blow. And it certainly is not a positive development. But neither is it the end of the investigation."

"I hope not."

"Good. A positive attitude can be a real help in times such as these."

Edward stared at Sheriff Blazer for a long moment, trying to measure the man in the crisp uniform behind the desk framed by a wall of accolades.

"I'm glad you're up to date on the search warrant. The specifics of that search warrant are what I wanted to talk to you about."

The sheriff leaned forward. "What do you want to know? I approved the search warrant on our side and Detective Rafferty took it to the courthouse for a judge's signature."

Edward could taste a small amount of bile in the back of his throat.

"You handled the search warrant?"

"I approved it."

"For Palmetto Windows?"

"That's right."

Edward's breath became shallow and rapid. "And that search warrant was served this morning?"

"That was my understanding. I wasn't on the premises at the time, but I believe that was the case."

"Well, that's interesting. Because I just went down to the courthouse and asked to see a copy of the search warrant. They didn't have one. In fact, they showed me a list of all of the search warrants issued this week. All of them are a matter of public record. There were no search warrants filed by anyone from the Lee County Sheriff's Department for Palmetto Windows."

Sheriff Blazer leaned all the way back in his chair. The leather made an audible crunch and the springs of the chair squeaked. Edward thought he noticed the sheriff clench his jaw.

"I'm sure there must be a mistake."

"Perhaps. Though I'm not sure where that would have occurred."

"Paperwork at the courthouse," the sheriff answered.

"Maybe. That's the obvious answer. But Detective Rafferty claimed he served that warrant this morning. So, after checking at the courthouse, I went over to Palmetto Windows."

"Did you speak with Darlene?"

"No. I spoke with one of the window installers. I didn't get the man's name but he told me no search warrant was executed. At least not on his truck."

"Maybe he didn't know. You should have asked Darlene. She is the brains of the operation."

"I met her yesterday. She was very helpful. Solid Southern hospitality."

"We all try to extend Southern hospitality here in Tupelo. We pride ourselves on it."

Edward didn't respond and Sheriff Blazer stared across his desk.

"Are you aware the missing Palmetto Windows truck was stolen from a locked parking lot behind the building?" Edward asked.

"I heard something to that effect."

"And the gate on the parking lot was locked when the first employee arrived the next day, meaning whoever stole the truck either threw the vehicle over the fence or they had a key."

Sheriff Blazer seemed to stare even harder at Edward. "I'll tell you what, Mr. Winston. Why don't you let me handle this? You've done enough detective work for the day. I'll look into it personally. Maybe there was a miscommunication of the timing of the search warrant. Maybe the search warrant is scheduled for tomorrow."

"That would be a relief."

"Indeed it would be. Let me check into it. In the meantime, I'm going to ask you to stand down. We don't need you stepping on any more toes.

Hampering an active police investigation. That could look a little awkward. A man hampering the police investigation of his missing wife."

Edward felt chills run up the back of his neck. Even his nerve-damaged left arm tingled.

"I can see the conflict of interest from your perspective," Edward replied, realizing any productive relationship with the sheriff's department had just crossed the point of no return.

"What do you say I throw my weight around a little and see if I can't get to the bottom of things? I'll have Detective Rafferty contact you after I shake the trees and chew a little ass."

Edward stood from his seat and extended his hand. Sheriff Blazer shook it without looking him directly in the eyes.

"Thank you for your time," Edward said, backing out of the room slowly.

*

Edward picked up his pace as he headed for the double doors at the front of the building. Stepping outside, he lost the battle with his nerves and vomited in the bushes adjacent to the main entrance. An additional bout of dry heaves strained his stomach as he shuffled towards his car, lightheaded.

Behind the wheel, Edward wiped his mouth with his forearm. No longer able to contain his emotions, Edward slammed both hands into the steering wheel and unleashed a guttural yell. Then he strung together a stream of curses before his voice faded and he fell into deep sobs of helplessness.

CHAPTER 12

EDWARD STEPPED FROM the shower and heard knocking on the front door. He slipped into a pair of shorts and a T-shirt and headed for the living room with wet hair. With a towel over his shoulder, Edward greeted Detective Rafferty through the screen door.

"Do you have a minute?" the detective asked from the front porch. His detective's badge hung from the leather belt on his slacks.

"Let's talk outside," Edward replied, throwing his towel on the arm of the sofa.

Both men stepped off the porch and onto the concrete sidewalk that ran from the front door to the driveway. Halfway down the walk, Detective Rafferty turned around, leaving the two men standing face-to-face, a few yards apart.

"Sheriff Blazer wanted me to come out and apologize for the mishap with the search warrant."

"I'm not sure I'd call it a mishap."

"A misunderstanding."

"A lie."

"We were hoping you wouldn't see it that way. Your wife's disappearance is still active. We need to focus on that."

"I think the investigation took a hit when Pervis Wade decided to burn his work truck. I'm going to venture a guess that some kind of pertinent evidence was destroyed."

"As I said before, we may never know. And if you hadn't gone to the Brew Ha acting like a detective…"

"You keep accusing me of acting like a detective. You could be accused of the same thing. *Acting* like a detective."

Detective Rafferty inhaled through his nose and hocked a loogie into Edward's front yard. When Rafferty looked back at Edward, his apologetic tone had vacated.

"Mr. Winston, I came here this evening as a gesture of good faith. It's apparent that sentiment won't be reciprocated."

"I think goodwill left when you told me you served a search warrant you didn't actually serve."

"Ahh. I see. For the record, I believe that's where the confusion is. Where our misunderstanding is coming from. I distinctly remember telling you that we were going to get a search warrant to search the Palmetto Windows trucks. I don't recall saying the warrant had been executed."

"Well you did. And so did Sheriff Blazer."

"I think the facts of the matter are a bit different. But I guess we won't be seeing eye-to-eye on that communication."

"I'll agree to that."

"For what it's worth, I've been told the search warrant is now on record at the courthouse."

"Oh, I'm sure it is. You created the evidence to support your version of the story. To support your claim that it was all a miscommunication."

"I'd be careful with that accusation."

Edward paused. "Suddenly everyone's telling me to be careful."

"Good advice."

"I'm not soliciting advice."

"That doesn't make it wrong."

The two men stared at each other before Detective Rafferty broke the silence. "Mr. Winston, did you have a life insurance policy on your wife?"

"I did."

"Was it a large one? And before you answer, know that I can obtain this information with or without your cooperation."

"She had a million-dollar policy on me. I had a million-dollar policy on her."

Detective Rafferty whistled. "Those are really big policies for a young couple."

"We were hoping to have kids. And the younger you get a life insurance policy, the cheaper it is."

"It's still a lot of money. And you know what they say, money is motive."

"Is that what they say?"

"It is."

"Are we done here, Detective?"

"If that's how you want this conversation to end."

"I think you just made that decision."

Detective Rafferty slowly turned towards the driveway and paused. "Sheriff Blazer also wanted me to pass along his regrets on the lost evidence."

"He already did. When I was at the station."

"Oh. Good. Good. Evidence is a funny thing, you know. At any moment it can be lost or found. It can disappear and reappear."

"Excuse me?" Edward asked.

"I think you heard me. Oh, and one more thing…"

"What's that?"

"Check out the eleven o'clock news tonight. The sheriff's department is preparing to announce a person of interest in your wife's disappearance."

"What are you saying, Detective?"

"Tune in at eleven."

CHAPTER 13

DETECTIVE RAFFERTY WAS back at Edward's door a little after seven in the morning. Behind the detective's freshly combed red hair, four marked sheriff cars were visible: two in the driveway and two on the street.

"Search warrant," Detective Rafferty said tersely as Edward opened his front door.

"Really?"

"Standard procedure for a missing person."

"I would've let you in without the warrant. Besides, Officer Gooden searched my house the night Holly went missing. You also toured the house, if I remember correctly."

"This is going to be a bit more detailed. A bit more invasive, if you will. We will be removing items from your home as part of the investigation."

Edward motioned for the detective and his entourage to enter. Detective Rafferty smiled and pushed the search warrant into Edward's chest.

"That was a nice press conference last night," Edward said.

"Did you catch it live?"

"Yes, and it's been replaying all morning. I'm sure naming me as a person of interest is going to make me popular around town."

"The sheriff is responsible for maintaining the peace in this county. Naming a person of interest calms people down."

"We both know I had nothing to do with my wife's disappearance."

"Time will tell," Detective Rafferty replied, heading down the hall in the direction of the bedrooms.

Two hours later, the team of officers left the premises with a dozen boxes of clothes, personal care items from the bathroom, and two laptops. Rafferty handed Edward a property voucher with a list of items being confiscated.

"Are these the only computers you have?" the detective asked, motioning towards the two laptops in a shallow box.

"Yes. One is Holly's. The other is mine. Mine is used primarily for surfing the Internet and accessing my work email. My wife uses hers to check Facebook, send email, and shop online. I already checked her computer. There's nothing there. Nothing to indicate she was planning to go missing."

The detective stared stoically at Edward. Then he asked, "Are they password protected?"

"Yes."

"What are the passwords?"

"I don't have to provide that."

"Yes, you do."

"No, I don't. The courts have ruled that a password is legally equivalent to testimony. It's protected by the Fifth Amendment. It cannot be coerced."

"Now, how would you know that, Mr. Winston?"

"Because I work with computers all day."

Detective Rafferty glanced around at his departing colleagues. "I really think it's time you asked yourself if you would like to cooperate with this police investigation."

"I was cooperating. Right up until your speech last night about evidence being lost and found. And before naming me as a person of interest."

"And now you won't provide us with your password?"

"Not at this time."

"You want to play hardball, we can play hardball. But I'm warning you, your lack of cooperation will be noted."

"You're wasting your time, Detective. There's nothing on either of those computers that will be of use to you."

"I'll let our forensic guys determine that."

"Your forensic guys will never get into those computers."

"Oh yeah? Why's that?"

"Because they're protected by 2048-bit encryption. Something you probably don't understand."

"So they can't be broken into?"

"No, they can. But not by the Lee County Sheriff's Department. Not in this lifetime."

"We can always get help. We can go to your ISP. Or we can take your computers to the Feds."

"You can get all the data you want from our ISP, but they won't get you into the machines themselves."

"Then we will take them to the Feds."

Edward considered the threat and a smirk slowly spread across his face. "Go ahead and do that. Take them to the Feds."

Detective Rafferty glared at Edward with a cold stare, his face turning a shade of crimson. "We'll be in touch," Rafferty added, his eyes narrowing as he stepped out the door.

Edward watched the sheriff vehicles pull away from his house and sat down to read the list of confiscated items on the property voucher. Sitting on the couch, Edward replayed the last two exchanges he had had with the detective in charge of his wife's disappearance.

"*Good advice, Detective. Let's take it to the Feds,*" Edward whispered to himself as he reached for his phone.

CHAPTER 14

THE MAYFLOWER CAFE sat two blocks from the governor's mansion, on the corner of Roach and Capitol Streets in downtown Jackson, Mississippi. Easily identified by the vintage neon sign clinging to the façade, for eighty years the restaurant had built its reputation on serving Greek-inspired seafood, their success flying in the face of conventional wisdom that traditional Southern fare ruled the roost. Tables brimmed with customers—lunch and dinner—seven days a week.

Edward stepped into the Mayflower and was directed towards one of the booths near the rear of the floor. The din from the lunchtime crowd was punctuated by the bustle of the partially exposed kitchen. Tables and booths boasted a cross-section of the local populace. Retirees rubbing elbows with men in suits. A group of young men in workshop coveralls sitting next to a pair of elderly gentlemen who looked as if they had just stepped off a bass boat. A quartet of college students eating amidst a spread of books and open laptops.

The waitress, a Southern blonde in her late twenties, stopped by the table and took Edward's drink order.

"Iced tea, please."

"One sweet tea, coming right up."

Edward kept one eye on the restaurant's bustling crowd and his other eye on the front door until a woman matching the description of his lunch date entered. He stood from his booth and waved his hand as the tall, professionally dressed black woman pushed her sunglasses onto the top of her head. A moment later the woman joined Edward at the table.

"You must be Mrs. Washington," Edward said.

"Special Agent Camille Washington, FBI," she replied, extending her hand and her badge.

Edward read the badge and then motioned towards the seat. "Please."

Agent Washington put her car keys and phone on the corner of the table and sat down.

"Thank you for meeting me," Edward said.

"It's my job, Mr. Winston."

"You could have insisted I meet with you in the office."

"I could have. But I'm a Special Agent for Color of Law investigations. Typically these investigations require a bit more sensitivity than other crimes under the purview of the FBI. Meeting off-site is not uncommon in my area of expertise."

"What does Color of Law cover exactly?"

"Color of Law deals with the abuse of power by authority. Judges, police, wardens, guards. We investigate everything from excessive force, to false arrest, to fabrication of evidence."

"How about the disappearance of evidence?"

"The destruction of evidence? We cover that too."

"Have you ever dealt with the Lee County Sheriff's Department?"

"Personally, no. But I know Lee County is one of the largest counties in Mississippi. Most of its population resides in the city of Tupelo. The city also has its own police force, whose jurisdiction ends at the city limits. The Lee County Sheriff's Department has jurisdiction for the entire county, including the city."

"What does that really mean?"

"That means both the sheriff's department and the city police can arrest someone in the city of Tupelo. But there are some things the sheriff's department is responsible for that the city police are not involved with. This includes running the jail and handling security for the courts. Lee County Sheriff's Department and the Tupelo City Police have overlapping jurisdiction within the city limits, but they try to divvy up the tasks."

"I don't know if that's good or bad news for my wife's investigation. I've only dealt with the Lee County Sheriff's Department."

"Generally speaking, we see less corruption with sheriff's offices. We see more problems with larger police forces. The flip side to that is the typical sheriff's department is smaller and the people who work there are often more tight-knit. It can be harder to get evidence against a sheriff's department."

"So that falls into the category of bad news."

"Every case is different."

"I guess," Edward replied, reaching for the menu on the table.

"Have you ever been here before?" Agent Washington asked.

"I've never been to Jackson."

"How did you like the drive?"

"It's a straight shot, three hours. Not much to see out the window."

"Well, if you've never been to Jackson, at least you're starting at the right spot. The Mayflower Cafe is famous for their seafood."

"I think I'm going with the chicken lunch special. I stay away from seafood when I'm not near the coast."

"You do know seafood can be shipped in refrigerated trucks? Sometimes they even fly it in via plane."

"I don't want my fish to fly."

Agent Washington raised a single eyebrow in a look of curiosity. "To each his own. But before you leave, you should get some Comeback Sauce to take with you."

"What's that?"

"The Mayflower's secret sauce."

"And it's named Comeback Sauce? If I take it with me, I don't have to come back."

"Clever, Mr. Winston."

After placing their order with their waitress, Agent Washington restarted the conversation.

"You mentioned something about missing evidence when we spoke on the phone. A truck from a window company. You think it was used in your wife's disappearance?"

"I do. I just don't have any proof."

"But you believe it."

"Yes. And I realize if it boils down to a believability issue, the Lee County Sheriff's Department is going to have the upper hand."

"Help me to believe you. Tell me what you're thinking."

Edward explained the timing of the search warrant, revisited the stolen red truck that turned up torched, and covered the highlights of the ensuing conversation with the sheriff, and the detective's subsequent claim of a miscommunication. He concluded with the search warrant that was served at his residence, the dire warnings from a guy at the local bar, all topped by being named as a person of interest in his wife's disappearance.

Agent Washington scribbled onto a legal pad for a moment and then looked up. "For what it's worth, some of the things you just shared concern me."

"So you believe me?"

"I believe you believe what you're saying is true. And that's a good thing."

"I get the feeling you're going to follow that with 'but…'"

"I am. What I'm wondering is whether you've considered the police could be telling the truth?"

"I assumed they were. At first. Not anymore. And if you need proof, let me wear a wire."

"That would be step Z. We are on step A. There are quite a few bridges to cross before we get there."

"Like?"

"Motive, evidence. Explaining your behavior."

"My behavior?"

"Yes. As much as I want to believe you, I'm concerned you may have acted a little too impulsively. You admitted you approached the person you thought was the prime suspect in your wife's disappearance and confronted him before the police could interview him?"

"I did."

"At a bar?"

"That's right."

"And this may have led to the destruction of evidence?"

Edward tilted his head to the side and then nodded. "It's possible."

"Do you see how confronting a suspect could be construed by the police as hindering an active investigation?"

"I guess."

"It wouldn't be a hard case for the Lee County Sheriff's Department to prove."

"So you're naturally on their side. That was my concern."

"Don't get ahead of yourself, Mr. Winston. I work for the FBI."

"Which means your first reaction is to support other law enforcement officers."

"Mr. Winston, have you ever heard of investigative protocol?"

"No, but I can imagine what it means."

"What it means is that criminal cases are built through hard work, evidence, testimony, and corroborating witnesses. A grieving husband with a missing wife is not the most rational investigator."

"Understood."

"Let me ask a question that any good defense attorney would ask. Who do you think destroyed whatever evidence may have been in this red truck?"

"Pervis Wade."

"Not the police?"

"No."

"So the police didn't destroy evidence at all, as far as you know? The suspect did?"

Edward recognized the flaw in his accusations and he stewed in his own defeat. He could feel his right armpit starting to perspire and his face turn flush. He took a sip of tea and crushed a single ice cube in his rear molars.

"And what about the witness in the case?" Agent Washington asked.

"Mr. Poole. He's a neighbor. Says he saw the red truck leave my house. The last contractor to leave the day Holly disappeared."

"And did he see your wife in the truck?"

"No."

"And there have been contractors at your house most days?"

"Most days for a month."

"And what can you tell me about this Bartlett character you met at the bar? The one who warned you about Pervis Wade."

"I get the feeling you're not going to like my answer."

"Give me a try."

"He may be the local drunk, of sorts."

"He *may* be?"

"Well, he could be just one of many local drunks."

"And this local drunk informed you that your prime suspect, Pervis Wade, had a history of crime but he had never been convicted?"

"Something like that."

The food arrived and Agent Washington briefly dipped her head in a moment of prayer, her lips silently moving. She shook a little pepper over her plate and then looked back up at Edward.

"Mr. Winston, I think we're going to need to start over with your claim that the sheriff's department is somehow, shall we say, negligent or remiss in performing their duties with regard to your wife's disappearance. We're going to need evidence and a motive."

"Which is why I've come to you."

"And I understand that. But you also have to cease and desist. You need to let me do my job. I cannot have you hindering any investigation. Their investigation or my investigation."

"I'll stay out of your way. But to be clear, as far as the Lee County Sheriff's Department is concerned, I didn't interfere with their investigation because they weren't actually investigating anything. Nor were they going to investigate. I don't think the sheriff's office had any intention of questioning Pervis Wade."

"The police's intent is nearly impossible to prove. It may not be a useful avenue to pursue."

"What about the lack of a search warrant?"

"You mean the delayed search warrant."

"It was filed after the fact."

"As true as that may be, official court documents support the claim that a search warrant was filed. The sheriff's department could easily argue the search warrant was filed on time. Whether the police intended for the search warrant to be served on the day *you* thought, that is another question. That would be unsubstantiated without evidence."

"Sounds like another point in favor of the sheriff's office."

"I operate on facts."

"What I've told you are the facts."

"Then what you're missing is the why."

"The why?"

"Yes. Why would the sheriff's department let a suspect in a missing person case walk?"

"I don't know."

"If we can answer that question, we may have the key to getting all the answers."

"So what's next?"

"I'm going back to the lone witness. I want to talk to your neighbor."

"I can introduce you to him."

"Mr. Winston, are you not listening? I want you to step back from the investigation. I have a badge. I don't need an introduction."

CHAPTER 15

AGENT CAMILLE WASHINGTON parked her car in the driveway in front of the pickup truck with the For Sale sign in the windshield. She looked over at the number on the mailbox across the street and her eyes jumped to the Winston residence beyond the manicured lawn.

Turning away, she made her way to Mr. Poole's front door and knocked, sending Tarzan the watchdog into a barking fit. Standing in the heat of the sun on the front porch, she waited until the dog quieted before knocking a second time with the same result.

"Yappy dogs," she said aloud, slowly shaking her head. She stepped back from the small front porch and peeked through the bay window as best she could from her disadvantaged perspective. She kept her attention on the front windows as she headed back towards her car, but when her black pumps hit the equally black asphalt of the driveway, she stopped in her tracks. She inhaled deeply, leaned towards the garage, and inhaled again.

With a sinking feeling in her stomach, she approached the garage and rose to her toes to peer through a window in the door. The unmoving pair of legs protruding from beneath a white '72 Chevelle was the omen she had hoped not to find. She knocked on the garage door, announced herself per protocol, and then reached down and twisted the handle. Yanking upward, the unmistakable fetid stench of decomposition and feces assaulted her olfactory senses. She turned away and gagged before moving in the direction of the yard for air. Hands on her hips, she took several deep breaths before heading back to the interior of the garage.

She approached the legs and gently tapped the closest one with her toe before stooping down and peeking under the vehicle. Standing, she removed her phone from her pocket and called 911.

*

The ambulance arrived within ten minutes and the lead EMT shook Agent Washington's hand in the driveway without breaking pace. Two other EMTs in matching blue jumpers opened the back door of the vehicle and began preparing emergency equipment on the stretcher.

Agent Washington walked next to the lead EMT—a vertically challenged man with broad shoulders and curly hair—and the pair stopped at the threshold of the garage. The scent of Mr. Poole's decomposition had already begun to attract flies.

"This is how you found it?" the EMT asked.

"I took a quick look and called 911. The smell was a pretty good indicator of the situation."

"You deal with many dead bodies?"

"In a previous life. Not these days. But one good sniff of a decomposing body is hard to forget. The nasal equivalent of something you can't unsee."

"Any reason the FBI is interested in this guy?"

"Nothing that would explain why he has a car parked on his chest."

"Fair enough. Let's take a look," the EMT said, donning gloves. He kneeled down and peered under the vehicle. "Ouch."

"I'm sure he said more than that."

"Hopefully he didn't have time to."

The EMT shimmied himself under the edge of the car and checked the body for a pulse. Lying on the ground, half under the vehicle and fully engulfed in the stench of death, the EMT confirmed Mr. Poole was, indeed, deceased. Moving away from the body, the EMT took inventory of the underbelly of the vehicle. Eyes darting, he spotted the car jack lying on its side.

"Looks like the jack slipped," the EMT said matter-of-factly.

"That's the obvious guess."

The EMT stood, his gaze roaming the inside of the garage. "Judging from the garage here, and the car he's working on, I'd say the victim is a mechanic. He certainly has all the fancy tools."

"He could have used a better jack," Washington retorted.

The lead EMT whistled to his colleagues who had just started pushing the gurney up the driveway. The EMT ran his hands across his throat and gently shook his head.

Agent Washington motioned downward at the legs still sticking out from beneath the car. "Who's going to extract our friend here?"

"Fire and rescue."

"And when will they arrive? Don't you work out of the same station?"

The EMT checked his watch. "We happened to be around the corner when this particular call came in. We'd just finished with a false alarm on a heart attack. Lee County covers a lot of land. Police and fire shouldn't be but a couple more minutes."

Agent Washington looked at the EMT's hands. "Do you have a pair of gloves I can borrow?"

"Sure. In the ambulance. We have booties, too, if you want them."

"Please."

*

Agent Washington and the three EMTS got onto all fours and peered under the vehicle. A tireless rim rested firmly on Brent Poole's groin, the location soliciting a groan from one of the EMTs near the front of the car. The right half of the front suspension was resting on the dead man's sternum. Dried blood stained the corner of his mouth. A matching puddle had formed and coagulated on the concrete floor. A screwdriver and a wrench rested next to the man's right hand.

Agent Washington took pictures of the body from ground level with her cell phone, moving past and over the EMTs as they worked. She completed her first lap of the vehicle and finished at the front of the car.

She touched the chrome trim of the antique automobile with her gloved hand and noticed half a shoeprint on the shiny front bumper. She focused her phone on the shoeprint and snapped a series of photos.

Curiosity piqued, she nonchalantly took another lap around the vehicle, checking the shoes of each EMT and confirming that everyone in the garage was wearing booties.

She detoured around Mr. Poole's protruding legs and checked the treads on the bottom of deceased man's shoes. She snapped another picture and stood in the middle of the garage, deep in thought.

Agent Washington switched her cell phone to video mode and took a third tour around the exterior of the car. Finished with the vehicle, she methodically covered every corner of the garage, videoing the dizzying array of automotive gadgets. On the workbench near the door to the house, she noted a stainless steel travel coffee cup next to a red Ole Miss baseball cap. She picked up the cup and felt its heft. She opened it, sniffed at the remains, and then returned the top with a twist.

She completed her crime scene collection with a 360-degree panoramic shot of the inside of the garage in its entirety.

The lead EMT stood again and Agent Washington posed a question. "Do you know anything about cars?"

"Driving them or fixing them?"

"Fixing them."

"Not much. You?"

"Nothing. When something breaks on my car, I take it to Shady Tree Eddy down the street. But when I look around this garage I see tens of thousands of dollars' worth of tools."

"Point being?"

"This dead guy has all the fancy tools, and he doesn't set the jack up properly? On top of that, he's under the car with only a screwdriver and a wrench?"

"Maybe that's all he needed."

"Let me ask my question in a different way. Have you ever known someone with a serious hobby?"

"Sure. My brother's into photography. Serious photography. More serious than he can afford."

"And what happens when someone asks your brother about photography? Or what happens when you ask him about one of his latest photographs?"

The EMT nodded. "He pulls out his camera, his lenses, his tripod. And that's for starters. If you don't nip it in the bud, you'll get a lesson on pixel count, lighting, composition, and field of depth."

"The whole nine yards," Washington confirmed.

"Oh yeah."

"So he never just hands you a simple four-by-six photograph and says 'check this out'?"

"Never."

"Exactly my point. So imagine this guy under the car is the mechanic equivalent of your brother and his photography. Why would this guy, a guy with a professional-grade home automotive garage, take two of the most basic tools to work on a car? I'd think he would at least have a toolbox on the floor nearby."

The EMT looked around and then replied. "I hear what you're saying, but you're crossing into an area where I can only speculate."

Agent Washington and the EMT turned their heads at the sound of another vehicle door shutting in front of the house.

"The police are here," the EMT said. "I think they might be better suited to answer your questions."

*

"Are you the individual who found the body?" Detective Rafferty said, coming up the driveway. His pale skin and red hair announced his arrival as much as his voice.

"I am," Agent Washington replied, holding her badge at shoulder height. With her hand raised, the butt of her handgun was visible in its holster. "Special Agent Camille Washington, FBI."

Rafferty leaned in for a quick glance of the badge. "Detective Rafferty, Lee County Sheriff's Department," he said, extending his hand.

Agent Washington shook his hand and smiled, staring directly into the detective's eyes.

"I didn't expect to find the FBI on the scene."

"And I wouldn't expect a detective to show up before the fire department or a patrol car."

"I was nearby."

"Tough break for the victim. Both the police and the EMTs were nearby and he still didn't make it."

Rafferty ignored Agent Washington's comment and continued to the garage.

"Can I ask what you were doing here?" he asked.

"I'm working a case."

"What kind of case?"

"A federal case."

"You work out of Jackson?"

"That's right."

"I don't want to get off on the wrong foot, but here in Lee County we believe friendly cooperation is one of the tenets of law enforcement."

"I'm not at liberty to discuss what brought me here at this time."

"Okay, then. Did you take a look at the body?"

"I peeked."

"What do you think happened?"

"I think the deceased was fixing a car and the jack failed. He was most likely crushed to death. My best guess is the time of death occurred sometime last night, but I can't say for sure. Between the heat and humidity, decomposition sets in fast during the summer."

Agent Rafferty looked down at the legs protruding from the car and then stooped to one knee. "I'm not sure there's much of a mystery here to solve."

"Probably not. But then again, I'm a pessimist, so I'll officially say it's too early to tell for sure."

Rafferty raised an eyebrow. "I think it's time to call the body ferries," he said.

"The body ferries?"

""Sorry, that's what we call them. The company's real name is Natural Transportation Services, or something close to that."

Agent Washington nodded. "While you make your call, I'm going to continue poking around."

Detective Rafferty paused. "What about this scene bothers you?"

"Look at this garage. This guy was a serious mechanic. I just don't see him working on a car without putting it on blocks, and I don't see him not setting the jack correctly."

"Accidents happen," Detective Rafferty said.

"They do," Agent Washington replied. The phone in her pocket vibrated and she stepped towards the yard to take the call. "Excuse me for a moment," she said, leaving the detective with the EMTs.

*

The fire truck arrived with four rescue personnel, followed by two additional patrol cars from the Lee County Sheriff's Department.

Agent Washington stood in the driveway, leaning against the front of her government-issued sedan. She watched as the three EMTs, four firemen, and two uniformed police officers assessed the best way to extract the body from its current predicament. After a Who's On First meeting in the garage, a new jack was retrieved from the trunk of a patrol car and placed on the concrete floor. Moments later, the antique vehicle was raised high enough for the deceased to be removed.

Agent Washington returned to the interior of the garage to join in the inspection of the body. More photographs were taken and the deceased was identified by the driver's license in the wallet in the pocket of his jeans. Then the body was unceremoniously zipped into a large black body bag.

The body ferries—two college-age kids in a white van—pulled up to the end of the driveway. Within minutes of their arrival, the body was placed on a stretcher, the associated paperwork tucked under the belt that crossed the middle of the gurney to hold the deceased firmly in place.

As the two young men headed back towards the van with their lone passenger, Agent Washington raised her badge.

"Gentlemen, hold on a second."

The gurney's wheels ground to a halt.

"Are you guys the body ferries?"

"Yes."

"First, let me say it's an awful name."

The driver nodded. "I didn't like it at first either. Now I don't care. It's pretty accurate, really. All we do is pick up bodies and take them to the coroner or a funeral parlor. Sometimes from a crime scene. Heck, we even take bodies from the morgue to the airport."

"Where are you taking this one?"

"The detective ordered the body to be sent to the coroner."

"Where is that?"

"Over on Troy Street. Green office building. You can't miss it."

Agent Washington reached into her breast pocket and handed the driver her business card. "Would you be kind enough to tell the coroner that I'll be stopping by shortly?"

"I can do that."

"Let the coroner know the FBI will be requesting a full autopsy. All the bells and whistles. The whole CSI episode. In addition to toxicology."

The young man looked at the paperwork on the stretcher next to the body bag.

"I'll give your card to the coroner and tell him what you said, but really, ma'am, we just deliver the bodies. We don't tell anyone to do anything."

"Just relay the message. I'll be there in an hour. In the meantime, I don't want the body being sent for a premature cremation."

"Yes, ma'am. I'll tell him."

*

Agent Washington returned to the garage. Detective Rafferty stood near the front of the car, looking like a prospective buyer. Tarzan could again be heard barking inside the house.

"Someone's going to need to get inside and take care of that dog."

"I heard it," Detective Rafferty said. "We should have access in a minute. The neighbor two houses down just came over. Says she has an extra key to the place."

"I assume the victim also has a key around here somewhere. At some point he was going to have to go back inside."

"I checked his pockets," Detective Rafferty said.

"I'm sure it'll turn up."

"I'll look for it when I do an inventory of the garage."

"Good. I also wanted to take you up on your previous offer," Agent Washington said.

"Which offer was that?"

"When you told me cooperation is the tenant of law enforcement here in Tupelo."

"It is."

"Great. In the name of law enforcement cooperation, I'm letting you know that I'm requesting a full autopsy on the victim."

"That's your prerogative. Typically we don't order autopsies on accident victims, unless the family is requesting it, or if there are other aggravating circumstances."

"I'll give you an aggravating circumstance. I don't like it when a person I'm trying to interview dies before I get a chance to meet with them."

"As I said, it's your prerogative."

"And being that the deceased can no longer grant an interview, I want a copy of the original witness statement the deceased provided to the Lee County Sheriff's Department. Specifically, the witness statement where the deceased identified a red Palmetto Windows truck as the last vehicle leaving the Winston residence the night Mrs. Winston disappeared."

Detective Rafferty gritted his teeth with enough gusto for Agent Washington to notice.

"That can be provided."

"I also want a copy of all the photographs and videos taken today and the official incident report for what transpired here. Including an inventory list."

"I can have them for you tomorrow."

"Excellent. I'll stop by headquarters and pick them up."

*

Agent Washington walked back to her car and noticed the growing crowd of onlookers in the street. Among the group she spotted Edward, standing defiantly in the heat with his arms crossed. Staring at him as she dialed, Agent Washington watched as Edward pulled his phone from his pocket and put it to his ear.

"Have you been there long?" Agent Washington asked from her position no more than twenty yards away.

"Long enough. What's going on in there?"

"Looks like your neighbor had an accident. He didn't make it, I'm afraid."

"Did you have a chance to talk to him?"

"Unfortunately, no."

"Are you sure it was an accident?"

"It looks like one. I'll know more when I talk to the coroner and get the official police report."

"So the jury's still out?"

"He had three thousand pounds fall on him. It was most likely an accident."

"And an uncanny coincidence."

Agent Washington quietly sighed. "Can I ask a favor, Edward?"

"Sure."

"Can you go back to your house and sit tight? I'll give you a call later. Maybe I can stop by tomorrow. I have some other information for you about your case, and a couple of questions."

"Does that mean you're taking the case?"

Agent Washington looked back up the driveway towards the garage. "Yes. I'm taking the case. We'll see where it leads us."

"Then let me get out of your way," Edward said, hanging up the phone.

Agent Washington looked back towards the crowd as Edward started walking in the direction of his house. Then she whispered, "*I get the feeling you don't know how to stay out of the way.*"

CHAPTER 16

EDWARD PUT HIS eye to the peephole and then opened the front door.

"Good morning."

Agent Washington stepped into the living room. "Sorry I'm late. An eighteen-wheeler turned over outside of Winona."

"You didn't stay in Tupelo last night?"

"I can't stay in Tupelo. I have meetings in Jackson and open investigations all the way to Gulf Shores."

"That sounds like a lot of driving."

"It's not all bad."

"Well, excuse the mess," Edward said, pointing his chin in the direction of several large boxes on his dining room table.

"Are you packing to move?"

"That's the stuff the Lee County Sheriff's Department took with their search warrant a couple of days ago. They returned it all last night."

"Anything missing?"

"I don't think so, but I didn't go through every item. Should I?"

"I would."

Edward grunted softly. "Can I get you some coffee? It's made."

"Please. Black is fine."

"Have a seat."

Agent Washington placed a manila folder on the table and looked up at the Japanese character in a frame on the wall.

"Can you read that?"

Edward popped his head over the kitchen counter. "I can."

"What does it mean?"

"It means happiness. My wife always liked that one."

"So you read Japanese?"

"I do. That particular character is also used in Chinese. Japanese borrowed a lot of its written characters from Chinese."

"Was it hard to learn?"

"Japanese pronunciation is really easy but the alphabet can be tricky."

"How do you go about remembering all those symbols?"

"I think I'm just wired for it. I have a strong visual cortex. Or so they say."

"It must be something."

Edward delivered two coffees to the table.

"Which do you want to hear about first, your neighbor across the street, or follow-up information on Pervis Wade?"

"Let's start close to home."

"Mr. Poole it is. Long story short, I came by yesterday to interview Mr. Poole regarding your wife's disappearance. I arrived, found his body, and called 911."

"And we lost our only eyewitness," Edward stated.

"We did."

"Convenient for the Pervis Wade case. Has it officially been ruled an accident?"

Agent Washington took a sip of her coffee. "The ME was confident Mr. Poole died of asphyxiation. Which is what you would expect with a car on your chest."

"Rumor is that part of the car was also resting on his manhood. That'll make you wish you were dead."

Agent Washington almost smiled.

"We still have to wait for toxicology to see if there were any extenuating circumstances."

"So you're not entirely convinced it was an accident."

"Until I have evidence to the contrary, I'm going to consider it an accident. An accident with very unfortunate timing."

"Is anyone questioning how a car ends up falling on a mechanic with decades of experience?"

"The jack slipped."

"It slipped?"

"It happens."

"I doubt it happens to mechanics as anal as Mr. Poole. He never struck me as the careless type."

Agent Washington paused and tilted her head. "Just how well did you know Mr. Poole?"

"We were friendly, but we weren't really friends. We had him over for a barbecue once. Usually I just caught him in the street taking out the trash or picking up the mail. Cutting the grass. Every once in a while he would invite me into his garage to take a look at the latest car he was fixing up. I know he worked on some pretty cool cars. A lot of muscle cars from the sixties and seventies."

"And when was the last time you were in his garage?"

"A month or two ago. When he was working on the truck that's now for sale in the driveway. Why?"

"Because I took some photographs and videos of the inside of his garage yesterday after I found his body. I was wondering if you would agree to take a look at them. Tell me if you see anything out of the ordinary."

"That doesn't sound like the type of thing you would ask if you believed Mr. Poole died in an accident."

"Consider me skeptical by nature."

"Uh-huh," Edward said, locking eyes with the agent.

"What do you say? Will you take a look?"

"Not if they're gruesome. I have enough trouble sleeping as it is."

"Are you squeamish?"

"A little."

"The photos aren't too graphic. The body wasn't mangled in any way. There was a minimal amount of blood. You can skip the photos of the body, if you want. I'm more interested in what you think of the garage."

Agent Washington pulled out her mobile phone and sat down next to Edward on the sofa.

"The photographs are first. I took videos at the end. You probably know how my phone works better than I do."

Edward flipped through the photographs, wincing at the close-up shots of Mr. Poole's face and the blood on the floor. He watched as the first video showed Mr. Poole's body under the vehicle, the hands and arms of the EMTs poking in and out of the scene.

The final two videos were of the garage. Edward watched each twice.

"Did you see anything out of place? Anything unusual?"

"Just one thing."

"What?'

"There's an Ole Miss cap on the back workbench."

Agent Washington rolled her eyes. "This is Mississippi."

"That may be, but Mr. Poole hated Ole Miss. His whole family roots for Mississippi State."

"Are you sure?"

"Absolutely. I wore my Ole Miss cap over to his house one day when he invited me to take a look at a car he was working on. He gave me hell."

"You don't strike me as an Ole Miss fan either."

"I'm not. But Holly and I drove up to Oxford for a game one weekend. I bought a cap at the stadium. Half of the state's population loves Ole Miss, so I figured I had a fifty percent chance of being welcomed wherever I go with an Ole Miss cap on."

"How did that work out for you?"

"I got a free dessert once. But I think the waitress knew I was from out of town."

"I'm sure she did," Agent Washington replied. "You wear caps often?"

"Hardly ever. I probably wouldn't have even thought about the cap if I hadn't seen it an hour ago in one of the boxes the police returned."

Agent Washington sat up straight. "The police returned your Ole Miss cap to you last night?"

"That's right."

"Can I see it?"

"Sure," Edward replied. He stood, went to one of the boxes on the dining room table, and reached his hand in. He removed the cap in question and returned to the sofa.

"Here you go."

Agent Washington played the video she had taken in the garage again and paused it when the baseball cap appeared on the screen. "It looks the same."

"I think they have a couple of styles, but they're all basically the same except for the color scheme. Red seems to be the most popular."

"And I bet every man, woman, and child in Oxford owns one." Agent Washington fell silent for a long moment. "And you're absolutely sure Mr. Poole was not an Ole Miss fan?"

"He told me he once refused to sell a car to an Ole Miss fan who started getting a little mouthy about the last Egg Bowl. So, yeah, Mr. Poole didn't have any love for the Runnin' Rebels."

"Can I keep this cap?"

"Can I ask why?"

"I want to run it through our forensic lab."

"Why in God's name do you want to do that?"

"Because I don't like the fact that your cap was in the possession of the Lee County Sheriff's Department at the same time an identical cap was seen at the scene of an accidental death, just across the street."

"Are you saying the police could have tried to make it look as if I had been in Mr. Poole's garage yesterday?"

"Let's say it's a coincidence I can't overlook."

Edward could feel a tightening in his neck. "Jesus. Are they trying to frame me?"

"Relax, Edward. Relax. If they were, they wouldn't have given the cap back to you. They would need it as evidence."

"And that's supposed to make me feel better?"

"A little."

Edward stared across the room with a blank look on his face before finally saying, "I sure hope you're good at your job."

"I am."

"You better be, because if that cap was at a staged accident scene yesterday, it's time for me to move out of the state."

"Let me get the cap in an evidence bag and take some swabs of the workbench across the street. There could be residual microscopic evidence that transferred."

"Do it."

"But in all likelihood, we're just talking about an Ole Miss cap. Probably the best-selling piece of paraphernalia in the entire state."

"And if forensics proves that particular cap was on the scene yesterday?"

"It helps start building our case."

Edward nodded. "Nice positive spin."

"I try."

"So what's next on your agenda?"

"I've requested a copy of the official witness statement Mr. Poole provided to the police for the night your wife went missing. Along with some other documents, photographs, and reports. I'm heading to the sheriff's department after this."

"Don't be surprised if you don't get what you expect."

"If they don't give it to me, I'll subpoena it."

"You can subpoena anything you want, but if it doesn't exist, it doesn't matter."

"Destroying official records is a very dangerous game to play with a federal agent, particularly one tasked with busting dirty cops, judges, and politicians."

"Maybe. Out of curiosity, when you were across the street yesterday, did you tell Detective Rafferty your area of expertise?"

"If Detective Rafferty is worth his salt, he would have ascertained that information as soon as I left the scene. Maybe even before I left. Either way, by now, I'm sure the entire Lee County Sheriff's Department knows I'm in town, poking around."

"Which means they know I contacted you."

"I assume that to be the case."

"Wonderful."

"The bright side is that everything is out in the open. I have your back, and they know I have your back."

"Who has yours?"

"The Federal Bureau of Investigation."

"Uh-uh," Edward replied.

"You don't sound convinced."

"Jackson is awfully far away."

*

Agent Washington secured the Ole Miss cap in an evidence bag retrieved from her car and returned to the sofa.

"Do you want to go over what I learned about Pervis Wade, Sheriff Blazer, and Detective Rafferty?"

"I think being framed by the police might be all I can take for one day."

"We don't know that's what occurred. It may turn out to be nothing."

"For the record, I don't think *you think* it's nothing."

Agent Washington raised an eyebrow as if protesting Edward's accusation. "Do you want to hear what I've got on the sheriff's department and the Wade family or not?"

"Sure. Tell me what's happing with our case?"

"*My* case. My investigation and my case," Agent Washington clarified.

"Your case."

"Well, for starters, Detective Rafferty and Sheriff Blazer go way back. They were in high school together."

"That's way back."

"Nearly thirty years. They may go back even further, but high school is as far as I could get without doing interviews. That's my next step."

"So the lead detective and the sheriff have a history. I'm not surprised."

"Yes. As you know, in Lee County, as in most jurisdictions, the sheriff is an elected official. As such, Sheriff Blazer was elected to his position. The sheriff, in turn, hired Detective Rafferty. Nothing untoward there. Both men have been in law enforcement in Tupelo for over two decades. Both men have had clean careers. There are no blemishes on either man's record. There have been no lawsuits filed against either man. There have been no lawsuits or accusations against any department or direct employees that either man has overseen."

"So they're clean?"

"With regard to legal records, they're clean. Someone doesn't get to be sheriff without a relatively clean record."

"That sucks."

"For your case, it's not the best news. But for the rest of the population who depend on the Lee County Sheriff's Department, law enforcement officers with clean records are a good thing."

Edward nodded.

"Pervis Wade, on the other hand, is not so law-abiding. As you know, he has had multiple arrests. But I haven't found a direct relationship between Pervis Wade and either Detective Rafferty or Sheriff Blazer. They are approximately twenty-five years apart in age."

"A generation apart."

"That's exactly right. And that may prove to be relevant. Because while I can't find a direct connection between Pervis and Lee County Sheriff's Department, there was once a connection between the Palmetto Windows company and Detective Rafferty and Sheriff Blazer."

"Again, I'm not surprised."

"I said 'was.' As in past tense."

"Meaning?"

"Palmetto Windows has been around for forty years here in Tupelo. It was founded by Pervis's grandfather. After he passed away, Pervis's father, Troy Wade, ran the company for the better part of twenty-five years. He died ten years ago. Heart Attack."

"Sounds like the Wade men don't live too long. Who runs Palmetto Windows now?"

"Sonny Frisk."

"Who the hell is Sonny Frisk?"

"He's Pervis's uncle. Pervis's father's half-brother. Same mother. Different father. Different last name."

"Pervis Wade's father passed away and left the company to his half-brother and not to his son?"

"That's right. Pervis was only twenty or twenty-one when his father passed away. He was probably too young to run the family business."

"What about Pervis's mother?"

"Records indicate she died when he was in elementary school."

"So Pervis Wade works for his uncle at Palmetto Windows."

"That's right."

"How is that relationship?"

"Hard to tell until I interview some people, but it's not difficult to imagine there could be animosity there."

Edward took a sip from his mug. "Maybe if Pervis wanted his father to leave him in control of the company, Pervis should have learned to behave."

"That's an interesting point. Pervis was never really in trouble with the law until after his father passed away."

"Did his father's passing trigger his legal trouble?"

"We don't know if that was the reason, but the timing is correct."

"And the connection between the sheriff, the detective, and Pervis's father?"

"Troy Wade, Pervis's father, also went to high school with Sheriff Blazer and Detective Rafferty. It seems like they were friends, back in the day. Played on the high school baseball team together."

"Good friends?"

"Friendly enough."

Agent Washington pulled out two copies of a large photograph and put them on the coffee table.

"Here's a photo of the three men together, many years after high school. It's the only photograph I could find of the three. It was in the archives of the *Daily Journal*. I made a copy for you to keep."

Edward looked at the photograph as Agent Washington explained the image.

"It was taken at a fishing competition out at Natchez Trace State Park. Detective Will Rafferty and Sheriff Blazer won the competition. At the time, Detective Rafferty was a patrol officer and Sheriff Blazer was a detective. The article stated they pulled in over forty pounds of bass that day for the title. I'm sure you recognize both men."

"I do."

"The third man, standing behind them, is Troy Wade. Pervis's father. And if you look at the wall in the background of the photo, you can see that Palmetto Windows was one of the sponsors of the fishing tournament. There are a couple of other local sponsors. The Tire Shack. Tupelo Hardware. You can also see the sheriff and detective have Palmetto Windows written on their shirts."

"Meaning the Lee County Sheriff's Department was friendly with Pervis's father before he died and before Pervis started becoming a problem?"

"Sponsorship doesn't necessarily mean friendship, but they certainly knew each other."

"But you can't find a connection between Pervis and the Lee County Sheriff's Department."

"I'm working on it. But so far, phone records indicate that Pervis Wade hasn't called either the sheriff or the detective since he started using a new cell phone carrier two years ago. Prior to that, I don't have data."

"Do you think the detective and the sheriff are protecting Pervis Wade because they're somehow indebted to Pervis's dead father?"

"I don't know. But when I do, we'll have a case."

"Not if I'm framed and in prison first."

"That's not going to happen on my watch."

"Maybe you'll be with me," Edward added.

"Not funny."

"So where do you go from here?"

"I need to see who in town is willing to talk to me. I was thinking about chasing down the local drunk you mentioned. If I catch him in a moment of clarity, who knows what he could tell me."

"Probably not much, but it's worth a shot. In the meantime, I was considering another talk with Pervis. Maybe he'll have a change of heart and spill the beans about what he knows," Edward said.

"Edward, I like you. But don't think for a second I won't slap you with a charge for interfering with a federal investigation."

CHAPTER 17

THURSDAY NIGHT AT the Brew Ha Bar and Grill was Ladies' Night. All cocktails and box wines were half-price for women until ten. Buckets of Rolling Rock went for five dollars. With the bar's beckoning neon lights in sight, Edward stumbled out of a yellow cab and shuffled across the gravel lot towards the entrance. He stepped inside and took a brief moment to steady himself before letting the double doors shut behind him, then walked directly towards the bar at the back of the establishment. Through the smoke and dim light, he recognized Bartlett from the backside, his acquaintance sitting on the same stool, wearing the same overalls and white T-shirt.

Edward pulled out a stool, sat down, and ordered a beer.

"I thought we agreed you wouldn't be coming around here anymore," Bartlett said.

"Pretend you don't know me."

Both men stared straight ahead and the bartender delivered Edward's beer.

Bartlett spoke again, still talking into the mirror behind the bar. "Your boy Pervis is not here tonight."

"Oh yeah?"

"I've been here since it opened. Haven't seen him."

"I thought he was here every night."

"Most nights. No one's here every night."

"You seem to be."

Bartlett shrugged and looked up at the clock. "It's only nine. He could still come around. Which means you need to drink your beer and leave."

"Not if I came to see him."

"And why would you do that?"

"Because we have something to discuss."

"Finish your beer and skedaddle."

Edward let the advice fall onto the bar. "Is there any other place in town I can find him? A second place he goes drinking?"

"Sometimes he and his friends do their drinking at Pervis's house. He lives on the other side of the airport. From what I understand, he built a big patio last year with an even bigger fire pit. Some nights they sit around drinking and shooting off their guns."

"You ever been there?"

"To Pervis Wade's house? Hell no. I'm just telling you what I heard sitting right here on this stool. But where he lives ain't a secret. You can probably check it out on your fancy phone."

"Probably."

A lull in the conversation ended with Bartlett asking, "Any word on your wife?"

"Nothing."

"Sorry to hear that. Real sorry. And don't take this the wrong way, but you look like shit."

"I haven't been sleeping too well. And I don't sleep well in general. It's gotten worse since my wife went missing."

Bartlett watched in the mirror as Edward turned his beer upward.

"Drinking won't help," Bartlett said.

"Is that advice you're giving and not taking?"

"Shit, drinking doesn't help me. Nothing does. That's why I drink."

"Only an insane person would try to argue with that statement."

The two men sat in silence watching a reality show on Alaskan survival airing on the small TV behind the bar, the volume on mute. In the reflection of the mirror, Edward could see the pool tables, dartboards lanes, and tables were mostly occupied. Two waitresses were hustling, ferrying drinks from the bar to the thirsty. Edward pulled out his phone and checked his email.

Without notice, Bartlett barked out a warning. "Your boy just showed up."

Edward turned to see Pervis Wade coming in the room. Edward flipped his fingers across the screen of his phone for several seconds and put it in his pocket. He grabbed his beer and took a sip.

"Time to take a leak," Bartlett announced, standing. "Remember what I said before. Cat and mouse. Don't be the mouse," he added, disappearing into the short hall at the back of the bar.

Edward watched in the mirror as Pervis meandered through the crowd, stopping to chat with a couple at a small table. He waved to a group of guys playing pool in the far corner.

By the time Pervis neared the bar, Edward had turned in his seat and was facing the man he had come to see.

There was a flash of surprise on Pervis's face, which quickly faded as he raised his voice and ordered a Bud in a bottle.

"I sure didn't expect to see you in here," Pervis said, waiting for his drink.

"I was here first. So don't start complaining that I followed you."

Pervis took his beer from the bartender's grasp and guzzled a third of the bottle.

"Careful there, Eddie. Running off at the mouth around here can get you in trouble."

"A lot of things can get you in trouble."

"That's right. Especially here in Tupelo."

Edward took a gulp of beer. "Do you have a couple of minutes to talk?"

"Talk?"

"Yeah. You and me. Let's talk outside."

"Outside? You want to take me outside, Eddie?"

"That's right."

Pervis drank thirstily and placed the almost-empty bottle on the counter. "I'll follow you."

Edward weaved towards the front door of the bar and Pervis trailed several paces back.

*

Edward stepped outside as an old Camaro pulled into the gravel lot, sending dust into the dark sky. A frisky couple, drunk on Ladies' night discounts, was making out between a pair of parked trucks to the left.

Edward moved away from the entrance. "This way. We don't need an audience."

Pervis continued to follow as Edward walked to the corner and stopped. From the corner Edward could see both the front entrance and a large Dumpster behind the building. A smattering of cars was parked on the dimly lit perimeter of the lot.

Pervis inserted a pinch of tobacco between his cheek and gum. He glanced around furtively and spit onto the gravel.

"Nice spot, Eddie. You looking to cop a feel out here?"

"No."

"Ain't any shame in it. I've gotten laid a couple of times in this parking lot over the years."

"Nothing classier than a parking lot behind a dive bar."

"What's your preference? A picnic table by the lake?"

"I didn't come here to talk about your sex life. I came here to talk about your relationship with the Lee County Sheriff's Department."

Pervis's face turned serious and he seemed to let the statement sink in before he replied. "What relationship is that?"

"Well, I know your father was friends with the sheriff and Detective Rafferty, who happens to be working my wife's case."

"You do?"

"I do."

"And how did you come across this information?"

"I have my ways."

"You mean the bitch with the FBI badge? The one poking her nose where it don't belong."

"That's an interesting thing to say, Pervis. How could you possibly know about her, unless the sheriff or Detective Rafferty told you?"

Pervis turned as another car entered parking lot. Then he turned back towards Edward. "I guess you got me there."

"So you admit you have a relationship with Sheriff Blazer and Detective Rafferty of the Lee County Sheriff's Department?"

Pervis squinted. "I don't admit anything."

"Sooner or later I'm going to figure it out. So why don't we agree to save me the time of looking and save you the effort of keeping it hidden. Just tell me what kind of relationship you have with Sheriff Blazer and Detective Will Rafferty of the Lee County Sheriff's Department, here in the great state of Mississippi."

Pervis shook his head slowly and his expression turned stoic.

"Why don't you run that question by me one more time."

"Do you admit you have a relationship with Sheriff Blazer and Detective Rafferty of the Lee County Sheriff's Department?"

"Are you sure you don't want to throw my name in that question, too? Make sure you get it on record?"

Edward's eyes opened in surprise as Pervis reached out and grabbed his shoulder. With strength that belied his medium frame, Pervis twisted Edward's shirt and pulled him onto his toes.

"Get your hands off me."

Pervis ignored the plea and wrestled Edward's shirt out of his pants with his free hand. As Edward pawed at the vice-like grip on his shirt, Pervis shoved him into wall of the building.

"Where is it?"

"Where's what?"

"Where's your wire?"

"I don't know what you're talking about," Edward yelled. "Get your hands off me."

"Shut up," Pervis hissed, bad breath and spittle blasting Edward's face.

Pervis yanked Edward's shirt up to his chin, let it go, and then ran his hands over Edward's pants pockets. A second later he had Edward's phone in his hand, lifting it to his eyes while his other hand maintained its grip on Edward's twisted shirt. Pervis looked at the screen on the phone, and then his eyes met Edward's. Pervis let go of his shirt and Edward regained his footing before lunging for his phone. With one quick strike, Pervis landed a right hook to Edward's rib cage.

Edward crumpled to the ground and Pervis stood over him. As Edward groaned, Pervis examined the phone more closely. The screen clearly showed a voice recording application was engaged. A digitized needle gauge and red button indicated the phone was actively recording.

"You little shit," Pervis said, kicking Edward's hands as they cradled his ribs.

Pervis carefully pressed the icons on the screen of the phone and stopped the recording. With Edward in the fetal position, Pervis deleted the recording. Spitting on the ground, he turned and threw the phone towards the wood line at the back of the bar, not far from the Dumpster.

"Get up," Pervis said.

"Leave me alone, asshole."

"Damn, you have a lot of balls. Not much else. But a lot of balls."

Edward tried to stand but only made it to one knee.

"Here in Tupelo, some people might see what you just did as a lack of common courtesy. A lack of manners. Recording someone without their permission."

"Recording a conversation is not against the law. Assault and destruction of property is."

Pervis spit again, a brown tobacco stain splattering near Edward's shoes. "I don't need a law lesson."

"I think you do. And I think it's coming."

"Lookie here, I don't know where you're from, but things work differently down here."

Edward stood and placed his butt against the wall of the building. He put his hands on his knees and took several deep breaths.

"I'm just looking for answers. I'm just looking for my wife."

"Is that all?"

"Yes."

Pervis looked around suspiciously. "You want to know what happened to your wife?"

"Yes."

"You think that's going to make you feel better?"

"I deserve to know."

"I see. I see. You *deserve* to know."

"That's right."

"Did you ever consider that maybe your wife ran off with another man? Maybe she's well and fine in another man's bed."

"Fuck you, Pervis."

"There it is. I was wondering when the piss and vinegar would spill over."

"Fuck you," Edward said again, his voice trailing off.

"Who knows? Maybe your wife's been running around behind your back while you've been at work. Maybe she's been servicing all the contractors out at your house."

"You're a real tough guy, Pervis. A bar full of friends and a sheriff's department keeping you out of trouble."

"Right now, right here, it's just you and me, Eddie. Just you and me."

Edward made a fist with his right hand and the pain from being kicked shot up his arm.

"I'll tell you what, Eddie. Let's make this easy for you." Pervis reached into the back of his pants and pulled out a pistol from his waistband holster.

Edward felt his bowels loosen.

"You ever shot a gun before, Eddie?"

"No."

"Well, here's your chance," Pervis said, turning the barrel towards himself and passing the handle to Edward.

Edward shook his head.

"Go ahead. Grab it. Take it. You want to find your wife, take it."

Edward grabbed the gun and its weight caught him by surprise.

"There you go. Now you're the tough guy. Now the tables have turned. The playing field is even."

"Where's my wife?"

"I don't know. Why don't you go ask your neighbor the mechanic?"

"Did you kill him, too?"

"From what I hear, he had an accident."

"I'm sure the Lee County sheriff wants everyone to believe that."

"I hear that's what the evidence shows. And evidence is the only thing that really counts."

"You're a lowlife."

"And yet both of us are here at the same place, at the same time. Outside a shitty bar on a weeknight. And one of us has a gun."

"You're a son of a bitch."

"And one of us has a foul mouth. When I was little, my momma told me not to swear too much. She said it makes you sound uneducated."

"I heard your mother died when you were young. That must be one of the only memories you have of her."

There was a long pause and Edward could feel his hand shaking. Pervis stared into Edward's face.

"Don't go talking about my momma."

"You're right, Pervis. You're right. I'm sure your momma was a real winner. She gave birth to you, after all."

Pervis flashed a demented half-smile. "Damn, that gun is giving you confidence. Amazing what a piece of metal can do for you. Now, let me ask this, Eddie, how long has your wife been missing?"

"A week."

"And don't you think it's time you moved on?"

"She's still missing."

"She isn't missing, Eddie."

"Why's that?"

Pervis leaned in, the gun in Edward's hand almost resting against his ribcage. "Because no one can hold their breath that long."

Edward's eyes filled with water.

"Go ahead, do it, big boy," Pervis egged.

Edward gritted his teeth. His finger quivered on the trigger. He stared at Pervis Wade with hatred through blurred vision. Edward's finger slowly pulled back on the trigger.

Pervis snatched the gun and turned it in a more favorable direction.

"Damn, boy. Damn. You almost did it. You almost shot me. I didn't think you had it in you."

Edward could feel his pulse rising and felt faint.

"But you gotta have one in the chamber," Pervis said sliding the rack back and releasing it. "And then you have to take the safety off," he added, flicking the metal tab down.

Edward froze. His eyesight narrowed into tunnel vision. Pervis's voice faded as if he were speaking through a thick pane of glass.

Pervis smiled and spit. "I really didn't think you had it in you, but I'm not so sure anymore. And now that the gun has one in the chamber and the safety is off, I don't think it would be too smart to give you a second chance."

The sound of the slide on a shotgun interrupted the conversation and Pervis seemed rattled by the firearm to his rear.

"I don't know what we got going on here, but enough is enough," the voice said.

Pervis didn't turn around. He looked straight at Edward.

"Who's that back there, Eddie? One of your buddies?"

Bartlett stepped forward and Edward heard the man's feet crushing the gravel of the parking lot.

"Put the gun, down," Bartlett said.

Pervis aimed his handgun downward, pressed the release on the magazine, and popped the round out of the chamber.

"Drop it on the ground to your right."

Pervis followed the instructions he was given.

"Edward, I want you to pick up the gun and wipe your fingerprints off it," Bartlett said.

"What?"

"Pick up the gun and use your shirt to wipe your prints off. Then drop it on the ground."

Edward did as he was told.

"Now, Pervis, grab your gun. Leave the magazine on the ground."

"Bartlett, you should have minded your own business."

"Just pick up your gun, Pervis."

Pervis reached down, grabbed his gun, and returned it to his holster in the back of his waistband.

"Okay. Good. Good. Now everyone's back to even. Pervis, you go inside. Edward, you're going home. Pervis, you can come back outside and get your magazine after Edward here leaves."

Edward nodded and Pervis grunted.

"And none of this ever happened," Bartlett added. "I'm too old and too tired to deal with this shit. And I have no intention of looking for a new place to drink. So the two of you take your problems elsewhere or I'll use this damn thing on both of you, so help me God."

CHAPTER 18

EDWARD'S HEAD POUNDED in unison with the thudding on his front door. He opened his eyes and his gaze fell to the coffee table. A bottle of Advil rested next to a bottle of Gatorade, which was surrounded by several empty bottles of beer. His eyes burned. He sat up and swallowed, his tongue coated in a thick film.

A second barrage of knocks brought Edward off the sofa and to his feet. He took several paces and opened the door to find Agent Washington standing on his front porch. The obvious displeasure on the agent's face made Edward's hangover immediately worse.

Agent Washington entered without an invitation.

"Why don't you answer your phone? I've been calling all morning."

"I lost my phone."

"You lost it?"

"Yes. What time is it?" Edward asked.

"Eleven."

"Oh, I usually don't sleep in."

"Do you know why I'm here?"

"I hope I don't, but I probably do."

"Tell me you didn't go back to the Brew Ha Bar and Grill last night and confront Pervis Wade."

"I may have gone for a beer."

"And did you confront him?"

"I just wanted to talk to him. He wanted a confrontation."

"Explain yourself."

"I tried to get him to admit that he knew the sheriff and Detective Rafferty."

"And did he?"

"No. He figured out I was trying to record the conversation."

"He figured it out, did he? Imagine that. Then what happened?"

Edward lifted his shirt. A large bruise covered the left side of his ribs. "It went downhill from there."

"Jesus."

Edward looked down at his torso. "It hurts worse than it looks."

"And let me ask, did this assault occur before or after you pulled your gun on him?"

"I didn't pull my gun on him."

"There was an anonymous call to the police from an unnamed patron at the bar who saw a man fitting your description standing outside, holding a gun on Pervis Wade. They also said a third man was holding a shotgun to the person fitting your description and Pervis Wade."

"An anonymous call to the police? How convenient."

"Please tell me this is all a misunderstanding and there wasn't a gun."

Edward sighed. "There was a gun, but it wasn't mine. It was Pervis's gun."

Agent Washington shut her eyes and her lips quivered.

"You are truly unbelievable. Unbelievable. I told you if you interfered with this investigation I would slap you with obstruction. Do you remember me saying this?"

"I do."

"Well guess what? That's exactly what I'm going to do this afternoon when I get back to Jackson."

"Don't you want to hear the whole story?"

"No. No, I don't."

Edward continued anyway. "Pervis handed me his gun and tried to bait me into pulling the trigger."

"And did you?"

"I couldn't. I wanted to."

"How much did you have to drink?"

"I only had one drink at the bar. I had a couple before I went."

Agent Washington looked at the empty bottles on the table and shook her head.

"Pervis also confessed to me that my wife was dead. He told me no one can hold their breath for a week."

"He said this?"

"He did."

"And you recorded this?"

"No, by that point, he'd already taken my phone and disposed of it."

Agent Washington took a break from staring at Edward and her eyes bounced around the room.

"You look like hell. And you don't smell much better."

"I wasn't expecting visitors."

Agent Washington frowned. "Edward, dammit. Why can't you listen? Why can't you follow instructions?"

"Because I love my wife and she would do the same for me."

CHAPTER 19

EDWARD SPENT THE better part of an hour pulling himself from his hangover. After a shower, several bottles of water, and a double-dose of Advil, he emerged from the bedroom with a quickened pace. He made coffee and toast for lunch, and as he pulled butter from the fridge, the house phone rang. He grabbed the handset off the cradle on the kitchen's small pass-through and answered.

"Hello."

"Mr. Winston. This is Sheriff Blazer with the Lee County Sheriff's Department."

Edward prepared himself to be admonished for his behavior at the Brew Ha. Perhaps a warning for forthcoming criminal charges.

"Yes, Sheriff," he answered.

"Mr. Winston. Are you sitting down?"

Edward recognized those four innocuous words as anything but. He could feel himself go faint. He stumbled towards the small dining room table and sat down on a chair.

"Where was she found?" he asked, his voice cracking.

"Why would you ask that?"

"Where was she found?" Edward repeated.

The sheriff cleared his throat and then answered the question. "I'm sorry to be the bearer of this news. Your wife's body was found in a local fishing hole just off Flat Creek."

"Where is that?"

"Two miles north of your house."

"Are the police on the scene now?"

"They are. A full response unit."

"How do I get there?"

"From what I understand, there's not much to see. It's an active crime scene."

"I'll find it myself."

Edward hung up the phone, his shoulders shaking as he sobbed. His wife's face floated through his mind as the tears flowed down his cheeks. He stood from the dining room chair and took the phone to the small office at the end of the hall. He spent a minute on his laptop with Google Maps and printed out directions to Flat Creek and a fishing pond located in a small public park.

Satisfied the coordinates were correct, Edward called Agent Washington.

"Special Agent Washington."

"It's Edward. They found Holly's body," he said, before breaking into audible sobs.

"Where?"

"A fishing pond near some place called Flat Creek. Not far from here."

"A pond?"

"Just like Pervis said. No one can hold their breath for a week. He wasn't just talking. He was taunting me. He knew."

"I'm turning the car around," Agent Washington said. "See you as soon as I can get back there."

"I'm going to the pond," Edward responded, hanging up.

*

Edward tried to focus through his watery vision. He gripped the map he had printed in his right hand while his left hand steered the car. His eyes danced back and forth between the paper and the double yellow lines on County Road 681.

He slowed the car on a curve and blinked away tears to read the next road sign. He turned the wheel right onto Edgewater Drive, and followed the unpaved road for a quarter of a mile before he saw the first police car. In the distance, nestled among old pine trees, Edward could see a plethora of emergency vehicles. A hundred yards beyond the vehicles, light shimmered on the surface of what Edward assumed to be the fishing hole.

Edward pulled his car off the gravel road and exited his car. Officer Gooden, the initial patrol officer who had come to Edward's house the night Holly had gone missing, approached as Edward neared the crime scene tape.

"Mr. Winston. I'm sorry for your loss, but you really shouldn't be here."

"Where should I be?"

"This is an active crime scene investigation."

"I won't get in the way."

The officer relented. "Stay behind the tape."

"Where's my wife?"

"Her body has been transported to the coroner."

"That was fast."

"Mr. Winston, your wife's body—and we are assuming it is your wife's body—has likely been in the water since she went missing."

Edward bit his lip. "Who identified her?"

"Detective Rafferty offered the initial identification based upon clothing and jewelry. Dental records and DNA will confirm the identification. Unfortunately the body was in no condition to be identified visually."

"Well, I'm sure it's her," Edward said, wiping a new tear off his face as it reached his jawline.

"Once again, Mr. Winston, I'm sorry."

"I'm going to take a walk around."

"For the sake of the investigation, please stay behind the crime scene tape."

"Yeah, yeah," Edward replied, waving his hand back over his shoulder as he turned away.

*

The yellow tape stretched in a crescent down the west side of the pond, wrapping around pine trees and the support beam of a picnic pavilion near the shore.

Edward slowly walked around the perimeter of the tape until he had an unobstructed view of the water. He estimated the size of the pond at no more than three acres. The lights of the remaining emergency vehicles were extinguished, the sirens long-since silenced. A quartet of uniformed police officers stood in a group, talking to a larger group of EMTs. Several plain-clothed officers took pictures of the shoreline. Others plucked small items from the wet clay near the bank and deposited them in evidence bags.

Stunned, shocked, and in a daze, Edward didn't notice Detective Rafferty until he was within speaking distance.

"Sheriff Blazer told me you were coming out here."

"Why is anyone surprised by this?"

"Because most people listen to law enforcement."

"What law am I breaking?"

"None."

"Then carry on with your law enforcement."

"What can I do for you, Mr. Winston?"

"Who found the body?"

"Some guy fishing on his day off. Says he comes out here a couple times a month. Has a valid fishing license."

"And this is a county park?"

"County land. It's not much of a park."

"There's a picnic table over there under the pavilion."

"That's it. A pavilion with a picnic table. And a switch for a light bulb that vandals break as soon as a new one is installed. There's nothing else out here. Not even a toilet."

"I understand that my wife's body has been taken to the coroner's office."

"It has."

"What's the preliminary cause of death?"

"It's too early to speculate on that."

"No guess?"

"Not at this time."

"Then I'll leave it up to the coroner to fill me in. I'm heading there next."

"Mr. Winston, have you ever seen a body that's been submerged for a week?"

"No, I haven't."

"It's not for the faint of heart."

Edward scowled and stared off at the water. Without looking back at the detective, he said, "There are a lot of things in this world that aren't for the faint of heart."

"I'm sorry for your loss, Mr. Winston. I truly am."

"You know that Pervis Wade told me my wife was dead. Told me there was no way she could hold her breath for a week."

"Would you like to make an official statement with the police regarding this verbal exchange? I'd be happy to take your statement."

"I'll pass. Somehow I think it'd be a waste of time."

Detective Rafferty checked the phone in his hand.

"Officer Gooden says you provided the initial identification?" Edward said.

"I did. I was the first detective on the scene. My preliminary identification was based on her physical description. Clothes. Jewelry. Of course, dental records and DNA will provide confirmation. But we're pretty confident it's your wife."

"I'm curious, how many detectives serve in the same capacity as you for the Lee County Sheriff's Department?"

"Three others."

"And are you guys on call?"

"On a rotation, 24/7. Why?"

"I'm just wondering what the odds are that the same detective who took over my wife's case was first to show up at my neighbor's garage when he was killed, and was the first to arrive and identify my wife's body at this location?"

"Just lucky, I guess."

"I don't believe in luck," Edward said.

"Are you leaving?" Rafferty asked towards Edward's backside.

"I'm going to the coroner's. I assume you'll be there too."

"I was just fixing to head in that direction."

"You'd better hurry up. If you hang around here too long, the coroner may say something you don't want me to hear."

CHAPTER 20

EDWARD ENTERED THROUGH the main lobby and was directed towards the backside of the green office building on Troy Street. He followed a series of hallways and stepped into the gray walls of a stairwell. One floor down, he arrived in the small waiting vestibule, four plastic chairs lined in a row across from an empty desk. For a moment he pondered proper morgue protocol before his eyes landed on a sign near the large double doors that read *Official Personnel Only Beyond this Point.* Another sign beneath a buzzer on the wall read *Press for Attention.*

Edward pressed the buzzer, waited, and then pressed it again. He stood in the windowless hallway for a long minute, the smell of chemicals turning his stomach sour. He touched his abdomen and lowered himself onto one of the plastic chairs. His right hand reached for his pocket, the usual location for his cell phone, and he cursed under his breath.

Sitting in silence, his mind turned to his wife and a wave of loss and loneliness washed over him. He dipped his head and silently let his tears fall to the floor.

Twenty minutes later, Agent Washington entered through a pair of automatic doors at the end of the hall. Edward stood from his chair and wiped his face.

"I'm sorry for your loss, Edward."

Edward nodded.

"I called Detective Rafferty and heard you stopped by the pond where the body was discovered."

"I did. Her body had been moved already. Did you visit the crime scene?"

"No. I came here. I'm going to the lake in a few hours with a forensic team from Jackson."

"After Lee County forensics have trampled everything?"

"This is Lee County. The park where the body was found was in Lee County. The sheriff's department is obligated to respond to all emergency calls. I have no evidence that the sheriff's office has done anything wrong with regard to today's discovery. But once I have their reports I can compare it to my own forensic team's evidence. Perhaps we will see a meaningful discrepancy there."

"Two dozen people were walking around that pond when I was out there."

"It'll be all right."

"I doubt it."

Agent Washington touched him on the shoulder. "Why don't you give me a few minutes in the back with the coroner? Just let me see what the status is."

"I pressed the buzzer but no one answered."

"Let me go in."

"I'll wait here."

*

Edward sat on a plastic chair, stewing in grief and anger, until Agent Washington reappeared through the double doors to the morgue. Her eyes were wet and Edward stood as she dabbed each cheek with a tissue.

"What did the coroner say?"

"Why don't you sit back down?"

Edward took the agent's advice.

"The body that was brought in today had been submerged for some time. It cannot be identified visually."

"So I heard. Can I see her?"

"You can, but I don't think you want to."

Edward put his head in his hands. Without looking up he asked, "Can you tell me what she looks like?"

"Edward, it's not pretty."

"Tell me anyway."

Agent Washington sighed and her mind seemed to shift into an analytical gear, void of emotion.

"The body pulled from the pond is in a serious state of decomposition. Massive tissue loss. In some locations, all tissue."

"Meaning you can see bone."

"That's correct," Agent Washington said. "In certain locations."

Edward's shoulders shook and Agent Washington waited.

"What else?"

"Severe bloating of the torso. Massive discoloration."

"What was the cause of death?"

"Right now, it's too early to tell, but it looks like she was strangled and then drowned. Perhaps strangled until she was unconscious and then drowned. She may have also been beaten."

"Fucking animal," Edward said.

"We'll get whoever did this."

Edward slowly raised his head. "Is there any chance it's not her?"

"Maybe you can answer that question," Agent Washington replied. She removed her phone from her jacket pocket and swiped at the screen. Then she handed the phone to Edward.

"I just took these pictures. It's one of the key pieces of evidence. It was found on the finger of the deceased. The ring finger."

Edward looked at the ring and then swiped to the next photo. On the third photo, he handed the phone back to Agent Washington.

"That's Holly's ring. Her wedding ring."

"And you're sure?"

"I'm sure. It has the date of our anniversary and a Japanese character engraved on the inside."

"What does the Japanese say?"

"What does it matter?" Edward replied. "It's her ring," he said, his voice cracking.

Agent Washington sat down and stared at the desk across from the waiting vestibule.

After a long minute, Edward said, "I get the feeling there's something else you're not telling me."

"There is."

"What is it?"

"The initial blood test indicates your wife was pregnant."

"I thought you said there was serious decomposition."

"There was. But only a small amount of blood is necessary for some tests."

Edward lowered his head onto his hands for several long seconds. Without speaking, he stood and walked towards the exit door and the light outside.

"Where are you going, Edward?"

"None of your business."

*

"Good afternoon," the tall man said, looking down his nose. A Smith & Wesson baseball cap sat high on his head. Brown hair flared out near each massive ear.

Edward looked up. Dark half-circles sagged under his puffy, blood-shot eyes.

"What can I do you for?" the man behind the counter asked.

"Looking for a gun," Edward said.

"I can't sell firearms to anyone under the influence."

"I'm not under the influence. I have allergies and don't sleep well."

The salesman raised his hands slowly, as if to invite Edward to look around. Firearms and accessories filled every available surface. "You've come to the right spot. If you can hunt it, we carry something to shoot it with. And if you're only shooting targets, we have even more options."

Edward took a few seconds to let his eyes wander. Handguns and pistols lined the clear glass case to his right. Rifles hung on racks on the wall behind the counter to his left.

"I think I'm looking for a handgun."

"Self-defense or home defense?"

"Both," Edward lied.

"Are you familiar with firearms?"

"Just what I read on the Internet and saw on YouTube," Edward replied without smiling.

The salesman leaned back as if trying to gain a different perspective on his first customer of the day. "YouTube? Okay, then. Let's bring it back to reality. For home defense purposes, you can't beat a shotgun. Eight or nine pellets in a single round, if you're using one of the more popular shells like a double-aught. To someone with no gun experience, those extra projectiles may help hit the target."

"Eight or nine pellets per shot. I can see how that would be useful."

"Two of the most popular models are the Remington 870 and the Mossberg 500. Mossberg holds more rounds. Remington has been used by law enforcement forever. Both have their advantages and disadvantages."

"Which do you prefer?"

"The one that is close at hand and is loaded."

Edward forced a smile.

"You have to remember, in a typical home defense situation, it's probably going to be dark. Your hands may be shaking. The shotgun takes some of the needed precision away. But it doesn't mean you can start shooting with your eyes closed. There are a lot of people out there who think you can."

"I can see the advantage of the shotgun, but I still think I want a handgun."

"That's what you said when you came in, so let's give the customer what he wants. We have a good selection of pistols and handguns. Are you planning to carry?"

"Yes, and I was hoping to take it with me today."

"Well, there's no waiting period to purchase a handgun in the great state of Mississippi. I just electronically send in a form 4473, and the weapon is yours."

"What's form 4473?"

"A federal firearm transaction record. Basically it informs Uncle Sam that I sold you a gun."

"What about a gun license?"

"Don't need one in Mississippi. And you only need the 4473 because you're buying a gun from a registered firearm licensee."

"I assume that's a fancy name for a gun shop."

"Indeed it is. I should also mention that if you plan on carrying the weapon, the law requires handguns be in a holster, or under lock and key.

Used to need a conceal and carry permit, but they eased off that regulation a few years back."

"I guess I'll take a holster, too."

"All right, then," the man replied, moving to the collection of firearms in the glass display case. He removed several unloaded handguns and put them on top of the counter. "Now, let's see what feels good in your hands."

"I want something that's point and shoot. I don't want the hassle of a magazine or a safety."

"You got kids in your house?"

"No."

"Then let your finger be your safety."

"Meaning?"

"If you don't want to fire the gun, don't put your finger on the trigger."

"I just don't want to forget to put the magazine in, rack the slide, or flick off the safety. I'm looking for something less complicated."

The salesman smiled. "If you want point and shoot with no fuss, then you need a revolver. A .357 has enough firepower to stop anything short of a raging bull. It kicks a little, but all you need to do is aim and shoot."

"What's the maximum distance for accuracy?"

"For self-defense, I can't imagine a scenario where you would be shooting more than ten or fifteen feet. Much farther than that and it gets harder to prove it's defensive. But a .357 is accurate out to thirty yards with a little practice."

The salesman removed a .357 from the cabinet and checked the cylinder. He confirmed the gun was unloaded and put it on the counter.

Edward picked it up. "It's heavier than I thought it would be."

"Stainless steel cylinder. Stainless steel frame."

"How much is it?"

"A little under a grand. More if you want to dress it up."

"I think I'll just stick with the basic configuration, whatever that is."

"KISS. Keep it simple stupid. There's nothing wrong with simple."

The salesman watched as Edward took aim around the store with the gun.

"If you haven't shot before, I strongly suggest going to a range and learning how. Maybe take a gun safety course to boot."

Edward didn't reply as he raised the gun to eye level and stared down the short barrel. "I'll take it and a box of bullets."

"Step around the counter and let's fill out some paperwork."

*

Thirty minutes later, Edward walked out of the Dixie Gun Shop with a black plastic case in one hand and two boxes of ammo and a new holster in a bag in the other hand. He placed the gun case on the roof of his car and dug his hand around in his pocket for his car keys.

"Please tell me that's not what I think it is," Agent Washington said, startling Edward as he unlocked his car door.

"That depends on what you think it is."

Agent Washington surveyed the parking lot and the company sign perched near the road.

"Looks like the case for a Smith & Wesson. I have one myself."

"Just exercising my right to bear arms, as guaranteed by the second amendment of the US Constitution. What are you doing here? Were you following me?"

"You're damn right, I followed you. What do you need a gun for, Edward?"

"I don't know, let's see… My wife was murdered and the man who murdered her is still running around town. And if that weren't enough, the police either covered it up or blew the investigation. And my neighbor, the only eyewitness in Holly's disappearance, was found dead. I'm feeling a little vulnerable."

"You should leave protection to law enforcement. At least until you feel more emotionally stable."

"Leave protection to law enforcement? Do you know who answers the phone if I call 911? The Lee County Sheriff's Department. I'm thinking about moving into a hotel in the next county over just to be in another jurisdiction."

Edward opened the door to his car and placed the gun and ammo in the passenger seat. A lone tear ran down his cheek.

"Edward, listen to me for a minute."

"What?"

"I need you to promise me that you're not going to do anything rash."

"Such as?"

"Such as taking your new toy down to the window company and having another talk with Pervis Wade."

"I wouldn't do that at the window company. Too many people around."

"Not funny."

"None of this is funny. Nothing has been funny in ten days."

"Let me finish my investigation."

"I'm not standing in your way."

"Edward, you're a smart guy. An IT engineer who speaks Japanese. You're smart enough to know that you can't kill Pervis Wade and get away with it. There's no way you can get away with shooting a man you suspect in your wife's disappearance with a gun you just purchased in your own name. Especially someone with police connections. Not to mention you were seen drawing a weapon on Pervis outside a bar on the other side of town. Come on. I know you're smarter than that. You know you're smarter than that."

Edward's lone tear turned to a series of quiet sobs and he put his head into his folded arms on top of his car.

Agent Washington put one arm across his shoulders and gently squeezed. She waited as his torso heaved and then his head rose from his arms.

"Edward, I think once this settles down a little, you should get out of town. Get some rest somewhere. Take a break. Get far away. Take a vacation."

Edward looked at the wet tears trailing through the scars on the back of his left hand and something stirred in his subconscious. "As soon as I finish putting my wife to rest."

*

Edward thrashed in bed, unable to wake from the nightmare. The only consolation was tonight's dream differed from the norm. Gone was the fire that usually engulfed him. For one night, his fiery tomb had been replaced by water. In lieu of the pain of burning flesh, his lungs burned for oxygen.

Edward thrashed and rolled over, water on all sides, pressing him down.

He fought to swim upward, the moonlight shimmering on the surface, out of reach, taunting him. He kicked his legs and swam, each stroke sending him deeper into the water. He could feel himself crying, his tears almost indistinguishable from the water that was threatening to become his grave. He swam harder, sunk deeper, and then spotted his wife's face through the darkening water. Thicker tears blurred his vision as Edward tried to swim towards her.

He tried to yell for help and then inhaled, water flooding his lungs and filling his nose and mouth. And then he felt himself rising in the water. He felt a firm grasp on his elbow, an unseen power pulling him upward. Through the murky water, a large tattooed arm came into focus then disappeared where a shoulder and body should have been. As Edward broke the surface of the water he awoke. Perspiration covered the sheets and pillowcase. He sat up, panting, tears on his face.

He turned on the light and took a drink of water. He grabbed the jar of lotion and rubbed the moisturizer into his scarred skin. He shut his eyes for a moment and could still see the arm pulling him out of the water to safety.

He rubbed more lotion into the back of his hand and replaced the jar on the bedside table.

"Time to be smart," Edward said to himself aloud.

CHAPTER 21

EDWARD LEFT THE last meeting of the day with a series of bows, a pocketful of business cards, and a preliminary agreement for a job transfer out of Tupelo. He stepped through the revolving door on the ground level of Fujita Automotive headquarters and merged into the heavy foot traffic on the sidewalk, not far from Shinjuku in downtown Tokyo, Japan.

A train ride and short walk later, Edward strolled through the lobby of the Sunroute Hotel and rode the small elevator to the fifth floor. He nervously peeled off his business suit and redressed in a less formal combination of slacks, dress shirt, and sports jacket, sans tie.

He stared at himself in the mirror over the dresser, wondering if the nerves he could clearly see in his reflection would be equally apparent to others. He placed his phone on the dresser and left the room, unsure of how the most important evening of his life would unfold.

*

The Yamanote train line encircled downtown Tokyo, the entire loop taking just under an hour. The twenty-nine stations on the Yamanote line included some of the busiest in the world. Three-and-a-half million riders daily made it one of the most densely traveled tracks ever laid.

Edward left his hotel as a Yamanote train came to a halt on the elevated platform of the Takadanobaba station in the distance. He crossed the heavily trafficked street and casually wandered into the small drugstore on the corner. A minute later he was back on the bustling sidewalk, bag in hand.

On the next block he entered the sliding glass doors of a large bookstore and meandered through the labyrinth of aisles. He found the bathroom in the back of the building, entered a stall, and removed the contents of the bag from the drugstore.

In the privacy of his public stall, he methodically wrapped his hand in an ace bandage and confirmed it was firmly in place. He exited the stall and threw the bag and receipt into the trashcan in the corner near the sink.

Two turns from the bathroom, Edward entered the staircase and headed to the third floor. Moments later, he stepped back into the bookstore with a sigh of relief as he recognized the extensive display of stationary and calendars. If his memory was correct, the selection of English language books was mere steps away. Glancing around while trying to appear nonchalant, he spotted a collection of postcards not too far from the register and plucked one with a glossy photo of Tokyo Tower on the front.

The young woman at the register watched as Edward counted exact change for the postcard and then thanked him for his purchase. Edward looked around sheepishly. Confirming no other customers were nearby, he asked the woman for a favor in the most polite Japanese he could muster.

"I've injured my hand. I was wondering if you would be kind enough to address this postcard for me. I wanted to send it to my brother back home but I just can't hold the pen very well."

"In English?" the woman answered in Japanese with great trepidation.

"Yes."

"English is not one of my strong suits. Perhaps I can get another employee to help."

"I only need you to write the name and address. I'll spell it out for you."

The woman's face flushed as she agreed. Two minutes of letter-by-letter and number-by-number dictation followed before the woman laid down her pen. Edward slipped the postcard into his breast pocket and thanked the woman profusely with multiple bows.

Back on the street, Edward made his way downhill in the direction of the Edogawa River. Cherry trees lined the riverbanks at the top of steep, moss-covered walls. A block further, Edward ducked into a liquor shop and headed towards the whiskey section. Edward quickly found what he was looking for, and as he doled out payment, the storekeeper placed Edward's expensive boxed whiskey in a plain plastic bag. From a doorway at the rear of the shop, the storekeeper's wife watched over the transaction before she suddenly admonished her husband for his rudeness. Apologizing to Edward, the woman disappeared through the rear doorway and reappeared seconds later.

"You can't carry expensive whiskey in a cheap bag," she said, slipping the whiskey box into a fancy cloth-handled bag with the name of a high-end department store printed on the side.

"Thank you very much," Edward said, stepping outside and disappearing into the setting sun.

*

Edward meandered in the direction of Waseda University and then headed north at one of the myriad small bridges that crossed the river. Trudging up a steep hill, decorative bag in hand, Edward tried to envision the path to his destination. Extreme caution had convinced him to leave his phone behind. Paranoia had coerced him not to Google his destination or print out a map.

He was flying blind on the streets of Tokyo, heading into the heart of Bunkyo ward, a wealthy section of town that boasted the Tokyo Dome and the University of Tokyo. Well-known gardens and expensive boutiques were nestled along the gingko-lined streets. Given its proximity and cultural offerings, as well as the respite from the bustle, Bunkyo was home to some of the finest residential streets in all of Tokyo.

Unfortunately for the lost, the finest residential streets of Bunkyo ward had no names, as was the case with most Japanese roads. For that simple reason, Edward's goal of locating an address he had been to exactly once, nearly a decade ago, was going to require persistence sprinkled with luck.

At the top of the hill, Edward stopped at the first intersection. He wiped sweat from his brow and looked down the road in each direction. He recognized the schoolyard catty-corner to his location and turned left. Minutes later he had a stronger recollection of the small rice shop at the bend in the road. He took two more turns in quick succession and then paused to gain his bearings. He looked up at the stars and the nearly full moon above, peeking out through light cloud cover. The size of the houses on each side of the road indicated he was on the right path. Whereas most of Japan lived in modest abodes with multi-use rooms, Edward was currently strolling among residences with private quarters for everyone and their guests. Large walls around each property offered privacy and soundproofing from the noise of the city and its thirty million inhabitants.

As Edward stared upward, a well-dressed elderly woman appeared at the front gate of a home on the left. The woman froze in her tracks as Edward looked over from his position on the far side of the narrow street.

"Excuse me," Edward said in polite Japanese.

In the dim light the woman's eyes seemed to assess Edward's presence, her penetrating stare eventually coming to rest on the gift bag in his hand.

"Yes," the woman responded, seemingly disarmed by the fact the well-dressed foreigner who spoke her native tongue also had good taste in department stores.

"I'm looking for a residence in this area. I don't have the address, but I have been there before. It has two large lion-dog statues on each side of the main entranceway."

The woman stepped back. "Lion-dogs?"

"Yes. About this size," Edward replied, holding his free hand above his head.

The woman seemed to hold her breath for a moment. "Do you know the owner of the house?"

"I do," Edward replied stoically.

"Two streets over," the woman replied, pointing her finger into the air over the wall of her neighbor's property.

"Thank you very much," Edward replied.

"You should be careful," the woman added, disappearing back through the gate from which she had appeared.

Two blocks further into the neighborhood, Edward peeked down a street to his left. Halfway down the block, two men stood in the middle of the road, bookended by large lion-dog statues.

Edward took a deep breath and turned down the narrow street.

*

The two men in the middle of the road turned to face Edward as he approached. Still thirty yards away, Edward walked slowly, not wanting to stir alarm.

Lights from residences on both sides of the street peeked over privacy walls. A lone streetlight shone overhead not far from Edward's destination. The illumination seemed to allow the two men in the street to identify Edward as a non-Japanese from three houses away.

"Good evening," Edward announced in Japanese as he closed the distance to the men.

He was ten feet away when he realized nothing in the men's posture indicated they were anticipating him to stop. Certainly neither man seemed to consider the non-Japanese person approaching on the narrow street was there to discuss business.

Edward stopped walking. His eyes danced across the two lion-dog statues and the modern wood fence enclosing the front of the property. A menacing metal gate in the middle of the fence was firmly shut.

Clearing his throat, Edward introduced himself. "Good evening. My name is Edward Winston. I'm an engineer from the United States. I would like to speak with Mr. Fukuzawa."

"Get the hell out of here," the larger of the two men offered in reply. Both men, dressed in nearly identical black suits, stepped forward.

Edward placed his gift bag on the ground and raised his hands as if he were being robbed. The men seemed to enjoy the gesture and the shorter of the two men snickered. The larger man sneered as if to convey that Edward's reaction was pathetic.

"Is Mr. Fukuzawa home?" Edward asked.

"What business is it of yours?"

"It's personal. Just let me reach into my pocket and get a business card for you to present to Mr. Fukuzawa."

"What's in the bag?" the larger man asked, stepping closer. Five feet separated the two parties and Edward could see the details of the larger man's crooked nose and rough skin. His hair was short and scars crisscrossed the man's head where hair refused to grow. His appearance gave Edward the impression that the man had considerable experience enduring physical punishment. Edward estimated both men were in their mid-twenties.

"I have whiskey in the bag. It's for Mr. Fukuzawa."

"Why don't you leave the bag and your business card and move along."

For a split second Edward thought about taking the advice. But there was nowhere else to turn. The narrow street in the swanky section of Bunkyo Ward was his last alternative. Tupelo to Tokyo. There was no next stop.

Edward clenched his fist and ground his teeth.

"No. I'm not leaving until I speak with Mr. Fukuzawa."

"Or what?" the larger man said, stepping yet closer and poking his finger into Edward's chest with the force of a metal bar.

Edward staggered back before regaining his footing. Then he stepped forward and reached into his breast pocket. Using both hands he presented his business card to the man, simultaneously dipping his head in a bow while providing his full name and title. It was the perfect execution of a Japanese custom performed millions of times a day in every city and town in the country.

The larger man smacked the business card out of Edward's hand and grabbed the gift bag with the whiskey off the pavement.

"What do you think you're doing?" Edward asked.

"Time to move on, foreigner."

"Give me the bag back."

"If you want the whiskey, you're going to have to take it back."

"I don't think Mr. Fukuzawa is going to approve of what's going on here."

"And how's he going to know?"

"Because you're either going to tell Mr. Fukuzawa someone is here to see him, or you're going to have to kill me right here, right now, in the middle of this street. And I don't plan on dying quietly."

"Suit yourself," the shorter man said, perking up at the prospect of violence.

Edward could feel the adrenaline surging through his veins and his hands began to shake. "If that's how you want it. But first let me take off my jacket," Edward said.

The two men watched as Edward began to disrobe. He removed his jacket and gently placed it on the head of the nearest lion-dog statue. With unsteady hands he began unbuttoning the cuff on his shirt.

"Your shirt too?" the larger man asked.

Edward rolled up his sleeve and displayed the scars on his left arm for the nearest man.

The man looked at Edward's arm and then back to Edward's face. Edward offered a grin.

"Is that supposed to tell me something?" the taller man asked.

Edward didn't respond and instead moved his hands to the buttons on the front of his dress shirt. His fingers undid each button slowly as he turned his body away, concealing his left side. Hands still trembling, he placed his shirt on top of his jacket. Then he turned towards the light to give the two men full view of his scars on his scrawny physique.

"Ever been burned before?" Edward asked. He moved closer so the men could see the extent of the damage.

The larger man seemed to wince and the smaller man bowed his head ever so slightly.

"More importantly: Do you know anyone else who has ever been burned?" Edward asked, his eyes piercing both men.

"I'll be right back," the larger man said, picking Edward's business card off the asphalt before vanishing through the gate in the direction of the house.

Edward took several minutes to put his clothes back on, the smaller man holding Edward's jacket. Once Edward was dressed, the man returned the gift bag with an extended bow.

The larger of the two men reappeared through the gate in the fence, rattling the knob. Blood trickled from his nose and a cut over his left eye. Through a stream of apologies, Edward noticed the man's front tooth had been broken in half.

"Please, follow me. Mr. Fukuzawa is waiting for you."

Edward followed the bleeding man across a series of large gray stone slabs, each the size of a small mattress. Lights illuminated the path from each side. Edward noticed the perfectly manicured lawn; a mix of grass and stone gardens. A koi pond was nestled in the far corner, next to an arc of artistically pruned trees.

Beyond the garden, Edward's attention turned towards the front of the house, a combination of modern wood panels and large glass windows. The home's front door was identical to the metal one in the fence facing the street. Two steps up, the tall man held the front door open and Edward stepped into the traditional sunken foyer of the home. A middle-aged Japanese woman on the far side of the foyer bowed deeply.

"Welcome," the woman said.

Edward responded with a bow and traditional Japanese greeting that loosely translated as "pardon my intrusion."

The woman bowed again and then placed a pair of guest slippers on the floor, toes pointing towards the interior of the home. Edward removed his shoes and the woman quickly bent down and turned the vacated footwear around so they pointed towards the door.

Edward nodded in appreciation and, with his downward glance, spotted several drops of blood on the stone tiles. He stepped up to the floor and slipped his feet into the guest slippers. Shuffling down the hall, the woman escorted Edward into the next room and bowed again. Two large sofas faced each other. A glass table sat between them. A white carpet spread beneath the table. The exposed wood of the ceiling stretched two stories above.

Through the glass windows, Edward could see the outline of the bleeding guard heading back through the yard, presumably returning to his position on the street. The orange glow from a lit cigarette cut through the darkness of the property.

"Please sit down," the woman said, motioning towards the far seat on the sofa. "Mr. Fukuzawa will be here momentarily. Can I get you something to drink?"

"No, thank you. I'm fine."

"Very well."

Edward looked around the well-appointed room and struggled to recall what it had looked like on his previous visit. The table looked familiar. The sofas were new. Beyond that, his recall was surprisingly gray. Or not surprisingly, given his physical state the only time he had been in the house.

CHAPTER 22

THE DEEP VOICE of Yusuke Fukuzawa cut through the stillness of the room and Edward immediately stiffened and stood from his seat.

"Please. Please. Sit down," Fukuzawa said, his hands patting the air in front of his torso as if to calm it down.

Fukuzawa was wearing black slacks and a beige shirt with a gold cravat. His gray hair was neatly trimmed. The wire-framed glasses resting on his nose gave the impression he was an avid reader. His skin hosted several liver spots, the one near his left ear the size of a silver dollar. A large watch weighed down his left wrist, balanced out by several missing fingers. Edward noticed the fresh cuts on Fukuzawa's first knuckles and quickly averted his eyes.

"I'm very sorry for coming to your home unannounced," Edward said, bowing as deeply as possible while still standing.

"Nonsense," Fukuzawa replied with feigned disgust.

"I thought about coming to your office, but I didn't want to be seen by too many people."

"Then I'm glad you came here."

"I brought you something," Edward said, extending the gift bag.

Fukuzawa placed the bag on the table and gently removed the bottle of whiskey.

"Johnny Walker Blue. One of my favorites."

"Then I'm relieved my memory was accurate."

"You didn't have to bring me anything. You would never have to bring me anything."

"Unannounced without a gift would have been exceptionally rude."

"Being threatened by my one of my guards is equally rude."

"I'm sure they were just trying to do their jobs."

"By forcing you to disrobe in order to see me?"

Edward shrugged his shoulders. "Disrobing was my idea."

"Forgive me for their behavior. They are relatively young. They are not aware of our history together. They were still in high school when we last met."

"I understand."

Fukuzawa motioned for Edward to sit back down on the sofa and then he bellowed into the air, "Oi."

The middle-aged woman reentered the room and Fukuzawa ordered two glasses and ice. Moments later the two men touched the edges of their crystal tumblers, arms stretched over the table between them.

"How have you been?" Fukuzawa asked. "Your business card says you work for Fujita in America."

"That's right. I'm an engineer. I live in Mississippi. I have a house. The job is good."

"A steady job with a good company. It's a good life. A good life for a good man."

"I accomplished what I wanted to accomplish."

"How about family? Did you ever get married? Have kids?"

"I was married. My wife recently passed away. No children," Edward managed to say without losing his composure.

"I'm sorry to hear that. My wife passed away long ago. But at least we had children. Children will change how you look at life. Give you a reason to live. Give you a reason to make better decisions."

"Maybe someday I will find out."

"I hope you do."

Both men took long sips of their drinks.

"How do you feel about seeing my daughter?" Fukuzawa asked. "You could even meet my grandson."

"I would love to."

"They live in the house behind this one. There's a path through the back garden."

"Sounds perfect."

Fukuzawa reached into his pocket and removed a cell phone. He pressed a couple of buttons, mumbled a sentence or two, and then returned the phone to his pocket.

"Shall we?"

*

Edward followed Fukuzawa from the back door of the house through an elaborate Japanese garden. A gate in the back fence adjoined his daughter's property. Just inside the gate, another man in a dark suit stood at attention. Fukuzawa nodded and the man bowed to his boss.

Light from the home filtered through the trees near the back of the property. The green grass was sprinkled with toys.

Edward followed Fukuzawa through the yard and onto a patio where Fukuzawa opened the back door of his daughter's house. Edward bowed and followed him into the kitchen. Another man in a suit stood in the far corner of the room, motionlessly staring out the front window.

The patter of a child's feet running against the wood floor caught Edward's attention. Fukuzawa bent at the waist and intercepted the boy as he tried to pass.

"This is my grandson, Koichiro," Fukuzawa said. The young boy nodded and said, "Nice to meet you."

Another set of feet came down the hallway and Fukuzawa's daughter appeared in the kitchen. She took in the sight of her father playing with her son, smiled, and then gasped in surprise at Edward's presence.

"We have a guest," Fukuzawa said calmly, motioning in Edward's direction.

Fukuzawa's daughter seemed to wobble and she grabbed the corner of the counter for support. Then she started to cry.

*

An hour later, Edward and Fukuzawa were back on the white sofas in Fukuzawa's living room. One of the guards from his daughter's home had escorted them back through the yard and the man was now walking around the perimeter of the house, his silhouette appearing and disappearing through the frames of various windows.

"So, what brought you here tonight, Edward-san?"

"I came for a favor."

"I suspected as much."

"Maybe I shouldn't have come."

"Nonsense. Are you oblivious to where we spent the last hour?"

"At your daughter's house."

"A daughter who wouldn't be here if you hadn't saved her."

"Perhaps."

"There is no perhaps. There were four cars in that accident the night you saved my daughter. Five people died. No one helped, except you. The only person who saved a life that night was a foreigner who happened to be in a taxi cab behind the accident when it occurred."

"I did what anyone would do."

"Bullshit. No one else did anything. It takes courage to force your body into a burning vehicle. I can only imagine the pain."

Fukuzawa paused and held up his hand to display his missing digits.

"You see, I'm no stranger to pain. Losing these fingers hurt. The sharp pain lasted a second. The intense pain lasted for hours. Severe pain lasted for days. Then it faded. But burns, they take a long time to heal. I know, I have watched my daughter try to recover for years. But I can tell you she still has moments where there's pain."

Fukuzawa motioned towards his hand again. "But these hands. They don't hurt anymore."

Edward nodded.

"Are you still in pain, Edward-san?"

"Sometimes. And I have nightmares."

"So does my daughter."

"I'm not sure they will ever go away."

"Maybe not."

There was another long pause and Edward took a sip from the whiskey glass still on the table.

"So what does the man who sacrificed his flesh retrieving my daughter from a burning vehicle, while others watched, need from me? What does the man who gave life to my daughter need? The man who gave life to my daughter and in turn gave life to my grandson. What would a man who has given me so much need in return?"

Edward steadied himself and leaned back into the sofa.

"My wife died recently."

"So you mentioned. I'm sorry for your loss. Was she ill?"

"No."

"It wasn't a car accident, was it? Even God wouldn't dare be that cruel."

"No. It wasn't an accident."

"Then how?"

"She was murdered."

"Murdered?"

"Yes. Beaten, strangled, and then drowned."

"Did they catch the person responsible?"

Edward looked up and his eyes met Fukuzawa's with an intensity the yakuza boss immediately recognized.

"They didn't catch him. But I know who did it. He admitted as much to me."

"Did you go to the police?"

"I went to the police and the FBI. The police are corrupt and the FBI hasn't done anything."

"And you came all this way to ask me for help?"

"That's right. You once said I could come to you for anything. For any favor."

"What do you want me to do for you?"

Edward paused. "I think you know."

"Edward-san. You have come this far. My door is open to you. My gratitude for your sacrifice cannot be measured. Any favor you ask will be granted. But you are going to have to ask. There can be no misunderstanding about what is being decided."

Edward moved his glass to his lips and downed the remaining liquid in one gulp.

"I need to have someone killed."

Fukuzawa removed his eyeglasses, wiped them, and then returned them to his face.

"Where is this person?"

"In Tupelo, Mississippi."

"And I assume this person is a man."

"It is."

"And do you care how it is done?"

"I do not."

Fukuzawa nodded.

"Do you have a name?"

"I have a name and an address."

Edward removed the postcard of Tokyo Tower from his breast pocket and placed it on the table.

Fukuzawa picked up the postcard and his eyes moved over the name and address on the back.

"Is there anything else I need to know?"

"The man who murdered my wife works as a window installer for a company called Palmetto Windows. He drives a red truck for work. He drinks at a bar called the Brew Ha, and he lives on a quiet road just outside of town. That's his name and his home address."

Edward paused.

"And he owns a few guns."

"So he's dangerous."

"Yes."

Edward stared at Fukuzawa and wondered for a moment what the man was thinking.

Then Fukuzawa reached into his pocket and retrieved his cell phone for the second time.

"Come inside," was all he said, placing the phone on the table.

A moment later the front door to the house opened and the man in the suit who had escorted Edward and Fukuzawa from his daughter's house entered the room.

A wave of nerves washed over Edward and he felt ill.

The man walked around the backside of the sofa and stood at attention next to Fukuzawa. A large, unsightly scar ran down the man's neck from his ear to the collar of his shirt. Edward marveled at how the man had survived a wound that ran through so many vital parts of anatomy. Unlike the two men at the front gate, Edward guessed the gentleman standing at attention in the living room was in his fifties. He exuded an air of complete loyalty and Edward felt certain that if Fukuzawa handed him the postcard, the man would be on a plane for Tupelo tomorrow.

"This is Nagata."

Edward nodded at the man who bowed back.

"Where are you staying?" Fukuzawa asked.

The question caught Edward by surprise. He had just asked for someone to be killed and in response he was being asked where he was staying.

"A small hotel near Takadanobaba. Sunroute Hotel."

"There are no good places to stay in Baba," Fukuzawa said.

"It's fine."

Fukuzawa motioned towards Nagata who was standing unmoved next to the sofa. "Nagata will see to it that you have a room someplace a little more deserving. You will never see the bill. Order room service. Get a massage. Relax. You need to relax."

Edward didn't argue with the offer, though he had no intention of actually staying in a hotel room sponsored by the yakuza.

"What about that?" Edward asked, pointing down at the postcard on the table.

"I said it's time for you to relax," Fukuzawa repeated.

Edward bowed his head and tried to calm his shaking hands. A moment later he asked to use the restroom.

Fukuzawa yelled out to his in-house help and the woman appeared at the doorway to escort Edward from the room.

*

Fukuzawa sat in silence, again removing his glasses and wiping them clean.

"Is everything okay?" Nagata asked pensively, unaware of the conversation that had taken place before he had been beckoned into the house.

"We shall see," Fukuzawa said, standing. Crossing the living room floor, Fukuzawa provided instructions to Nagata. "When our visitor is out of the bathroom, retrieve the car and take him to the Ritz-Carlton in Shinjuku. Get him a suite."

The employee nodded and then Fukuzawa added. "When you're done moving him to the Ritz, find Shiro Ose and bring him to me."

CHAPTER 23

SHIRO'S MUSCULAR FOREARM grabbed the wooden sword from the umbrella stand as shouting erupted down the narrow hall. Shiro flew down the corridor and pushed aside the thick red curtain to the smoke-filled room as two patrons exploded in an exchange of punches. The four other gamblers at the poker table scrambled from their stools, grasping for their chips and seeking refuge on the dealer's side of the table.

"You son of a bitch," a businessman yelled as he landed a punch to the head of a younger man in running pants and a T-shirt. The man in running pants raised his hands to protect himself from the assault and the business-man kicked towards his groin, hitting his target's thigh.

Shiro's entrance paused the room for a split second, and the man in the running pants pulled out a knife with a long serrated edge and a sharp tip. Shiro glared at the man, his eyes like lasers, and then slowly raised his wooden sword, pointing it at the man standing half a room away.

The man in running pants sneered and then lunged, blade first, at the businessman in the suit.

The sound of the wooden sword cutting through the smoke-filled room ended with a resounding crack. A blood-curdling scream pierced the air and the men huddling on the dealer's side of the table clawed their way out of the room and down the hallway.

The man in running pants looked down at his arm, his hand hanging at an unnatural angle, only still attached by damaged tendons and pulverized bone. The knife rested at the foot of a poker stool. Shiro stepped forward and kicked the blade in the direction of the dealer, who picked it up.

"What's going on in here?" Shiro asked.

The businessman answered. "I caught him with his hand on my chips when I was lighting a cigarette. Quick-fingered son of a bitch. I don't imagine it's the first time he's done it."

Shiro stared at the injured man as he cradled his badly damaged arm. "Is this true?"

"I never touched his chips," the man choked out.

Shiro looked at the dealer for clarification.

"I didn't see anything."

"Who was ahead?" Shiro asked.

The dealer motioned towards the man in the suit. "He was up thirty thousand yen tonight."

"And this guy?" Shiro asked, using his *bokken* to point at the injured man, whose face was turning ashen.

"Down twenty thousand. Maybe twenty-five."

Shiro kept his wooden sword pointed at the man with the broken wrist.

"If this were forty years ago, I would be throwing your body out the back window into the river behind the building. And that would be the end of it. Lucky for you, the police are more diligent these days and there's an apartment building across the way. Someone watching television in their living room might notice a body hitting the water."

The man audibly sucked in air.

"Let's move," Shiro ordered. The man in running pants headed through the curtained partition and into the hall. Shiro walked behind the man, the point of his *bokken* near the floor. In the corner of the lounge at the front of the establishment, the four men who had escaped from the altercation gathered near the small bar.

"Sit down," Shiro said to the injured man, pointing towards a leather chair along the wall with his wooden sword. "And stay put."

Shiro approached the men at the bar and apologized for the disturbance with a series of bows and formal expressions of regret. Then he turned towards the lone bartender. "Send them back to their room with a bottle of Hennessey, on the house."

The bartender nodded and Shiro walked back down the hall to soothe the other patrons on the business side of the establishment. He apologized to the men around the poker tables in the two other small rooms, then popped into the larger Mahjong parlor and repeated himself to the dozen patrons seated four to a table, tiles littered in front of them.

Back in the lounge, Shiro sat down in the chair across from the injured man who was groaning through his pain.

"What's your story?"

"I needed to win to pay my son's tuition. My wife refuses to send him to public school."

"If you need money, don't come here."

"I had no choice."

"And now you're going to need money to have your hand fixed."

The man grunted like an animal as he stared down at his mangled limb. Shiro noticed a bone pushing at the skin, threatening to punch through.

"How many times have you been in here?"

"I don't know."

"Well, I do. Too many. Twice a month for the last year or two. Probably close to fifty times."

"Maybe," the man said.

"Do you know who runs this establishment?"

"You run this establishment."

"Do you know who owns this establishment?"

"I can guess."

"If you can guess, then you don't need to."

Someone rang the front door buzzer and Shiro looked up at the security camera next to the entrance. He made eye contact with the bartender and flicked his head in the direction of the door. The bartender covered the carpeted floor in quick strides and undid the locks for the visitor.

Shiro turned back towards the man in the chair. "Unfortunately, your behavior has put me in a difficult position. If I let you live, I have to explain why I was weak. Why I let you go. If I kill you, I'll have to spend the rest of my evening dealing with your body. And I have an important game later tonight."

The man's shoulders began to shake uncontrollably.

"What do you suggest I do?" Shiro asked.

"Let me go. I'll repay you for the inconvenience."

"Fifty thousand yen. Tomorrow. And I don't want you back in here. Ever."

"I can do that."

"That's the first thing. The second thing I want is for you to tell all your friends with money that you know the best place to find honest, upright gambling. Right here."

"I can do that."

"I know you can. I know you will. And don't go sending any trash in my direction."

Shiro reached into his front pocket and pulled out ten thousand yen, holding it between two fingers. "Take this money to get a cab. And add it to what you owe me tomorrow. Go see a doctor. Tell them you fell."

Shiro flipped the money into the man's lap. "Do we understand each other?"

The man nodded. "Yes."

*

Nagata was at the bar, pouring himself a drink as the bartender stood to the side, out of the way. He filled the glass three-quarters full and then took a drink.

Shiro approached and the two men exchanged respectful bows.

"What's up with the guy with the damaged hand?" Nagata asked.

"He may have tried to steal another player's chips."

"And you're letting him walk away?"

"He lost twenty-five thousand yen in here this evening. He owes us another fifty for the disturbance. And I don't have time to deal with anything else tonight. We're hosting Cho-han. Invitation only. I need to start getting ready."

"How's business this evening?"

"Good for a Thursday."

"Not many people are playing Cho-han these days."

"Not too many. Just a few yakuza. But it's good business. No matter who wins, the house wins."

"How many players usually come?"

"We have ten or so. Guys from Tokyo, mostly."

"You're going to have to cancel it."

"Why?"

"Fukuzawa wants to see you."

"Where?"

"His house."

"Tonight?"

"Tonight."

"The Cho-han guests are already on their way. I can't cancel."

"Then I'll stay in your place," Nagata said.

"Have you ever proctored a Cho-han game?"

"Many times. Starting before you were born."

Shiro reached into his pocket and handed Nagata the keys to the second-floor gambling house. "If I'm not back, close up when you leave."

Nagata returned the favor and handed Shiro his car keys. "Take my car. It's parked illegally in front of the building. Come back after you meet with Fukuzawa."

Shiro nodded and exhaled. "That's good news for me. If you expect me to bring your car back, then Fukuzawa probably doesn't have it in for me."

"Not tonight," Nagata answered without a hint of sarcasm.

CHAPTER 24

SHIRO BOWED TO Fukuzawa's live-in help at edge of the foyer. The woman returned the bow and showed Shiro into the living room where Fukuzawa was on the sofa watching baseball on TV, the volume turned low. As Fukuzawa stood, Shiro offered his boss a series of deep bows, his head almost parallel to the floor.

"Please have a seat," Fukuzawa said.

Shiro bowed a final time and then sat down at the end of the sofa. His posture remained perfectly upright. His eyes straight ahead.

"How was work tonight?" Fukuzawa asked.

"Not bad for a weeknight. We had a little trouble with a customer but it was handled. We're hosting Cho-han tonight. Nagata offered to run the game in my absence."

Fukuzawa waved the conversation off with a flick of his wrist.

"I've always liked you, Shiro. You've always performed honorably. And there's no doubt you know how to run a gambling den. Not everyone can strike a balance between host and enforcer. You bring them in. A nice steady sum of money. I've never had to worry about you producing. Never."

"Thanks to your guidance."

Fukuzawa exhaled loudly. "And you've managed to have a successful career while avoiding arrest."

"Also thanks to you."

Fukuzawa glanced down towards the missing half of Shiro's left pinkie finger. A single cut for a single mistake.

Shiro followed Fukuzawa's eyes to his left hand. "Had you not sent Ito-san to confess to a crime I committed, I would be in prison now."

"Ito-san did as he was required."

"I'm as thankful today as I was then."

"It was a business decision. Ito simply didn't make the money you did. Like all business ventures, our family would fail without income."

"I am still grateful."

"Ito's sacrifice is part of the life we lead."

"Indeed."

"I'm curious, Shiro. Do you have a passport?"

"No. I've never left the country."

"Good. Good," Fukuzawa replied.

Shiro was unsure of where the conversation was leading as an awkward moment of silence fell over the two men.

"If I recall correctly, you speak some English," Fukuzawa said.

"I do. My mother dragged me to English conversation schools from a very young age. She thought it would lead me to a promising career. Later, in high school, I had an American girlfriend here in Tokyo. An exchange student from Boston who was staying with a classmate down the street."

"How's your English these days?" Fukuzawa asked.

"That's difficult to answer."

"There's a rumor you frequent certain clubs in Kabukicho that employ foreign women."

Shiro nodded without shame. "I do."

"That can't be cheap."

"I make ends meet."

"And I understand you have a few favorites in the clubs. One is Australian. A girl you've been seen with outside the club as well."

"You are very well informed."

"There's hardly a whisper in Tokyo that the wind doesn't bring to my ears," Fukuzawa replied. "I have four thousand men under my control and I keep tabs on all of them."

"Of course."

"It's my understanding that this Australian woman from the club doesn't speak Japanese very well."

"Yes, not very well."

"So do you get to practice your English with her?"

"Conversation isn't required for fucking."

Fukuzawa unleashed a deep bellowing laugh. "So true. So true. Who needs the conversation?"

Shiro nodded.

Fukuzawa's expression turned to stone as quickly as the laugh had appeared. "You didn't answer the question."

"We speak English when we're together."

"Can you handle simple conversation?"

"Yes. And I can brush up if you need me to."

Shiro felt the inkling of nerves setting in. Violence, negotiations, and gambling were his specialty. If he had wanted to study, he would have stayed in school.

"Perhaps. Perhaps we can get you a few lessons," Fukuzawa said, staring off through the living room window for a moment.

"How are your wife and daughter?" Fukuzawa asked.

"They're good. Everyone is healthy. My daughter is in the first grade."

"And how's your wife dealing with her life? I know she was once unhappy with your career in our family."

"I was yakuza before I married her."

"That doesn't mean she's happy about it. I was married once. There were many discussions about me finding a different career. A legitimate career. And as much as my wife wanted me to start another life, I couldn't. I had no other skills. I'd been in the yakuza for twenty years by the time I was married. There were no other options."

"I see," Shiro replied.

"So your wife is content with your life?"

"All is well in my house," Shiro stated.

"I've also heard rumors you could be interested in returning to a regular life. Returning to society."

"I'm not sure where that rumor came from."

"It doesn't matter where it came from. I want to know if it's true."

Shiro treaded lightly, answering without answering. "I think one should always keep their options open without betraying their loyalty. Loyalty is paramount."

"I see. I see. Out of curiosity, what would you do without your yakuza family?"

"I would fix cars."

"Fix cars?"

"Yes. When I was a boy, my father was a mechanic. I learned from him. I enjoyed it."

"So your father taught you two things. How to fight and how to fix cars."

"My father taught me kendo. My uncle taught me karate. I learned to fight on the street."

"As do we all."

"My dad taught me how to survive," Shiro conceded, hoping to end the conversation with a positive image of his father.

"And you have," Fukuzawa agreed. He grunted and seemed to consider his next sentence carefully. "I have a proposal for you, Shiro. A task for you. A task I'm willing to reward you for."

"I don't need a reward. You're family. I will do whatever is required."

"This is different. This is a personal favor."

"I'll still do whatever is asked."

"I need to have a problem eliminated."

Shiro stared straight into his boss's eyes. "I understand."

"What do you know about Mississippi?"

"Not much."

"Buy a guide book. You have an appointment tomorrow at the finger doctor. You'll need your photo taken. Then we'll work on getting you a passport."

"I have a negotiation tomorrow."

"Go see the finger doctor when you're done."

CHAPTER 25

SHIRO SAT AT the head of the table in the two-room suite at the Tokyo Hyatt. To his left was a man in his fifties, impeccably dressed in a business suit that Shiro imagined had last been worn at a funeral. The man pressed a handkerchief to his cheek, wiping perspiration from his face.

The woman to his right, opposite the man at the table, was wrapped in a black *tomesode*, a traditional kimono worn by married women. She appeared to be in her sixties, her perfectly applied makeup masking her true age.

The negotiation at hand was in its final stages. Both parties had agreed, with Shiro's gentle guidance, to accept some responsibility for the accident that had brought them all together. It was an unfortunate mishap, an expensive car pulling out of a parking garage and clipping a bicyclist as he passed. Unfortunately, both parties had been drunk. More unfortunate for the woman's husband, he had not been in a vehicle and had lost the battle of physics.

The ensuing fall from the bicycle had incapacitated the older man, effectively ending his ability to work. The husband's ability to feed himself had only recently recovered. Bathing, dressing, and walking more than a few steps were still ahead on the rehabilitation checklist.

A civil case had been initiated by the woman, who sought damages for her husband's debilitation. Her husband's state of inebriation at the time of the accident had diminished the strength of her case and the courts had ruled against any judgment. Faced with the prospect of a long appeals process, with mounting legal costs, the woman had sought an off-the-record resolution to her sudden loss of household income. It merely required the woman to look up the address of the nearest yakuza headquarters and make an appointment.

*

"Please," Shiro said, motioning with an upturned palm at the man on the left. The man opened the top on a decorative box and began handing money to Shiro. With deliberate movement, the man held each stack of one million yen in both hands as he presented his settlement offering.

Shiro, in turn, nodded as he accepted each stack of money and piled the inch-thick bundles on the table in front of him. As the man passed the last stack, Shiro double-checked the amount.

Satisfied, Shiro rotated towards the woman. It was now his turn to pass the money to his right, one stack at a time, two hands on each stack. When slightly more than half of the pile had been transferred to the woman, Shiro's hands stopped. The woman again bowed her head and then slowly added her portion of the money to a handbag that matched her kimono.

"That concludes the business at hand today," Shiro said. "Thank you both for coming to this meeting with an open mind."

The man to Shiro's left grunted quietly in apparent disagreement and Shiro paused long enough for the man to bury any further objections he had on his "volunteered" participation in the proceedings at hand.

"I hope both parties are satisfied with the result of the negotiation. Please feel free to contact us again if another issue arises that cannot be resolved through traditional means."

The payee stood, bowing to Shiro first, then to the woman, before disappearing out the door. The woman, recipient of sixty percent of the negotiated settlement, bowed a final time, rising from the floor in her kimono through a precise set of movements.

Ten minutes later, Shiro handed the proceeds from the day's mediation to a coworker in the lobby of the hotel. "Pay the bill for the room. Take this back to the office," Shiro said.

*

Shiro fought through traffic before parking his car in a private spot next to a *yakiniku* restaurant just north of Shinjuku. The ever-present rumble of trains from the busiest station in the world reverberated down the street and sidewalks, the towering buildings funneling the noise away from the bustle.

With the echo of mass transit behind him, Shiro disappeared into the labyrinth of ill-repute known as Kabukicho. On streets no wider than the average car, Shiro passed a stretch of venues specializing in male hosts for female clientele. Around the corner, two men stood at the entrance to a club with a nurse theme, the door illuminated by neon lighting, the archway shaped as a pair of stethoscopes. The two men in front of the entrance had corralled a potential customer and were assuring the drunken man that the girls in the establishment were first-rate. The doormen nodded as Shiro passed and Shiro heard them offer their prospective client a discounted blowjob, with two drinks on the house.

Several streets later, with law-abiding Japan lurking a hundred yards away at the end of the block, Shiro entered the middle door in a string of identical gray seven-story buildings. He stepped into the lobby, nodded at an elderly gentleman in a security uniform and approached the elevator bank.

Without prompting, the security guard took one step forward and pressed the elevator button for Shiro.

"Fifth floor," the man said confidently before returning to his position next to the elevator doors.

*

A woman in a white lab coat cracked opened the door to an apartment on the fifth floor and Shiro considered whether he had the wrong address. The woman's bangs were cut perfectly straight across her forehead, parallel to the perfection of the hair that stopped just above her shoulders. Her face was round and kind. Her eyes were neither. Shiro watched as the woman visually felt him up, her stare running from his shoes to his head, pausing at his groin, and eventually landing on his left hand.

"Please come in," she replied, pulling the door open wide.

Shiro stepped in and removed his shoes in the small foyer. He followed the woman into a large white room with windows facing the street. Neon lights from the establishments below flickered and reflected against the façade of the building across the street. Shiro surveyed the open space and noted a second room towards the rear of the converted apartment.

"Welcome," the woman said. "My name Nakamura. You must be Shiro Ose."

Shiro nodded.

"That is the first and last time I will use your name. And at no point will I ever write your name down. There will never be a traceable record of you visiting this location or of any work I may do for you. I will provide you with an identifying number and you will refer to that number for all of our transactions."

Shiro shrugged his shoulders. "That's fine."

The woman motioned towards a large white seat that resembled a dental chair.

"You don't have any help?" Shiro asked, puzzled by the lack of a receptionist, a rarity in Tokyo.

"A couple evenings a week I work here by myself and for myself. I also work at a larger well-known clinic. We make a variety of custom prosthetics. Arms. Hands. Legs. Ears. You name it."

"Interesting."

"Here, I only make fingers."

"And are all of your clients like me?"

"Yes."

"Good, then I don't have to explain anything."

"No, you do not. But *I* have to explain a few things. I have rules. Rules that will be followed. Without exception."

Shiro could feel Nakamura's eyes sizing him up by his reaction. "Such as?" he asked.

"First, you don't talk about this place. What I do is not illegal, but I don't need the hassle of being hassled for what I do."

"Okay."

"Secondly, there is a queue. Everyone is in the same line. All of my patients are equal. I will not accept a bribe for expedited or special service, so don't offer me one."

"Understood."

"Third, I always get paid in advance, for all of my work. In your case, the bill has already been paid in full."

"Do people not pay you?"

"Why, are you going to offer to help me out with that? Maybe shake someone down for me?"

"I could."

"No thanks. But to answer your question, yes, people don't pay me. The problem with providing services to the clients I serve is that most of them are leaving a profession where they were well paid. Most often, my clients are in a transitional phase of their life and that transition means they won't be receiving the same salary they once did."

"Unreliable clients are a tough way to make it in business."

"Yes. They are. My fourth rule is simple. Never threaten me in any way. Do not threaten my life, my family, my work, my home."

"I wouldn't."

"And I would like to believe that. I really would. But you are from a mold, Shiro Ose. Most men from your mold only understand power that comes with money, threats, or violence. I refuse to operate in that world."

"You said you weren't going to use my name again."

Nakamura scowled. "Do you understand my rules?"

"Yes."

"Good. What we're going to do today is pretty straightforward. All we have to do is size you up, make a mold, take some photographs, choose an appropriate skin color, count the number of hairs you have on your knuckles, and then I can get to work. When I'm finished, no one will be able to tell you have a finger prosthesis without very close inspection. Unless, of course, you go to the beach and get a tan. Or spend all winter inside."

"What can you do about that?"

"I can make you a summer and a winter finger. But the seasonal fingers are in a different queue. I provide every client with one finger up front, and then I make extras."

"How long will it take?"

"A week to ten days. Then you come back for a fitting and we check the color and make any final adjustments."

"Do I make an appointment?" Shiro asked.

"No. I call you when it's done. Just leave your number and I'll call when it's ready."

Nakamura smiled and raised the armrest on the chair where Shiro was sitting. She turned on an overhead light and reached out with her dainty hands. "Now, let me take a look at that finger."

CHAPTER 26

EDWARD STOOD IN his living room, empty boxes piled in the corner, threatening to fall. A stack of flat cardboard covered the coffee table. Edward pulled a strip of shipping tape across two cardboard seams and seconds later transformed another cardboard sheet into a moving box. He threw the box at the stack in the corner and the Jenga tower of cardboard came crashing down.

Edward heard the muffled ringtone of his new cell phone and dug through his temporary assembly line on the coffee table. Removing the phone from under a roll of bubble wrap, Edward answered.

"Edward Winston."

"This is Special Agent Washington, are you home?"

"I am."

"Can I stop by?"

Edward looked around his living room. "Sure, but it's a bit of a mess. I'm in the middle of organizing. Packing things."

"How about meeting downtown? I just left the courthouse. I'm in my car." Agent Washington's breath was audible, her voice vibrating with a sense of urgency.

"Café 212? It's around the corner from the courthouse."

"I'll find it," she said.

"Just give me a couple of minutes to change my shirt and wade through my living room."

"I'll be waiting."

*

Edward sat down at a table for two across from Agent Washington. On the wall over their heads, a faux black-and-white French café awning cast an equally faux shadow downward towards the table.

"You want something?" Agent Washington asked, pointing at her coffee.

"No. I'm good."

"How was your vacation?"

Edward shifted his weight in his chair. "I'd probably call it bereavement travel. It's hard to have a funeral and consider it a vacation."

"I'm sorry. You're absolutely right. That was poor wording on my part."

"Don't worry about it."

A coffee mug crashing to the floor somewhere behind the barista counter broke the ensuing silence.

"I scattered my wife's ashes in Lake Michigan. Along a nice stretch of beach called Lake Bluff."

"Is that what she wanted?"

"You know, we never discussed it in detail, but I know she wanted to be cremated. She mentioned once that she wanted her remains to be scattered in Lake Michigan. She had a framed photograph with her mother that had been taken in Lake Bluff. It sounded like a good place. And it was. It was beautiful."

Edward almost let his emotions get the better of him and then reined them in.

"And then I took a quick trip to Japan. Met with some people at headquarters to see about other job opportunities. Some place away from here. I also saw some friends. Went to a hot spring resort. Tried to take my mind off things. Tokyo and Tupelo are on different planets."

"You look rested."

"I'm officially on a leave of absence from work. Fully paid. I've started to pack my things. I'm not sure where I'm going, but I know Tupelo isn't in my future."

Agent Washington turned her head in both directions and then dropped her voice to a near whisper.

"I asked you to come her because I have some news regarding your wife's case. The Lee County Sheriff's Department is preparing to announce they have solved your wife's murder."

"They are? Did Pervis's luck finally run out?"

"No. They're not naming Pervis."

"Who then?"

"Your neighbor. Brent Poole. The mechanic."

"They think Mr. Poole killed Holly?"

"They claim they have evidence to that effect."

"What evidence?"

"Are you sure you want to hear it?"

"Are you going to tell me anything worse than what I've already heard? Could there be anything worse?"

"They found articles of your wife's clothing in Mr. Poole's house, including a pair of her underwear in his bedroom."

"Am I supposed to take that to mean Mr. Poole killed her? Need I remind you the police had access to my wife's belongings? It seems obvious that the police took my wife's underwear and planted them at my neighbor's."

"The sheriff's department also claims to have found a tire rim from a 1974 Cadillac. The rim was pulled from the fishing pond where your wife's body was found. It had a length of chain attached to it. Something you might find in an automotive garage. They're going through Mr. Poole's records to see if he ever worked on a similar vehicle."

"Un-fucking believable," Edward said, his voice rising. Two mothers at the next table glared in his direction and then rolled their baby strollers further away.

"I know it's not what you want to hear."

"And what's the FBI doing about it?"

"I've requested copies of all the evidence."

"That doesn't sound promising."

"No one's perfect, Edward. Sooner or later they're going to trip up, and I'm going to catch them."

"I'm not sure how many shots you're going to get at it."

"Why's that?"

"Because if they can make it look like Mr. Poole committed murder, and you don't find anything to contradict them, it's over. The case is closed."

"There's always the next time."

"Not always," Edward said, perturbed. "Do you have any good news?"

"No and yes. The forensics report came back on your Ole Miss cap. Nothing was found on the cap indicating it was the same cap found in Mr. Poole's garage. In fact, no DNA was found on the cap at all. Not even a single hair from your head, which was unexpected. After all, a cap should have its owner's DNA on it. Further examination of the cap identified trace residual chemicals indicating it had been thoroughly cleaned."

"So they could have been trying to set me up with the cap but aborted the plan when you started poking around."

"It's possible."

"So what's the good news?"

"The good news is that there's a silver lining to the police naming your neighbor as a suspect."

"What's that?"

"If Mr. Poole is the prime suspect, you'll no longer be considered a person of interest."

"Until they create evidence showing Mr. Poole and I were actually working together."

"Don't be ridiculous."

"No offense, but I think the ridiculous market has been cornered by the Lee County Sheriff's Department."

Agent Washington wrung her hands on the table. "I called you because I wanted you to hear it from me first. The sheriff said he'll be reaching out to you personally, but I'd also expect a full story in the papers and on the news. The sheriff is planning to hold a press conference on the steps of the courthouse."

"I'll be sure to tune in."

CHAPTER 27

THE BLUE FORD Taurus with a Tupelo Realtors magnet on the door pulled slowly into the driveway and stopped behind Edward's Camry. A brunette in her forties got out of the car with a leather satchel and ambled up the sidewalk as she eyed the neighborhood of her next potential listing. Minutes later, folders and brochures were stacked neatly across Edward's small dining room table. As Edward poured coffee into matching cups, the real estate agent began her spiel.

"With most clients, I dig a little into the reason why they're interested in selling. It's a big decision, after all. But I don't think that conversation is necessary here. You were very clear over the phone."

Edward nodded.

"And once again, I'm sorry for your loss, Mr. Winston," the real estate agent added.

"Thanks," Edward replied. "Hopefully I can sell it quickly and take a small step towards moving on. That's the plan anyway."

"Where are you heading?"

"Not sure yet. My company is going to let me transfer to another facility. Maybe Texas or Kentucky."

"It's nice your company can accommodate your situation."

"It's a Japanese company. Its relationship with its employees is a little different."

"I'll have to take your word for it. So, what's your timeframe for moving?"

"I hope to be out of Tupelo by the end of the summer."

"I can work with that. How about a quick tour of the house and then we can sit down, check out some comps, talk numbers, and come up with an asking price?"

"That sounds fine."

"I'll also need proof of homeowners insurance. I know you probably have some, but if you don't, I can get you a deal."

The real estate agent smiled and slid a folder in Edward's direction.

Edward read the professionally done cover of the insurance folder and pointed to the name on top.

"I recognize the company name and logo."

A capital *S* and *I* were enclosed in a white pentagon.

"Sterling Insurance has been in Tupelo forever. The original founder is no longer with us, but two other local agents bought his practice. They kept the name for its brand."

"It looks familiar."

"They advertise. You'll see the logo from time to time. They have a billboard and a few bus stop advertisements. They used to do TV spots, but I haven't seen any in a while."

"Maybe that's it."

"You haven't been around long enough to know, but a lot of people remember the company from the news. The founder of Sterling Insurance was beaten to death over a parking space at a restaurant. A real tragedy. It was in all the papers."

The light bulb that had flickered in Edward's mind moments before reached full illumination. "I've heard the story," Edward managed to reply, almost choking. "I'll get you the info on our homeowners policy. I'm pretty sure we pay it all at once, one time a year."

"Let me know."

Edward stood and motioned with his hand towards the living room, ten feet away. "We can start the tour here. Excuse the mess."

*

In the aftermath of losing a loved one, simple things can be the hardest to endure. Edward felt the day's first stab of loneliness standing in front of the yogurt selection in the refrigerated aisle of Piggly Wiggly. With orange juice to his left and eggs to his right, Edward stood motionless, staring at the Greek yogurt options, with fruit on the bottom. He could see his wife's face, a spoon in hand, smiling as she consumed the yogurt she ate first thing in the morning and again every afternoon.

Similar moments of mourning struck Edward's psyche in the cereal aisle and again in the bakery. A half-dozen aisles later, among freezers stocked with pizza, Edward grabbed a six-pack from a display on the precipice of the beer and wine section. As he put the beer in his cart, a voice called out from his rear.

"Well, I'll be damned," Pervis said, his cackle bellowing, echoing into the tall ceiling. "Imagine the chances of meeting you here. I usually don't shop at Piggly Wiggly, myself. But they have Miller Light on sale. A case for thirteen bucks. Can't beat that price anywhere."

Edward glared as Pervis pushed his cart closer. Edward could feel his blood pressure rising as Pervis approached and eyeballed the contents of his shopping cart.

"I see you have a nice selection of healthy food alternatives."

Edward caught a whiff of Pervis's breath and moved back a half-step. "Fuck off, Pervis."

"Why do we always have to go down the road of unpleasantries?"

"I said fuck off."

"I really don't understand the hostility. Especially after yesterday. The Lee County sheriff announced your dead neighbor was the prime suspect in your wife's murder. I'd have thought that would smooth things over between us."

Edward glared at Pervis. Clenching his teeth, he began pushing his cart towards the front of the store.

Pervis raised his voice as Edward stepped away. "I don't see any ingredients for making chili in your cart. That's too bad. Your wife had a good recipe."

Edward stopped and turned around.

"Uh-oh. I seen that look before. Here comes piss-and-vinegar Eddie," Pervis said, maniacally.

Edward dropped his voice, as if he had a secret. "Say, Pervis, I was wondering something. When's your birthday?"

"Why? Are you going to buy me a present?"

"Nope."

"Then I'm not sure I want to tell you."

"Come on. Be a sport. I just want to make a friendly wager."

"A wager? I'm in. I don't know what you have in mind, but I'm in."

"I'm going to need your birthday."

"October thirtieth."

"And how old are you going to be this year?"

"Thirty-one."

"All right. Easy enough to remember."

Edward paused as a woman with a child in her cart rounded the corner and then disappeared down the aisle.

"So, what's the bet?" Pervis asked.

"I've got a thousand dollars that says you don't make it to your next birthday."

Pervis stopped smiling for a moment. Slowly, a demented grin returned to his face.

"That's an interesting bet, Eddie. And what's going to happen to me before my next birthday?"

"Hard to say. But a thousand dollars says you don't make it."

"And just how are you going to get paid if I don't make it?"

"Good point. Let's consider it a win-win. If you're alive, you win. If you're dead, you don't have to pay, and you still win."

"But *you* won't get paid. What kind of a bet is that?"

"You dying would be payment enough."

"What are you going to do, shoot me? I heard you were out at the gun shop a while back and got yourself a .357."

"I did."

"Well, you had your chance to pull the trigger on me and you couldn't. Buying a gun isn't going to change that."

"I'm not going to shoot you, Pervis."

"Then what?"

"I'm not going to do anything. Now, do you want to take the bet or not?"

Edward extended his hand and Pervis sneered.

"Ticktock, Pervis," Edward said, turning back to push his cart in the direction of the cashier. Several paces away, Edward added a parting comment over his shoulder. "There's a sale on Listerine in aisle six. Your breath smells like you ate the ass of a dead skunk."

*

Edward stared at the ceiling of the bedroom, immune to the effect of the Ambien he had taken ninety minutes before. Closing his eyes, his mind turned towards his supermarket run-in with Pervis. He replayed the conversation in his mind, regretting he had said anything. In retrospect, he should have paid for his groceries and left. But he hadn't. Now he was lying in bed, trying to convince himself he hadn't said anything incriminating.

He forced Pervis from his mind and a new anxiety immediately replaced the old. He spent the next half an hour in darkness, fretting over his recent trip to visit a man named Fukuzawa. *Having nightmares when you're awake is worse than having them when you're asleep.*

With anxiety conquering sleep, Edward got out of bed. He ambled to the kitchen, poured a glass of milk, and drank half. Eyeing the dining room table from the kitchen, he moved into the next room, grabbed a box of documents, and took them to the sofa. Finding his seat, he plucked the papers off the top of the box and flipped through the real estate listing agreement he had signed that morning. Next, he fished around in the box and removed an accordion file stuffed with documents related to Pervis Wade.

He perused a copy of a police report he had purchased at the courthouse nearly a month before. A short month ago, when ignorance had still been bliss. Reading the document, Edward noted Pervis's date of birth in the upper right-hand corner of the page.

"October thirtieth," Edward said aloud, flicking the corner of the paper with his finger. "I can't believe it. You do know how to tell the truth."

Edward spread the contents of the Pervis folder on the table in front of the sofa. He plucked the photograph from the fishing tournament taken a decade before and his eyes ran across Sheriff Blazer and Detective Rafferty celebrating their victory on stage while Pervis Wade's father stood to their rear.

Edward's eyes moved from the three men's faces to the large sponsor board at the rear of the stage. Pulling the photo closer, Edward focused on the large *S* and *I* enclosed in a white pentagon, the logo peppered among others for the Tire Shack, Tupelo Hardware, and Palmetto Windows.

"I knew I had seen you before," Edward said.

Curiosity percolating, Edward turned his attention to the details of the arrest report for Pervis Wade and the manslaughter of one Charlie Sterling. Edward's eyes dropped to the blue insurance folder with the embossed lettering.

"What exactly happened to you, Charlie Sterling?" he asked, talking to himself aloud for the third time since climbing out of bed.

He stood up and retrieved his laptop from the bedroom. Sitting back down, he leaned towards the screen of his computer, his fingers dancing across the keyboard. He filtered through a series of Google search results and scribbled notes on the outside of a manila folder. An hour later he checked the time on the computer screen, laid back on the sofa, and closed his eyes.

CHAPTER 28

A WAITRESS IN a yukata led Shiro down the hall, stopped at the threshold to the private room, and slid open the door. Fukuzawa was seated alone on the left side of the table. Shiro bowed deeply before removing his shoes and stepping onto the elevated tatami floor. Another member of the extended Fukuzawa family was at the far end of the large table, pouring sake into their boss's cup. The waitress excused herself, slid the *shoji* door closed, and disappeared, her feet shuffling quietly on the dark wood floors.

"Have some sushi," Fukuzawa ordered.

"Thank you," Shiro replied, touching his hands together in front of him and bowing again.

"How is the new finger?"

"Fine. I've been wearing it for the last week. No issues." Shiro raised his hand and rotated his wrist so his boss could see both sides.

"Put in on the table," Fukuzawa said.

Shiro did as he was asked and Fukuzawa put on his glasses.

"It looks real," Fukuzawa said.

"It does."

"Good. Good."

Fukuzawa turned to the man at the end of the table and nodded his head in a quick motion. The man reached down and grabbed a small leather bag. He handed the satchel to Fukuzawa, who placed it on the corner of the table. Fukuzawa put his hand into the bag, removed a burgundy-covered passport, and handed it to Shiro with one hand.

Shiro received the passport with two hands and nodded his head.

"Take a look," Fukuzawa commanded.

Shiro opened the passport and stared at a photograph of himself above the name Shinji Yoshida.

"That's an official passport from the Japan Ministry of Foreign Affairs. It's getting more difficult to obtain official passports these days. Every time they introduce new anti-counterfeit measures, we have to bribe or compromise someone else at the ministry."

"Who is Shinji Yoshida?"

"A dead guy who never had a passport."

"Thank you," Shiro said.

"You'll be fingerprinted upon your arrival in the US. At immigration at the airport. Until then, Shinji Yoshida will not have fingerprints associated with his new passport."

"And my new finger?"

"It will scan."

"Are we sure?"

"Yes," Fukuzawa scoffed. "It will scan. Someone will meet you at the airport and handle the details of the rest of your trip. Money. Reservations. It will all be taken care of."

"How will I recognize this person?"

"You won't have to. They will recognize you."

"Very well."

"You will be traveling as part of a tour group."

"Where am I going?"

"As far as the authorities are concerned, you're going to Disneyland. Where every Japanese tourist wants to go."

*

Shiro pushed the pink bicycle with training wheels to the community storage under the stairs. He paused at the front door of his seventh-floor apartment and stared in the direction of Tokyo Bay. A stream of ships bisected the bay, the lights on their decks flickering against the black water. When the weather was clear, daytime views from the right side of the building offered glimpses of Mount Fuji. To his left, a dozen identical apartment buildings stood like dominoes, ready to fall. Between frequent earthquakes and the land reclamation effort that had given birth to the entire apartment development, the domino analogy took on a sense of real possibility most residents tried to ignore.

Shiro slid his key into the lock and turned the knob. He removed his shoes and socks and walked barefoot down the short hall in the direction of the kitchen. His wife stood from her seat at a small table.

"Welcome home. Are you hungry?"

"Always."

"You missed Yoko-chan. She's already asleep."

"I'll peek in on her in a minute."

"You didn't come home last night."

"Work."

"It's always work."

His wife sighed and turned towards the kitchen sink. She dropped an apron over her head and began preparing a plate of food for her husband.

"Is mackerel all right?"

"Fine."

"And miso soup?"

"Yes. Do we have any pickled vegetables?"

"We do."

"I'll take some."

His wife opened the rice cooker on the counter and began filling the bowl with warm rice.

"I'm going to check on our daughter."

"Don't wake her."

Shiro ignored his wife's request and walked back down the hall. He pushed open the door to his daughter's room, approached the small bed, and quietly sat down on the mattress. His daughter opened her eyes.

"Papa."

"Sssshhhh."

"I missed you."

"I missed you, too. How was school today?"

"You mean, how was school yesterday and today?"

"You're right. How was school yesterday and today?"

"Today was good. Yesterday wasn't good. Kyosuke made fun of me."

"And what did I tell you to do when someone makes fun of you?"

"You told me if I liked the person, I could ignore it."

"Do you like Kyosuke?"

"No. So I punched him in the nose. Just like you told me."

"And did he tease you today?"

"No. Today was a good day."

Shiro smiled and stroked his hand through his daughter's hair.

"Go to bed, Yoko-chan."

"Okay, Papa."

Shiro stood.

"Papa, are you going to be here in the morning when I wake up?"

"I am."

"Good. We can have breakfast together. I like it when we eat together."

"Me too. Maybe soon we can start having dinner together more often."

"You're funny, Papa. Everyone knows you work at night."

"Good night," Shiro said, exiting the room and shutting the door behind him. By the time he returned to the table in the kitchen, his dinner was waiting for him, replete with a glass of sake, his nightly ritual, the temperature of his drink adjusted for the heat of the summer or dead of winter.

*

Shiro's wife spoke as he sipped his sake. "Yoko-chan got into trouble at school. She punched another child."

"I just heard."

"She said you told her hitting was okay."

"Sometimes it is."

"Not in the first grade. Not in school. Please don't teach her these things."

"Sounds like she solved the problem."

"No, Shiro. She created a problem. And the other parents are looking at me as if I am a problem."

Shiro shoveled a bit of rice into his mouth with his chopsticks. "I will speak to her again."

"Please."

A long silence followed as Shiro's wife watched him consume his late dinner. He ate with verve, pushing food into his mouth at a rhythmic pace. He took another sip of sake and his wife spoke again.

"The car needs to be fixed. It's making a screeching sound."

"Probably the brakes. I can take a look tomorrow."

"I need the car tomorrow."

"All day?"

"No."

"I'll take a look when you're not driving it. If tomorrow doesn't work, you'll have to take it to the shop. I have to go out of town for a while."

"Where are you going?"

Shiro answered without looking up. "Overseas."

"Bullshit," she replied.

"I have to go to the USA."

"For what?"

"I can't say."

"For how long?"

"I don't know."

"Are you going someplace interesting?"

"I'm going to Mississippi. I'm not sure what's there."

"Bring back a souvenir. Whatever is popular."

"We'll see."

Shiro stared pensively out the window at the back of the apartment. "I don't know if this is a good time to bring this up, but there's a chance I may be able to start a new career soon."

"You mean something other than gambling? Something with daytime hours?"

"There's a chance. That's all I can say. A chance to leave this life behind. A chance to be a real husband and father."

"Don't make promises you can't keep. I don't want to hear them."

"It's not a promise. It's a possibility."

"And how does that work? Fukuzawa is not going to let you just walk away without something in return."

"You're right. He's not going to let me walk away without doing something for him first."

"I don't like the sound of it."

"That's why I didn't want to tell you."

"You don't understand."

"What don't I understand?"

"Even if you do what he's asking you to do, he still may not let you go."

CHAPTER 29

EDWARD WALKED UP to the square white house with the sweeping front porch and knocked on the door. A young man in jeans and a faded T-shirt was buzzing the lawn next door, perched on a John Deere riding mower. Edward knocked a second time and the neighbor cut the engine, silence falling on the residential street.

"No one's home," the young man said.

"I'm looking for Rose Sterling."

"Mrs. Sterling hasn't lived in that house for years."

"I Googled her. It said this was her address."

"Oh, she still owns it. But she rents it out most of the time. Right now, it's empty. The last tenants moved out a month ago. I think she's going to have the place painted before the next ones move in."

"You seem to be in the know."

"She pays me to cut the yard, but I'm just a neighbor."

"When exactly did she move out?"

"A few years after her husband died."

"Did you know him?"

"I lived next door to him when I was little."

"What was he like?"

"Mr. Sterling?"

"Yes."

The young man on the riding mower scowled. "Who wants to know?"

"My name is Edward Winston. I wanted to talk to Rose about her husband and Pervis Wade."

"Why would you want to go stirring that pot?"

"I wouldn't say I'm stirring anything."

"You aren't from around here, are you?"

"No. Does that matter?"

"Sometimes. It seems like people from other places don't understand that some stories just end the way they end. No one can rewrite history."

Edward considered the John Deere rider's pontification. "I'm not trying to rewrite history."

"You're trying to do something. There's no other reason to be coming 'round asking about Charlie Sterling."

"It's important," Edward said.

The young man leaned back in the seat of the mower, the hot sun searing the tension in the air.

"If you want to find Mrs. Sterling, she moved over to Sixth Street. Across from the Baptist Church. She wanted to get closer to Jesus. She was never quite the same after she lost her husband."

"What about her husband? You never answered what you thought of him."

"Charlie Sterling was everyone's friend."

"Apparently, not everyone's," Edward replied, stepping off the porch.

*

Edward knocked on his second door of the hour, this time a small brick shotgun house with a clothesline in the side yard. The porch on the front of the house faced north, providing an element of cool shade, even on a hot Mississippi afternoon. From the metal chairs on the porch, the sign for Verona Baptist Church was squarely in view, just across the street. The pastor's message of the week—posted on the signboard—was short and simple: "Sinners Wanted."

Rose Sterling answered her interior wooden door but left the screen door closed and locked.

Edward spoke through the screen as if in a confessional.

"Good afternoon, Mrs. Sterling. My name is Edward Winston. You may have heard my name on the news recently. I was hoping to have a few words with you."

"What did you want to have a few words about?"

"It's a little awkward to come right out and say."

"Give it a try."

Edward took a deep breath. "I believe my wife was murdered by the same man who murdered your husband."

Rose Sterling reached for the doorknob but didn't turn it.

"It's been a long time since anyone wanted to talk about Charlie's murder."

Edward stood motionless as Rose seemed to consider the presence of the man on her front porch. She slowly took her hand off the doorknob and nodded in the direction of the porch chairs. "Take a seat. I'll bring out some tea."

"Thank you."

Edward gleamed with sweat by the time a full pitcher of tea found a spot on the wrought iron table. Without the screen door between them, Rose Sterling looked much younger than Edward initially thought. He guessed she was in her early fifties, though her radiant skin made pinpointing her age difficult. She smiled through red lipstick and poured two glasses of tea before sitting down on the other side of the table.

"I'm sorry about your wife," she said.

"Thank you," Edward replied, unsure whether Rose had recognized him, or if she were offering condolences based upon what he had said.

"I know how hard it can be to lose someone close," she added.

"I'm sure you do."

"You know, it's not something you ever completely get over."

"I imagine that's true. I feel like I've been walking around in a haze."

"Honey, I walked around in a haze for years. Even now, all these years later, I still find myself lost in the world from time to time. Not sure exactly what triggers it. It can hit me taking a walk or while I'm watching TV. Sometimes when I'm doing something as simple as cutting carrots."

"Carrots?"

"I know that probably sounds crazy. My husband loved carrots. Probably has something to do with that."

"It doesn't sound crazy at all. The yogurt section of the supermarket froze me in my tracks yesterday. I keep telling myself I'm just suffering from a lack of sleep."

"When I hit a sleeping rut, red wine tucks me into bed and Ambien makes sure I stay there."

"I've tried Ambien and it doesn't really help."

"Don't forget the wine."

Rose and Edward took simultaneous sips of tea from their respective glasses. Edward noticed his host glancing at his scarred hand and then looking away.

"I wanted to talk to you about your husband and Pervis Wade," Edward said.

"You said you think Pervis Wade killed your wife?"

"I did. I do."

"I followed your wife's disappearance on the news. I never heard anything about Pervis Wade being a suspect. The last I heard a neighbor was responsible."

"So you're familiar with what happened to my wife?"

"This *is* Tupelo. News travels fast and sticks around for a while. Secrets are hard to keep."

"Well, regardless of what you heard, my neighbor had nothing to do with my wife's murder. Pervis Wade did."

"And he's not going to be charged?"

"Not in this lifetime."

"That's too bad," Rose replied. "Because he's a murdering son of a bitch."

"I agree. Maybe he'll get what's coming to him someday."

"I'm counting on it."

"Did you know him?"

"Never laid eyes on him before he killed my husband."

"And do you believe the story of how your husband died?"

"I believe he was beaten to death. I don't think there's much debate about that."

"What about the fight over a parking space? The police report and all the newspapers say your husband was killed over a parking space at the Down Home Cooking restaurant."

"That's what they say. They say my husband pulled out a tire iron and then ended up being beaten to death. But everyone knows that's horseshit. Excuse my language."

"Why?"

"Because Down Home Cooking has plenty of parking and my husband was killed on a weeknight, near closing time. Around back, not far from the Dumpsters. No one in their right mind has ever fought for a parking spot near a Dumpster."

Edward found it difficult to argue with Rose's rationale. "Do you think it was random?"

"No. I don't believe for a second my husband was randomly killed by the son of a business client."

Edward's eyebrows rose involuntarily. "Pervis Wade's father was one of your husband's clients?"

"You sound surprised. My husband had a lot of clients. Thousands. He was the president of Sterling Insurance for over twenty years. Built the company from nothing."

"Sounds like he was successful."

"He did well. He knew most of the town."

"You said you never met Pervis Wade. Did you ever meet his father?"

"Troy Wade? Once or twice. Most everyone in town knew him, too. Most knew he ran Palmetto Windows."

"What did people think of him?"

"A regular guy, I guess. He was also pretty successful. I know his wife died a long time ago. At any rate, after my husband was killed, I heard plenty about Pervis Wade and his father. Nothing makes a Southern town like humidity, cheating husbands, sweet tea, and rumors."

"What were the rumors?"

"Rumor was that Pervis was smart. He just never applied himself to anything. Some people say his father spoiled him on account of him not having a mother around. All I know for sure is that he killed my husband, was charged with manslaughter, and was later released for lack of evidence."

"I see," Edward said.

Rose smiled with a heavy dose of Southern charm twinkling in her eyes. "When someone answers 'I see,' I always figure they got something on their mind they don't want to share."

Edward smiled back. "Let me ask a question that may seem a bit unrelated."

"Go ahead."

"How was your husband with computers?"

"Why's that important?"

"It might not be. I don't know."

"My husband was an insurance salesman. When he started out in the business, no one was using computers. Over time that changed, of course. When his clients and other insurance companies started using computers, my husband jumped on the bandwagon like everyone else."

"The reason I ask is the police report indicates a laptop was found in your husband's car the night he was killed. That means your husband wasn't killed for his computer."

"I don't think anyone thought it was a robbery. Nothing was reported missing from his car. It wasn't common knowledge, but my husband also had a fair amount of money on him, in addition to the computer."

"How much money?"

"He had withdrawn ten thousand dollars from the bank a couple of days before he was murdered."

"And it wasn't taken?"

"No. It was still in the car. In the glove box."

"Did he always carry around so much money?"

"Occasionally he had cash on him, but nothing near that amount." Rose picked up her glass of tea but didn't drink. "What are you digging for, Mr. Winston?"

"I'm just wondering why your husband was killed. If you're sure he wasn't killed over a parking space, and nothing seems to have been stolen, including cash, why was he killed?"

"I don't think anyone really knows. A couple of theories floated around for a while."

"Like?"

"For starters, the police wondered if my husband was killed because of a lost watch."

"A lost watch? I don't follow."

Rose's gaze faded to the church across the street and she spoke without any expression, her eyes fixed. "You know, for two decades my husband sold all kinds of insurance, in every city and town in this state. Yes, indeed. All kinds of insurance. Life. Annuities. Disability. Auto. Home. Boat. A one stop shop for all of your insurance needs."

Rose paused as if reminiscing. "Listen to me, I sound like a TV commercial."

"And how does the lost watch fit in?"

Rose ignored the question and continued to speak as if reciting from some unseen script. "The insurance business was good to my husband. And it was good to me. My husband had a lot of happy clients. Business was good. Business was so good, somewhere along the line my husband decided he was going to start hosting insurance seminars, on top of his regular business endeavors. Weekend seminars to show his appreciation to his clients. Of course, it was also an opportunity to sell more insurance."

"Of course."

"For many years my husband held these insurance seminars out at the Cedar Creek Conference Center."

"I've never heard of it."

"Well, it's nice. In the northeast corner of the county. There isn't a creek in sight—despite the name—but it's nice. They have golf. Fishing. Drinking was its own activity, too. On the big weekends, as we called them, Charlie would make a few presentations, open the bar, and let the boys loose. And it got loose, too, let me tell you. Eventually it got out of hand. The year Charlie was killed, Cedar Creek told him he needed to find a new venue to host seminars."

"Did you ever go to one of these seminars with your husband?"

"I went once. I stayed until a bunch of the guys brought out their guns for some target practice in the field behind the lodge. Men taking turns throwing beer cans into the air with shotguns blasting."

"Sounds dangerous."

"Oh, it was. The seminars may have been good business, but they also seemed like an excuse to drink beer and talk shit. Excuse my language, again. I think when you're an insurance salesman, a lot of business is drinking and running off at the mouth. Don't get me wrong, my husband sold honest products, but drinking and talking nonsense seemed to help clients pull out their checkbooks."

"I can see that," Edward said. He let the conversation settle into a calm pace and then gently nudged Rose back to his original question.

"And why do you think your husband may have been killed over a lost watch?"

"It was the only possible explanation I ever heard. It sure made more sense than dying for a parking spot."

Edward changed the angle of his inquiry. "What can you tell me about your husband's watch?"

"It wasn't my husband's watch. It was Troy Wade's watch."

"Your husband was killed because Troy Wade lost his watch?"

"That's the theory the police shared with me. As the story went, Troy Wade attended the last insurance seminar my husband held at Cedar Creek."

"Before your husband was asked to find another venue?"

"That's right."

"Do you know if Troy Wade had ever come to one of your husband's seminars before?"

"I'm sure he had. But he'd never lost a really expensive Rolex before, which apparently is what happened the night in question. According to my husband, Troy Wade lost his watch and a big stink followed. To hear my husband talk about it, people were accused of being thieves. Naturally some people were insulted by the accusation. A lot of things were said in the heat of the moment and the ugly side of a few drunken men bubbled to the surface. Punches were thrown."

"Did your husband ever indicate he knew anything about the watch or know who took it?"

"No. But my husband did remember that Mr. Wade owned a Rolex. At least from a distance it looked like a real Rolex."

Edward took a moment to let the dust settle, his mind mulling over the possibilities of Rose Sterling's watch theory. "So at your husband's last seminar, Troy Wade lost an expensive watch and caused a hubbub. Any idea if Troy Wade had insurance on the watch?"

"He didn't. A fact that was not lost on the participants of the seminar. My husband sold thirty personal item policies in the week after the seminar. Clients suddenly felt a need to insure their guns, their wedding rings, all their wives' jewelry. There were some rumblings that the whole thing was a setup by my husband as a way to drum up business. That was all hogwash."

"Was the watch ever found?"

"Not that I know of. It was a hot topic of conversation for a couple of weeks."

"And then?"

"And then Troy Wade died of a heart attack. Dead men don't care about lost watches."

"But maybe their sons do. Did you ever think that your husband was carrying a large amount of cash to pay Pervis Wade for his father's lost watch?"

"The thought occurred to me. Pervis Wade could have been angry that he lost out on the watch and thought it was somehow my husband's fault. But Troy Wade had a life insurance policy, so Pervis received money from that. He wasn't hurting for money."

"People always want more."

"Yes, they do. And less than a month after Troy Wade passed away, Pervis Wade killed my husband in a parking lot."

Edward shook his head.

"And the police investigated this lost watch theory?"

"Of course they did. It was their theory."

"Do you remember which police officers were involved?" Edward asked, knowing the answer.

"Sheriff Blazer was one of them. But he wasn't a sheriff just yet. He was running for the position around that time. He made sure he got his face on television. Part of me got the feeling that my husband's death was another photo opportunity for him."

"Did you ever get the feeling Sheriff Blazer wasn't doing his job? Or not doing his job to the best of his ability?"

Rose put her tea back on the table and looked directly into Edward's eyes. "Be careful where you go with that question, Mr. Winston. A lot of people in this town love Sheriff Blazer. There's a reason he's been reelected several times."

"Are you one of those people who love the sheriff?"

"I'm not. But that doesn't mean I shouldn't warn you to be careful."

"Then thank you for the warning."

Edward took a deep breath and noticed the cross on the top of the church was casting a shadow across the parking lot.

"I have a photograph of Sheriff Blazer and a detective named Rafferty winning a fishing competition many years ago. One of the sponsors for the fishing competition was Sterling Insurance. Were you aware of this?"

"I wasn't. I didn't get involved with my husband's business. He did a fair bit of advertising. He sponsored little league baseball teams every year. He supported football, too. I'm not surprised he sponsored a fishing tournament."

"Would it surprise you if some of the law enforcement officers who investigated your husband's death may have also been your husband's clients?"

"It wouldn't surprise me one bit. Like I said, my husband had thousands of clients. Thousands."

Edward wasn't sure if there was any more meat on that particular bone, so he asked a different question. "When the police were investigating your husband's death, did they ever search your husband's belongings? Come to your house?"

"They did."

"Did they have a search warrant?"

"No. And I wouldn't have asked them for one."

"Did they take anything with them?"

"They took a lot of stuff. But they returned it all a few days later."

"Were they looking for the watch?"

"I assumed they were."

"Did you ever check to see if everything was brought back to you?"

"No, not really. Should I have paid more attention to what was taken?"

"I don't think it matters at this point."

"Good. Because between you and me, I don't want to relive any of it.

Nothing is going to bring my husband back and nothing's going to bring Pervis Wade to trial."

Edward finished his tea and admired the stained glass windows on the church reflecting the afternoon sun.

"I like the view you have here from the front porch, Mrs. Sterling."

"I do, too. It's hard to forget God is watching over you when you live right across the street from one of his houses."

Edward stood and smiled. "Well, Mrs. Sterling, thank you for your time, for the conversation, and for the tea."

"You're welcome, Mr. Winston. I hope you learn to take life by the horns again. You're still young enough to pull it off."

"Would you mind if I came back for more tea some time?"

"Only if you bring good news with you and leave your questions at home."

CHAPTER 30

SHIRO OSE STOOD in an immigration line for the first time in his life, shoulder to shoulder and back to front with a full flight of Japanese tourists. Touching down at LAX, with a tour guide leading the way, the group boasted a ten-day itinerary, including sightseeing through Beverly Hills, three days at Disneyland, and the obligatory side trip to Vegas.

The tour guide with the small purple flag motioned for Shiro to step forward, gesturing towards an open immigration counter window. Shiro bowed slightly, shuffled ahead, and placed his passport on the counter. The immigration officer, a man with white hair and a matching moustache, picked up Shiro's passport and then stared him in the eyes.

"You speak English?"

"A little"

"What brings you to the US?" the uniformed man asked.

"Sightseeing. I am part of the tour group," Shiro said, motioning towards the people behind him sporting a myriad of matching caps, lapel pins, and shirts.

The immigration officer nodded. "How long are you staying?"

"Ten days."

"Put your hands on the scanner. Fingers first, then thumbs."

Shiro Ose did as he was told while the immigration officer stamped his passport.

"Welcome to the US," he said. "Enjoy your stay."

*

The group of tourists stood in a circle just beyond customs, waiting for the tour guide to appear through the automatic doors. Shiro carried his leather bag on his shoulder, his gaze scanning the variety of people as they passed.

The tour guide appeared and again raised his small purple flag. He needlessly announced the name of his group and the circle of Japanese tourists under his guidance tightened around him.

"Our bus will be waiting at exit number four. Everyone please make their way to exit number four."

The group began herding themselves in the prescribed direction and Shiro joined the procession, unsure of his next move. The tour guide fell to the back of the group, turned, and grabbed Shiro by the arm.

"The man you need to see is over there," the tour guide said, motioning with his head at a Japanese man in a business suit standing near the hotel transportation counter.

The man in the suit glanced down at a piece of paper in his hand, and then his eyes rose to meet Shiro's. He seemingly confirmed Shiro's face a second time against the paper in his hand, and then slipped the copy of the photograph into his suit pocket.

Shiro peeled away from his tour group and approached the man.

"Ose?" the man asked.

"Yes."

"Welcome to California" the man said in Japanese.

"Thank you."

"May I take your bag?"

Shiro half-bowed, grabbed the strap on his bag, and handed it to the man in the suit.

"This way," the man replied without offering his name.

Outside, Shiro stopped on the sidewalk outside the terminal as the man holding his bag made a phone call. A minute later a black executive sedan pulled to the curb and the trunk popped open.

The man motioned for Shiro to get into the back seat and then deposited the leather bag in the trunk, shutting the lid with a resounding thud.

The man slipped into the front passenger seat, and the driver pulled the black sedan into the choking mix of cars, taxis, and rental car shuttle buses.

"How was your flight?" the man in the passenger seat asked, looking over his shoulder.

"Fine," Shiro responded. "Long," he added.

"Any trouble at immigration?"

"None."

"The tour groups usually don't have trouble, but LA can be a little tricky for yakuza. The airport has a lot of experience spotting Japanese mafia. They're almost as good as Honolulu airport, but not quite."

Shiro noticed the man's Japanese had a hint of a dialect he couldn't place.

"I see," Shiro replied.

"Do you have tattoos?"

"Both arms and shoulders."

"Keep your shirt on. Too bad it's summer and you're heading to Mississippi. It's going to be hot."

"I brought long-sleeve linen shirts. I'll manage."

"They said you speak English."

"A little. I've had a few English-speaking girlfriends."

"That's one way to learn."

The man reached down onto the car floor near his feet then passed a large manila envelope to Shiro.

Shiro undid the metal clasp on the envelope and peeked in. A bulging, smaller envelope caught Shiro's attention and he plucked it from the larger envelope.

"Cash?" Shiro said, his fingers wrapping around a stack of money several inches thick. "How much?"

"The dollar equivalent of a million yen. Completely clean, untraceable money. Use it anyway you like."

Shiro reached in the larger envelope again and removed a passport.

"Your new name for the next ten days is Taro Ishida."

"I just arrived on a new passport that was also in someone else's name."

"And now you have another name. That's a valid passport with a valid visa. It's the real name and photo of a Japanese citizen who legally entered the United States. The visa won't expire until you are long gone. The resemblance is close enough to fool most people you will encounter."

"Does Taro Ishida know that I have his passport?"

"Does that matter?"

"I'm just curious. A stolen passport could lead to trouble."

"It's not stolen. It's being rented."

"Rented?"

"Let's just say that Taro was recruited because he looked like you. He is now being paid to stay on vacation. All expenses paid. For the next ten days, he has agreed to stay put and enjoy the high-life, free of charge. If, for some reason, his passport doesn't make it back to him, he'll contact the local police and report that it was stolen. The Japanese Consulate will issue him another passport for his return home."

"And he agreed to this?"

"He was persuaded. And he was paid. Someone has spent a lot of money financing your trip here to the US."

Shiro reached back into the envelope and removed a small booklet. Taro Ishida's information was handwritten on one side of the page. A copy of Taro Ishida's passport photo had been stapled to the other page.

"An international driving permit?"

"Yes. It allows you to drive in the US. It's not an official document. You will only need it if you get stopped by the police while driving. Otherwise it's worthless."

"I see."

"You may need to show the driving permit when you pick up your rental car at the Memphis airport. The rental car is also under the name Taro Ishida. There are two credit cards at the bottom of the envelope with the same name. Both cards are activated and valid."

"Memphis?"

"Yes. There are no direct flights from LA to Tupelo. You have to drive from Memphis. Two hours tops. Easy enough."

Shiro was unmoved by the assurance of an easy trip. He reached into the envelope and collected the credit cards.

"Between the cards and the cash, you should have more money than you could possibly need," the man said.

Shiro grunted, again unimpressed by what he considered a baseless claim.

"You have a room at the Gum Tree Inn in Tupelo. The place has a kitchen. You can get food and make it. It's a small motel. They take cash or credit, but will probably require a credit card to check in."

Shiro peeled his eyes away from the envelope and looked out the window. He realized the car he was riding in had completed a loop and was again passing in front of the international terminal.

"Now, put your other passport and documents in the envelope and hand it to me," the man said.

"Why?"

"Because for the next ten days you are Taro Ishida. And Taro Ishida has no reason to be carrying anyone else's documents."

Shiro Ose put Shinji Yoshida's passport into the envelope and cleaned out his wallet, removing everything except a photo of his wife and daughter. He inserted several hundred-dollar bills and the two credit cards into his billfold.

"Do you have a phone on you?"

"I left it in Japan."

The man produced a phone and charging cord from the console between the front seats and handed them to Shiro. "The phone is prepaid. It should allow you to get on the Internet if you need a map or something."

Shiro looked at the screen and then at the man in the passenger seat. "Do you have a number I'm supposed to call when this is all done?"

"No. No number."

"How am I supposed to reach you?"

"You finish your business and come back to Los Angeles. Find your way to Benkei in Little Tokyo. It's a small izakaya restaurant off the pedestrian mall. Make a lunch reservation for one at the counter under your real name."

"And then?"

"And then you will be hooked up with your tour guide for your return trip home."

The driver of the black sedan pulled over at the curb in front of the domestic terminal and the man in the front seat got out and retrieved the bag from the trunk. He pulled the back door open and Shiro got out.

"Thanks for the tour of the airport," Shiro replied.

The man handed Shiro his bag and then pulled a boarding pass from his jacket.

"Your flight to Memphis leaves in two hours. Have a safe trip. Good luck."

*

Seven hours later, Shiro turned off Main Street in Tupelo and followed the paved but narrow road as it ran along a strip of warehouses. He squinted at the small sign near a driveway to the left and a two-story building came into view through the canopy of southern live oaks and gum trees. Shiro pulled into the parking lot, his eyes darting around his new home. The door to each room of the inn looked out over the large, shaded gravel parking lot. A shared balcony ran along the length of the second floor.

Shiro got out of the car and stretched. He entered the office at the end of the first floor, just under a neon sign indicating No Vacancy. An old woman wearing pajamas eyed Shiro as the bell hanging on the back of the door announced his arrival.

"Good evening. How can I help you?" the woman asked. Deep wrinkles from decades of smoking added years to the woman's appearance.

"I have a reservation," Shiro said.

"You must be Mr. Taro."

"Ishida. Taro is my first name."

"Are you Japanese?"

"Yes."

"You in town for work or for the festival?"

"The festival."

"I figured. You know we had nearly fifty thousand people last year for the Elvis Festival. People from all over the world. Most stayed somewhere a little nicer. I think people like a place with a pool. I told my husband we should put one in, but he won't listen."

Shiro was still digesting the number of festival attendees from last year by the time the manager had finished her pool discussion. He smiled and grunted.

The woman rested her cigarette on the edge of the ashtray. "I need a credit card for a security deposit. I also need to see an ID."

Shiro reached into his pocket and handed her the first card he felt. Then he slipped her the passport from his other pocket. A twinge of nerves ran through him as the woman took the credit card and passport and turned away. A minute later she handed both items back to Shiro.

"And the only thing left is a signature," the woman added.

Shiro scribbled on the line and the woman reached into a cubbyhole behind the counter. She placed a room key on the counter, the key ring attached to a large block of wood engraved with 203.

"You're in 203. Second floor. Second from the end."

"Is there a place to eat around here? Or a supermarket?"

"We're only a few blocks from Main Street. Five minutes or so on foot. I mean, I know it doesn't feel like it back here in the trees. Anyhow, there's a supermarket at each end of Main Street. A few places to eat in between. Walmart and the super stores are out on the highways. It's going to be dark soon, but you can walk to the local grocery stores. Not a lot of violent crime in Tupelo."

There may be before I leave, Shiro thought. "Thanks."

CHAPTER 31

SHIRO WOKE BEFORE dawn, ate a bowl of instant ramen, and went back to bed hoping to shake his first experience with jet lag. He woke for a second time in the afternoon, ate a premade sandwich wrapped in cellophane, and turned on the TV.

He surfed through the cable lineup, settled on ESPN, and eventually dozed off just long enough for the sun to set. He woke again as daylight disappeared through the limbs of the large tree in front of the inn. Feeling better, he opened the interior door to his room and looked through the screen of the old wooden storm door. Fireflies flickered in the darkness of the parking lot, dancing near the trees that ringed the edge of the property.

Enticed by the view, Shiro dragged a folding lawn chair from the corner of his room and carried it outside to the balcony. He went back inside and walked through the glamour of a Gum Tree Inn suite on his way to the small refrigerator. A queen mattress with a jungle motif bedcover sat on the right. A small kitchenette with a single burner was to the rear. A lumpy sofa and old table was just to the left, next to the bathroom. Large square tiles, mostly white, some cracked, covered the floor.

Shiro grabbed his cigarettes off the small kitchenette counter and swiped the ashtray from his bedside table. He grabbed a cold canned beer from the mini-fridge and headed towards the door. Back outside, he set his loot on the floor of the balcony and tugged on the aluminum frame of the lawn chair until it opened. He lit a cigarette and placed it in the ashtray under his chair, smoke wafting upward in the desired effect.

Sitting down, he put his legs against the rails of the balcony, lit a second cigarette, and took a long, slow drag. He closed his eyes and listened to the sounds of summer: a cacophony of crickets, a TV playing through an open window, the sound of his neighbor's squeaky box spring getting a workout. As darkness gained momentum, he turned his attention towards the mosquitos and moths dive-bombing the light on the wall near the stairs.

Halfway through his beer, the screen door to the room on his right opened, its rusty hinges protesting. A handsome man in cowboy boots and a black baseball cap exited the room and was startled by Shiro's presence on the balcony. Shiro nodded and took a drink of his beer, followed by another drag off his cigarette. The startled man pulled his cap down to his eyebrows and ambled down the stairs. Shiro watched as the man crossed the parking lot, walked off the property, and climbed into a tow truck parked on the street fifty yards from the motel.

Shiro was finishing his second beer when his neighbor's door opened again and a curvy blonde stepped onto the balcony.

"Hey, neighbor," the woman said.

Shiro nodded, his eyes landing on the woman's black shorts and snug-fitting pink tank top. Her painted toenails framed the top of her matching flip-flops.

"Hello," Shiro replied.

"My name's Mindy."

"My name's Shiro," he said before catching himself. "Everyone calls me Taro."

"Nice to meet you Taro. You mind some company?"

Shiro shrugged.

Without waiting for an answer, Mindy went back into her room and returned with a folding lawn chair identical to the one Shiro was sitting in. The woman disappeared for a second time and then reappeared, blasting herself with a cloud of mosquito spray from a green can.

"You want some?" she asked, looking as if she had recently applied lipstick in addition to bug repellent.

"I'm okay," Shiro replied, gesturing towards the burning cigarette in the ashtray under his chair. "That keeps most of the bugs away."

"So does this," Mindy retorted, holding up the can. "And it doesn't waste a perfectly good cigarette."

Shiro borrowed the can, sprayed his exposed legs, and handed it back.

"You want a beer?" Shiro asked, getting lost in Mindy's hypnotic blue eyes for a brief second. He inhaled the sweet smell of her perfume mixing with the pungent scent of bug spray.

"If you have an extra. I don't want to drink your last beer."

Shiro went inside and returned with another cold can.

"How long have you been here?" Mindy asked. "I heard the shower running in your room, and then the TV, but I haven't seen you around."

"I came last night."

"Where are you from?"

"Japan."

"Are you here for the festival?"

"I am."

"The festival is a busy time for the city. Good for business."

Shiro took a sip of his beer.

"It's awfully hot out here for a long-sleeve shirt," Mindy said, commenting on Shiro's choice of an outfit.

"Helps with the bugs," Shiro said. "How long have you been here?" he asked.

"Four months."

"That's a long time."

"It may not look like much, but this place is a lot better than where I lived before. The owners take care of things around here when they break. That's pretty much all you can ask for."

"I guess so."

"You'll be thankful they fix things when the AC goes out. And it probably will."

"I'll manage."

"Is it hot in Japan?"

"Summer in Tokyo is hot and humid."

"Then you should be right at home here in Tupelo."

Shiro shrugged again.

"Do you know anyone in town?"

"No. I'm just here for the festival."

"Then I'll be your first friend," Mindy replied, holding the beer can up and waiting for Shiro to touch her can with his.

"Cheers," Mindy added, forcing Shiro to reply.

Shiro took a sip. "I think I scared your boyfriend."

"My boyfriend?"

"The guy in the boots with the black cap. He drives a wrecker."

"You mean a tow truck?"

"If that's what you call it."

"He wasn't my boyfriend."

"Oh," Shiro replied. "Sorry."

"Don't be sorry. I like the guy, he's just not my boyfriend."

"I shouldn't have said anything."

"Let's both forget it."

Shiro took another look at his neighbor, eyes running over her hair, breasts, and legs. "How old are you?"

"I don't know how it works in Japan, but here in the US of A, you can't just ask a woman how old she is. It's rude."

"It's rude in Japan, too."

"There you go," Mindy replied, sulking. "How old are you?" she asked.

"Almost forty."

"Thirty-five," Mindy admitted. She raised her beer can again and offered a toast. "Here's to forty and thirty-five."

Shiro raised his can again and took a long drink.

"What do you do in Japan?"

"I'm a negotiator."

"A negotiator? That sounds interesting. What do you negotiate?"

"I negotiate agreements between people who can't agree."

Mindy laughed and ran strands of hair behind her ear.

Shiro and Mindy sat in silence for a moment, listening to the sounds of summer.

"Are you done working for the night?" Shiro asked.

Mindy seemed insulted. "I thought Japanese people were supposed to be polite. Indirect."

"Not everyone."

"Apparently."

"Am I wrong?" Shiro asked.

"Does it matter?"

"Not to me. I don't care what you do," Shiro said.

"Good."

"I'm going to get another beer. Do you want one more?"

"Sure. One for the road."

Shiro went inside, used the bathroom, and returned with two more beers.

Mindy restarted the conversation. "If you don't care what I do, then I'll just come out and tell you that you're right. The guy who left here in the tow truck was a customer. A customer I've had for a very long time. One of my favorites, really."

"If he was a customer, that explains why he tried to hide his face when he was leaving. A boyfriend would be proud to be with someone who looks like you."

Mindy smiled and Shiro noticed her dimples. Between her eyes, dimples, and curves, he was sure his neighbor had no trouble attracting clients.

Mindy reached out and tapped Shiro on the leg. "I'm glad you don't care."

"I know a few hookers."

"Oh, really?"

Shiro nodded.

"Does Japan have a lot of working girls?"

"Working girls?" he asked.

"Hookers."

"Japan has hookers. Mostly in the big cities."

"I'm curious. How much do they charge?" Mindy asked.

"Thirty thousand yen an hour."

"How much is that?"

Shiro stared upward as if performing a calculation in his head. "Three hundred and twenty dollars."

"Maybe I should move to Japan."

"You would make more than that."

"Really? Why?"

"Because you're blonde."

"I'll keep that in mind. Maybe I need to take a vacation to check it out."

"Let me know if you do. We can work something out. I can introduce you to people."

"I will."

Shiro finished the beer in his hand. "I have to go to work."

"I thought you were in town for the festival?"

"I am," Shiro replied, regretting he had mentioned working.

Mindy watched as Shiro cleaned up the balcony in front of his room. As he fought with the folding lawn chair, the phone in Mindy's lap buzzed. She looked down, picked up the phone, and read the screen.

"It looks like you're not the only one who has to work tonight," she said.

"You've already been working."

Mindy stood and started to text a reply on her phone. "It was nice to meet you," she said. "Stop by if you want to talk. Or do more than talk."

CHAPTER 32

EDWARD SAT IN a chair across from the records alcove at the Lee County Justice Center, waiting for it to open. At precisely nine, the small metal shutter rolled quietly upward and the same young woman with the same diamond stud in her nose smiled.

"I recognize you," the woman said.

"I've been getting that a lot lately."

"I thought I recognized you from the news the first time you were in here, but I wasn't sure. I'm real sorry to hear about your wife."

"Thanks."

"What can I help you with?"

"I'm looking to get my hands on some more records."

"You've come to the right spot," the woman replied, pointing upward at the sign hanging from the ceiling.

"I'm looking for information on the search warrants issued in the investigation of the death of Charlie Sterling. He was killed a decade ago."

"That sounds like it could be related to the information you requested before."

"That's a pretty good memory."

"We don't get a lot of requests from the public for arrest records. A lot of attorneys and law enforcement officials, but not many walk-ups. Otherwise I may not have remembered you."

"That's better than saying you remembered me because I was labeled a person of interest in my wife's disappearance."

"I did see that on the news. I also saw the police now say your neighbor was involved."

Edward nodded and made the conscious decision to end the conversation with silence.

"Let me see what I can find," the office clerk said.

Edward sat in the chair across from the counter, contemplating Pervis Wade and reflecting on his visit to Fukuzawa. He wondered if his request had been ignored, or if the execution of his request had run into unseen problems. In all likelihood, if there were trouble, he would never know. He was left sitting squarely between impatience and doubt with no way out. But what he didn't feel was remorse. And part of him wanted to feel it. Regret. Guilt. Something. But for a man who had requested the death of another, Edward surprisingly felt nothing.

The clerk returned to the window with several folders. "I brought everything I could find on the Charlie Sterling case," she said, snapping Edward from his trance.

"What do we have?"

"Court records. All the police interviews. All the search warrants served in the case."

"How many search warrants were served?"

"Let's see… We have a search warrant for Pervis Wade's residence. We have a search warrant for a piece of property north of the city that was owned by the Wade family. We have another search warrant for the Cedar Creek Conference Center."

"Hard to believe all of these are a result of a fight over a parking spot at a restaurant."

The woman furled her brows as if trying to understand the gravity of the statement.

Edward flipped through the first search warrant. "I'll take everything you have."

The woman tallied the total, her fingers running through corners of the folders. "Twenty-eight even."

Edward paid in cash and thanked the clerk.

"I have another question," he said, one step away from the counter.

"Shoot."

"Had you ever heard the name Pervis Wade before I came to this window the first time?"

"No. But, I'll admit that after you left, I Googled him. Then I asked my mom if she had ever heard of him."

"What did she say?"

"She knew about the Charlie Sterling case. Apparently everyone did. I was only twelve at the time. I wasn't paying attention to the news. I was probably busy watching *Hanna Montana*."

"Did your mom mention anything about a missing Rolex watch?" Edward asked.

"Huh?" the woman replied.

"Never mind."

CHAPTER 33

BETWEEN A COMMERCIAL for a nonstick frying pan and a robotic vacuum cleaner, the bedsprings stopped their rhythmic squeaking. In near darkness, Shiro practiced his English by repeating phrases on a rerun of *Friends*.

A slamming door shook the wall behind the TV and distracted Shiro from his impromptu studies. He listened as the bathroom pipes in the wall came to life, rattling and humming. English practice thwarted, Shiro turned the TV off with the remote and rolled over. He shut his eyes and a second thunderous crash from the room next door knocked a picture off his wall.

Shiro cursed in Japanese and put his feet on the floor, still sitting on the bed. The sound of breaking glass cut through the night, followed by a woman's scream. Shiro stood and stepped towards the wall as a deep voice bellowed a string of profanities.

Shiro heard Mindy respond, her words too muffled by emotion to understand. Shiro pressed closer to the wall. Another crash was followed by heavy footsteps across the floor. Shiro moved towards the front window of his room and listened as Mindy's screen door opened and slammed closed.

Standing in silence, Shiro peeked out the front curtains and saw a silhouette lighting a cigarette on the balcony. Blood pumping, he thought he heard the sound of Mindy crying through the hotel wall. Decision made, he rolled his neck in all directions, grabbed his pack of cigarettes from the dresser, and slipped his lighter into his pocket. A second later, he stepped onto the balcony wearing flip-flops, a T-shirt, and a pair of baggy shorts.

Shiro placed a cigarette between his lips. A bald man with broad shoulders was leaning against the rail of the balcony, taking in the scenery of the gravel parking lot below. A leather belt with a large buckle was restraining a pronounced beer gut. A single stud was in his left earlobe. A cloud of bugs danced in the light bulb near the motel staircase. The man turned and grunted. Shiro could feel the man's eyes on the tattoos covering both of his exposed arms.

"Do you have a light?" Shiro asked.

In one smooth motion, the man pulled out a zippo, flipped it open with his thumb, and lit Shiro's cigarette.

"Everything okay?" Shiro asked, motioning towards Mindy's door with his head. The door was half open, light escaping from the room onto the balcony.

"Mind your own business."

Shiro exhaled. "I was minding my own business. I was trying to sleep."

"Go back and try harder."

"I'm not finished with my cigarette," Shiro replied, his face stern.

"Then smoke."

Shiro stepped towards Mindy's door and the bald man blocked his way, putting his foot against the doorframe.

"Where do you think you're going?"

"Checking on a neighbor."

"For the next twenty-five minutes, that's my room."

Shiro looked down at the man's foot against the door. Raising his eyes, he cleared his throat. "Excuse me, please."

"I said, mind your own business."

Shiro ignored the warning, put his cigarette in his mouth, and leaned past the man's large torso to steal a glance into Mindy's room. He could see Mindy on the bed, pressing a white towel to the side of her face.

Shiro felt his adrenaline surge as a hand crashed down on his shoulder, spinning him around, backing him onto the rail of the veranda. A punch to Shiro's ribs knocked his cigarette out of his mouth. A second blow to the opposite side of his torso had no effect beyond straightening his posture.

The bald man threw his third punch high, and Shiro casually raised his arm to block it. The man tried again with a right hook, followed by another left. Shiro barely moved, thwarting the assault as if he were swatting a gnat.

The man grabbed Shiro's left shoulder and moved his other hand towards his pocket.

Shiro let the man maintain his grasp on his shoulder and jammed a thumb into the skin under the man's jawline. He quickly moved his hand to the man's neck and latched on, squeezing the cross section of flesh that contained one of the man's carotids. The man's hands immediately flew upward, trying to pry Shiro's fingers loose.

Shiro stared into the man's eyes as he squeezed. Emotionless, he watched as the man's face contorted. His throat gurgled and his complexion turned deep red. Shiro held the man's neck for a ten count and could feel the man's consciousness begin to fade.

Mindy's hand on his arm shook Shiro from his tunnel vision.

"Let him go," she said.

Shiro released his grip and the man fell to the ground, gagging and coughing.

Mindy looked down at her latest customer. "I called my manager. He's on his way over. You better not be here when he gets here."

The man struggled to get to his feet and stumbled to the steps. Shiro reached down, picked up his still-lit cigarette, and blew off the filtered end.

Shiro and Mindy watched her customer stumble down the stairs and into his truck parked below. As the red taillights of the vehicle faded into the darkness, Shiro turned towards Mindy.

"Are you okay?"

"I'm fine. It happens. Some of these guys pay for sex and think that gives them the right to get rough."

Mindy seemed to take a moment to digest her first look at Shiro's tattoos and a concerned look washed across her face. She hurried back into her room and Shiro stood at the doorway, watching through the screen as Mindy rifled through her purse. She moved to the dresser and her hands frantically dug through the contents of the top drawer. Then she slammed both hands down on the dresser.

"That son of a bitch took my money," she said, pushing the screen door open and coming back on the balcony.

Shiro took a long drag from his cigarette. "Do you want me to go after him? I have a car."

"No. Forget about it."

"Do you know him?"

"No. He was a new client."

"I imagine new clients make you nervous."

"They do. And I don't get too many. I get clients I haven't seen in a long time, but not many new ones."

Shiro nodded. "How much money did he take?"

"Three hundred."

Shiro stared at the shadow of the trees in the darkness of the Gum Tree Inn property. "Hold on."

He returned to the threshold of his neighbor's door and extended his hand. "Here's six hundred dollars. Three for tonight. Three more for tomorrow. Take the day off."

"I can't take your money."

Shiro shrugged his shoulders. "It's not really my money."

Mindy cocked her head to the side. "Whose money is it?"

"I can't say."

"Did you steal it?"

"No."

"Well, I guess we all have secrets," she replied.

"Pay your manager and take the day off."

"I don't really have a manager," Mindy admitted. "Not an actual manager, anyway."

"I don't understand."

"I tell customers I have a manager when I need to have a customer leave. No one wants to meet a pimp."

"What's a pimp?"

"A hooker's manager."

"Oh."

Mindy noticed the Tupelo City Police car rolling down the narrow street in the direction of the Gum Tree Inn.

"Here comes the cops," Mindy said.

"I'm going inside," Shiro said, not waiting for a reply.

*

Mindy smoked a cigarette on the balcony in front of her room and watched as the police car crawled to a halt in front of the manager's office. A policeman in his forties stepped from the car, put on his cap, and disappeared into the office.

Mindy was near the end of her cigarette when the officer stepped from the manager's office. The policeman surveyed the property and Mindy could feel his eyes stop when they reached her position at the end of the second-floor balcony. Mindy took a drag and waved her hand before exhaling a blue cloud of smoke.

The police officer nodded, got into his car, and left.

Two minutes later, Mindy entered the manager's office and the bell on the door announced her arrival. The old woman in her favorite pajamas came around the corner and approached the desk.

"Are you all right, dear?" the woman asked, peering at the side of Mindy's face and the fresh red mark.

"I'm fine."

"Someone heard a ruckus and called the cops. I told the officer it was probably the two teenage brothers upstairs roughhousing."

Mindy placed a hundred-dollar bill on the counter. "That's a hundred for your trouble."

The woman swiped her hand over the money and it disappeared.

"And I appreciate you letting me work here," Mindy added.

"If none of the other guests at the Gum Tree don't mind, I don't. Just try to keep things quiet. We've had a good run. We'll see how long it lasts."

"Thanks."

"You know, I try my best to keep the room next to yours empty. Give you a little buffer. But with the festival, everything's booked. I had to put the Asian fella in the next room. It was the last one available."

"Don't worry about it."

"Have you met him?"

"Who?"

"Your neighbor."

"I have. Seems like a nice guy. Says he's in town for the festival."

"It's going to be busy this weekend."

"I sure hope so," Mindy said, smiling.

"Honey, can I ask you a personal question?" the old woman asked.

"Sure."

"How did you end up doing what you're doing? I mean, a pretty girl like yourself. You seem to have a good head on your shoulders."

"It just happened. I left my house after high school. Got married and divorced before I knew it. Eventually I started stripping. A cousin's friend got me the job. The money was good. But as you get older and things start sagging, you have to step down from the stage. You can't stay on the pole forever. No one wants to see an aging woman gyrating to songs she doesn't even know. Stripping is a young woman's game. The move from stripper to hooker wasn't as hard as you think."

"Oh, honey, I know it's not."

"I figured you might know something about it."

"I do. And I didn't mean to pry into your business."

"It's okay. I don't plan on doing this forever."

"I'm rooting for you."

CHAPTER 34

CEDAR CREEK CONFERENCE Center was twenty minutes past Elvis Presley Lake and Campgrounds, a swath of beautiful land decimated by an F-4 tornado that uprooted trees and blew away trailers. The land was still recovering, tall pines replaced with saplings reaching for the sky as fast as the earth, water, and sunshine would allow.

The last half of the drive to Cedar Creek passed over two hills, commonly referred to in Mississippi as highway overpasses. At the top of the third peak, Edward took the exit and headed north. Ten minutes from the highway he turned at a large Cedar Creek sign supported on each side by massive stone columns.

The entrance road to Cedar Creek meandered through manicured grass and large shade trees, ending in front of a two-story lodge. Shorter side buildings stretched in either direction for fifty yards. A lone car sat near the front entrance and Edward parked several spaces away. He climbed the wide steps and entered the lobby. A massive stone fireplace filled the main room. The Lord's Prayer hung in a frame from the stone, just beneath a wooden cross. A check-in counter stood on the left side of the lobby. Edward approached and rang the bell for service.

A man with a dazzling white beard stepped from the office just behind the counter. Eyes on the man's facial hair, Edward couldn't help thinking of Christmas.

"Good afternoon. Welcome to Cedar Creek."

"Good afternoon," Edward replied, smiling. "I was hoping to talk to someone in charge."

"That would be me. Douglas Graham. Proprietor of this establishment. My friends call me Digger."

"Nice to meet you, Mr. Graham. My name's Edward Winston."

Digger squinted for a brief second. "I've seen you on the news. You're the man whose wife went missing."

"That's right."

Digger's eyes closed and his head dipped. "May the Lord Jesus Christ, our savior, fill you with his peace and love." Digger's lips continued to move in silence and Edward forced himself to look down at the floor.

Finished with his prayer, Digger raised his head. "What can I help you with, Mr. Winston?"

"I wanted to ask a few questions about Cedar Creek and Charlie Sterling."

"What business is that of yours, if I may ask?"

"It has to do with my wife's murder."

"Oh, boy," Digger replied. "Sounds like we'd better have a seat. Let's head over to the comfortable chairs."

Edward followed Digger across the lobby to a quartet of deep leather chairs on the far side of the stone fireplace. Digger motioned for Edward to have the chair with a view looking out the large windows on the back of the building.

Edward waited for Digger to sit and then said, "Tell me about Cedar Creek."

"Cedar Creek is what my family and I refer to as a casual resort and conference center. We have a banquet hall that seats a hundred and fifty, four dozen guest rooms on the property, a three-acre lake, a pool, and two hundred acres of riding and hiking trails."

"Sounds nice."

"We host weddings and wedding receptions, as well as business events and seminars."

"It's quiet here today."

"During the week, that's usually the case. We have a couple coming later today to check out the property for a possible wedding. But there's always someone here. We have an on-call staff and, of course, we have security on site, around the clock. For events, we bring in as many people as we need. We know every caterer in the state and a few in Alabama. We regularly drive Memphis barbecue down from Corky's or The Rendezvous."

"I drove to Memphis with my wife once, just to eat at The Rendezvous."

"Two hours for good ribs is perfectly reasonable. I prefer the dry rub. Wet rub gets in my beard and looks something awful."

"I like both."

"Pragmatic. I appreciate that. Anything else you want to know about Cedar Creek, or did I hit enough of the highlights for you? I'd be happy to show you around the lodge and the rooms. Or you can take a self-guided tour, if that's more your speed."

"I might take a walk around after we finish talking. What can you tell me about Charlie Sterling, the former president of Sterling Insurance?"

"God rest his soul," Digger responded, head dipping again.

"So you remember him?"

"Of course, I do. He came out here at least once a year for the better part of a decade."

"And he rented the whole place?"

"Yes, he did. Packed them in, wall-to-wall. Lots of who's who from Tupelo."

"I talked to Charlie's wife and she told me you asked Charlie to take his business elsewhere."

"Oh, boy," Digger said again, stroking his white beard.

"Can you tell me what happened?"

"I don't want to sound rude, but what exactly does this have to do with your wife's murder?"

Edward paused. "I believe the same person who killed Charlie Sterling killed my wife."

"Pervis Wade?"

"That's right."

"The news said the police had solved your wife's murder. And it wasn't Pervis Wade."

"The news has it wrong. The police have accused an innocent man. A man who is now deceased and who cannot defend himself. A man whose family now carries the stigma of their loved one being labeled a murderer."

Digger cast his gaze skyward and his lips moved in silence. Then he said, "I asked Charlie Sterling to take his business elsewhere because of an issue we had with some of the guests during his last seminar here."

"What kind of issue?"

"We are a Christian establishment here at Cedar Creek. We have rules that we expect our guests to follow. These are the same rules the Bible expects us to follow."

"Rose Sterling told me things occasionally got out of hand at these seminars. She mentioned she came out here with her husband once. She said some of the men had been drinking and that a group of Charlie's clients were outside shooting off their guns."

"Guns?"

"That's what she said."

"Well, Mr. Winston, guns aren't prohibited in the Bible. And neither is drinking. In moderation."

"Oh," Edward replied. "Then why did you ask Charlie Sterling to take his business elsewhere?"

Digger took a deep breath. "Several guests made some of my female employees very uncomfortable with inappropriate sexual comments. Allegedly. Another guest urinated in one of the potted plants in the lobby. We found vomit on one of the sofas. There was a brief fistfight."

"I get the idea. It was unruly."

"I didn't want to get rid of Charlie Sterling. I didn't. But I had warned Charlie before. He knew his guests needed to rein it in. The weekend I just described to you was the straw that broke the camel's back. Cedar Creek can't host wedding receptions if the place smells like a frat house. As a Christian businessman, I couldn't let Cedar Creek get that kind of reputation."

Edward sat back in his chair. "And that particular weekend was the same one where Troy Wade lost his Rolex watch."

"It was."

"I thought that was the case. I was at the Lee County Courthouse earlier and I obtained records indicating a search warrant had been served on Cedar Creek following Charlie Sterling's death. The search warrant indicated the police were looking for additional information regarding the missing watch."

"That's right."

Edward nodded his head slowly several times.

"I assume you knew about the missing watch before the police showed up with the search warrant."

"Of course. On top of all the other shenanigans that weekend, when Troy Wade realized his watch was missing, he became, shall we say, a little upset. He accused other guests of taking it and then he accused my staff. I was called early the next morning."

Edward fell back into silence, his mind trying to get a handle on a story that was becoming more slippery at every turn.

"And six weeks later the police arrived with a search warrant looking for the missing watch?"

"That's right. After Charlie Sterling was killed, the police came looking for the watch. They thought there might have been a connection between Pervis Wade killing Charlie and the missing watch. Nothing was ever proven, as far as I know."

"Were you here when the search warrant was served?"

"No. My wife was here. But she called me. Put me on speakerphone. I told the police they didn't need a search warrant. I mean, we're God-fearing, church-going Christians. We had nothing to hide because you can't hide anything from God."

"Do you know which members of the police force served the warrant?"

"Like I said, I wasn't here, I was on the phone. But one of the guys was Detective Blazer. Better known these days as Sheriff Blazer. I can't remember the other one."

"Bill Rafferty?" Edward offered.

"Yeah. That's sounds about right."

"And did you know these officers?"

"I knew Sheriff Blazer. He had been a guest at some of the Sterling Insurance seminars in the past."

"So he had stayed here before. As a guest?"

"Yes."

"Was he here the night of the missing watch and the other shenanigans?"

"I don't recall his name on any of the guest rooms for that evening. After the watch went missing, security checked everyone in attendance."

"So they could have been here and left?"

"Not all of the people at the seminar stayed overnight. Most went home."

"And when the police arrived with their search warrant, what did they do?"

"They wanted to see all of our surveillance videos."

"Did the security videos help the police find out who took the watch?"

"By the time the police came with the search warrant, we no longer had the security videos from the night in question. It had been over a month since the watch had gone missing. We just don't keep our security tapes that long."

Edward raised his eyebrows. "Sounds like an eventful month and a half."

"We did a lot of praying that summer. A lot. Boy, oh boy."

"You mentioned you have security personnel on site twenty-four hours a day."

"We do."

"Would you mind if I spoke with them?"

"About what?"

"About the night the watch went missing. I just want to hear their perspective."

Digger stared hard at Edward.

"The head of security at the time the watch went missing was a man named Reggie Taylor. He no longer works here. He started his own security company. Antebellum Security. Seems to be doing well. I have a number for him around here somewhere. But you can probably find it online, too."

CHAPTER 35

SHIRO WAS SWEATING through an already drenched white sleeveless shirt. His door was open and a spread of maps and brochures covered the bedspread.

Mindy knocked on the doorframe and Shiro looked up.

"Come in," he said, folding the maps and stacking them with the brochures.

Mindy eyed the perspiration glistening on her neighbor's well-defined muscles. "My, my. You do have some colorful tattoos."

"Japanese tattoos are the best in the world," Shiro replied.

"I've never seen one in person before, but they just might be."

"The air-conditioning stopped working."

"Mine too. It happens. Our rooms share a compressor. I talked to the office and they're sending someone over to fix it."

Mindy seemed interested in the spread of material Shiro was looking through and he moved the sightseeing paraphernalia and maps to the kitchenette in the back of the room.

"You want to go out and get something to eat?" she asked.

"I can't. I have some work to do."

"There you go again, saying you have work. You told me you were in town for the festival."

"I am."

"Well, how about we go down to the festival then? It starts tonight. They've already closed off the streets. They should have some places to eat."

"Okay. For a while. But I have things to do later," Shiro said.

"So will I, hopefully. In the meantime, let's grab dinner and check out all the Elvis impersonators."

"What's that?"

"People dressed up like Elvis. You'll love it."

*

Shiro and Mindy walked down the road in the direction of Main Street, taking a left, a right, and another left. The back of several warehouses were visible off in the distance, the top of the roofs catching the day's last rays of sun.

At the end of the next street, Mindy pointed left. They followed the back of the shops on Main Street, walking past the Dumpsters and rear exits of brick buildings that had served as the backbone of the city's commerce for a hundred years.

At a break in the buildings, Mindy motioned in the direction of a concrete alley that led to Main Street and the festivities. Seconds later, Tupelo's most unlikely pair stepped onto the main drag and eyed the plethora of festival booths lining both sides of the asphalt in each direction. Barricades blocked the road to automobile traffic and throngs of people milled about, moving from booth to booth. The smell of food drifted down the street through the strings of lights overhead.

Shiro bought turkey legs and Mindy purchased beer in red plastic cups. Dinner in hand, Mindy pulled Shiro in the direction of a small stage near the middle of the second block. They sat down in folding chairs amidst a growing audience and waited for the next Elvis impersonator to take the stage.

"This is just the beginning of the contest," Mindy said. "The finalists do a show over at the coliseum at the end of the festival."

Shiro ate his turkey leg and drank his beer while Mindy carried most of the conversation.

"It looks like you want to do some sightseeing," Mindy said. "I saw the brochures and maps on your bed."

"I do."

"What did you have in mind?"

"I'm going to take the Trolley Tour."

"Those are good. They only run during the week of the festival. You can jump on and off as many times as you want. They make stops all over town. What do you want to see?"

"Elvis Presley's house and the Automobile Museum. Maybe the battlefield."

"It's actually the house where Elvis Presley was born. The house he built and lived in is called Graceland. It's in Memphis. The Automobile Museum is good if you like cars. The battlefield is boring."

"I went to a battlefield in Japan once. It was boring, too."

Shiro and Mindy watched a half-dozen Elvis impersonators grind and gyrate through several Elvis classics before Shiro announced, "Let's go."

Back among the booths, Mindy stopped to get cotton candy. She pinched off a piece, put it in her mouth, and swirled it around with her tongue.

"Do they have cotton candy in Japan?"

"They do."

"Cool. Because if they didn't, you could start a business selling it. Everyone loves cotton candy."

Shiro shrugged his shoulders and Mindy beelined it to a booth burgeoning with handcrafted, wooden knickknacks.

"What are these?" she asked the attendant, cotton candy mangling her words.

"Wood puzzle boxes," the man behind the table answered. "There's only one way to put them together and one way to take them apart."

Shiro stepped to the table and picked one up. "How much?"

"Twenty bucks."

"I'll take it. And whatever she wants," he added.

A minute later, they exited the booth and Shiro eyed a stack of hiking sticks standing upright in an old barrel.

"Thanks for the gift," Mindy said, drawing Shiro's attention away from the barrel.

"You're welcome."

"You want to come out again tomorrow evening? There's something different every day."

"Maybe after I go sightseeing."

"Okay," Mindy replied, pointing in the direction of the alley from which they'd come.

As they turned the corner from the alley at the rear of Main Street, the overweight, bald john from the night before stepped out from between two Dumpsters.

"I was hoping you two would come back this way. I've been waiting for you. I saw you leave the motel earlier. I hope you had a good date."

"Keep walking," Shiro whispered to Mindy.

The man reached out for Mindy, and Shiro kicked the man in his pudgy midsection.

"Don't touch," Shiro said.

Mindy stopped and turned around. "Keep walking," Shiro repeated, pointing in the direction of the motel.

The man took several deep breaths, removed his hands from his stomach, and stood straight. Shiro casually backpedaled until he was near the entrance to the alley.

"I don't want to fight," Shiro lied.

"You sure seem like you want to."

"I don't want to. We can both just walk away."

"I don't think so."

"No?"

"No," the man said, flicking open a large buck knife as easily as he had flicked open his zippo lighter the night before. The man flashed the blade of the knife so Shiro could see it.

Shiro stood with his arms by his side, staring at the man. "Just remember, I gave you a chance."

The man came to life, slashing wildly with the knife. Shiro casually flanked him with slow, deliberate steps. Unsuccessful with his first attack, the man lunged forward. Shiro sidestepped the lunge and kicked, his foot catching the man on the nose.

The man staggered backwards but regained his balance.

Shiro spotted a piece of wood wedged in the top of a Dumpster to keep the lid open. He feigned a series of kicks to drive the man in the opposite direction and then tugged the wood from its position. The Dumpster lid slammed shut.

Shiro looked down at the broken broomstick in his hand and smiled. It was shorter than his favorite weapon, but it was long enough to put an end to the question of who was going to win the fight in the alley.

"This is really your last chance," Shiro said, holding the stick as if it were a sword.

"Fuck you," the man said, lunging forward again with the knife.

Shiro struck the man's right collarbone as the knife passed by. He struck the left collarbone as the man retracted the blade. A third blow to the top of the head caused the man to drop his weapon. Without a sound, the john stumbled back, beginning a staggering fall that concluded with the back of his head bouncing on the concrete pad near the Dumpster.

Shiro's attention returned to the old broom handle, which had broken nearly in two. He quickly surveyed the man on the ground, the knife just beyond the reach of his outstretched hands.

Shiro finished snapping the shortened, partially broken broomstick into two pieces. He slipped both pieces into the front of his pants, and pulled his long-sleeve shirt over his waist. He traveled down the alley for the third time, again joining the throngs of revelers on Main Street as the night turned a darker black.

At the far end of the festival, the scent of food was replaced by the scent of urine, Shiro stood third in line. He entered the first available blue Porta-Potty and locked the door behind him. Standing in the confines of the portable toilet, he wiped off the two ends of the sticks and dropped them into the abyss of human waste.

*

Mindy was standing at the top of the stairs as Shiro walked up.

"Where have you been?"

"I had to take the long way back."

"What happened?"

"He pulled a knife."

"Are you okay?"

"I'm fine."

"How about the other guy?"

"He was breathing when I left him."

"That wasn't a good idea."

"What should I have done? Run away? Let him stab me?"

"He'll probably go to the police."

"No, he won't."

"Why not?"

"He was wearing a wedding ring."

"So."

"What's he going to say? That he got into a fight with a man who was walking with a hooker he had sex with the night before. The same hooker he beat up. The same hooker he stole money from?"

"Good point."

Mindy wrung her hands. "I thought you were a negotiator. There wasn't much negotiating going on back there."

Shiro smirked.

"Don't smile. Even if that guy doesn't want to say what happened to him, if he ends up in the back of an ambulance, they'll still probably come around here asking questions."

"If they do, I'll tell them the truth. I went down to the festival with you. We drank a beer, ate a turkey leg, watched some guys dressed like Elvis, bought a souvenir, and then came back."

CHAPTER 36

EDWARD WOKE EARLY and spent the better part of an hour research-ing Reggie Taylor and Antebellum Security. A professional website and a list of clients from across Tupelo painted a favorable picture of the com-pany and the legitimacy of its operations. From what he could ascertain, Reggie Taylor's post-Cedar Creek career seemed to be doing well, though a fancy website alone meant nothing.

With an empty coffee carafe on the table, Edward confirmed the phone number that Digger from Cedar Creek had given him. He scrolled far-ther down the page and perused a series of customer testimonials. On the second-to-last entry, Edward froze.

"What the hell?" he said to the stack of boxes in the living room. He read the screen twice, leaned back in his chair, and shut his computer. He stood to tame the surging bout of nerves and jumped when his phone on the table rang.

"Edward Winston," he panted.

"Good morning, Mr. Winston," his real estate agent responded with her unwavering cheer. "I have good news for you. We've received a full-asking price offer with an agreement for a quick close. The new owners want to close in two weeks and they agreed to rent the house back to you if you need it."

"That's great," Edward replied, his thoughts still on Reggie Taylor.

"If you're available, I'll bring the contract over later today and you can sign it."

"That sounds great," Edward responded. "And if you pick up lunch, I'll buy."

"Deal."

*

Edward finished choking down his tuna sandwich and signed the contract for the offer on his house.

"Have you decided where you're going next?" his realtor asked.

"It looks like I'm heading to Lexington, Kentucky, until the end of the year. Then I'm going to go back to corporate headquarters in Tokyo."

"I hope it works out for you."

Edward felt his phone on the table begin to vibrate and he checked the number. "I should take this," he said to the real estate agent, raising a single finger into the air.

The real estate agent nodded and began gathering the documents on the table in front of her.

Edward pressed his phone to his ear.

"This is the North Mississippi Medical Center. We're looking for a Japanese translator. Is there any chance you're available?"

Edward looked around at the state of his living room and at his real estate agent stacking papers. "I'm available," he said. "I can be there in thirty minutes."

*

The receptionist at the emergency room entrance led Edward into an area identified as triage by the sign on the wall and markings on the tile floor.

He was handed off to a nurse in her early sixties who shook Edward's hand and gave him the rundown.

"Thanks for coming. This guy is a little hostile. We tried to get him in a gown, but he didn't want to take off his clothes. He's been sitting there for the last hour, refusing treatment."

"What's his ailment?"

"One of the Trolley Tour drivers had a medical emergency. He crashed one of the trolley buses into a ditch out near the battlefield. We had a dozen people injured. Two of them are in serious condition. There are no real seatbelts on those trolley buses. Everyone on board was brought to the hospital. The patient you are about to meet seems to be one of the lucky ones. He has a contusion on his head."

"So he hit his head?"

"That's right. We wanted to do a CT scan and he's refusing treatment."

"Maybe he's afraid of the medical bill."

The nurse faked a smile. "We've already been contacted by the tour company's attorney and president. Everyone's medical treatment is covered. Payment is not an issue. This week is a big money maker for the tours in town. I'm sure that factored into it."

"What did the patient say when he refused treatment?"

"'No, thank you.'"

"At least he's polite."

"When one of the doctors tried to forcibly take off his shirt he added 'fuck you' to his politeness."

"So he speaks some English."

"I guess you could say that."

"Don't be too offended. Sometimes Japanese people hear things in movies and think it's acceptable to repeat them."

"Then he needs to watch different movies. Anyhow, after he cursed the doctor out he clearly stated he was Japanese. That was the last thing he said."

"So he came in with a bump on his head?"

"And a possible concussion. No ID. Just a pocket full of cash. The trolley picks up in a couple of places in town. You can hop on and hop off."

"So you don't know anything about him?"

"That's what you're here for."

"What do you want me to ask him?"

"We would like to perform a CT scan. Just to be on the safe side. But we can't let him leave until we can identify him, confirm he has a place to go, and a ride to get there."

"Okay. Let's see what I can do," Edward replied. The nurse pulled the curtained partition open and Edward stepped towards the bed.

A Japanese man with a stern expression and rugged good looks raised his head.

A doctor joined the nurse at the entrance to the room and the nurse whispered something into the doctor's ear.

"You're our translator?" the doctor confirmed.

"I am. If there's anything specific you want me to ask, let me know."

Edward started speaking Japanese and the doctor and nurse looked on in curiosity.

"Nice to meet you. My name is Edward Winston," Edward said to the man in the bed, bowing slightly.

"You're not a doctor?" the man replied in standard Japanese. The man's choice of words and pronunciation offered no hint of a regional dialect. From a single sentence, Edward assumed the man was from Tokyo, or not too far from the capital.

"No. I'm a volunteer translator."

"Where did you learn Japanese?"

"In Japan."

"Tokyo?"

"Yes. I worked in Tokyo for a Japanese company."

"And what do you do now?"

"I still work for a Japanese company. I'm an engineer."

The man in the bed nodded. "I see."

"Do you live in town?" Edward asked.

"I'm in town for the festival. Please tell the doctors I want to leave. Please translate that."

"They have a few questions for you."

"You're the translator. I just told you to translate that I want to leave. You didn't translate that to the doctor."

Edward turned towards the doctor and nurse. "He said he would like to be released."

"Please tell him that we cannot release him until we have an identity, a destination, and a ride."

Edward turned and relayed the message in Japanese.

"Tell them my name is Nobu Matsuhisa."

"Nobu Matsuhisa?"

"That's right."

"The famous chef?" Edward confirmed with suspicion.

"Oh, you know him?"

"I do. Well, I know of him."

"Do you think the doctors will recognize the name, or shall I choose a different one?"

"I don't know. I guess that's up to you."

"Why don't you translate my answer and see what they say?"

Edward turned towards the nurse and translated. "He said his name is Nobu Matsuhisa."

The nurse scribbled the name on the white board on the wall.

"How old is he?" she asked.

Edward turned back towards the man and translated the next question.

"Make up an age," the man said. "Tell them whatever comes to mind."

"I'm really just the translator."

"Tell them that I'm thirty-eight."

"He says he's thirty-eight," Edward relayed.

The nurse added the age next to the name.

"Okay. It's obvious you're not interested in answering any questions. And I understand. But that's going to make this difficult because they don't want to let you leave until they get a few answers."

"Are they planning to keep me here forever? For a bump on the head?"

"Probably not."

"I haven't done anything wrong. I'm not a criminal. I can wait in this bed for a very long time."

"And then what?"

The doctor interrupted the exchange between Edward and the patient. "What did he say?"

"He said he wants to leave and that he hasn't done anything wrong."

"Tell him to answer our questions and he can leave."

Edward turned back towards the bed. He could feel the man's attention on his scarred left hand. Edward moved his unblemished hand to cover his left. The patient's eyes rose to meet Edward's.

"I understand what the doctor said. I don't need you to translate it," he said.

"You speak English?" Edward asked, in Japanese.

"Some. But I have no intention of speaking it right now."

"Where did you learn English?"

"Tokyo."

"At school?'

"Not really. Tell me, are there a lot of Americans who speak Japanese here in Tupelo?"

"No. I have a coworker who does. His wife is Japanese."

The man squinted from the bed as if trying to peer into Edward's soul. "You said you spent time in Tokyo?"

"That's right."

"Any chance you've ever been to Bunkyo ward?"

Edward glanced back over at the doctor and smiled. Then he turned back towards the bed. "I've been to Bunkyo ward a couple of times. They have a nice woodblock print museum there."

"Have you ever visited any place other than the museum?"

Edward paused, staring into the man's eyes without blinking. "I have an acquaintance who lives in Bunkyo ward," Edward replied, his pulse quickening.

"So do I," the man replied. "What a small world."

The patient reached over to the side table with his right hand and took a sip of water.

"It *is* a small world," Edward agreed, his eyes dropping to the man's left hand, which sported five full fingers.

The patient took another sip of water. "The man I know in Bunkyo ward lives in a house with two large lion-dog statues at the gate. Have you ever seen such a house?" A smirk flashed across the man's face and disappeared.

Edward wiped sweat from his forehead and the doctor interjected himself into the conversation for a second time. "What's he saying?"

"Just small talk. He's from Tokyo. I'm trying to build a little rapport with him."

"Can you at least ask him how he feels?"

"Sure," Edward answered.

"Tell him I'm fine," the man said before being asked.

Edward turned back towards the doctor. "He says he's fine."

"Can you get any more information from him?"

The patient ignored the doctor and continued his conversation with

Edward in Japanese. "You didn't answer my question. Have you ever seen a house in Bunkyo ward with two large lion-dog statues at the gate?"

Edward swallowed hard. He noticed the patient was covering his left hand with his right, just as Edward had done with his own scars seconds before. Edward's eyes darted to the man's collar and then along the cuff of his sleeve. The man's effort to conceal his hand and large swathes of his skin sent goosebumps up the back of Edward's neck.

"I've been to the house you're describing. A man of his word lives there," Edward replied.

The patient smiled. "Yes. A man of his word. A man who expects and receives complete loyalty."

"I imagine he does."

"And I cannot imagine why a man like that would have any business in a small town like this. Can you?"

"Because he is a man of his word," Edward replied.

The patient nodded.

"Where are you staying?" Edward asked.

"I think it's better for both of us if you don't know. In fact, we probably shouldn't be seen together, don't you agree?"

"Oh, I agree. But we've already been seen together."

"And now it's up to you to get me out of here. Tell them whatever you have to tell them." The patient shut his eyes for a moment, waiting to hear what Edward was going to translate.

Edward turned back towards the doctor and nurse. "He said he's a tourist in town and was just coming for the festival. He says he's a huge Elvis fan. Always has been."

"And where's he staying?"

"He says he's staying at the Hilton Garden Inn."

The nurse wrote down the information on the clipboard and the doctor looked over at the patient.

"And what did he say about allowing the CT scan?"

"He wanted me to thank you for your concern, but he feels fine. He wants the medical team to focus on other people who were more seriously injured on the trolley."

The doctor and the nurse stepped away and exchanged a series of whispers. The nurse turned and provided the only stipulations keeping the patient in bed.

"We can't let him leave without a ride and a destination."

Edward turned towards the patient. "I think we're almost out of here."

*

Edward pulled his Toyota Camry to the front of the ER as the nurse pushed Shiro in a wheelchair towards the car. Edward got out of the vehicle and opened the passenger door.

A minute later Edward exited the hospital property.

"Where to?" Edward asked.

"Take me near the festival on Main Street."

"Most of the roads are closed downtown. I can get you a couple of blocks away."

"That's fine."

"And then?"

"And then nothing. You and I never met. You and I will never meet again."

"Fine by me. What about your visit to Tupelo?"

"What about it?"

"How long will you be in town?"

"Not long."

Edward drove in silence for several minutes. Then he asked, "How are you going to do what you came here to do?"

Shiro slowly turned his head in Edward's direction and scowled. "If you care, then you should do it yourself."

"Just trying to be helpful."

Shiro grunted. "I don't need help. And I don't want help."

"Do you know where to find the guy you're looking for?"

Shiro stared straight ahead. "You need to stop talking."

Edward did as suggested. Minutes later he motioned towards the police cars blocking the road on the next street.

"This is as close as I can get to Main Street," Edward said, looking for a place to pull over. He slowed down for a yellow light and before his car came to a complete halt, Shiro casually pulled on the door handle.

"Let me pull over first."

Edward brought his car to the curb and Shiro opened the door. Edward exited the driver's side and stood.

"Hey neighbor," Mindy's voice echoed, cutting through the din of the festival two blocks away. She approached the car and Shiro stole a nervous glance in Edward's direction.

"Is this a friend of yours?" Mindy asked Shiro.

"We're not friends," Shiro replied, shutting the door. "We just met. He just gave me a ride."

"I thought you were taking the Trolley Tour today."

"There was an accident," Edward offered from afar.

"Oh. Are you okay?" Mindy asked.

"Fine."

"He's fine," Edward confirmed while trying to figure out the relationship between Shiro and the bouncy blonde on the sidewalk.

"Thanks for the ride," Shiro said over the roof of the car.

"You're welcome," Edward responded, before adding in Japanese, "Be careful and have a safe trip back."

Mindy's mouth gaped over the white guy speaking Japanese. Shiro quickly turned to walk away.

"Thanks for helping him," Mindy added, hurrying down the sidewalk after her neighbor.

Edward got in the car and pulled away from the curb. He looked in the rearview mirror and watched as the Japanese man and the blonde walked side by side and disappeared around the corner.

CHAPTER 37

MINDY AND SHIRO sat in a row of empty chairs as another Elvis imper-sonator took the stage. A weak summer breeze offered the contestants a muted respite from the heat.

"I heard some interesting news today," Mindy said, leaning in close to Shiro.

"What did you hear?"

"The news reported a man was found in the alley not too far from here. He was seriously injured. The doctors put him in a coma to reduce the swell-ing on his brain."

"That doesn't sound good."

"No, it doesn't," Mindy replied. "They say he may not make it."

Shiro could feel Mindy crying but he didn't turn to face her.

"I'm worried," she added.

"Like I said, I had no choice. It was self-defense. The man pulled a knife."

Mindy wiped her face.

"Besides, I'm leaving soon. And that will be the end of it," Shiro said.

"That doesn't make me feel any better."

The two sat without speaking as another rendition of "Heartbreak Hotel" screeched from the stage. Mindy grabbed her phone and looked at the screen.

"I have a customer. I have to go."

Shiro looked up as she stood. "Okay. I'm going to take a walk and then go back to the hotel."

"Maybe we can have a beer later. I'll knock on your door if I'm free," Mindy said.

*

Shiro waited through two more Elvis impersonators and then started down the street. He passed the same woodworking booth he and Mindy had visited previously and eyed the walking sticks standing vertically in a large barrel.

Two blocks later, Shiro stood in a thick line that snaked into the Tupelo Hardware store. On a busy corner of Main Street, Tupelo Hardware had been in business since 1926. But it wasn't until 1945 that Tupelo Hardware planted the seed that would bloom into decades of notoriety.

Like many hardware stores of its era, Tupelo Hardware sold a little bit of everything. Hammers, nails, boards, and rakes were mainstays. Little red wagons, piggy banks, and baseball bats were almost as popular. As luck would have it for the future of Rock n' Roll, in 1945, the store's inventory happened to include one guitar in a glass display and a .22 rifle hanging on the wall.

According to lore, Elvis Presley's mother, with her eleven-year-old son in tow, entered the front door of Tupelo Hardware and strolled across the creaky wood floor to the counter. She reportedly inquired about a bicycle for her son, whose interest quickly focused on the rifle hanging on the wall. Sensing an opportunity for a diplomatic resolution, the man behind the counter suggested the young man try the guitar. Minutes later, on a hot summer afternoon, Elvis Presley became the proud owner of his first guitar for a whopping seven dollars and fifty-nine cents.

*

Shiro followed a couple with matching festival T-shirts through the front door of Tupelo Hardware and meandered along the crowded aisles until he found the knife display in the back corner. Under the watchful eye of a store employee, Shiro perused his knife alternatives and settled on a mid-size Benchmade with a folding blade.

"Do you need a sharpening stone?" the man behind the counter asked.

"No," Shiro replied.

The man entered the sale into the register. "One hundred fifteen sixty-three."

Shiro placed a pair of hundred-dollar bills on the counter, received his change, and headed out the door.

Back on the street, Shiro returned to the woodcarving booth and began parsing through the hiking sticks in the old barrel. He removed one stick at a time, grasping them with two hands, and testing their weight. He nodded as the middle-aged craftsman in an apron appeared on the other side of the display table.

"Are you looking for a walking stick?"

"Yes. Souvenirs for my friends."

"How tall are your friends?"

Shiro kept his hands moving as he answered the question. "Some of them are tall. Some are shorter than me."

"I see," the man answered.

"Did you make these yourself?" Shiro asked.

"I did."

"What kind of wood?"

"American Appalachian Hickory. Very strong. But flexible. It doesn't warp easily."

"Strong is good," Shiro replied. He pulled out a taller stick and shook it in his hands. Satisfied, he placed the stick outside the barrel and repeated the process two more times. Shiro motioned towards his three selections.

"The hiking sticks are buy one, get the second one half off. So if you buy one more, you get an additional discount."

"Just these."

"I tell you what. I'll be here through the weekend. If you change your mind and come back, I'll sell you one more at half price."

"How much for these?"

"Ninety."

Shiro doled out another Ben Franklin and pocketed the ten dollars in change. With his white Tupelo Hardware bag in one hand, and three walking sticks in the other, Shiro ambled down the street before turning left in the direction of the Gum Tree Inn.

CHAPTER 38

SHIRO SAT IN his rental car with the window open and the ignition off. His car was backed into a turn around, just off the dirt road at the edge of a swath of trees. The trampled earth around the car was littered with beer cans and bottles, discarded clothes, and at least one condom wrapper, offering clues as to what the secluded offshoot of the rural road was often used for.

He sucked on his cigarette and exhaled slowly, savoring the taste. Sitting in the darkness and silence, he reeked of mosquito spray and sweat. In the hour and a half he had been parked, incoming dark clouds had swallowed a waning moon. He stole a glance at the sky as he took another slow drag, then looked over at the passenger seat. The top of a walking stick rested in the foot well, rising upwards until it met the frame of the passenger door, just under the window.

Out the passenger side window, a vast stretch of freshly tilled Mississippi earth disappeared into the darkness, the silhouette of a barn the only indication that life existed beyond the field.

Across the street, over a hundred yards away, a small party raged on in the form of three young men, copious quantities of beer, a fire pit, and occasional gunfire. It was the latter that had kept Shiro in his car as an observer. The quiet of the last few minutes gave him hope the evening's target practice was over. A rumble from the clouds above meant the window of opportunity for the evening was threatening to close.

From behind the wheel, Shiro could see the back of Pervis's house, the large patio with the fire pit in the center, and a number of outbuildings in the expansive backyard. The three men were seated in chairs facing the fire, the outline of their backs visible against the backdrop of the flames. With the proper weapon and stealth, a true assassin could have approached the men from the rear and struck without being seen.

Shiro was waiting for the right time. The advantage to his current position was his ability to be patient and identify the routine of the group. And there was a routine: remove beer from cooler, drink beer, take a leak in the yard, throw wood onto the fire, shoot guns at targets. Oddly, somewhere deep inside, Shiro felt a kindred spirit with the three men. The familiarity with a life of nonconformity.

A faint hint of music wafted across the long stretch of ground between Shiro's position in the car and the house. He watched as a rumble of thunder sent the faces of the men skyward. As the thunder faded, a silhouette stood, strolled into the yard near the grove of trees, and relieved himself. With a lightened bladder, the man returned to the patio and smacked his friend on the shoulder. Shiro squinted as the man who had just relieved himself rounded the side of the house, climbed into his car, and disappeared down the dirt road towards civilization.

And then there were two, Shiro thought. *And that might be as good as it gets.*

He tried to play the scenario out in his mind. Beyond the inherent danger that comes with approaching armed men, the ground he needed to cover without being seen was a major impediment. His first order of business was to maneuver through a drainage swale and thirty yards of tall grass to the grove of trees on the edge of the yard. From there, the crux of the problem remained. The distance between the relative protection of the trees on the side of the yard and the patio was a no-man's-land without refuge. If the men remained seated, facing the fire pit, they wouldn't see him unless they turned around. If they did turn, the jig was up.

Get to the trees, Shiro thought. *Then decide.*

He could feel the adrenaline beginning to percolate in his veins. He reached for his water bottle in the console between the front seats and twisted the top. He reassessed the darkening clouds, considered the implication of impending rain as potentially advantageous, and finished off his cigarette, dropping the butt into a second water bottle. Breathing deeply, he took the keys out of the ignition and carefully placed them on the passenger seat. He reached up and confirmed that the light on the ceiling of the car wouldn't illuminate the darkness of his position when he opened the door. He pushed aside thoughts of his wife and daughter, ran through his mental checklist, and whispered a Japanese phrase for inspiration. He quietly opened the car door, reached over for his hiking stick, and then exited the vehicle.

*

Shiro moved slowly in the darkness, his knees bent to remain low to the ground as he walked. He kept his eyes on the back of the targets and the larger of the two men threw something into the fire without getting out of his chair. The music got louder as Shiro approached, the view to the house and patio intermittently obstructed by tree trunks in the grove.

Minutes later, Shiro lowered himself to one knee behind the trunk of the largest oak. He moved his head to the side, far enough to observe the men with one eye. Now thirty yards away, the men sat in their chairs, laughing, cursing, and calling each other names.

Based on his previous observations, Shiro was confident the man seated in the chair nearest the back door was the owner of the house. The other man, he assumed, was a friend who was about to pay dearly for his friendship. Unless he departed in the very near future. Either way, Shiro knew he had passed the point of no return. Time was up. There would be no retreat.

Shiro crouched in the darkness and his mind flashed back to memories of sitting around a summer campfire with his own rough-and-tumble friends. The sound of shattering glass echoed across the yard, ending Shiro's moment of nostalgia and sending his pulse higher.

"Don't fucking break bottles on the patio, asshole," Pervis Wade yelled to the man in the chair next to him. "I walk around back here in my bare feet. All this space out here and you have to break shit on the patio? Dickhead."

"Then you'd better sweep it up."

"You're fucking cleaning it up."

Pervis's friend stood from his chair and the outline of his massive body was framed by the fire. "I have to take a piss."

"Asshole. I'll get the broom. You can clean it up when you're done."

"I'm going to take a leak and then I'm outta here," the man replied, wobbling in his first step off the patio.

"I hope you piss down your leg and catch your dick in your zipper."

Pervis headed into the house and the back door slammed shut behind him.

Shiro positioned himself squarely behind the trunk of the tree as the drunken man stomped across the grass. The image of a sumo wrestler flashed in Shiro's mind as the man staggered in his direction, struggling to navigate the final stretch of uneven yard towards the unofficial, open-air outhouse.

Shiro froze every muscle as the man approached. Then he held his breath. For the better part of a minute Shiro listened to the man hum as the sound of a healthy urine stream bounced off the trunk of a tree less than ten feet away. Finished, the man swayed as he fiddled with his fly. When the man staggered sideways in a large clumsy step, his new angle brought Shiro's silhouette into view.

The man's eyes squinted and his mouth opened preparing to announce his discovery. Shiro leapt upward and brought down his hiking stick with the speed and power of three decades of experience. A resounding crack echoed across the yard, melting into the music. A lone grunt escaped the man's mouth as he crumbled to the ground.

Shiro moved back behind the tree from which he had just struck. The entire assault had taken seconds yet he was completely covered in sweat.

Pervis came out of the back door of his house with a broom and dustpan. He looked over at the grove of trees and saw the frame of his large friend lying on the ground.

"Get up, you drunk bitch. I brought the broom so you can clean up your mess."

Pervis stood on the patio, waiting for his friend to move.

"Don't think I'm coming over there to help you, either. I couldn't pick your fat ass up even if I wanted to."

Pervis stared out towards the tree and his friend's arm flailed once into the air and then returned to the earth.

From his position behind the tree, Shiro watched as the large man's effort to regain consciousness faded.

"Fine. I'm going to leave your drunk ass right there in the grass. See how you like a night with the mosquitos."

Pervis began sweeping up the glass on the patio, cursing under his breath. Glass clinked into the metal dustpan until most of the debris had been accounted for. With a broom in one hand and a dustpan in the other, Pervis again turned to face the trees.

The swoosh of the hiking stick cutting through the darkness ended with the dustpan and broom flying across the patio.

Startled, Pervis looked down at his empty hands. His focus moved from his hands to a pair of shoes several feet away. Slowly his gaze rose and met Shiro's face.

The two men locked eyes and both reached the same conclusion. Uncompromising trouble stood before each of them.

"Who the fuck are you?" Pervis asked.

Shiro brought the stick down in two rapid strikes, one on each of Pervis's collarbones.

Pervis howled, his arms rendered ineffective.

"Are you Wade?"

"Yes."

"Pervis Wade?"

"Yeah. Who the hell are you?"

"The man sent to kill you."

"Who sent you? Eddie?"

"My boss."

Pervis took a step back and looked over at his handgun on the patio near his chair.

"There's nothing out here that's going to save you," Shiro said calmly.

"I wouldn't be so sure."

Shiro stepped closer, pointing the hiking stick at Pervis's neck.

"What is that? A stick?"

"Yes."

"You came here with a toy?"

Shiro raised his hands and struck downward at Pervis's head hard enough to split his scalp. Immediately blood began trickling down Pervis's forehead and nose.

"What do you want?" Pervis groaned.

"I don't want anything. But I do have a question."

"Kiss my ass."

Another blow landed on Pervis's head.

"I'll give you another chance."

Pervis didn't respond and Shiro asked his question. "Are you sorry for what you've done?"

"Would it matter?" Pervis asked, blood cascading down his face.

"No," Shiro answered, his hands once again lifting the stick above his head for another strike downward.

*

Shiro walked quickly back in the direction of his car, glancing over at the feet of the large body lying among the grove of trees. Lightning momentarily lit up the sky as Shiro approached the drainage ditch on the side of the road.

The sound of the bullet being fired reached Shiro's ears as the impact of the round pierced his shoulder. The bullet ripped through his shirt and Shiro cursed.

Shiro stumbled, regained his balance, and turned around. The large man on the ground fired a second shot in Shiro's direction and Shiro veered left to put a tree between himself and the injured man on the ground. A third and fourth shot echoed across the yard before the firing stopped.

Keeping the trees between himself and the man, Shiro tightened his grip on his hiking stick. He moved from trunk to trunk out of prudence, and could see the man's feet as he approached the last tree. Shiro quickly poked his head around the last trunk, stealing a glance of the man as he lay sprawled on the ground, gun still in hand. Shiro moved to the other side of the trunk and prepared himself for a final assault. He took another deep breath, stepped from his position, and brought the stick down onto the man's arm. Pain shot through Shiro's shoulder as the man eyes thrust opened, his mouth gasping. Shiro grunted, raised his stick again with one arm and drove the Appalachian Hickory downward with all his might.

CHAPTER 39

SHIRO SLOWLY CLIMBED the stairs to the balcony on the second floor of the Gum Tree Inn as the rain starting falling in large drops. He passed his neighbor's room, the interior door cracked open wide enough for him to hear the television. He fumbled with his motel key, the block of wood with the room number on it knocking against the door as it swung back and forth.

Mindy stepped onto the balcony and Shiro turned his head.

"Howdy neighbor."

"Hi," Shiro said.

Mindy immediately noticed Shiro's pallor.

"Are you feeling all right?"

"Fine." He twisted the key in the lock, and as he reached for the light switch inside the room, the bloodstain on the back of his shoulder flashed into Mindy's line of sight.

"Holy shit!" Mindy said, as Shiro attempted to shut the door behind him. She forced herself into the doorway, and Shiro tried to shove her from the room. Undeterred, Mindy shoved back.

"Get out," Shiro said.

"No. What happened?"

"None of your business," Shiro replied. "Now step back."

"No," Mindy said, standing firm at the doorway.

Flecks of blood covered Shiro's forehead. Her eyes dropped to his shoulder and then his chest. Her inspection stopped on his shoes, which were standing on a folded towel just inside the front door.

Shiro noticed Mindy staring at his makeshift welcome mat. "I'm Japanese, we take off our shoes when we enter the house," Shiro said. He slipped off his shoes and left them on the towel. A drop of blood fell from his hand and landed next to his shoes.

"Let me call you an ambulance or take you to the emergency room."

"No. No ambulance. No hospital." Shiro paused and added, "And no police."

"Then let me help you."

Shiro glanced down as a second drop of blood landed on the towel under his shoes, complicating a predicament he hadn't foreseen. The fact was he had nearly lost consciousness twice on the drive back, and only had a hazy recollection of stopping his car on the bridge over Tom's Creek to dispose of the murder weapon.

"If you call the police or an ambulance, it won't be good for you," Shiro replied, his eyes opening wide, trying to threaten Mindy with his expression.

"Yeah, yeah," she replied. "Don't threaten people who are trying to help you."

"I don't need help."

"Oh, you don't?"

Shiro stared hard at Mindy with his dark eyes. She ignored him and turned her attention to his shoulder and shirt, both stained with blood.

"Come inside and close the door," he relented.

Shiro stepped from the doorway but remained over the towel.

"Maybe we should take you to the bathroom," Mindy offered. "It'll be easier to clean up in there."

Shiro nodded and walked towards the bathroom. Mindy quickly approached from behind and stopped him near the doorway.

"Wait here," she said, leaving him to stand on the tile floor in the small kitchenette near the entrance to the bathroom. His posture slumped. With waning focus, he watched as Mindy entered the bathroom and closed the lid on the toilet. She pulled the shower curtain to one side and tied it around the rail in the upper corner, out of the way.

She turned back to the doorway and motioned for Shiro to enter.

"Grab a seat."

Shiro slowly lowered himself onto the closed toilet. Mindy reached over to the bathtub and turned on the faucet. A stream of water rushed from the lower spout.

"Time to get cleaned up."

Shiro almost stood and then sat back down.

"A little dizzy, are we?"

"Fine," he replied, his bravado fading.

Mindy shuffled to his side and gently pulled upward until Shiro rose to his feet.

"Get in," she commanded.

Shiro stepped over the edge of the tub. He gripped the soap dish mounted to the tile wall for balance.

"Just stand there. I'll get you undressed," Mindy said.

Water continued to pour from the tub's spigot as she gently removed his shirt. Water sprayed her face, ricocheting off Shiro's body and the wall of the shower. Shiro grimaced as she pulled the fabric off the fresh wound. She dropped the shirt into the bottom of the tub and then reached for Shiro's pants.

Shiro looked down as Mindy undid the button on his pants and unzipped his zipper. She slowly pulled his pants off his right leg, followed by his left.

"You know, some guys really like me to undress them. And to tell you the truth, I kind of enjoy it. It's better than just showing up and climbing on board."

Shiro tried to smile. Seconds later he was naked, warm water running through his hair and down his body.

"Let the water wash out that wound. As much as you can take."

Mindy stared at Shiro's body as the water ran over his skin, his taught muscles wrapped in elaborate tattoos, both accentuated by the water. Her eyes paused on the brilliant colors of the carp on his left side and the dragon on his right.

Shiro stood with his hand on the soap dish, watching through the cascading water as Mindy investigated his body.

"Are you all right to stand there for a minute? I need to run to my room and get a few things?" She asked.

"Go."

*

Shiro could hear Mindy through the bathroom wall, cabinets opening and shutting. Then she appeared back at the bathroom door with a stack of towels, a bottle of bleach, a handful of trash bags, a bag of sugar, and a box of maxi pads.

Shiro looked at his neighbor and her accouterments.

She shrugged her shoulders. "I've been living next door for four months. I keep a few things around."

Shiro nodded.

"How are you holding up?"

"Better," Shiro responded. "But you shouldn't get involved with this."

"Too late," Mindy said. She reached down and grabbed Shiro's wet clothes from the bottom of the tub, wrung them out, and placed them in one of the trash bags.

"Now, let's see that injury," Mindy said.

Shiro turned and Mindy tried to assess the wound. "Tell me what happened."

"Gunshot."

Mindy paused her inspection.

"Shot?"

"Yes."

"By who?"

"I don't know and I wouldn't say if I did."

"If you were shot, you need to call the police."

"No police. No ambulance. No hospital."

Mindy cocked her head to the side. "You're putting me in a tough spot, Taro."

"No, you are. I didn't ask you to help me."

Mindy's head drooped as if considering her options. When she looked up she asked, "Tell me, was anyone else shot tonight?"

Shiro understood the question Mindy didn't want to directly ask. "No. I've never fired a gun in my life."

"What about a knife? Did anyone get stabbed tonight?"

"Not by me."

Mindy paused for another long moment. "If we're not going to the hospital, then you're going to have to put up with a home repair job on that shoulder."

"Do your best. It doesn't have to be perfect. I'm not sticking around. My trip to Tupelo is over. I'm leaving."

"Of course you are. I mean, you were only here for the festival, after all, right?" Mindy replied with sarcasm.

"That's right."

Mindy focused on the wound. "I really have no idea what I'm looking at here. There's definitely a hole. The bullet could still be in there. Doesn't look like there's an exit wound. But I can't really tell if the skin was just ripped off and the bullet kept going. But I do know your tattoo is going to need a repair job."

Mindy pressed gently next to the wound and blood oozed out. A stream of burgundy ran across the bottom of the tub and disappeared down the drain.

"For someone who was shot, you're not bleeding as much as I thought you would. Now let's dry you off and see if we can get it to stop completely."

*

Mindy towel-dried Shiro as he stood in the bathtub. Finished, she looped the towel around his waist.

"Hold that," she said, grabbing Shiro's free hand and placing it on the seam in the towel where the two ends met.

She reached over and picked up the pound bag of sugar she kept in her kitchenette.

"I saw this in a movie once," she said.

"So have I."

"It may hurt. I don't know."

"Just put it on."

Mindy placed her hand against Shiro's skin under the wound and poured sugar from the bag into her palm. She pushed the pile of sugar into the wound and waited for a reaction from Shiro that never materialized. She shoved another handful against the skin, the excess sugar granules falling into the tub.

"Don't move," she said.

She reached down, stuck her hand into a flower-covered box on the floor, and pulled out several maxi pads. She set them against the wound and then told Shiro to hold them in place.

Shiro dropped the towel around his waist and moved his hand.

Mindy picked up the towel and placed it on the closed toilet. "To the bed," she said, watching as Shiro stepped from the tub and walked past, completely naked.

*

Shiro was half-dressed, sitting up in bed, his back and head on a stack of pillows leaning against the headboard.

"I'm going to clean this place up and then go to the store for proper bandages."

"Okay."

"Is there anything else you need?"

"No. You've done enough."

Shiro turned on the local news with the remote control, his eyes glued to the screen as Mindy cleaned the bathroom. By the time the weather report started, Mindy was preparing to leave with a trash bag in each hand. A heavy scent of bleach wafted from the bathroom and filled the room.

"Everything is spic-and-span in here. I have everything you were wearing in this bag," she said, lifting it up. "And everything I used to clean up in this one."

Shiro nodded.

"Anything else?"

"Can you take the shoes and the towel near the door?"

Without questioning, Mindy reached down and put the shoes and towel-turned-welcome-mat into one of the bags.

"That's all," Shiro replied. "I have cash in the top drawer. Take some for whatever you need."

Mindy opened the drawer and peeled off several hundred dollars.

"I'll be back in an hour or so. I'm going to find a place to throw these out and then stop by a drugstore."

"I'll be here," Shiro replied, his eyes reverting back to the TV.

*

Shiro sat on the bed, eyes closed, listening to the television. The pain in his shoulder was growing, the adrenaline that had numbed him in the heat of battle almost completely gone. He pulled the homemade bandages off the wound and examined the crimson stain on the absorbent side of the feminine pad.

Looking down at the pad in his left hand, Shiro cursed. He placed the maxi pad on the bedspread, bloody side up, and raised his left hand to eye level. He cursed again, punched his hand into the mattress, and then stared back at the missing half of his left pinkie.

*

Shiro's door opened and a dripping green poncho filled the entrance. Sheets of rain cascaded off the roof of the motel, forming a waterfall just beyond the edge of the balcony. Mindy shut the door as thunder boomed across the night sky.

"It's really pouring out there," she said, removing the hood of her poncho to reveal shoulder-length, jet-black hair. Dark sunglasses covered her eyes.

"A disguise?"

"Seemed like a good idea. And I drove to Booneville for what we needed. Sorry it took longer than I expected. It is really raining."

"Did you get rid of everything?"

"I did. I put them in separate Dumpsters. One in Saltillo. One in Booneville." Mindy removed the poncho and sunglasses and left them on the floor near the door.

"We may have a problem," Shiro said, holding his hand up.

Mindy stepped forward for a closer look. "You lost a finger?"

"I did. It wasn't real, but I may need it. Any chance you saw it when you were cleaning up?"

Mindy shook her head. "I didn't even know you had a fake finger."

"That was the idea."

"Why do you need it?"

"When I came into the country, they scanned my fingerprints. At the time I had ten fingers. I assume they're going to match the scan when I leave."

"Oh," Mindy replied. "Maybe they won't."

"The United States pays attention to Japanese men with missing fingers, or partial fingers."

Mindy's eyes opened. "Like in the movie *Black Rain*?"

"I don't know that movie."

"Oh, you should definitely see it some time."

Shiro just stared at his hand.

"So, what are you going to do?" she asked.

"Tonight, I'm going to sleep. Tomorrow, I'll think of something."

Mindy dug through the plastic shopping bag and pulled out several drugstore boxes and a bottle of peroxide. "Before you go to bed, let's put a proper bandage on that wound."

Shiro grunted, his mind on his missing prosthetic.

Mindy cleaned his wound with peroxide then wrapped it with a combination of gauze and medical tape.

"I also picked up some superglue. If it's still bleeding in the morning, I can try gluing it."

"Did you see that in a movie, too?"

"That's right."

Shiro checked out the bandages covering his wound. Then he asked, "Why did you help me?"

She shrugged her shoulders. "Why did you help me earlier this week with my client who got out of hand?"

"I'm not sure it's the same thing."

"It is where I come from."

Shiro nodded, reflecting on the code by which he lived his life.

"Besides, if you don't tell me anything, I'm not doing anything wrong," Mindy justified.

"Once I'm gone, you can tell anybody anything you want."

"I'll cross that bridge when I get to it."

"Thank you for your help," Shiro said, bowing his head.

Mindy leaned in, kissed him on the cheek, and then stood. "I have antibiotics in my room. I had a urinary tract infection a while ago but I only used half a bottle. I know you're supposed to finish all the medication, but no one does. Medicine is just way too expensive these days. And if you're not going to see a doctor, you should start taking them, just in case."

CHAPTER 40

SHERIFF BLAZER'S COUNTY-ISSUED Ford Explorer pulled to a halt in front of the Wade residence. He walked around to the back of the house and surveyed the crime scene. Police tape crisscrossed the yard, cordoning off the massive patio and fire pit. A second section of yellow tape wrapped around the trunks of several trees on the edge of the property. A team of officers under the tree canopy was collecting evidence in the morning shade.

Sheriff Blazer crossed the wet grass, approached the men near the trees, and stopped just short of the tape. One of the officers paused his search and nodded at the sheriff.

"What do we have?"

"Two dead. One here by the trees. The other on the patio."

"Cause of death?"

"It looks like blunt force trauma."

"For both?"

"Yes, sir. Of course, the ME has final say."

"I hear one of them is Pervis Wade."

"That's correct. The other here by the tree is Big Barry Lawson."

"Someone beat Big Barry to death?"

"Apparently."

"How in the hell did that happen? He goes six-four and two-seventy."

The officer nodded. "That's not even the crazy part. Big Barry had two guns on him. A .22 and a 9-millimeter. Both of them were short of full magazines. We found four casings on the ground near the body with the weapon. All from a .22 handgun."

"So the perpetrator could have been shot?"

"It's a possibility. We're looking for evidence to that effect. But a .22 handgun isn't going to blow a hole through anyone. Blood loss depends on whether or not it catches an artery. Also depends on clothing. May not bleed initially, or much at all. Makes it hard to get DNA. The rain last night didn't do us any favors in that regard, either. It looks like both men were killed outside prior to the rain. And it really came down last night. We have a fair bit of debris across the yard. Broken branches. Some runaway trash."

Sheriff Blazer turned his head for a panoramic view of the property as he contemplated what he'd just heard. "Get word to the emergency room to be on the lookout for a gunshot wound. A .22 might not blow a hole through someone, but they still may need medical treatment."

"Yes, sir."

"Is Detective Rafferty on site?" he asked.

"He's in the house."

"Keep me posted."

Sheriff Blazer strolled back towards the house and paused at the large circular patio. A faint bloodstain was visible between the chairs on the perimeter and the fire pit in the middle. Forensic evidence markers stood on several locations around the patio.

Detective Rafferty exited the back of the house as Sheriff Blazer stared at the patio, imagining what took place.

"Good morning, Sheriff," Detective Rafferty said, approaching.

"Good morning, Will. Have you been in the house long?"

"A half hour."

Sheriff Blazer looked around in all directions and then asked, "Any signs of it?"

"No. And the place isn't that big. The bedroom has a dresser and a bed. The living room has a couple of chairs and a small sofa. No bookcases. No office. I was going through the kitchen cabinets when you arrived."

"So nothing?"

"Nope. I was planning on hitting the attic next."

"It has to be here somewhere."

"Probably."

Sheriff Blazer pointed at the patio and then at the grove of trees. "What in God's name happened out there?"

"Looks like Pervis and two of his friends were out here drinking and target shooting."

"Help me with my math. Pervis and two friends make three. We only have two bodies."

"That's right. Herman Dyer was the third. I talked to him on the phone. He claims he was out here with both Pervis and Barry. Claims he left around ten. Went home and went to bed. Says when he left both of his friends were alive and well. He's heading downtown as we speak."

"Any reason not to believe him?"

"Not at this point. Herman, Pervis, and Barry have been friends for an awfully long time."

"I heard Barry had two guns on him, both of them had been fired."

"That's right. And it fits with what Herman Dyer said. He said it was standard drinking protocol to put targets down in the yard and take shots at it. Pervis even had a light rigged up down in the field."

"What were they shooting?"

"All kinds of stuff. There are bits of bottles and cans. An old frying pan is hanging from a metal cross, fifty yards out. There's half a mannequin, or what's left of it. Parts of an old red wagon. A scarecrow with more holes in it than Swiss cheese."

"I get the picture. Has anyone talked to any of the neighbors?"

"We did. There are five houses on the street past this one. The smallest lot on the street is forty acres. Four of the neighbors on the street have provided statements. None of them saw anything suspicious."

"Anyone hear anything?"

"They did. But they said it was normal. The closest neighbor says he heard several shots fired. He's a gun owner himself and seems a bit hard of hearing. He didn't seem to care about the noise. His driveway is more than a half-mile down the road. Probably another quarter mile to his house."

"No eyewitnesses?"

"Not at this time."

The sheriff looked back at the patio. "Big Barry was killed in the yard and Pervis was killed here on the patio, is that right?"

"Yep. A loaded gun was found on the patio. It's registered to Pervis. It had also been fired."

"Both Pervis and Barry had loaded guns and someone killed them?"

"That's right. And whoever beat Pervis did it with authority. Probably used a baseball bat or a lead pipe. We didn't find the weapon on the scene. Initial indications are that Pervis had over two dozen broken bones. His face was not recognizable."

"Sounds like a perpetrator with anger issues."

"It does."

"Where's our engineer friend, Edward Winston, this morning? Do we have a bead on him?"

"We had a patrol car drive over this morning. No one answered the door. His Toyota Camry was parked in the driveway."

"See if you can find out where he was last night."

Detective Rafferty nodded. "I'm on it."

Sheriff Blazer again looked around. "Do you have anything that can place our friend Edward at the crime scene here, if the opportunity presents itself?"

"I still have a box with some of his things we collected with the search warrant. I'm sure there's something that could be incriminating."

"Good. Maybe we can kill two birds with one stone."

"Understood. Anything else?"

"Search the house again."

CHAPTER 41

"HOW DO YOU feel?" Mindy asked, sitting on the foot of the bed. "I checked in on you last night and you were snoring away."

"Not great," Shiro answered, grunting as he sat up in bed.

"Let me take a look."

Mindy unwound the bandage she had put on the night before, peeling the gauze away like the layers of an onion. She reached the entry wound and touched it lightly. Coagulated blood stuck to the gauze and Shiro's shirt.

"What a mess," she whispered before raising her voice. "The wound looks better. Seems like most of the bleeding has stopped."

Shiro slowly got out of bed, ambled to the dresser, and examined the wound in the mirror.

Mindy stood and followed him. "We still don't know if the bullet is in there."

Shiro groaned. "I need to get dressed."

"Where do you think you're going?"

"I have to go and look for something."

Mindy shook her head. "Oh, no you're not."

"I have to."

"Just call and get another finger sent to you. Or let me go to a store and buy you one."

"It's not that easy."

Shiro returned his focus to his shoulder. "I'm not asking you to do anything else. You've done enough. I'll handle it."

"Don't treat me like I don't know what's going on. Give me a little credit."

Shiro turned towards Mindy. "What *do* you think this is about?"

"I think you got into a fight with someone and this time they had a gun and not a knife. You probably lost your finger somewhere along the way."

Shiro mumbled in Japanese.

"And if that's not right, I don't care. I don't really care what happened, other than you're injured."

Shiro tapped the bedspread with his good arm. "Sit down."

Mindy flopped her bottom onto the bed. Shiro grabbed the remote control, turned on the television, and stopped on a local channel. For ten minutes they sat in silence, suffering through the morning news. An entire segment was spent covering the plethora of downed trees from the previous night's storm and the associated flashfloods. A tornado reportedly touched down just outside Lee County.

"What are we waiting for, exactly?"

"You'll know it when you see it," Shiro replied. He went to the bathroom, and when he stepped out Mindy was staring at the television, mouth open. On the screen, news cameras were focused on a large backyard being pecked at by a team of uniformed officers. A wide-angle view showed a barricade erected in the middle of the street. Yellow police tape cordoned off sections of the property. The camera switched from the crime scene to a young reporter in a new suit who cobbled together the story based on the limited available information.

Mindy slowly turned towards Shiro, who stood completely still, emotionless.

"Was that you?"

Shiro never took his attention off the TV.

"Holy shit," Mindy said, standing from the bed as if the surface of the mattress had suddenly become hot.

Shiro grabbed the remote from the bed and turned off the TV.

"Did you know those two men?"

"No."

"Then why?"

"Because I was asked to."

"You can't just go around killing people."

"My job doesn't let me make that decision."

"You mean you were ordered to do this?"

Shiro nodded. "I was offered a way out of my life. This is what I was asked to do."

"Which was it?"

"I don't understand your question."

"You said you were ordered to do it *and* you said you were offered a way out of your current life. Were you ordered, or did you volunteer?"

"In my world, there's no difference."

A tear ran down Mindy's face and hung on the curve of her jaw.

"What did they do? What did those two men do?"

"One of them killed a man's wife. That man knew my boss. My boss sent me."

"You make it sound simple."

"It is."

"What about the other man? Two are dead."

"The other man was unlucky."

Another tear ran down Mindy's cheek, following the wet trail of the first. She paced back and forth, her lips quivering. She stopped pacing in front of Shiro. "And now you're free to choose a different life?"

"If I can get back to Japan."

"Then I'll help you get back. There's no sense in both of us being stuck in our current lives forever."

Shiro dipped his head and then he raised his hand with nine-and-a-half digits. "And now you understand why I have to go look for something."

"I understand why, but you can't. The police here in the US, even in small towns like Tupelo, keep an eye on people who show up at crime scenes. For whatever reason, coming back to the scene of the crime is something a lot of criminals do. It's one of the easiest ways for the police to identify potential suspects. So whatever happened last night, you can't go back."

"How do you know this?"

"I watch a lot of movies."

"I have to go."

"You can't. But I can."

"Why you?" Shiro asked.

"Because just about anybody in this town could be a client of mine."

Shiro didn't respond and Mindy ended the conversation. "But neither of us is going to go looking for anything today. Today we let things cool down. Tomorrow, I'll give it a drive by in the morning."

CHAPTER 42

FOR THE FIFTH time in an hour, Edward listened to his mobile phone vibrate on the small table in front of the sofa. Unlike his response to the previous calls, Edward stood from his bed and took three steps towards the large window. He answered the phone as he opened the curtains, the sun pouring into the room.

"This is Edward," he said, in a raspy morning voice.

"This is Agent Washington. I've been trying to reach you."

"You're not the only one."

"Where are you?"

"Why? What's going on?"

"Pervis Wade was killed last night."

Edward felt a pang of nerves wash over him and he flopped down onto the small sofa. "You're kidding."

"The Lee County sheriff personally called me and asked if I could contact you out of professional courtesy. He says they've been trying to reach you but haven't had any luck."

"Then I guess I'm the only one feeling lucky."

"What's that supposed to mean?"

"The guy who killed my wife is dead. Some people would call that good fortune."

"Be careful what you say, Edward. Be very careful."

Edward looked out the window at the boats on the water in the distance.

"So the Lee County Sheriff's Department has you doing their dirty work now? I didn't see that coming."

"If you weren't ducking them, I wouldn't be calling."

"I wasn't ducking anyone. I was sleeping."

"Then consider this your wake up call. In more ways than one. I don't need to tell you who the Lee County Sheriff's Department is going to consider as their prime suspect."

"There's no evidence I had anything to do with Pervis Wade's murder. None whatsoever."

"I hope not."

"Of course, evidence doesn't seem to stop the good old boys from Lee County. But I think the amount of evidence they would need to fabricate to frame me for Pervis Wade's murder just isn't possible. Not even for them."

"At any point, feel free to tell me you didn't do it. You haven't said that yet. You've told me there is no evidence. Twice."

"I didn't do it."

"I think it's time you and I had another face-to-face. I can be in Tupelo by lunch."

"I'm not in Tupelo."

"Where are you?"

"Biloxi."

Agent Washington cursed under her breath. "What are you doing in Biloxi?"

"Looking out the window at the Gulf of Mexico from my suite at the Beau Rivage Resort and Casino."

"Stay put. I'll be there in a few hours."

*

Edward turned on the TV and flipped through the news channels before realizing the three hundred miles of red clay between Biloxi and Tupelo meant local news remained local. Edward opened his laptop, hopped on the WiFi, and typed in the URL for the *Daily Journal*, Tupelo's online newspaper.

The right side of the *Daily Journal's* homepage hosted the breaking news column. Edward quickly scanned the screen beneath a flashing banner advertisement. Halfway down the page a mug shot photo of Pervis Wade stared back at him. Edward rushed through the story, his eyes devouring every word as fast as he could read them. Finished, Edward scrolled up to stare at the photos of Pervis Wade and a man named Barry Lawson.

"Goddammit," he said, shutting his laptop.

*

Edward watched from the lobby as Agent Washington parked her government-issued sedan in front of the main door and waved off the valet with a flash of her badge.

Edward stood from one of the wing-back chairs in the middle of the marble-floored lobby and raised his hand. Agent Washington nodded, slipped her sunglasses onto the top of her head, and walked over. The two shook hands in the bustling lobby as a busload of senior citizens with heavy wallets trekked their way to the front desk from the parking lot.

"Let's go somewhere we can speak more privately," Agent Washington said.

"Out back," Edward replied. "There's a quiet garden with seats."

Edward led Agent Washington across the marble floor and through a set of double doors at the rear of the lobby. He took a left at the bar near the pool and followed a short walkway past an unoccupied shuffleboard court. Edward motioned to several tables and chairs under an elaborate white pergola. Agent Washington sat across from him and placed her keys and phone on the table. Edward could see the butt of Agent Washington's pistol resting in its holster near her armpit.

"Did you get a chance to check the news?"

"I did."

"Did you get in touch with the Lee County Sheriff's Department?"

"I returned their calls. They want to talk to me face-to-face as soon as I get back into town."

"I'm sure they do." Agent Washington stared stoically at Edward until he squirmed in his seat.

"Why are you looking at me like that?"

"How did you do it, Edward?"

"Do what?"

"Kill Pervis Wade."

"I don't know what you're talking about. I'm as shocked as anyone."

"Are you?"

"I am."

"We'll see about that. How long have you been in Biloxi?"

"Three days."

"That's very fortuitous timing. The Lee County Sheriff's Department estimates the murders occurred sometime between ten and twelve last night. The bodies weren't found until this morning."

"I saw some photos and video on the *Daily Journal*. I assume that's where Pervis lived."

"You tell me. Is that where he lived?"

"I don't know. He never invited me over for dinner. Not even after killing my wife and unborn child. Some people have no manners at all."

Agent Washington flashed a look of incredulity. "This is not a joke. Two men were killed last night. Both were beaten to death."

Edward stifled a second wave of nerves. "Beaten to death? Two men? Certainly no one is going to believe I was physically capable of that."

"Crime scene investigators are looking into it."

"What would you like to hear, Agent Washington? That I'm sorry? Because I'm not."

"What about the second man who was murdered?"

"Who was he?"

"Pervis Wade's friend. A man named Barry Lawson."

"Was he married?"

Agent Washington cocked her head to the side. "Why? Does that matter?"

"Just curious. Doesn't matter to me. But as a husband who lost his wife, I can empathize with the death of someone's spouse."

"Can you?"

"Of course."

"You know, a trip to Biloxi isn't going to keep you from being investigated as the prime suspect in this thing. The Lee County Sheriff's Department is going to prove you could have driven back to Tupelo, committed the murders, and then returned to Biloxi. It's only a four-and-a-half-hour drive. And that's going the speed limit. You can make it in under four, if you push it."

"That sounds good in theory, but it's going to be very, very difficult to prove."

Agent Washington seemed to notice the increased bravado in Edward's demeanor.

"For starters, my car is in Tupelo," Edward continued. "That kind of throws a wrench in anyone's plan to prove I drove to Tupelo and back. I mean, I could have rented a car, I guess, but there would be a paper trail. I could have even hitchhiked, really. I mean, it's possible."

"Your car is in Tupelo? How did you get here?"

"Greyhound."

The jaw muscles in Agent Washington's face tightened. "You took a Greyhound bus?"

"I did. I have the ticket receipt if you need to see it. And let me tell you something about Greyhound. There's no direct route between Tupelo and Biloxi. I had to go through Birmingham. As in Birmingham, Alabama. It wasn't a short trip. Over eight hours."

Agent Washington gritted her teeth. "Tell me, Edward, why would someone like yourself take a Greyhound Bus from Tupelo to Biloxi?"

"Why not?"

"A lot of reasons. Most Greyhound patrons are either senior citizens, students, destitute, or criminals."

"That sounds like stereotyping."

"I'm not playing with you. I've warned you once this is not a joke."

"That's right. It's not. If you want an explanation as to why I'm in Biloxi without a car, I have one. I'm ashamed to admit it, but I've been drinking a little more than I should as of late. For reasons most people would probably understand. I decided to come to a resort and I wanted a professional to handle all the driving duties. And you know what? It's been nice here without worrying about a car. Did you know they have free public transportation in town called the Casino Hopper? It takes you up and down the drag to any of the casinos. Miles of nice beaches. Gambling and drinking all hours of the night."

"Fine, you want to practice your alibi? Let's do it. Where were you last night between ten and twelve?"

"In the casino, at the Pai Gow Poker table."

"Pai Gow Poker?"

"Yes."

"Never heard of it."

"It's a split-hand game popular in Asia. In order to win, you have to win both sides of your hand against the dealer. There are a lot of pushes, meaning no one wins. You can play for a long time without losing much money. Of course, you don't win much money either. But all the drinks are free while you play."

"You came eight hours by Greyhound to lose money gambling so you could drink for free?"

"I'm actually up two hundred dollars. Anyhow, the evening Pai Gow dealer is a guy named Sean. He splits time with another dealer named Hernan. Last night between ten and twelve, Sean was dealing cards at the Pai Gow poker table and I was sitting directly across from him. I've been down there for a few hours every night since I arrived."

"What time did you leave the Pai Gow table?"

"I cashed in my chips around 12:30 or so. Then I had a couple drinks in the bar. The bartender is a blonde named Janet. I've gotten to know her well. I went to bed at around 2:30. I was in my room all night. Until you called."

"Why do I get the feeling that no matter the time of day I inquire about, you're going to have an airtight alibi?"

"I never said 'alibi,' you did. It's not my fault the casinos have an interest in providing a secure environment for their business and their patrons. You can't blame me for the security cameras that cover the entire casino and every floor of the hotel."

"No, I couldn't blame you for that."

"And you can't blame me for the security key pass to my room that logs every entry and exit."

"I assume you had room service as well."

"A couple of times. Not to mention golf. Do you want to hear about the Sheltons? John and Gerry. They're a nice couple from Beaufort, South Carolina, who like to vacation in Biloxi. They own a bed and breakfast back in South Carolina that their daughter runs most of the time. I played golf with them yesterday and the day before that."

"Enough, Edward."

"I've been in Biloxi, Mississippi, for the last three nights. I've had a nice room at the Beau Rivage Resort and Casino. I've been gambling, playing golf, and drinking. I would say my vacation time can be accounted for by numerous hotel staff and other guests. I've tried to tip well."

"Are you finished?"

"Do I need to continue?"

"No matter what you say, I'm not buying your story. I don't believe it was a coincidence that you happened to be here when the man you believe is responsible for your wife's death was savagely murdered."

"Life is fragile. No one knows the hour or minute of their death."

"And now we're quoting scripture?"

"They say it can help people to get through the tough times."

Agent Washington stared at Edward, who didn't blink or look away.

"Just so we are clear about where we stand, if I find out you had anything to do with Pervis Wade's demise, I will do everything required of me by law to assist in putting you behind bars for the rest of your life."

"I understand. As a special agent working Color of Law investigations, I would expect nothing less."

"I'm warning you, Mr. Winston, don't screw with me. Murder is serious business with serious consequences."

"There's no evidence to prove I was involved in Pervis Wade's death in any way. Search my house. Search my cars. Search my computers. Subpoena my phone records. I was here. He was killed there. Period."

"You can bet they'll leave no stone unturned."

"Won't matter," Edward said. "Do you remember what you told me in the parking lot of the gun shop in Tupelo?"

"I told you that shooting Pervis Wade would be a waste of a good life. Yours."

"Actually, you said I was too smart to walk up to Pervis Wade and shoot him with a gun I had purchased in my own name."

"I recall."

"Well, you were right."

CHAPTER 43

THE CAB DROPPED Edward off at his house and thirty minutes later Sheriff Blazer's Ford Explorer pulled into the driveway. Edward heard the doors to the large vehicle shut and he peeked out the front window as Sheriff Blazer and Detective Rafferty started up the short walkway. Edward met them at the front door and welcomed the two men into his living room.

"Excuse the mess," Edward offered, observing the two officers as their eyes pried into the nooks and crannies of his home.

"I certainly never thought the sheriff of Lee County would be standing in my living room," Edward said, breaking the silence.

"Mr. Winston, we can do without the theatrics. You're the one who suggested we meet here," the sheriff answered. He was in full uniform, shirt pressed, badge shined, gray hair combed.

"Indeed I did. You can understand my apprehension about coming down to the station, under the circumstances. Given our history."

"Actually, I don't understand, but in the interest of solving a murder, I agreed to come out here. Detective Rafferty didn't think it was a good idea."

"I guess that makes you the good cop."

"I would prefer to say I'm pragmatic."

Edward smiled. "Sure. Sure. Please have a seat."

Sheriff Blazer and Detective Rafferty sat on the sofa.

"If it's okay with the Lee County Sheriff's Department, I would like to record this discussion. So as to eliminate any potential misunderstandings. I don't want a repeat of the confusion we had over the search warrant for the trucks at Palmetto Windows. I assume that's agreeable to everyone," Edward said.

"I don't think that's really necessary," Detective Rafferty replied.

"And I can appreciate that position. But if you want to speak with me, we can either record the conversation, or you can have me come down to the station with my lawyer and you can listen to me say nothing."

Sheriff Blazer nodded at the phone in Edward's hand. "Go ahead."

Edward pressed the icon to start recording and placed his phone on the table.

"Good evening Sheriff Blazer and Detective Rafferty," Edward said, leaning down towards the phone. "Welcome to my home."

Detective Rafferty rolled his eyes.

"I see you're in the process of moving," Sheriff Blazer said.

Edward joined the officers in another glance around the room. Boxes were stacked along every available wall. Each box had a piece of paper attached to it, listing the contents of each container.

"I'm moving. I've already accepted an offer on the house. Closing is next week. Almost everything has been boxed. I have a few clothes still in the dresser and a set of dishes in the kitchen. Other than that, I'm ready to go."

Detective Rafferty pointed to Edward's gun on the small table on the far end of the sofa. "I wouldn't have taken you as a gun owner."

"I guess you can't judge a book by its cover."

"Is it loaded?"

"It is."

"In the future, it's probably a good idea to let law enforcement know there's a loaded gun in the room when they enter," Sheriff Blazer interjected. "Good thing we're just here for a courtesy visit."

"I'm glad to hear this is just a courtesy call," Edward replied. "I assume you've had time to read over my itinerary for my recent trip to Biloxi? I sent it via email earlier today after speaking with you on the phone. I have an extra copy around here if you need it."

"We read it," Sheriff Blazer answered, peppering his response with sarcasm. "And let me compliment you on the most detailed recollection of an itinerary I have ever seen in my professional career."

"I have a good memory."

"Apparently."

"Do you have any additional questions concerning my whereabouts for the last several days? Anything that my itinerary doesn't adequately answer?"

"Just one" Detective Rafferty asked.

"Shoot."

"When did you decide to go to Biloxi? We checked with the Resort and Casino and they indicated you didn't have a reservation in advance. Ditto for your Greyhound ticket."

"It was spur of the moment."

"Is that usual for you? No offense, but you seem more like the planning type." Detective Rafferty motioned towards the boxes with an upturned palm as if offering evidence to prove his point.

"I'm sure you don't know me well enough to determine what kind of vacationer I am. My trip to Biloxi was spur of the moment, but I had been thinking about it. I'm on a leave of absence from work. I have the time."

"Yes. You have the time. Enough time to have planned things out very carefully, if that's what you wanted to do," Detective Rafferty said.

"Is that a question? I didn't hear a question in there."

"No, it was an observation."

"I see," Edward replied.

"Let me cut to the chase, Mr. Winston," the sheriff said.

"Please."

"The Lee County Sheriff's Department believes you were somehow involved in the murders of Pervis Wade and Barry Lawson."

"Even though I was in Biloxi at the time of the murders, with multiple alibis?"

"That's correct."

Edward looked down at his phone on the table. "Well, I'm sure glad I got that on record. Just so everyone knows where we stand."

"It's the responsibility of the Lee County Sheriff's Department to investigate all crimes to the best of our capability and to the fullest extent of the law."

"I think I've heard that before on a TV drama."

"We will be vetting every alibi you provided. We guarantee a thorough investigation."

"I hope you do a better job for Pervis than you did for my wife."

Sheriff Blazer nodded and stood up without warning. Detective Rafferty followed suit.

"Thank you for your time, Mr. Winston," the sheriff said.

Detective Rafferty pointed at the gun on the small side table. "You should practice proper gun safety. Keep it under lock and key. Avoid accidents."

"I would if I had a wife or kids. But seeing how I don't have either, I think my safety is best served by a loaded firearm."

Detective Rafferty scowled and followed Sheriff Blazer out of the house.

*

"Our engineer friend has grown some balls," the sheriff said, backing the car out of the driveway.

"And a mouth to go with them," Detective Rafferty retorted.

"What do you think?"

"Let's have another detective go down to Biloxi in person. See if we can find anyone soft on his alibi. See if there are loose boards there that can be pried up with the appropriate leverage. Run background checks on those corroborating his alibi."

"I'll have someone start poking around first thing in the morning."

"Good."

"Anything else?"

"Go back and take one last look through Pervis's house."

"There's nothing there."

"Take one more look. Then burn it to the ground. Make it look like an accident."

"Roger that."

The sheriff and detective rode in silence for a moment before the sheriff spoke again.

"You know what really bothers me?"

"I'm afraid to ask."

"Let's assume for a second this guy somehow actually murdered two people."

"Okay."

"Well, if that's true, why do we think he's going to stop there?"

CHAPTER 44

WITH THE RISING sun burning off the morning fog, Detective Rafferty exited through the front door of Pervis Wade's house empty-handed. He positioned the evidence seal on the doorframe and pressed the adhesive backing against the door.

He stepped off the front porch and removed his phone from his pocket. He listened to a trio of rings before Sheriff Blazer answered.

"Sheriff."

"Will."

"I'm out at Pervis Wade's. I just finished my third run through the house. There's nothing there."

"Well, that's not good."

"No, it's not. You still want me to follow through on the thing we discussed?"

"Yeah, but let the media clear out first. Give it another day."

"Roger that."

"Is the police tape still up out back?"

"No, it came down this morning. We ran through the whole scene multiple times with forensics. We got whatever was here to get."

"Let the circus begin."

"Oh, it has. Nothing like a double murder to bring them out. There's been a steady stream of onlookers—gawkers, neighbors, mourners, prayer groups. They've started a memorial in the backyard. Someone pounded a big cross into the ground. The flowers and signs are piling up."

"I'll send another car out there."

"That might help."

"Do we have anyone taking pictures of the crowd?"

"No. But we had someone taking photos all day yesterday."

"When are you coming back to the station? Forensics says there's a ton of evidence to go through."

"I'm going to take one last look around back and be on my way."

Five minutes later, Rafferty crossed the front yard to his unmarked car parked on the dirt road that ran along Pervis Wade's property. Flecks of red clay covered the side of the vehicle, as if the car had contracted measles. A white news van passed the detective and pulled over. A reporter and a cameraman stepped from the vehicle, preparing to film where two men had been slain thirty-six hours before.

A mile down the road, Rafferty came to a halt at the stop sign where the dirt and gravel met asphalt. As his tires gained traction, an old Civic approached from the opposite direction, braking to make the turn onto the dirt road. As the two cars passed each other, Rafferty stared into the other vehicle, catching a glimpse of the blonde behind the wheel. A half minute later, with the turnoff to the dirt road fading in the rearview mirror, the detective's memory served up the name of the woman he had just seen.

"Mindy the hooker," he said to himself out loud. "Now, all the freaks are out."

*

Mindy parked her old Civic in front of the small news van convoy. A mass of people milled about the property. Mindy's head bounced as she counted the people gathered in the yard and on the road. Her head stopped bobbing when she reached twenty-nine.

She got out of her car with a small bouquet of flowers in hand, and waved off a reporter who approached microphone first, cameraman in tow. She crossed the road, following two middle-aged men as they traversed the trampled grass at the bottom of the drainage gully on the edge of the property. With her flower bouquet resting in her arm like a baby, Mindy walked across the uncut grass with her eyes down. She added her flowers to the towering pile near the grove of trees and headed towards the patio, eyes scanning the ground as she walked. She stopped at the threshold of the patio and listened to the men next to her describe the crime scene as if they had witnessed it firsthand. Her eyes surveyed the large circular patio and one thing became clear. Whatever evidence Shiro may have left on the scene, it had been wiped clean by either Mother Nature or the sheriff's department.

Mindy took a second, deliberate lap around the yard and then slowly headed back to her car. A group from the Tupelo Bible Church, wearing matching T-shirts, poured from an extended van with the church's name printed down the side. Stepping up the far side of the drainage swale, Mindy lost her footing. A man stuck out his hand for the damsel in distress.

"Thanks,"

"Looks slippery," Edward said.

Mindy stepped onto the road, paused, and turned around.

"Hey, I know you," she said to Edward's backside as he headed into the gully.

Edward reached the far side of the ditch and looked back at the blonde he had just helped. "I get that a lot. I've been on the news."

Mindy and Edward locked gazes.

"No. You're the guy who spoke Japanese the other day downtown," Mindy said, beating him to the punch of recognition. "You gave a friend of mine a ride. A guy named Taro."

Mindy watched as Edward's complexion turned ashen.

"I think you've got the wrong guy," he replied, his voice shaking.

"I don't. I'm really good with faces. It's part of my job."

"Sorry, but you're mistaken," Edward repeated, ending the conversation by turning and walking in the direction of the back of the house.

*

Mindy returned to her car and watched from the driver's seat as Edward stood at the precipice of the patio, staring at the house and the large fire pit. He spent another ten minutes near the trees and the memorial, and then came back down the gentle slope towards the road.

Mindy stepped from her car and met him as he stepped back onto the road. The pair was immediately approached by a new tandem of reporters and Edward looked down and away. Mindy followed him up the street until the string of news vans was behind them.

"I hate to keep bothering you, but I'm absolutely sure I saw you the other day. You drive a burgundy Toyota Camry."

Edward pointed to his car parked twenty paces ahead. "Not much of a mystery there. That's the car I came in. And that's the car I'm going home in."

Edward kept his feet in motion as Mindy hustled to keep up.

"Wait," Mindy pleaded.

"I have to go," he said, picking up his pace.

"Why did you come out here?"

"The same reason everyone else did. Curiosity," he answered over his shoulder.

"What if I told you that's *not* why *I* came out here?"

"I'd say good for you."

Edward reached his car and opened the door. Mindy grabbed the top of the doorframe with both hands.

"Let go of the door."

"Let me ask one question. Then you can go."

"One question," Edward relented.

"Did your wife die recently?"

Edward's eyes squinted with disdain. "You used your one question."

"Please don't go. I need your help. And your friend needs your help," Mindy blurted.

"Who?"

"The Japanese guy you gave a ride to the other day. The day the Tupelo Tour Trolley crashed."

"I don't know what you're talking about."

"Sure you do."

"I have to go. Please take your hands off my door. I don't want to make a scene."

"Go ahead. Make a scene," she said, challenging him.

Edward glared and Mindy released her hands. Without a word he slipped into the front seat of his car.

"If you care, his name is Taro," Mindy said. "And he needs help. He's been shot. And if that doesn't concern you, then you should know he may have left something behind somewhere out there," Mindy added, cranking her neck to gaze out across Pervis's backyard.

Edward shut his eyes and gently shook his head in disbelief. "I can't help you, I'm sorry."

"My name's Mindy. I'm staying at the Gum Tree Inn. Number 201. Just in case you change your mind. Taro and I will be there tonight. I'm not sure about tomorrow."

"I hope things work out," Edward said, shutting the door.

Mindy watched as Edward drove away. Crying, she walked down the road, away from the house. A hundred yards from the crime scene, she searched the muddy patch of earth strewn with beer cans, clothes, and a lone condom wrapper. Ten minutes later she was back in her car.

*

Edward paced through his house like a caged animal, watching the local news on the TV and checking the Internet. At six in the evening, a single update on the double murder in West Tupelo came across the screen. With rapt attention, Edward listened to a reporter in a bow tie provide neither a motive nor a suspect in the slayings.

Just before 9:00 p.m., Edward lost the battle to the demons in his head. Sweating, hands shaking with nerves, he intentionally left his cell phone on the table, grabbed his car keys, and exited the house, stepping into the darkness.

CHAPTER 45

THE DRIVE TO the Gum Tree Inn was the most paranoid twenty-five minutes of Edward's life. Nerves rattling, he parked his car on the street near the inn's entrance and watched the flow of the property from a distance. A No Vacancy sign illuminated the wall near the manager's office. The blue hue of a TV shown through a wide-open curtain in a guest room on the first floor.

With trepidation, Edward exited his car and casually walked down the short drive to the motel parking lot. He could hear people talking somewhere outside, unable to pinpoint the exact location of the voices. He passed the manager's office, checked the number on the first room on his right, and quickly assumed room 201 was on the second floor.

He disappeared up the stairs behind an old Coke machine and traversed the second-floor balcony. Several slightly open doors offered glimpses into the lives of the tenants in a one-star Southern motel. At the end of the building, Edward knocked on room 201. No one answered and he knocked a second time, confirming the room number while standing in a swarm of bugs under the light.

He heard the knob on the door to his right rattle. Mindy pushed the screen door open and stepped outside.

"Hi," Edward managed to say.

"I didn't think you were coming."

"Neither did I. And apparently I just knocked on the wrong door."

"No, that's my room. This one is Taro's," Mindy said, looking back towards the room from which she had just appeared.

"How is he?"

"Come inside and see for yourself."

"I don't think he's going to be happy that I'm here."

"Why?"

"Because I'm not happy I'm here."

"From what I can figure, if he wants to get home, he's going to need help."

Mindy reached for the knob on the screen door and Edward gently grabbed her arm. "How did you get involved in all of this?"

"It just happened."

"And what do you think 'all of this' is?"

Mindy paused. "A very bad idea that went downhill from there."

Edward didn't have a reply.

"I helped him because I was returning a favor," Mindy added, entering the room.

Edward nervously looked over his shoulder before following Mindy inside. Taro was sitting in bed, a bandage wrapped around his shoulder. His torso was bare, and Edward took in the display of tattoos he had assumed were there when he had met Shiro in the emergency room the week before.

Shiro opened his eyes, looked at Edward, and scowled.

And then something occurred that had never happened in the annals of the Gum Tree Inn, or any other Southern dive motel.

"What the hell are you doing here?" Shiro said in Japanese.

"She said you needed help," Edward responded in English.

"No English. You and I speak Japanese," Shiro said. "You understand? Japanese only."

"Got it," Edward responded. "You're injured. What happened?"

"I was shot."

"Is it serious?"

"I don't know. I've never been shot before. Guns are rare in Japan. And if someone gets shot in my profession, they usually die."

There was a pause in the banter and Mindy interjected. "I don't know what the hell the two of you are talking about, but this is the most interesting conversation I've ever witnessed."

Edward ignored her. "The news says two men were killed."

"That's right."

"I only wanted one."

"Plans changed."

"Why?"

"Because they had to change. The time was right and the guy you wanted dead wasn't alone."

"Then the time wasn't right."

"Rain was in the forecast. The guys had been drinking. No one was around. It was my best opportunity. I'm not in town forever. I have a timeline. I need to leave. For several reasons."

"What happened exactly?

Shiro explained in detail what occurred at Pervis Wade's and finished by sucking air back through his clenched teeth in a mix of pain and conundrum. "Give me a cigarette," Shiro asked in English, pointing at his pack on the dresser. Mindy brought the smokes and a lighter to Shiro.

"Jesus. What a mess," Edward whispered in disbelief. "You need to get out of here. You can't hang out in Tupelo. If you stay, the police will eventually figure it out. You need to leave."

"My plan was to leave. But I ran into a problem," Shiro said, slowly raising his hand. "I lost my finger. It's a prosthetic. But I might need it. They scanned my fingerprints at the airport when I entered the country. They're going to scan them again when I leave. Not having a finger will raise a flag. It's all biometric."

"Where did you lose it?"

"I assume I lost it at the house. In the yard. Near the fire on the patio. Somewhere."

"When did you notice?"

"When I was back here. I checked the car, it wasn't there."

"You have a car?"

"A rental. Fake name."

"Where's your car?"

"Downstairs in the parking lot."

"Downstairs? You were injured. Did you bleed in the car?"

"It has a black interior. You can't see the blood unless you're looking carefully."

"Sounds like you're speaking from experience."

"I am. We may not have many guns in Japan, but we have a lot of knives. Knives make for a lot of blood."

"If the police find your car, I guarantee they'll look carefully enough to see the blood."

"It couldn't be helped. I couldn't walk home."

"What are you planning to do with the car?"

"Leave it."

"Here? I don't think that's a good idea."

A long list of possible outcomes to the current situation flashed through Edward's mind, none of which were good.

"What about the clothes you were wearing? Your shoes?"

"All gone. This room is clean. Mindy cleaned it."

"And now you're bleeding all over it."

"It's just my blood. There's nothing illegal about bleeding."

Edward ran his hands through his hair. "What was your plan for leaving town? You must have had a plan."

"I was to catch a flight from Memphis to LA. From LA to Tokyo."

"Can you fly with that shoulder?"

"Maybe. But if it starts bleeding, it could be a problem."

"I would say so."

Shiro touched his bandages. "Any ideas?"

"Yeah. Call your boss. Have him send someone to help you out."

"That's not possible."

"It may be the only way."

"I'd rather spend the rest of my life in jail. I was told I would be on my own. No matter what."

"Well, that might be okay with you, but that's not okay with me. If you end up in jail, I'm going to end up right next to you. You need to get out of town."

"I need to get out of the country."

"First we get you out of town, then we'll see what I can do about your finger and sending you home."

*

Edward created a plan on the fly as Mindy and Shiro chimed in. "It's almost ten now. Sunrise is just before six. I'm going to run out and get a few things for our road trip and then try to catch a few hours of sleep. I'll be back here at 5:30 a.m., sharp. I'll be driving my wife's car. It's a silver Honda Accord."

"Why are you switching cars?"

"It may give some people the impression that I'm still home. And if I need to get rid of it, people are less likely to give it a second thought. Anyhow, I'll be here at exactly 5:30 and I'll pull the car around to the bottom of the stairs. We load Shiro into the car, and I take off. In and out. Quiet. Before anyone is awake."

"Okay," Mindy replied.

"Got it?" Edward asked Shiro in Japanese.

"Yes," Shiro replied.

Edward turned to Mindy. "Once we're gone, you need to wipe down this room. Wipe down everything. Anywhere you think there could be fingerprints. The kitchenette. Glasses. Dishes. The toilet seat. The balcony rail. The doorknobs. Everything."

"Just like Jason Bourne," Mindy said.

"Better. Make Jason Bourne look sloppy by comparison."

"I'll wipe every square inch and every object. Then I'll use bleach. And I'll wipe down the rental car too."

"Good. And you said you know someone who can take care of the car, right?"

"I do. He's a customer. A long-time customer. He owns a tow truck company."

"Will he help you without asking too many questions?"

"He'll do anything I ask."

Edward's eyebrows jumped as he was struck with the first inclination as to what Mindy did for a living. "At the very least, see if he can tow the car somewhere else. It's a rental. Sooner or later the company will look for it. It probably has a GPS on it somewhere."

"Are you sure you can drive straight through to Los Angeles? It's a long way," Mindy asked.

"It's twenty-six hours from Tupelo. I don't sleep much anyway. A couple of Mountain Dews and I should be fine."

"And if not? What if you fall asleep behind the wheel and crash with a Japanese guy with a gunshot wound in your back seat?"

"Then we're screwed."

"I still think I should come with you."

"Absolutely not. You need to stay here and act normal. If you disappear, it would be suspicious. No one is going to miss a Japanese tourist who was in town for the festival."

Mindy nodded and looked over at Shiro in the bed.

"I'll be back in the morning. Five thirty. Be ready to go," Edward said, heading out the door.

CHAPTER 46

SHERIFF BLAZER CAME into the evidence room and his eyes scanned the two long tables covered in plastic sheets. Evidence bags stretched out to his right. Detective Rafferty stood with his back to the door, examining the bags, one by one.

"Did we bring back the whole farm?" the sheriff asked, approaching from behind.

Detective Rafferty turned around. "Almost."

"You said you had something to show me. And it better be good. I don't like spending my nights digging through evidence."

"I like it at night. No one's around."

"What do you have?" Sheriff Blazer asked.

Rafferty pointed to the far table. "I have something, but I'm not sure exactly what."

Rafferty stepped across the room and the sheriff followed him.

"Starting at the end of the table, we have three handguns and a ton of spent casings. Most of them, I assume, are from target practice. We have spent shells from all the weapons we collected at the scene, as well as from weapons not found at the location. We assume the other caliber casings are from shots fired prior to the night of the murders. All told, we collected over two hundred spent casings from seven different caliber weapons."

The sheriff nodded and pointed down at the bullet-riddled mannequin. "Is that what you wanted to show me?"

"No," Detective Rafferty replied.

He picked up the box of evidence gloves and offered them to the sheriff as if they were tissues. Detective Rafferty slipped his hand into an unsealed evidence bag and plucked out a chunk of flesh-colored rubber. He handed the object to the sheriff.

"What the hell is that?"

"It was found on the patio, near the fire pit. Looks like it was damaged from the heat."

"And what, exactly, do we think it is?"

"A finger. With a remnant of a nail on the back. As you can see, the front side, where the fingerprints would be, is melted and bubbled from the heat. The hole where the finger would slip on has also melted shut. You can tell by the detail on the nail that it probably looked pretty realistic before it was damaged."

"You don't think whoever killed Pervis Wade left behind a finger, do you?"

"I've never been that lucky in my life."

"Me either. Any chance it came off the mannequin?" the sheriff asked.

"I don't think so. They're made out of different material. Besides, the mannequin doesn't have any arms. No arms mean no wrists, no hands, no fingers."

"I get it. The anklebone is connected to the leg bone. Call around to the hospitals and see who makes fake fingers and who buys them. There can't be that many places in the finger business."

"I'll start asking."

"Speaking of hospitals, did we ever get a callback on any patients arriving with an unexplained gunshot wound?"

"The hospital called with a GSW yesterday. A guy in Plantersville who shot himself in the leg cleaning his weapon. He swears the gun was empty when it went off."

"Another immaculate self-shooting."

"Pretty much. The hospital is still on notice to let us know if anyone else shows up."

"Good. Any DNA among all the evidence?"

"The only blood found on scene so far is from either Pervis or Barry."

"That's not great news. Anything else?"

"Yeah," Detective Rafferty said, removing his gloves and moving to a clipboard at the end of the table.

"We ran through Edward Winston's phone records. There were records of calls to the resort in Biloxi, to the golf course, and to the rental car company where he rented the car he drove back from Biloxi."

"So his story is holding up?"

"It is. But there's something else of note."

"What?"

"It appears that Edward Winston also called a little place named Cedar Creek."

"And why would he do that?"

"I don't know, but we need to find out."

CHAPTER 47

EDWARD KNOCKED ON Mindy's door before dawn. She answered fully dressed in jeans, a T-shirt, and sneakers. Edward held out a new mobile phone and Mindy took it.

"That's a prepaid phone. If you need to reach us, call Shiro on his prepaid phone."

"You think of everything."

"No one thinks of everything," Edward replied. "That's why our prisons are full." He flicked his head in the direction of Shiro's room. "Is he ready?"

"Yes, but he's not doing well. He's burning up. His heart is racing. It's gotten worse in the last couple of hours."

"That's not good. That could be an infection. It could be the start of sepsis."

"Are you a doctor?"

"No. But my mom was an ER nurse."

"I'm pretty sure the bullet is still in him."

"There's nothing we can do about that right now."

"What happens when you get to LA?"

"Either our friend Taro tells me where I have to take him, or I call in a favor."

"The same kind of favor that got him here in the first place?" Mindy asked.

Edward felt the sting of her comment. "Something like that."

Mindy put her hands on her hips. "If you ask me, you're the one who got him into this mess so you need to get him out of it."

"That's what I'm doing. Help me get him into the car."

*

Edward shut the back door and walked around to the driver's side. He sat down behind the wheel and checked his view of Shiro sitting in the back. The injured man was resting against the rear passenger door, his legs stretched out across the back seat.

"Are you going to be all right back there?" Edward asked.

"Okay," Shiro responded, his face covered in perspiration.

"Do you need anything?"

"No."

"Your cell phone, passport, credit cards, international driver's license, and cash are in the pocket on the back of the seat in front of you. Your travel bag is in the trunk. If you need anything to drink or eat, let me know. I have everything up front here with me."

"I need my cigarettes."

"Those are back in the pocket, too."

Mindy poked her head in. "Are we all set here?"

"I think so," Edward replied. "I have water. I have food. I have extra bandages. We have cigarettes for the wounded. I have an empty two-liter bottle for emergency bathroom breaks, if needed."

"Nice."

"It's nineteen hundred miles to LA. This car is supposed to have a range of 474 miles per tank on the highway. If that's true, I only need to stop three times and I'll be there tomorrow morning."

Mindy climbed into the back seat, skillfully straddling Shiro's torso, and kissed him on the cheek.

"You be good, Taro."

"Come to Tokyo. I'll get you a job," he replied, his voice weak.

"Send me a postcard," she said, climbing out of the back seat in reverse.

"So we're clear on what you do?" Edward asked.

Mindy answered. "We're clear. Clean the room and then act normal."

"And tow the car."

"It's already gone," Mindy said, pointing to the spot in the lot where the rental had been.

"That was fast."

"I figured the sooner the better. Besides, no one was around at three in the morning."

"Where did he take it?"

"I didn't ask. He also took care of the GPS."

"Can you trust him?"

"I've known him a lot longer than I've known you, and look what I'm trusting you with."

"Good point."

"Besides, it's too late now."

Edward nodded.

"When will you be back?"

"I don't know. We'll see. I shouldn't be out there more than a couple of days."

"Don't just vanish on me. Let me know how it turns out. Deal?"

"Deal. Call if you need to. Don't call if you don't have to."

Mindy climbed the stairs towards her room as the silver Honda exited the Gum Tree Inn property and the lights came on.

From the balcony, Mindy watched the red taillights disappear into the morning darkness as tears streaked down her face.

*

Shiro slept for an hour and a half and opened his eyes as the early morning sunlight flashed through the steel trusses of the Memphis and Arkansas Bridge. A steady beat thumped on the car's suspension as it crossed the seams of the concrete slabs of the highway.

"Where are we?" Shiro asked in Japanese. Edward noticed his passenger's voice seemed to be weaker, more reserved.

"We're crossing the Mississippi River, heading into Arkansas."

Shiro sat up slightly, peering out the window. "The river is smaller than I thought it would be."

Edward peeked over the guardrail. "I guess. They probably built the bridge on a narrow section. You should see the Mississippi River up north in Minnesota. You can jump over it."

Shiro stared out the window and Edward glanced into the back seat.

"You need anything?"

"No. I'm okay."

"How do you feel?"

Shiro responded with a single grunt.

A sign for the West Memphis Dog Track whizzed by the passenger window and Edward cleared his throat.

"Can I ask you a couple of questions?"

"It's twenty-four hours to California, right?"

"More or less."

"Then let's talk."

"Who is Mindy? Just your neighbor at the motel?"

"Just my neighbor. She's a working girl."

"Are you sure?"

"Yes. She taught me the expression. She's definitely a working girl. I ran into a few of her clients."

"Really?"

"Yes."

"Can you trust her?"

"I can. She helped me clean up after the accident. She was a real pro."

"I don't know if that's a good thing, or a bad thing."

"I didn't ask her for help. She insisted on helping."

"Did you tell her what you did?"

"She knows what happened."

"Everything?"

"More or less."

"Let's hope she can keep her mouth shut."

"She can."

Edward paused. "What's your real name? I assume it's not Taro Ishida."

Shiro reached for a cigarette, lit it, and inhaled deeply. "Taro's not my real name."

"What is?"

"Shiro."

"Shiro what?"

"Shiro is enough. But I came into the country under a third name, Shinji Yoshida. A real passport with my real photograph."

"Okay. Shiro. What can you tell me about this finger you lost?"

Shiro raised both hands and Edward checked them out in the rearview mirror. "Can you see my hands?" Shiro asked.

"Yes."

Shiro made fists with both hands, leaving his pinkies extended. He rotated his hands in the air. "The finger I lost looks very similar to the real one still on my right hand."

"I assume it was professionally manufactured?"

"Of course. Custom made. Hand painted. Fine detail."

"Made in Japan?"

Shiro scoffed. "Of course."

"And it looked real?"

"Real enough to get past immigration in Los Angeles. Apparently they're on the lookout for me and my colleagues."

"How was the finger attached?"

"Suction."

"No glue?"

"No."

"And it never fell off before?"

"No. But I'd only had it for a few weeks. It was made for this trip."

"And you can't get a replacement sent to you?"

"No."

"Why not?"

"Because I won't ask for one and it wouldn't help if I did."

"You could try."

"No, I can't."

Edward merged into the fast lane to pass a large RV. Then he said, "I'm sorry for the trouble I got you into."

Shiro moved his eyes towards the rearview mirror where they met Edward's. "You didn't get me into anything."

"I feel like I did."

"My boss asked me to do something, and it was my duty to do it."

"Are you saying you couldn't refuse?"

Shiro glowered. "Do you know anything about the yakuza?"

"A few things. Mostly what I read after I met your boss for the first time."

Shiro chuckled and took another drag of his cigarette. "What did you read?"

"Different yakuza families run different areas of the country. Different families have different specialties. Unlike most organized crime in the world, the yakuza itself is not illegal. You have headquarters and business cards."

Shiro exhaled and nodded.

"I read the yakuza started out with two main groups: thieves and gamblers. Specialties, if you will. Later they branched out into labor unions and politics."

"You read that?"

"That was the gist of the book. These days the yakuza are into everything. Legitimate businesses. Moneylending. Entertainment"

"You forget to mention prostitution and drugs. Unless you were trying not to insult me."

"I didn't think I needed to mention them."

"What about killing people?" Shiro asked, almost tauntingly.

"I skipped that, too."

"I think we're past hurting each other's feelings, don't you?" Shiro asked.

"Maybe we are," Edward replied. "So, what's *your* specialty?"

"Gambling and negotiations."

"How's business?"

"Good."

Edward mulled over his next question. "If you're a gambler, why were you sent here to kill someone? It doesn't seem like the same line of business."

"My boss asked me to come here because I speak some English. It's a unique skill among my peers."

"Not many yakuza studying English?"

"Very, very few," Shiro said. "Studying is not our strong suit."

Edward looked into the rearview mirror as Shiro shut his eyes.

"Let me ask you a question," Shiro said, eyes unopened.

"Sure."

"There's a rumor you climbed into a burning car to save my boss's daughter."

"That's right."

"You were burned. I saw the scarring on your hand in the hospital."

"I received some burns, yes."

With his eyes shut, Shiro took a final drag off his cigarette. He removed the top from an empty water bottle and dropped the butt in. "So, how does someone who can force himself into flames to save a person he doesn't know not have the courage to kill the person who murdered his wife?"

"They're not the same. At all. One is saving a life. One is ending a life."

"Do you think asking someone to end a life for you is different than ending it yourself?"

"I did. But I don't now. And I had the chance to kill the man who murdered my wife but I couldn't do it. I had a loaded gun in my hand."

"So you called in a favor?"

"I did."

"And here we are."

"Here we are. And right now we need to put distance between you and Tupelo. Once I get you to LA, it'll work out. It should be fine."

"Maybe for you, but not for me."

"Why?"

"Because I failed. My boss asked me for a personal favor and I failed."

"Technically you didn't fail. Things happened."

"I was also under orders not to contact anyone if there was trouble. And the fact that I'm in the back seat of your car means I failed."

"I'll talk to your boss for you."

"No, you won't," Shiro said.

"Why not?"

"Because my failure is my failure. I can't have you begging my boss to forgive me. That's not how it works in my world. I'll keep my dignity and take what comes."

"And what if I try to help you anyway?"

Shiro cursed under his breath and leaned his head into the corner of the back seat. A coughing spasm racked his body.

"The cough is new," Edward commented. "How are you feeling?"

"Fuck you," Shiro replied.

"How about telling me where we're going in Los Angeles? I'm sure your boss doesn't want me to go to jail. And if you don't give me some direction, that becomes more likely."

"If you drive around long enough, I'll just die right here in the back of your car."

"Not if I can help it."

"Then I guess this is a stalemate," Shiro replied, turning his face towards the rear window of the car and leaving Edward with a view of the back of his head.

CHAPTER 48

DETECTIVE RAFFERTY ARRIVED at the North Mississippi Medical Rehabilitation Center a little after nine in the morning. With a small bag and his badge in hand, he stepped to the counter and smiled at the receptionist.

"My name is Detective Rafferty with the Lee County Sheriff's Department. I'm here to see Dr. Durand."

"Yes, Detective. Dr. Durand is expecting you." The woman stood from her chair and led the detective through a set of double doors with frosted glass. She approached an open office in a short hall and knocked on the doorframe.

"There's a detective here to see you," the woman said, speaking into the room.

"Send him in," Detective Rafferty heard the doctor tell the receptionist. Rafferty entered the room and Dr. Durand met him with a firm handshake that belied the man's diminutive stature.

"Thanks for seeing me on such short notice."

"Not a problem."

Dr. Durand pointed to the chair. Moments later Rafferty held a plastic bag over the desk at eye level.

"Have you ever seen one of these?" the detective asked.

The doctor squinted through the plastic of the evidence bag and asked, "Can we open it?"

"Do you have gloves?"

"I do, somewhere around here," Dr. Durand answered. He rifled through his desk and Detective Rafferty noticed a perfectly circular bald spot on the top of the doctor's head.

"Here we go," Dr. Durand said, placing a box of medical gloves on the desk.

Rafferty put on a pair of gloves, removed the finger from the bag, placed the bag on the desk, and then placed the finger on the bag. The doctor gently picked it up.

"It's severely damaged."

"As I said on the phone," Rafferty responded.

The doctor pursed his lips. He rotated the finger in his hand, moving his head in the opposite direction to see different views of the synthetic digit.

"It's not a toy."

"Why is that?"

"Too much detail. It has hairs, or it did before they were burned off. The nail has a cuticle. The folds on the skin on the back of the knuckle indicate skill not typically wasted on a toy or a costume."

The doctor flipped the finger over. "I assume there were fingerprints on this side before it got too close to a heat source."

"A fire pit."

"That would do it. The melting point for silicone is actually quite low. Unfortunately, silicone also makes the best prosthetics."

"Do you make fingers here on the premises?"

"We don't make anything here. Virtually all of our prosthetics are custom made by the University of Mississippi Medical Center in Jackson."

"Do they make fingers?"

"They do."

"Like this one?"

"Hard to say. Let me take a few pictures and send them over. I should get a response pretty quickly."

"That would be great."

The doctor spun in his chair, opened a drawer on the bookcase behind his desk, and pulled out a small digital camera.

"This might help capture more of the details," the doctor said, sounding almost apologetic for using a camera that wasn't embedded into a cell phone.

"Do you see many people at the clinic for prosthetic fingers?" the detective asked as the doctor took several photographs.

"That's a poignant question. We see our fair share of hands and arms here at the clinic. Most of our leg amputees are a result of military service or diabetes. Single fingers just aren't that common."

"In your experience, how do most patients lose a digit?"

"Farming accidents. Power tools. Carelessness. Alcohol. Sometimes a combination of all of the above. The last patient I recall with a prosthetic digit was a young boy who stuck his middle finger in the backside of an old pump on his grandfather's farm. Apparently the kid had grown up listening to his grandfather warn him to never put his finger in the hole while he was pumping water. Curiosity finally got the better of him."

"And they couldn't reattach it?"

"They couldn't or didn't. I don't remember exactly. I usually deal with patients after reattachment efforts have failed."

Rafferty motioned towards the finger on the desk. "What's your gut reaction when you look at this? Does anything spring to mind?"

"Well, it's small. A pinky finger for an averaged size man. Perhaps even a large woman. Either way that alone makes it curious."

"Why's that?"

"Because the function of a pinky finger isn't vital. For most tasks, people use their thumbs and either their index finger, middle finger or ring finger for grasping, holding, pinching, what have you."

"I get the idea."

"In broad strokes, a prosthetic pinky finger is more likely to be a cosmetic solution. Someone who wants to hide the fact they're missing a digit. There's minimal functionality to regain."

"I see."

"In fact, off the top of my head, the one group that springs to mind when I think about replacing pinkies is the Japanese mafia. As you've probably seen in the movies, they're infamous for lopping off fingers as a gesture of atonement. These days, from what I understand, the trend is starting to fade. Apparently, the yakuza is learning that missing digits makes it easy to identify a person."

"The yakuza?"

"You seem surprised."

"This is Tupelo. It's not something that comes up very often."

"It's well-known in my line of work that the Japanese make some of the finest custom prosthetics in the world," the doctor said. "Of course, given the condition of your finger here, it's hard to say if it's Japanese. The skin color on the less damaged side could be indicative of a non-Caucasian."

Detective Rafferty opened his bag and gestured for the doctor to return the digit to its storage receptacle.

"Thank you very much for your time, doctor," Rafferty said, reaching into his pocket for a business card. "Please let me know if you learn anything from the prosthetics group in Jackson."

"My pleasure. I'll pass along any information I receive."

*

Detective Rafferty walked out into the morning sun with his mobile phone in hand.

"Sheriff Blazer here."

"Sheriff, it's Will. I just paid a visit to the director of the amputee clinic over at the hospital."

"What did you learn?"

"I learned that we need to start calling every hotel in town and get a list of all of the Japanese tourists who have been staying here for the festival. We're looking for a man. Possibly a man with nine fingers."

"You're kidding."

"Nope. The good doctor seems to think the Japanese mafia could be behind the finger we found."

"In Tupelo?"

"That's what I said. It sounds crazy. Until you consider that our IT engineer friend Edward Winston speaks Japanese and works for a Japanese company."

"I'll have a group of officers get started on the hotels."

CHAPTER 49

SAN JON, NEW Mexico, population two hundred and three, hosts a sliver of historic Route 66, a gas station with a convenience store, a water tower with the town name on the side, and a nameless diner advertising itself to the world via the word "EATS" in neon.

Edward pulled into the gas station and parked his car on the far side of the building, away from the line of sight through the main window. He got out of the car, threw some trash into a garbage can, and headed for the front door, strolling past six unoccupied pumps. He stepped into the convenience store and spotted the sign for the bathroom in the back corner. He weaved through the snack aisle and past the beer fridge. A round security mirror hung from the ceiling in the corner. Edward observed the image in the mirror long enough to determine the teenager behind the counter was busy picking his nose and watching television.

Before heading back to his car, Edward purchased a pack of gum and an international calling card, the teenage boy behind the counter barely taking his eyes off the TV as he punched the keys on the register.

At his car, Edward peeked into his back seat from the outside of the vehicle. His passenger hadn't spoken since the sun had disappeared over the western horizon, dead ahead through the windshield on Interstate 40. For the last hour, the groans and moans from the rear seat had dissipated, leaving Edward to obsess over whether the man would even make it to Los Angeles.

He opened the driver's side door and reached into the back seat to check for a pulse. Perspiration covered Shiro's neck, evidence enough that his passenger was still alive. Dead men don't typically perspire.

Edward reached his hand into the pocket on the back of the passenger seat and removed Shiro's prepaid phone. He stepped from the car and sat down on the curb, his feet resting where cracked asphalt met the dry dirt of the New Mexico desert. He dialed the toll-free number on the front of the calling card, entered the pin from the reverse side, and then carefully punched in a twelve-digit number he had committed to memory.

"Good morning," an overly cheerful female receptionist responded in Japanese from six thousand miles away.

"Good morning," Edward responded, his free hand shaking. "I apologize for what I'm about to ask, but I need to speak with Mr. Fukuzawa."

"May I ask who is calling?"

Edward considered the question. "I probably shouldn't say."

"Mr. Fukuzawa is in the middle of a meeting at the moment. If you could leave your name and number, perhaps he can call you back."

"It's urgent. Please tell him it's a friend from the USA. The one with nightmares."

The woman repeated Edward's explanation for exactness, seemingly unfazed by the message's content.

"That's correct," Edward confirmed.

"Just a moment, please."

Several minutes later, the woman returned. "Mr. Fukuzawa would like you to call back to another number. Do you have something to write with?"

Edward wiped the dirt on the ground near his feet and then tested his makeshift paper by running his finger through it.

"I'm ready."

The receptionist provided the number. Edward traced it into the dirt and then made a second call. The phone rang once and Fukuzawa answered.

"I didn't expect to hear from you again."

"I have a problem."

"Your problem is being solved."

Edward could feel his stomach turn. "My problem was solved. I have another problem."

Fukuzawa grunted. "What is it?"

"I have a Japanese man in my back seat who has been shot. He's lost consciousness. He needs a doctor."

"Son of a bitch," Fukuzawa growled in disgust.

Edward pulled the phone away from his ear, unsure if the insult was directed at him or Shiro.

Fukuzawa dove into a tirade, his anger growing with each word. "What's he doing in your car? What are you doing with him? What happened?"

"It's a long story. We met by accident. Tupelo is a small city. There aren't many people who speak Japanese."

Fukuzawa repeated his insult, this time more quietly, as if he were accepting some level of responsibility for not foreseeing the possibility that Edward and Shiro could have crossed paths. "Can he speak?"

"Not anymore. He's been mumbling. He's covered in sweat. Breathing is rapid. We're in the car. I'm driving to California. He didn't tell me where I was supposed to take him. I only know he was planning to leave for Japan from Los Angeles."

"You're driving across the country with him in the back of your car?"

"Yes."

Edward cringed as Fukuzawa audibly sucked air backwards through his teeth. "Dumbasses."

"Where in Los Angeles should I take him?"

"Where are you now?"

"New Mexico. San Jon, New Mexico."

"Never heard of it."

"It's a small town."

"Good. Push him out of the car. Drive away. Don't look back."

Edward glanced over at his car and then around at the vastness that surrounded San Jon. His eyes rose to the water tower, the town's entire commercial skyline.

"I don't know if I can do that."

"Then take him home. It's your choice."

"I *know* I can't do that."

Fukuzawa hissed a series of guttural Japanese curses so creative Edward could only guess at their meaning. "The man in your car understood what he had to do and what would happen if something went wrong. If he could talk, he would tell you the same thing I'm telling you."

"I can't just push him out of the car like garbage."

"Do it anyway."

"No."

"No? Who do you think you're talking to?"

"Who do you think you're talking to?" Edward retorted, shocking himself. Edward could feel his pulse pounding, blood coursing through his veins. He could also hear Fukuzawa breathing heavily through the phone, as if the man were about to burst.

"Let me be very clear about what I say next," Fukuzawa whispered with a calm coolness that sent chills up Edward's spine. "If I help you with your new problem, you will owe me. Do you understand what this means?"

"I think I do."

"There is no thinking. You will owe me. When I ask for something, you will do it. And believe me, there will come a day when I ask for something."

Edward reconsidered shoving Shiro into the desert and driving off. Then he pushed the image from his mind.

"I understand," Edward replied.

"Good," Fukuzawa responded. "Call me back in ten minutes. I need to check on some things."

*

Edward called back precisely ten minutes later and Fukuzawa answered.

"I made a few calls."

"Thank you."

"Don't thank me now, because you won't be thanking me later. Understand?"

The tone of Fukuzawa's voice conveyed a deepening level of menace and Edward stammered, "Y-yes."

"Good. But, before we finalize our agreement, I have a question for you."

"Anything."

"Why do you care about this man in your car?"

"I don't know."

"You don't know?"

"Let's say I have a soft spot in my heart for Japanese people."

Fukuzawa expelled a bellowing laugh. "You're curious. I'll give you that. Very curious. You jumped into a burning car to save a Japanese stranger and now you're driving across the country to save another."

"I think it's what most people would do."

"I disagree. But at least you're consistent. I'm sure that's worth something to someone."

"Does that mean you're going to tell me where I need to take him?" Edward asked.

Fukuzawa sighed. "A restaurant called Benkei. It's in Little Tokyo. Los Angeles. Park in the alley behind the restaurant. Show up in person before lunch tomorrow and make a reservation for dinner."

"What name do I use?"

"Yours. You use your name. Your real name."

"That doesn't sound like a good idea."

"What? Suddenly you know what a good idea is? You wanted to be involved. Now you're involved."

*

Two pit stops and twelve hours later, Edward pulled into the alley behind the Japanese Village Plaza off East Second Street in Los Angeles. He reached into the back seat and touched Shiro's forehead. He placed his hand on the man's soaked shirt. He felt his passenger's lungs fight for oxygen through shallow, rapid breaths. Shiro mumbled aloud.

"I'm going to get help. We're here. Hang on."

Edward left the car in the alley, braved a narrow footpath lined with trashcans, rats, and tetanus, and appeared on the front side of his destination. He looked up and down the pedestrian-only walkway and spotted his destination on his right. At five before eleven, he entered the front door of a traditional Japanese restaurant and pushed aside the curtains hanging over the entranceway. A Japanese waitress stepped towards the door to greet him.

"One for lunch?" she asked.

"No, I would like to make a reservation."

"Certainly. For how many?"

"One. For dinner."

"What's the name?"

"Edward Winston."

For the briefest of moments, the woman's eyes opened wide. "Just a minute. Please have a seat," the waitress said, motioning towards a stool at the corner of the counter.

Edward sat and observed the rhythm of the restaurant preparing for lunch. A tall thin Asian man with a goatee and headband was standing behind the main counter, loading raw fish into the refrigerated glass that ran the length of the bar. A second employee grabbed a red lantern from a hook near the door and moved it to the exterior of the shop. A third man, as wide as he was tall, appeared from a curtained doorway, delivered a tray of vegetables to the counter, and returned to the kitchen. The sound of pots and pans banging together echoed from the rear of the restaurant.

*

An elderly Asian man stepped from the kitchen, barked a command in Japanese at the tall man with the goatee, and then came around the counter to Edward's seat. The man appeared to be in his late sixties, with a square face and wild eyebrows in need of a trim. He bowed his head slightly and pointed his hand, palm up, in the direction of a secluded corner of the restaurant.

Edward followed the man, removed his shoes, and stepped up onto an elevated tatami floor. A table with a built-in grill filled the middle of the room, the beige walls stained from years of smoke.

"Tea," the man yelled into the air. An unseen female's voice echoed an obedient reply.

Edward forced himself to sit *seiza*, with the soles of his feet under his butt, his knees completely bent.

"I understand you have something for me," the man said in a thick dialect of Japanese Edward didn't recognize. His words fired out in a blur, each syllable joined together in a verbal train. As he spoke, Edward noticed the flash of a gold-capped incisor.

"I do have something for you," Edward replied.

"Is he alive?"

"He was ten minutes ago."

"Can he walk?"

"Not at the moment."

The waitress brought a tray with a cast iron teapot and two matching broad-mouthed cups. She placed a cup in front of the man and Edward, and slowly filled each glass three-quarters full. The older man brought his cup to his lips, took a sip, and returned the cup to the table.

"Our mutual friend in Tokyo has gone through considerable effort to help you with your problem."

"I am appreciative."

"What you've asked for does not come without risk. Risk to our mutual friend in Tokyo. Risk to your passenger. Risk to yourself. And risk to me."

"I'm sorry for the inconvenience."

"And cost. Nothing is free."

"I am indebted to those who are helping."

"Our friend in Tokyo wanted me to remind you of your agreement."

"I have no doubt."

"Don't make a fool of anyone. Repay your debt."

"I will."

Edward took a drink of tea, the hot green liquid doing little to quench his dry throat.

The man nodded and pierced Edward with a cold stare. "Bring your car to the back of the New Daimaru Hotel. It's across the street. Park in the rear in one of the reserved spots. Someone will meet you there."

"And then what?"

"And then you stick around until I say you can leave. That's what Fuku-zawa asked and that's what you will do."

"Why?"

"Because that's what is being asked."

"I'm going to need some sleep. I've been driving for twenty-six hours straight."

"You can stay at the hotel across the street."

"Do they take cash? I'm trying to avoid leaving a paper trail."

"Don't worry about the paper trail," the old man replied, snarling in disgust at the request of another favor. "No one will remember you were ever there."

"Is the owner of the hotel a friend?" Edward asked.

"No. The owner of the hotel is sitting in front of you."

*

There was nothing new about the New Daimaru Hotel. Five stories high, the old brick façade sported an authentic fire escape down the front of the building. A ramen shop filled half of the first floor, the smell of boiling pork bones seeping through the walls and ceiling into the guest rooms above. In the sea of demolition and modernization engulfing the blocks around Little Tokyo, the New Daimaru clung to its history and architecture, staunchly winning the battle of survival but certain to lose the war.

Edward nervously pulled his car into one of the two available spots, both designated as reserved, per ominous white signs with red lettering. He again checked on Shiro, who neither moved nor groaned as Edward took his pulse and felt his temperature. Ten minutes later, two of the workers from the restaurant appeared at the back door of the hotel.

Edward stood from the car, nodded, and introduced himself.

Both men ignored him and pressed their heads against the window of the vehicle.

"Is he alive?" the tall man with the goatee asked in English.

"He's still breathing."

The man grabbed the handle on the rear door and tugged. The bulkier of the two men caught Shiro's head as it flopped backwards, no longer supported by the closed door. Without straining, the stocky man slowly pulled Shiro from the car while his partner with the goatee grabbed Shiro's ankles as they reached the end of the back seat.

In broad daylight, in an alley behind an old hotel, the two men carried an unresponsive Shiro up two concrete steps into the rear entrance of the hotel. Edward quickly shut his car door, gave a furtive glance at his surroundings, and followed the men inside.

In the back hall of the hotel, in front of what Edward assumed was an old service elevator, the men gently lowered Shiro to the floor. Edward joined the men as they watched a yellow light illuminate the floor numbers of the descending elevator.

When the doors opened, the stocky man stepped in and dragged Shiro into the antique elevator. From the hallway, the man with the goatee pushed Shiro's knees forward, folding Shiro into the confines of the elevator through force and contortion.

"I'll take him up and send the elevator back down," the stocky man said.

Edward watched as the elevator door shut; Shiro's head on the floor, facing up towards the groin of the man straddling him.

"Thanks for your help," Edward said to the man with the goatee as they waited for the elevator to return.

"No talking," the man answered, his eyes fixated on the changing floor numbers of the elevator.

The two stood shoulder to shoulder in complete silence until the elevator returned. Both men entered and the old elevator shook and shimmied its way to the top floor. The doors opened with a single mechanical ding and Edward followed the man down a long straight hallway with threadbare carpet. Squeaky boards announced their arrival before they reached the room at the end of the hall.

An old wooden door opened and the stocky man who had taken Shiro up in the elevator exited the room. In the confines of the narrow hall, Edward pressed his back to the wall. The two workers from the restaurant filed past, traversed the carpeted floor, and disappeared back into the service elevator.

Edward turned towards the open hotel room door, cautiously peering across the threshold.

"Come in," a voice beckoned in perfect English from the depths of the room.

Edward slowly stepped in. A bed, dresser, side table, and old chair completed the room's décor. A luggage cart was protruding from an open closet door. A light illuminated the dated bathroom in the corner. Shiro was on the bed, a stack of pillows supporting his head. A thin Asian man, dressed as if he had stepped straight off the putting green, was leaning over Shiro's body, pressing a stethoscope to his chest.

The doctor stood, his wireframe glasses slightly cockeyed. "It's good to see you again," he said to Edward.

Edward quietly gasped. "I know you," he replied. "You visited me when I was in the hospital in Tokyo."

"I did. How are the burns these days?"

Edward raised his hand. "As good as they're going to get."

The doctor continued his medical assessment of Shiro and Edward continued his questions. "Why? How? Why are you here?"

"Because I'm a doctor," the man replied, checking his watch. "You should know that."

"I do," Edward replied.

"Good. Now what can you tell me about this gentleman you just delivered?"

Edward mentally changed gears and he tried to provide as much detailed information as possible. "He lost consciousness twelve hours ago. He was in and out before that."

"And the wound?"

"He was shot two and a half days ago. Maybe sixty hours."

"And he was conscious until last night?

"Yes. He was in pain. And seemed to be getting worse. But he was conscious."

"Did you give him anything?"

"He took some old antibiotics originally prescribed for a female with a urinary tract infection."

"Anything else?" the doctor asked, swiping a digital thermometer across Shiro's forehead.

"Advil. I don't know how many."

"That shouldn't matter."

"I'm sorry, but I don't remember your name," Edward admitted.

"I never gave it to you. You can call me doctor. No sense in adding to the confusion at this point."

"Can I help you do anything?"

"Yes. Drag that luggage valet next to the bed."

The doctor moved a Nike gym bag from the chair in the corner and placed it at the foot of the mattress. "I'm going to give him a heavy round of antibiotics intravenously. Hopefully, he'll make it."

"What are his chances?"

"My best guess is that he's on the verge of becoming septic. If he has been unconscious for twelve hours I would put his chances at fifty-fifty."

"Shit," Edward replied.

The doctor cut Shiro out of his clothes and affixed an IV bag to the rail of the luggage cart. A steady drip started, disappearing into the vein in the crook of Shiro's arm.

"How long until you know anything?"

"If his condition doesn't worsen in the next twelve hours, then the odds start working in his favor."

"After that, how long until he's conscious?"

The doctor stared at Shiro on the bed, and when Edward realized he wasn't going to get an answer he changed the subject. "You've obviously been in the US for a very long time. Your English is impeccable."

The doctor adjusted the drip gauge on the IV bag. "Yes, I've been here a very long time. Over thirty years. I graduated from medical school here in the US. I was lucky enough to practice medicine at some of the finest hospitals in the country."

"And how exactly did you end up here?"

"You mean, why am I doing off-the-books medical treatment on a man who has been shot, is covered in tattoos, and is missing a finger?"

"You could put it that way."

"The short answer is I don't care who my patients are. The Hippocratic Oath doesn't mention anything about who I shouldn't treat. Years ago, some powerful people in Japan learned this about me. What you see me doing in this room has been a side job ever since. When I met you, it was an extension of my part-time employment. After the car accident where you received your burns, our friend in Tokyo was very concerned about your well-being. I flew to Japan just to see you."

"That is a fascinating part-time job."

"Almost as fascinating as why an American engineer just drove an injured member of the Japanese mafia across the country in the back of his car."

Edward sighed. "Then I guess I don't need to explain anything to you."

"Not to me," the doctor said, pulling up Shiro's eyelids and shining a light into his eyes. "But I do hope you know what you've gotten yourself into."

"I do."

"Are you sure? Do you know what yakuza stands for?"

"Mafia."

"No, that's not what I mean. I'm talking about the origin of the word yakuza."

"I don't."

"It was the losing hand in an old card came called *oichokabu*. As the losing hand, it had no points. It was often referred to as a 'useless' hand. Historically, a lot of yakuza had ties to gambling. Over time, this expression began to be used as a way to describe yakuza members themselves. To this day the yakuza embraced this identity as 'useless' people."

"They're embracing an insult?"

"They look at it as the symbol of what brings them together. Of what makes them unique. The yakuza accepts all losers into their brotherhood."

"And you work for them?"

"I do. And I can tell you this. Yakuza members are, in many ways, like a pack of feral dogs. And you need to understand the pack of dogs you're involved with doesn't play games. They make decisions and live by those decisions. And if you're going to be involved with them, you will have to live by those decisions. Doing what is right is not their concern. Doing what is loyal, what is asked, in the proper way, following tradition, that is what's right. It has nothing to do with reality, or the law."

"I appreciate the warning," Edward said. "But as you probably know, the guy on the bed just killed a man because I asked him to. That's probably not what most people consider the right thing to do."

The doctor nodded. "Either way, they owed you and now you owe them."

"Don't remind me."

"I have to remind you. That's part of my job."

Both men watched Shiro breathe, the traffic noise from the street in front of the hotel seeping through the old window behind them.

"What's the plan if he recovers?" Edward asked.

"We'll discuss that when he comes around. No sense in counting our chickens before they hatch."

Edward tried to stifle a yawn.

"How are you around blood?" the doctor asked.

"Not so good. Why?"

"Because I'm going to need help getting that bullet out and I was told to ask you."

"You were told to ask me?"

"That's right. As a reminder of what you've agreed to."

*

Shiro's body arched in a spasm of pain as the doctor's forceps disappeared into the wound on the back of Shiro's tattooed shoulder.

"Hold him steady," the doctor ordered as Edward splayed himself across Shiro's back, pinning him to the bed. Shiro grunted face first into the pillow.

"I'm trying to hold him," Edward strained. "Can't you give him something?"

"I did."

"Well, it's not working. I thought he was unconscious."

"Not anymore," the doctor replied, concentrating on the medical instrument in his hands and the blood seeping from the open wound.

The doctor removed the forceps, examined the wound, and reinserted them for the third time. Shiro almost bucked Edward onto the floor and the doctor sat on Shiro's buttocks to help keep the patient down.

Edward grabbed the arm attached to Shiro's uninjured shoulder and pulled it off the bed, effectively stealing the injured man's leverage.

The doctor delicately repositioned the forceps and then slowly removed them from Shiro's wound.

"Got it," the doctor said, holding the bullet up to the light. He dropped the projectile into a red solo cup and placed it on the bedside table.

"Don't let him go," the doctor added. "I need to clean out the wound and properly stitch it."

Edward winced at the blood that covered Shiro's tattooed back and arm.

Fifteen minutes later, the doctor finished the last stitch. He sat up from Shiro's buttocks and the patient turned his head towards the side and mumbled a curse, eyes still shut.

"That should do it," the doctor said.

"Oh, for me, too. In more ways than one."

"He's a lot tougher than I thought," the doctor added. "I'll bump up his odds of surviving. I give him a seventy-five percent chance of pulling through."

"You can make it a hundred percent."

The doctor stepped into the small bathroom and put his surgical accouterments into the basin of the pedestal sink.

"If you don't need my services any longer, I'm going to get some sleep," Edward said.

"Fine. Sleep well."

"Will you be around later?"

"I'm going to be around until he's either dead, or back in Japan."

CHAPTER 50

EDWARD SLEPT A dreamless sleep for fourteen hours straight, his longest stretch of shuteye since he had tripled his initial dose of Ambien. In the darkness of the predawn morning ruled by newspaper deliveries, trash trucks, and hookers finishing their shifts, he sat up in bed and checked his phone: 4:02 a.m.

He showered, dressed, and took the stairs down one flight to the lobby. A pair of worn leather chairs sat on opposite sides of a wood table offering a spread of tattered magazines. The small television on the wall was off. A cockroach scurried across the floor near the unmanned front desk as he headed outside.

Edward hit the onramp to the 101 with a coffee from McDonalds in his cup holder. He headed north and followed the coastline, the Pacific Ocean out his window to the west. He arrived in Santa Barbara a little after six thirty and drove to Stearns Wharf, navigating the streets via vague recollection. He spent ten minutes staring at the ocean, and then cruised the quaint main drag lined with culinary options both for the rich and the college students that constituted a large portion of the city's population.

It took him two passes to recognize the recently painted beige stucco duplex across from Alameda Park. He circled the block until he found a spot, and at five minutes past seven in the morning, Edward walked up the sidewalk to the left half of the duplex. On the small porch he took a deep breath and rang the doorbell.

A barrel-chested, curly haired man in his thirties answered the door in plaid pajama pants and a T-shirt. A small child, wearing only a diaper, clung to his shoulder.

"Edward. Jesus. What are you doing here?" his brother asked with a look of shock.

"I was in the neighborhood."

"Come in, come in. Ashley is still asleep upstairs, but I have coffee made."

"Just for a minute. I can't stay."

Edward stepped inside and his brother shut the door behind him. His brother turned in the direction of the kitchen and Edward followed.

"You want coffee?" his brother asked, reaching for a metal carafe on a counter littered with sippy cups.

"No, I'm good, thanks."

His brother bounced the baby in his arms. "Look, I'm real sorry I couldn't be more help with Holly. I really am."

Edward shook his head. "Don't worry about it."

"How are you holding up?"

"It hasn't been easy."

"I guess not. Not that I have room to talk, but you look like shit. Are you on something?"

"No, that's your area of expertise."

"And there's the brotherly love I've missed."

"You started it."

His brother nodded.

"How's Kevin?" Edward asked, reaching out to touch his nephew's chubby knee.

"He's good. Has a couple of teeth and is just starting to stand. The usual baby stuff. He'll be a big brother this fall."

"He's adorable," Edward added. "And congratulations."

"So you're really not going to tell me what you're doing out here, showing up unannounced at the crack of dawn?"

"I just wanted to see my brother and nephew. I had the time."

"We have a pull-out bed on the sofa in the living room. It's all yours if you want it."

"I really can't stay."

Edward felt his brother's stare deepen. "What kind of trouble did you get yourself in?"

"I'm not in trouble."

"Sure you are."

"I'm not."

"Then why does this feel like the time in sixth grade when you shot a bottle rocket into the intersection near the grocery store and then showed up at my baseball practice three blocks away just so you had an alibi?"

Edward didn't answer.

"How long are you going to be in town?"

"I'll be in LA for a day or two. Then I'm heading back."

Edward's brother seemed to know when to give up. By quarter after seven, Edward was at the front door, saying goodbye in the foyer.

With Edward in the doorway, his brother waved to a group of women jogging down the street with their baby strollers.

Edward glanced over at the fitness moms and then back at his brother. "If anyone asks, tell them I stopped by."

CHAPTER 51

DETECTIVE RAFFERTY SAT down across from Sheriff Blazer and handed his boss a list of names.

"What do we have?"

"We hit all the hotels in town looking for potential members of the Japanese mafia."

"And?" the Sherriff asked, eyes dropping to the list.

"Sixteen. We have sixteen names of Japanese men according to local hotel records. It may not account for everyone, but it's a good start."

"How many of the guests are still in town?"

"About half. We have officers canvassing the hotels, reaching out to the guests on the list who are still around."

"It shouldn't take long. We assume we're looking for a guy with a fake finger. Just check their hands."

"That's exactly what we're doing."

"What about the guests on the hotel lists who have already left town?"

"If we come up empty handed, we may have to contact the FBI for those who have already left town. They can put us in contact with the Japanese Embassy, DHS, and Border Protection."

"And our friend, Special Agent Washington?"

"I didn't inform her yet."

Sheriff Blazer rubbed his chin and handed Detective Rafferty a Post-it Note with a phone number on it.

"What's this?"

"A detective from the Tupelo City Police force called about an hour ago. I was out. He left a message. Wanted to talk to the detective in charge of the Pervis Wade investigation. Give him a call. See what he wants."

*

From the confines of his cubical in the corner of the first floor, Detective Rafferty leaned back in his chair. He plucked his phone off his desk and dialed the number on the Post-it Note.

"Detective Keating," a man answered, speaking through a wheeze.

"This is Detective Rafferty from the Lee County Sheriff's Department."

"You're working the Pervis Wade double murder case?"

"That's right."

"Well, I might have something for you."

"Shoot."

"I don't know if you heard, but a few days ago we found an unconscious guy in the alley just off Main Street. During the festival. The victim had multiple wounds. A broken nose and skull fracture, among other injuries."

"Beaten?"

"Badly beaten. Could have easily been killed."

"Robbery?"

"We don't think so. Nothing was taken. The victim was found with an open knife in his immediate vicinity. We ran a background check on him and he has a criminal record. Assault with a deadly weapon. Did six months for breaking and entering. Made it hard to determine whether he was the victim or the perpetrator in this case. Either way, he was put into a medically induced coma until the swelling on his brain subsided."

"Where does the Lee County Sheriff's Department fit into this?"

"Our captain provided us with an update on your double murder this morning. There wasn't much new to the case, but we were briefed on the details of the injuries of the deceased. According to what we heard from the ME report, it sounds like one of the guys in your double murder received a similar beating to the guy found in the alley."

"You think there's a connection?"

"The ME report indicated one of the deceased in the double murder had both of their collarbones broken. Is that correct?"

"That's right."

"The guy we found in the alley also had both collarbones broken."

"Really?"

"Yep."

"Do you have any suspects?"

"Not yet."

"And you said the guy is in a medically induced coma?"

"He was. The doctors brought him out of it this morning. The man's wife called and let me know her husband was finally able to speak with us. The wife wants to find whoever did this to her husband."

"Did you speak with him?"

"I did. We didn't talk too long. And he was a little out of it."

"Being in a coma probably does that to you."

"For sure. Physically, he looked rough. Black eyes. Bandages on his nose. On his head. Both arms in slings."

"What did he tell you?"

"He said he was jumped. An unprovoked attack. Claimed he pulled his knife to defend himself."

"And he saw the attacker?"

"He did. He claims it was an Asian guy with a stick. Says the guy was lurking in the alley."

"An Asian guy?"

"He seemed pretty sure. I got the feeling there was more to the story, but you know how that goes. You never get the whole truth."

"And where exactly was this guy found?"

"Behind the shops on Main Street. North side. A block down from Tupelo Hardware."

Detective Rafferty picked the list of names off his desk and perused the hotels that had provided the names of their Japanese guests.

"Just around the corner from the Gum Tree Inn," Rafferty stated.

"That's right. The Scottish Inn and Candlewood are also in the neighborhood. The Gum Tree Inn isn't far, but it's much smaller. Why do the hotels matter?"

Detective Rafferty didn't respond.

"You still there?" Detective Keating wheezed through the phone.

"I am. Thanks for the call."

"Let me know if it pans out."

CHAPTER 52

DETECTIVE RAFFERTY ARRIVED at the Gum Tree Inn and entered the manager's office. The old woman behind the counter pulled herself from her worn recliner in the corner.

"Good afternoon," Detective Rafferty said, lifting his badge.

"Good afternoon, Officer," the woman answered, cigarette dancing between her lips.

"Detective," he corrected.

"Good afternoon, *Detective*," the woman repeated, snuffing out her cigarette in the ashtray and readying herself for an inquiry into the hard-working blonde at the end of the second floor.

"As you probably know, we've been reaching out to most of the hotels in town, asking for assistance in locating a person of interest. Someone from the Lee County Sheriff's Department contacted you yesterday. You provided the name of a Japanese guest we would like to follow up with."

"Room 203," the woman answered without batting an eye. "Name is Taro Ishida."

"Is he here?"

"He hasn't checked out. But this ain't the Hyatt. The guests don't come through the lobby on their way in and out. People here try to mind their own business as much as possible."

"Did you check his ID?"

"I did. Made a copy of his passport when he arrived."

"May I see it?"

The woman nodded, disappeared, and came back with a photocopy of Taro Ishida's passport. Detective Rafferty stared at the face staring back at him. "Not the best picture in the world."

"Passport photos are a little like mug shots. And they don't get any prettier when you Xerox them on an old machine," she retorted.

"And you're sure he's staying in Room 203?"

"Yes, second floor, second from the end."

Rafferty paused and then asked a final question. "Did you notice if the guest in room 203 was missing a finger?"

"I'm sure I didn't," the woman replied with a look of bewilderment.

Rafferty grunted to himself and took another look at the copy of the passport photo. "I may be on the premises for a while," Rafferty said, turning away from the counter.

"Take as long as you want."

*

Mindy removed the top from a can of tuna, dumped it into a bowl, and added a spoonful of mayonnaise. Stirring the mix, she was startled by the pounding on the door of the next room. She froze, spoon in fist, and listened as a male voice barked with authority, "Lee County Sheriff's Department, open up."

Mindy stepped away from the kitchenette to peek in the direction of the balcony and Detective Rafferty's face suddenly appeared at her window, his nose almost pressed to the glass, his hand cupped on his forehead.

The detective saw Mindy through the window and banged on her door with the same verve he had displayed seconds before.

Mindy set down her lunch preparations, answered the door, and smiled. "Long time no see, Detective."

"Well, I'll be damned. Mindy," Detective Rafferty replied, grinning. "You staying out of trouble?"

"I'm trying to."

"You may need to try harder."

"Oh, yeah? What makes you say that?"

"Because I saw you the other day out at the scene of a double murder. I was leaving as you were arriving. And as luck would have it, you just happen to be staying in the same motel as a person of interest in the same case. What do you think the chances are of that?"

"Tupelo is a small town. And there were a lot of people out there."

"Why don't you tell me what *you* were doing out there?"

"Same as everyone else. Paying my respects."

"Let me guess, you and Pervis Wade had business together."

"Nope. I'd never heard of Pervis Wade until I saw his face on the news. But I did know Big Barry Lawson."

"You did?"

"I did. And between you and me, he was only Big Barry in height and weight."

The grin on Rafferty's face vanished. "I haven't seen you around the courthouse. Or in the back of a patrol car. Made me think you had turned the corner. Gotten a real job."

"I work here and there. What else can I do for you?" Mindy asked.

"I want to ask a few questions about one of your neighbors."

"Give me a second," she replied. "I have tuna fish on my hands. Come in and have a seat," she offered, nodding at the chair at the tiny table.

The detective entered and sat down.

"Can I get you something to drink?" she offered.

"No, I'm good. How long have you been staying here?"

"A couple of months," she answered.

The detective's eyes measured the room and Mindy nudged the conversation forward.

"Which neighbor do you want to know about?" she asked, stepping away from the sink and drying her hands.

"The one right next door," Rafferty answered. His red curly hair bounced as he flicked his head in the direction of Shiro's room. He put the photocopied page of Taro Ishida's passport on the table.

"Taro, the Japanese guy?"

"Yes. Have you met him?"

"I have. Seems like a nice guy. Says he came into town for the festival. Doesn't speak English very well. We walked down to the festival one day." Mindy leaned in to look at the photograph of the passport and immediately realized the man was a complete stranger. Whoever Taro Ishida was, it wasn't her neighbor.

"Is he in town by himself?" the detective asked.

"As far as I know. I haven't seen him with anyone else."

"Any chance you saw him with a white American guy? Average height. Brown hair, brown eyes. Speaks Japanese."

"No."

"Did your neighbor tell you anything about himself? Anything about his job? His family? Life in general?"

"Not really. Said he was on vacation. Said he liked Elvis. Always had."

"Did he have tattoos?"

"He did from his wrists up his arms."

"Anything memorable?"

"A hodge-podge of crazy Asian stuff. I think there was a guy with a sword and a fish."

"What about on the rest of his body?"

"I never saw him without a shirt so I don't know about the rest of him. But I wouldn't be surprised. Everyone has tattoos these days."

"How about his fingers? Did he have all his fingers?"

"Fingers?" Mindy replied, trying to sound surprised.

"Yes, fingers. Did he have all his fingers?"

"You're giving me the feeling this guy could be dangerous."

"He's a person of interest in a double murder. He could be very dangerous."

Mindy did her best to appear terrified.

"Did you notice whether or not he was missing a finger?" the detective pressed.

"I wasn't really looking, but I'm going to say he had all his fingers. We drank a couple of beers together. I probably would have noticed if one was missing."

The detective nodded, seeming to believe every word of every response.

"What about a car? Do you know how he got here?"

"I think he has a car downstairs. The hotel office probably has that information."

Rafferty nodded again.

"Do you recall whether or not your neighbor was home the night of the big storm a few days ago?"

"I don't recall what my neighbor was doing. I think I had an appointment that night with a teacher from East Tupelo High. I could be wrong."

"Keeping them all straight must be an occupational hazard," Rafferty replied.

Mindy smiled and ran a strand of hair behind her ear. "I think we're done here."

"I guess that's all for now," Detective Rafferty relented, knowing he had insulted his way out the door. He reached into his pocket and handed Mindy his business card. "Call me when your neighbor gets home. We'd like to talk to him."

"I'll let him know."

"And don't go too far. I'm putting you on my radar as well."

"Oh, I'm sure you are."

Rafferty walked out and Mindy shut the door behind him. She waited until he reached the bottom of the stairs before her hands started to tremble.

*

Rafferty left the motel manager's office with his phone in hand. "Sheriff, you're not going to believe this."

"What did you find?"

"You remember a stripper turned hooker named Mindy McCormick?"

"Sure."

"Well, I was checking on the lead from the Tupelo City Police and I think we have a possibility on our Asian guy. He's staying at the Gum Tree Inn. He's in the room next door to Mindy. I have a copy of his passport."

"Did she know him?"

"She says she met him. And that's not the best part. She stopped by the crime scene at Pervis Wade's."

"Curious."

"Claims she knew Big Barry."

"And what's she doing at the Gum Tree? Is she working out there?"

"Probably. I talked to the manager before and after I spoke with Mindy.

The manager claims to know nothing about Mindy or what she does for work. She's been there for a few months."

"Is our Asian guy still in town or did he skedaddle?"

"Apparently he's still around. He hasn't checked out."

"Did we get a finger count? Anyone notice a missing digit?"

"Not so far."

Sheriff Blazer sighed. "Put someone in the parking lot with an eye on the room."

"Roger that."

"And get back here with a copy of that passport."

CHAPTER 53

EDWARD RETURNED FROM Santa Barbara and parked in his reserved spot behind the New Daimaru Hotel. He rode the elevator to the top floor, walked down the hall, and knocked on the door to Shiro's room. With a quick turn of the knob, the doctor's face appeared in the entranceway and Edward stepped in.

"How is he?"

"Better than I imagined."

"Is he talking?"

"He strung together a few sentences earlier this morning."

"That's great. How long until he's up and about?"

"We'll have to wait and see."

"And then what?"

"Then I'm going to get him on a plane and escort him back to Japan."

"You're going to take him back?"

"Yes."

"I thought you were just a doctor."

"I am a doctor. But I have a medical license in the US and in Japan. And that gives me the ability to do a few other things. Like serving as a medical escort."

"How often does someone need that service?"

"On occasion, usually for legitimate reasons."

"Oh," Edward replied, his mind churning through possibilities.

"Grab a seat," the doctor said, pointing at the chair in the corner. "You and I need to have a conversation."

"About what?"

"About this missing finger."

Edward sat down. "I don't know what I can tell you. I never really saw it."

"Do you have any idea where it could be?"

"He said he lost it doing the job he was sent here to do."

"You mean he lost it at the scene of a crime?"

"That's right. Or on the way there. Or on the way back. He had been shot and didn't seem to know exactly where."

"But it's possible law enforcement is in possession of this finger?"

"It's possible but we don't know."

"Who is we?"

"I had some help getting him out of town. A woman he befriended on his own."

"Hmmm," the doctor replied pensively. "Anyone else in the picture we need to know about?"

"No."

"Good."

Edward motioned towards Shiro in the bed. "He mentioned something about needing the finger to get out of the country. Is that accurate?"

"Yes. Under normal circumstances."

"And what about under less-than-normal circumstances?"

"Every system has exceptions. Including US immigration."

"How do you know this?"

"Because this isn't my first rodeo, as they say. When a foreign national comes into the US, their passport information is scanned by US Customs and Border Protection or—as many people still call it—US Immigration."

"And fingerprints are also captured when they enter the US."

"That's right. Fingerprinting all visitors coming into the US has become standard in the last few years. So our friend here entered the US with a Japanese passport and ten fingerprints associated with it. He needed ten fingers to increase his odds of entering the country without raising suspicion. As you probably know, US Immigration keeps an eye out for Japanese men with missing fingers and tattoos."

"And now he only has nine fingerprints."

"Yes and because he scanned ten fingers to enter the country, he may need ten fingers to leave. Of course, if our friend here were in the US for legitimate reasons, we could just roll the dice and see what happens. Under normal circumstances, the worst-case scenario would be that US Immigration identifies him as yakuza and he is expelled from the country. Under normal circumstances that would be fine because he's leaving the country anyway. The missing finger throws a wrench in that scenario. Particularly if law enforcement has it. If law enforcement is actively looking for him, we can't rely on luck alone. Unless *you* want to risk it. I understand your neck may also be on the line."

"I'll pass."

"I figured as much," the doctor said, pushing his glasses up the bridge of his nose.

"Can't he just use another passport to get home? Just forget the passport he came into the country on? Get him another?"

"In theory, yes. I'm sure the information used to obtain the original passport is fraudulent. It's not his real name. But it is his photograph. And if that passport never receives an exit scan, eventually US immigration is going to add him to a list for people who entered the country and never left."

"That could be a problem."

"Yes, it could."

"He said a replacement prosthetic can't be sent to him. Is that true?"

"An exact replica would take time. But even an exact replica won't help. If the police have the finger, then they have an exact match to one of the ten fingerprints he used to enter the country. And all those fingerprints are tied together to one passport. That leaves us with several possible scenarios."

"Which are?"

"First, let's say our man attempts to leave the country with nine fingers. It's possible law enforcement could use the fingerprint from the lost prosthesis to produce a flag in the system when any of the other nine fingers are scanned."

"That's not a good scenario."

"The second possibility is that law enforcement just flags all people with nine fingers."

"I'm holding out for a third option."

The doctor pursed his lips. "The third scenario is where I come in. We create a medical exception."

"Which means?"

"Which means no system is perfect and we can use that to our advantage. The passport scanning system employed by US Immigration doesn't work one hundred percent of the time. Machines break down. Scanners don't scan. Network connectivity fails. Databases become corrupt. In these cases, a passport can be accepted without the associated scans. In fact, by law, approval from an Immigration officer is the only thing needed to enter the country. The standard US protocol is to scan all available information as often as it can be scanned. But, as they say, stuff happens."

"So there are exceptions to the passport scans."

"There are."

"Give me an example."

"Consider the case of an individual born without an arm or hand, or someone who has lost a hand in an accident. Do you think they can't travel?"

Edward mulled over the image in his mind.

The doctor didn't wait for an answer. "Of course they can. All it takes is the Immigration officer to allow that person to pass. It is completely subjective, really."

"Jesus, you're not planning on chopping off his arms, are you?" Edward said with a sinking feeling, pointing at Shiro in the bed.

"Don't be silly. Apparently your friend on the bed is quite adept at making money for his boss. I get the impression his gift for making money is the only thing keeping him alive. And he's going to need his hands and arms to pay back his boss for the cost of getting him home."

CHAPTER 54

SHIRO'S PREPAID PHONE rang as Edward sat in his sagging bed on the second floor of the hotel.

"Hello?"

"The cops were here earlier," Mindy whispered without segue.

"Here where?"

"At the motel."

"City police or the sheriff's department?"

"A detective with the sheriff's office. Rafferty."

"That's not good. I know him."

"So do I," Mindy answered.

"He's one of the dirty cops who helped cover up my wife's murder."

"Then we have a problem on top of a problem."

"What did he want?"

"He asked me about Taro Ishida, my neighbor for the last week."

"What did you tell him?"

"I told him I had met the guy. That Taro and I walked down to the festival together one day. I said he didn't speak much English so we didn't talk about much."

"Did he believe you?"

"I'm pretty sure he did. He also asked about you."

"What exactly did he ask?"

"He asked if I'd ever seen Taro talking to a brown-haired, brown-eyed

American guy who speaks Japanese. He didn't mention your name, but I assume by the description you were the person he had in mind."

"Probably."

"What should I do?"

"Nothing. Don't do anything at all. I figured sooner or later they would make their way to the motel. I just didn't think they would connect the dots that quickly."

"You were right to get out of town when you did."

"What else did he say?"

"He asked if Taro had a car. I told him I thought he did. He also asked if Taro had tattoos. I said I'd seen tattoos on his arms. I left it at that."

"Those are safe answers."

Mindy took a deep breath and exhaled. "He also asked whether or not Taro was missing a finger."

Edward cursed. "Shit."

"Pretty much."

"I guess we don't need to wonder whether the police have the missing prosthetic. They do."

"What's next?"

"I'm going to stay here one more night, try to get some sleep, and then I'm heading back to Mississippi."

"And what do I do?"

"Hang tight. I'll give you a call when I'm on my way back. Plan on meeting somewhere outside Lee County. Leave your cell phone at the motel and try not to be followed."

*

Edward woke with the doctor standing over his bed, gently shaking his shoulder.

"Wake up."

"What time is it?"

"Almost ten."

Edward sat up groggily. "I didn't get to bed until late."

"Time to get a move on. Decisions to be made," the doctor said, throwing Edward's pants onto the mattress.

"I have some bad news," Edward replied.

"What's that?"

"The lost finger is no longer lost. The police definitely have it."

The doctor seemed to digest the news with a hum. "That doesn't change our plan."

"What is the plan?"

"You'll find out as soon as you get dressed."

"I also need to get back to Mississippi."

"I don't think you're going anywhere until our friend in Tokyo agrees you can leave."

"Am I being held hostage?"

"Don't be ridiculous. But as I understand it, you're involved in what's going on here. And you will be involved until you're told your presence is no longer needed. Now get dressed. I'll meet you downstairs in the lobby."

Edward shoved his legs into his pants, zipped his fly, and rubbed his eyes. "How's our patient doing?"

"He's up," the doctor replied, before leaving the room.

Edward stood by the side of the bed as the door shut. He pulled a shirt over his head, ran his fingers through his hair, and stepped into the small bathroom to throw water on his face. Finished with his hygiene, Edward packed his belongings into his small duffle bag. Ten minutes after being awoken, Edward walked into the lobby.

Shiro looked up as Edward approached the worn leather chairs in the lobby.

"How do you feel?" Edward asked.

"Fine," Shiro responded, standing slowly with an audible groan. His arm hung in a sling. His face was clean-shaven and his hair was damp.

"You look a lot better than you did in the car. You had me worried there for a while."

The doctor approached from Edward's rear and interrupted the conversation. "I think he'll be fine from here on out. Another bolus of antibiotic and he should have no issues with an eleven-hour flight."

"Is that the plan?"

"That's what we're going to discuss," the doctor said, heading towards the front door and holding it open.

"Where are we going?"

"Across the street for an early lunch."

*

The private back room of the restaurant was an elevated tatami room that sat twenty people comfortably around two black tables placed end-to-end. The owner of the restaurant appeared at the entrance to the private room and flashed his gold-capped incisor and wild eyebrows. He motioned for Shiro and the doctor to find their seat and then steered Edward to a position across from the physician and his patient.

A waitress appeared at the doorway with a tray of ingredients, bowed once, and then gracefully slipped into the room without her shoes. She took up her position at the end of the table and silently removed the middle section of the tabletop, revealing a large stainless steel griddle. She turned the griddle on and placed several bowls of pancake-like batter on the wooden outer edge of the table. She dumped a large plate of seafood into the batter and stirred. She completed her preparation by pouring green tea for the four men at the table and then exited the room.

"Is okonomiyaki okay with you?" the owner of the restaurant asked Edward, referring to a Japanese dish cooked at the table that is often translated as a savory pancake not traditionally eaten for breakfast.

"Sure."

"Good. Our patient said he was looking forward to having some real Japanese food. He said there wasn't any in Tupelo."

"They have some, but it's not very good."

"As one would think," the old man said, taking a sip of his tea. "Now let's get down to business," he added with a sense of confidence that indicated he was the man in charge and everyone else, including the doctor, was along for the ride. Edward surmised whatever decision had been made, it was between the owner of the restaurant and Fukuzawa in Tokyo.

"After considering our options, we've decided the best-case scenario is for Shiro to return to Japan under the passport he entered the country with. He is part of a tour group and that tour group leaves the day after tomorrow."

"What about his finger?" Edward asked.

"The doctor will produce real medical documentation that should allow Shiro to pass through immigration with very limited risk."

Edward breathed a sigh of relief and the old man took another sip of green tea.

"We also want to make sure we have no other surprises. The doctor just informed me the missing finger could be in the possession of law enforcement. Is this right?"

"We have confirmation that it is," Edward replied solemnly.

"What else does law enforcement know?"

"It's hard to say for sure."

"Use your imagination."

"I assume they think a Japanese man killed two people in Tupelo, Mississippi. I assume they believe this Japanese man lost a fake finger in the commission of the crime."

"And he was staying at a cheap motel in town. Is that correct?"

"That's right."

"Was any evidence left in the room?"

Edward shrugged his shoulders. "The room was cleaned by a friend after we left."

The old man stared at Shiro across the table.

"He also had a rental car. It's been taken care of."

"How?"

"I assume it has been destroyed. Or chopped up and sold for parts."

"But you don't know?"

"I don't. All I know is the car was removed from hotel property."

"And what about the vehicle you came here in? He was in the back seat for the entire ride, correct?"

"Yes."

"Did anything happen on your ride? Did you get pulled over?"

"No. I stopped three times for gas and one time for a calling card."

"Do you think your car is clean?"

"It's my wife's car. She passed away. I was planning on getting rid of it out here. Maybe park it in a bad area of town with the windows down and the keys in it."

"What are you going to say when the police ask about your wife's car?"

"I'll tell them it was stolen."

"I see," the old man replied. "I have a better idea. There's a CarMax down the road. When we're done here, drive your car over there and sell it. Take whatever they offer you. Don't negotiate. Get the paperwork. Get in and out."

"And then what?"

"And then forget about it."

Edward considered asking why but was cut short by the second half of lunch preparations.

Apologizing for the interruption, the waitress reappeared at the door to the room and moved onto the tatami floor. She sprinkled several drops of water onto the griddle and watched them sizzle. She spread a small amount of oil and brushed it across the hot surface before pouring the batter into four equal pancakes. She wielded a small metal spatula to contain the batter as it ran towards the edges of the griddle. The aroma reminded Edward how hungry he was. Shiro removed his arm from the sling, picked up a pair of chopsticks, and broke them apart.

The waitress spent several minutes flipping the pancakes and covering them with a dark sauce, fish flakes, and mayonnaise. Finished, she lowered a pancake onto each man's plate. She reached under the table and turned off the heat to the griddle. She quickly gathered her cooking utensils and excused herself from the room, again closing the *shoji* door behind her.

The old man poured sake for everyone at the table and then offered a toast to a successful completion of their mission.

Edward raised his cup and took a healthy gulp of pre-lunch sake, forcing it into his empty stomach. He waited until everyone at the table finished their drink and placed their cups on the wooden outer edge of the table. Confident the meal was about to begin, Edward picked up his chopsticks.

Waiting for a cue to start eating, Edward noticed the old man lock eyes with Shiro and nod.

Shiro bowed, moved his plate to the side, and placed his hands squarely on the still piping-hot grill. A second later, Edward's brain registered what he was witnessing and he lunged forward to grab Shiro's hands. The old man snatched Edward by the scruff of the neck and pulled him onto his backside.

"Don't interfere," the old man said without any emotion.

Horror overwhelmed Edward as the acrid smell of burning flesh filled his nose. Shiro's face contorted, his eyes bulging in unison with the veins in his neck. For five nightmare-inducing seconds, Shiro kept his palms on the heat of the grill before he retracted his hands with a blood-curdling yell.

Edward scrambled for the exit to the room and managed to open the sliding door before vomiting on the floor.

*

Edward dragged himself back to the table after a lengthy intermission in the bathroom. He opened the door to the private room and the owner of the restaurant motioned for Edward to return to his position at the table. Edward sat and stared at Shiro, who had his eyes closed, each hand submerged in a bowl of ice water.

The doctor and the old man finished their plates, wolfing down their lunch with the stench of cooked human flesh still hanging in the air.

Feral dogs, Edward thought.

The doctor sensed Edward's uneasiness and pushed his plate to the side. He wiped his mouth with a napkin and cleared his throat. "I only said we wouldn't chop off his arms. Besides, there was only one way to be sure the lost prosthetic finger would never be matched. We just destroyed the other nine it matches to."

"There had to be a better way." Edward said.

The doctor shook his head. "He'll be well taken care of. I'll personally treat his burns and accompany him back to Japan with his tour group."

"And how do you explain the injuries?"

"Accidents happen. Too much to drink at a Japanese restaurant and he stumbled onto a hot griddle."

"And what about the missing finger?"

"I'll wrap both hands. Make it look like he has ten. No one will notice. And if anyone wants to see the wounds, I'll start by showing them the burns on his other hand. Combined with official medical forms from the UCLA emergency room it should be sufficient to pass any superficial scrutiny."

Shiro opened his eyes and closed them again, his head resting against the wall behind him.

Edward looked down at his own heavily scarred hand and shook his head. "He's going to regret those burns later," he said, almost tearing up.

"He did what he had to do. This is our best chance for him to get him home so he can heal and disappear back into his previous life."

The old man and the doctor finished another round of sake as Edward vowed never to eat anything from a griddle again.

"Before you leave and take care of your car," the old man said, "don't forget Mr. Fukuzawa is expecting you to repay your debt. I assume I don't need to remind you of how seriously he takes debt repayment."

Edward exchanged glances with everyone around the table and nodded, his hair standing on end.

CHAPTER 55

EDWARD STOOD IN line at the ticket counter, five people back from a blonde with a red scarf tied in her hair. He tried to relax as the line shuffled forward, one customer at a time. When he reached the front, he slipped a hundred dollar bill to the woman at the counter behind the security glass. The woman with the large Elvis Presley badge attached to her white shirt pushed a ticket and Graceland visitor guide to Edward through the pass-through of the window.

"The bus for the next tour leaves in five minutes, but you can board now."

Edward stopped at the door to the small shuttle bus and presented his ticket to the driver who waved him on. Looking at the half-full bus, Edward easily spotted Mindy sitting in the back row. Mindy looked up and seemed to immediately recognize Edward despite his disguise in an LA Lakers cap and oversized Hollywood sunglasses.

"Is this seat taken," Edward asked with a smile.

"It's yours," Mindy replied, playing along.

"Any trouble?"

"The police have had someone keeping an eye on the motel since Detective Rafferty paid me a visit."

"Did he see you leave?"

"He did. But I wasn't followed."

"Are you sure?"

"There are some long stretches of empty roads between Tupelo and Memphis. And I doubled back a couple of times."

"Good enough. Besides, even if you were followed, I don't think anyone is jumping on this tour to follow us."

"I hope not. How did it go out there in California? Did Taro make it?"

"He's alive, if that's what you mean," Edward answered with a cracking voice. "They said they're going to fly out tomorrow."

"I get the feeling you're not telling me everything."

"I'm not." Edward said. "And just so you know, his real name isn't Taro."

"He will always be Taro to me."

"Fine, Taro it is. This morning I watched our friend Taro intentionally place his hands and fingers on a burning-hot griddle. He sustained massive burns."

"He did this to himself?"

"He did," Edward said.

"In front of you?"

"There were four of us at the table, including Taro."

"That must've been awful."

"I may never sleep again. And I wasn't sleeping much to begin with."

A couple claimed the row of seats in front of them and Edward put his finger to his lips, shaking his head slightly. The door of the shuttle bus closed and the vehicle chugged through the parking lot before crossing four lanes of traffic on Highway 51, also known as Elvis Presley Boulevard. Ninety seconds after departing, the bus arrived at the large circular driveway to the Graceland Mansion. The patrons on the bus disembarked. Edward and Mindy slowed their pace until they were at the back of the tour group.

"Did he burn himself because of the missing finger?" Mindy whispered as the tour guide gave his introduction to Graceland for the thousandth time.

"Taro's boss figured the only real danger was if law enforcement or Immigration matched the fingerprint from the lost finger to his other nine fingers."

"So they took care of that."

"Permanently."

"What do we do now?"

"That's a good question. I'm considering some options. Either way, I don't think the police are done with you yet."

"I'm sure they're not."

"You're probably the only person who admitted to spending time with their prime murder suspect. They'll be back."

"I don't know what else I can tell them."

"Don't tell them anything else. Stick to what you said and leave it at that. You met the guy. You had a few beers with the guy. You went to the festival with the guy. That's all you know."

"What if they find out I'm lying?"

"About what?"

"Everything. For starters, the detective showed me the photo from Taro's passport. One glance told me it wasn't really him. It was someone else. What if they come back with another photo, Taro's real photo, and ask me why I didn't notice the passport photo wasn't him?"

"Don't sweat it. As stereotypical as it sounds, a lot of Americans have difficulty distinguishing between Asian faces, especially those sharing a close resemblance. I mean, you weren't the only one who didn't notice the photo in the passport wasn't Taro. It doesn't sound like the motel office paid much attention to the passport photo either."

"Unless it was a test. A setup."

"If the police come back to question you, hire an attorney before you say anything."

"You don't think hiring an attorney makes me look guilty?"

"I think going to prison makes you look guilty. If the police visit you again, tell them they're making you feel uncomfortable. Tell them they're making it seem as if you're guilty. Tell them if they continue asking questions that sound like accusations, you will hire an attorney."

"And then?"

"And then hire one."

"I'll think about it."

"Ultimately, it's your decision."

"Making good decisions isn't my strong suit. Obviously. Besides, I don't have money for an attorney."

"I'll cover it. But make sure they accept payment in cash."

"Oh, I like the sound of that. My own sugar daddy."

"You need an experienced defense attorney. Don't get some ambulance chaser or divorce lawyer."

"Okay."

Edward and Mindy followed the tour group into the Jungle Room. With most of the entourage taking selfies, Mindy turned towards Edward. "What do I say if someone asks if you and I have ever met? It's possible we've been seen together."

"By who?"

"I don't know, but this is the fifth time we've met. The first time was on the street when Taro got out of your car. The second time was at Pervis Wade's after the you-know-what. The third time was at the motel when you came to Taro's room. The fourth time was when you picked Taro up to take him to California. Today is the fifth."

"I don't think anyone is going to put us together."

"But they could."

"Maybe."

"I was thinking about it on the drive here. If you're okay with it, I could always imply you were one of my clients. That is, if anyone asks what our connection is."

"Are you suggesting that I admit to visiting prostitutes as a cover for murder?"

"Yes."

"First off, if anyone asks if we know each other, let your attorney answer. Or rather, not answer. But if we ever end up in court, under fire, with our lives on the line, you can imply I paid you for sex. Hopefully it won't come to that."

"But it might."

"It might. And it might not."

"Aren't you worried?" Mindy asked.

"The Lee County Sheriff's Department left me two voicemails yesterday and another this afternoon. It's safe to say they want to speak with me."

"That's not good."

"I have an alibi for the night Pervis Wade was murdered. The problem with the Lee County Sheriff's Department is they don't play by the rules."

Out of the corner of his eye, Edward thought he saw Mindy wiping tears from her face.

"Well, I'm *really* worried," she said.

"We're both guilty of something, but the only way we go to prison is if they catch our Japanese friend. I doubt they're going to find him."

"Anyone can be found."

"Which is why I have a backup plan."

"I'm all ears."

"I'm going to convince the Lee County Sheriff's Department to stop investigating."

"Is that all?"

"Seems pretty straightforward, actually."

"Oh, I'm sure it will be," Mindy said sarcastically.

CHAPTER 56

EDWARD PARKED HIS car in a gravel driveway and watched a broad-shouldered black man in a tank top carry a box from the back of a pickup truck to the front porch of a white farmhouse. A white van sat in the shade of a carport to the left of the house.

Edward got out of his car as the man returned to the truck and moved another box, muscles flexing.

"Good afternoon," Edward said across the yard.

The man wiped his hands on his jeans and came down the driveway. "You must be Edward."

"I am. Edward Winston. Nice to meet you."

"Reggie Taylor," the man replied, sweat on his chiseled face and strong jaw.

"Thanks for making the time."

"Not a problem. Took the morning off. Getting ready to redo a laundry room."

A train whistled in the distance and Edward craned his neck towards the field across the road.

"That's the ten o'clock from Tupelo to Memphis. Comes through everyone morning. Has for as long as I can remember."

"Are you from around here?"

"Not too far. Just across the way. Bought this place from my uncle after I got out of the army. Fixed it up so my mother would have a place to stay. Her health is failing. I've been working on the house for a couple of years now. Just need to put tile in the laundry room, install a new washer and dryer, and I'm done."

Edward looked up at the farmhouse with a silver metal roof. "It looks great from the outside."

"It's been renovated down to the studs. New electric system. New plumbing. My brother and some cousins did a lot of the heavy lifting. I did the electrical work myself."

"Are you an electrician?"

"I don't have a license, if that's what you mean. But I don't need one to work on my own house."

"I guess not."

"So you wanted to talk about my job when I worked at Cedar Creek," Reggie said.

"That's right. And I want to know about Pervis Wade and Charlie Sterling."

"Digger mentioned you were asking about Pervis, among other things."

"Did you know Pervis?"

Reggie pulled a blue handkerchief from his back pocket and wiped the perspiration off his forehead. "I know he's dead. And I know he killed Charlie Sterling. Everyone does."

Edward nodded. "Did Digger tell you why I was asking about Pervis?"

"He said you thought Pervis killed your wife."

"That's right."

"You'll have to forgive me for saying so, but the news never mentioned Pervis Wade in your wife's disappearance. *That* I would have remembered."

"The Lee County Sheriff's Department made sure everyone heard what they wanted them to hear."

The veins in Reggie's forehead pulsed. "I don't know what you're implying, but if you're going down the road I think you are, this conversation is over."

"And I think we're just getting started."

The two men stood face-to-face in the gravel driveway as if engaged in an impromptu blinking contest.

"I'll give you five minutes to say what you came here to say," Reggie relented. "For your wife's sake."

"I researched you and your company, Antebellum Security, before I came out here. Seems like you've done well since you left Cedar Creek. Looks like you've benefitted from several private consulting contracts with Lee County. Some security gigs for the sheriff's department and a couple for the Lee County School System as well."

"I've been lucky. Everyone needs security these days."

"Luck is part of it. But it's not everything. According to public records, the Lee County Sheriff's Department has steered over a hundred thousand dollars' worth of contracts in your direction over the last couple of years."

"There's nothing illegal about hiring a security professional with credentials."

"I'm sure. And you maintain a preferred contractor status with the county as both a veteran and a minority."

"Doesn't hurt."

"So you don't dispute you have a business relationship with the Lee County Sheriff's Department?"

"It's not a secret. There's nothing to dispute. And if the conversation wasn't over before, it is now."

"But you haven't heard my business offer yet."

Reggie crossed his arms and clenched his fist. "I'm not sure I need to."

"I think you do. Because the FBI is investigating the Lee County Sheriff's Department for abuse of power, falsifying evidence, murder, and whatever else they discover. And that means your gravy train is coming to an end."

Edward didn't take his eyes off Reggie. "Judging by the look on your face, I assume you didn't know they were under federal investigation. It's not public knowledge."

Reggie squinted as if trying to see the truth.

"Rest assured, the FBI is going to put someone in jail. The only real question is how many people," Edward said. He could see anguish growing across Reggie's face.

"You're engaging in dangerous talk for someone living in this county," Reggie said.

"I'm not going to be here much longer. I'm one moving truck away from leaving the great state of Mississippi forever."

"And I'm going to be here forever. At least as long as my momma is." Reggie set his gaze on the field across the street from his home. "How do you know for sure Pervis Wade killed your wife?"

"He admitted it to me. And the police covered it up. Then the Lee County Sheriff's Department altered evidence to make it look like my neighbor was responsible. "

Reggie again wiped his face with his handkerchief.

"And what's your business offer? What would someone who's leaving these parts need me for?" Reggie asked.

"I want to hire you as a security consultant. For the week."

"And what happens at the end of the week? As you pointed out, my contracts with Lee County provide a substantial chunk of my business. What am I going to do when you're gone?"

"What are you going to do when *all* of your contracts are gone?"

Perspiration glistened on Reggie's forehead.

"I'm willing to pay you a hundred grand for a week of work," Edward said.

"A hundred grand?"

"That's right. Seems like the appropriate amount of compensation given what you're likely to lose."

"Have you ever heard the expression 'if it sounds too good to be true, it probably is'?"

Edward reached into the pocket on his shirt and produced a cashier's check made out to Antebellum Security. He handed the check to Reggie, who held it up towards the sun.

"It's real. That's fifty grand," Edward said. "Part of my wife's life insurance settlement. I can't think of a better way to spend it."

"You must have had good insurance."

"We did."

"It looks legitimate," Reggie confirmed, lowering the check and folding it.

"It is. But feel free to call or visit the bank."

"I might do that."

"And I'll bring you another fifty grand after I've moved."

"And what do I have to do?"

"First, you need to start answering questions."

Reggie looked back at his house. "Wait here."

Edward watched as Reggie crossed the yard and stepped into the shade of his carport. Reggie opened the side door to the van parked on the concrete slab and minutes later returned to the yard carrying a yellow electronic device the size of a brick.

"What's that?" Edward asked nervously as Reggie approached.

"A scanner."

"For what?"

"Listening devices and cameras. Arms up."

Edward put his arms out to the side. Reggie ran the scanner over Edward's body, front, back, legs, arms.

"Where's your cell phone?" Reggie asked.

"In the car."

Reggie pointed the device in the direction of the car in his driveway and the device chirped.

"How accurate is that thing?" Edward asked.

"This one detects all radio frequency signals between one megahertz and six gigahertz. That covers all WiFi, DECT, GSM, Bluetooth, FM, VHF, UHF, and other audio and video transmission frequencies, including cell phones."

"Basically everything."

"I'd imagine the NSA or CIA has a few things this can't detect. Beyond that, within thirty feet, yeah, it catches everything."

"Do you use this on all your guests?"

"Nope. Just the ones who want to talk about things that make me nervous."

Reggie finished his scan and pointed to a pair of chairs in the front yard. "Let's grab a seat."

Edward followed Reggie through the grass, into the shade, and sat down. Reggie lowered himself into the chair across from Edward, scanner in his lap.

"Before we get started, if anyone ever asks me if we spoke, I'll deny it."

"Fair enough," Edward replied.

Reggie nodded. "What do you want to know?"

"I want to know what happened out at Cedar Creek during the last Sterling Insurance seminar. I want to know about this missing Rolex I've been hearing about. I want to know what happened between Charlie Sterling and Pervis Wade."

"That's a long list."

"Let's start with you. How did you end up at Cedar Creek?"

"I was in the army for eight years and when I got out, Cedar Creek was my first job."

"What did you do in the army?"

"I was a security specialist."

"What does a security specialist do?"

"Secures perimeters. Secures communications. Pretty much what you'd imagine. When I got out of the army I came back home and tried to put my skills to use."

"So Cedar Creek was your first job out of the army."

"Yeah."

"Were you working the night the Sterling Insurance seminar got out of hand?"

"Back then, I worked most every weekend. A lot of weddings. Some business events. It was usually pretty low-key."

"How long did you work there?"

"A couple of years. When I started, I set up most of Cedar Creek's security. They had had some problems with a few break-ins back in the day. Not surprising really. During the week, there weren't a lot of people around."

"What kind of security did you install?"

"Cameras. Alarm systems. The whole works. I'd just spent eight years doing essentially the same thing for the military. It wasn't hard. Most of it was standard stuff. Cameras on the corners of the buildings. Cameras in the lobby. Most of the common areas were covered. Bubble cameras in the ceiling of most of the halls."

"What about that last Sterling Insurance seminar at Cedar Creek? Digger said it was the straw that broke the camel's back. He said after that night he asked Charlie Sterling to take his business elsewhere."

"That's right."

"What exactly happened?"

"Someone brought a bit of moonshine and a couple of the gentlemen went after it harder than they should have. And it led to trouble."

"Digger said someone urinated in a potted plant. Other people vomited. He mentioned a fistfight."

"Like I said, people got a little drunk. All of the above happened. And more."

"Such as?"

"Most notably, someone called for late-night entertainment."

"Entertainment?"

"A van full of strippers, allegedly."

"You were in charge of security. Were they strippers or not?"

"Hard to say. I didn't ask them what they did for a living."

"But you saw them?"

"I did. A vanload of women arrived sometime around eleven in the evening."

"Did you see them on camera or in person?"

"Both. But I did most of my observing via security cameras."

"Did you catch any of these ladies performing?"

"Not a one. Digger refused to install surveillance in any of the guest rooms. The women I saw were mingling with guests in the common areas. That's it."

"Did you do anything?"

"Like what?"

"Call the authorities."

"The authorities were already there. Policemen. Lawyers. Politicians. A judge. The strippers weren't doing anything illegal that I could see. Just a half-dozen women in short shorts and even shorter skirts, coming late to an insurance seminar. It was tame, really. Although I'm sure Digger wouldn't have thought so."

"I take it you don't share Digger's religious convictions."

"I drive my mother to church on Sundays, but I'm in no position to cast the first stone. You wouldn't believe some of the stuff I saw on military bases when I was overseas. Besides, what was I supposed to do? These were grown-ass men. Pillars of the community."

"So you figured you'd let them have their fun."

"Whatever took place behind closed doors was between the adults who chose to enter those rooms. Hell, stripping by itself is not even illegal here in Mississippi."

"So then what happened?"

"The girls left a little after one."

"And that's it?"

"Pretty much. I kept an eye on them until they were back in their vehicle. By then, things had calmed down. Most of the drunks had passed out."

"Did you ever talk to Digger about what you saw?"

"I didn't have to. The bar and housekeeping staff started talking. The next day, Digger asked me if I saw anything illegal. I told him what I saw, and what I didn't see."

"And what did he say?"

"He said to get rid of the surveillance video."

"Did you?"

"I did."

"But that wasn't the end of the conversation, was it?"

"It was the end of the stripper conversation."

"At what point did Troy Wade's Rolex go missing?"

Reggie sighed. "Here we go with the mystery of the missing watch."

"What do you mean?"

"That damn watch was only missed for a few short hours. It may have gone missing, but by lunch the next day, I can tell you that watch wasn't being missed by anyone."

"It was my understanding the missing watch could have been the reason Charlie Sterling was killed."

"It wasn't."

"You seem sure."

"I am."

"It was also my understanding that the police came to Cedar Creek with a search warrant a month after the insurance seminar. After Charlie Sterling's death. Court records indicate the police served a warrant to search for evidence about a missing watch."

Reggie shook his head and swatted at a gnat buzzing near his face. "The police didn't come back to Cedar Creek looking for a watch."

"That's what they told Digger Graham. That's what the search warrant says."

"I don't care what they told Digger Graham or what was written on the search warrant. I spent a couple of hours with the police. They were only interested in one thing."

"Whether or not you caught them on tape with any of the strippers?"

Reggie paused. "Naw, but that's a good guess. I already told you there were no cameras in the guest rooms and the girls, if they did anything, only did it behind closed doors."

"Then what did the police want when they came back with the search warrant after Sterling was killed?"

"They wanted a copy of the surveillance camera feeds in other parts of the resort."

"Like?"

"Specifically, they wanted a copy of the surveillance video they thought I had given to Troy Wade."

"Surveillance video that you gave to Troy Wade?"

"That's right."

"Did you give a surveillance tape to Troy Wade? Did you have video surveillance of someone stealing his watch?"

"You're not listening. No one gave a shit about the watch. The only thing important about the missing watch was that it brought Troy Wade into my security office to look at surveillance tapes."

"And what did you see?"

"When Troy Wade discovered his watch was missing, he went drunk nuts. This was late. Two in the morning. After the strippers had left. I was called to the lobby to try to calm him down. Eventually he agreed to discuss it in the morning, when clearer heads could prevail. Sure enough, the next morning, before I finished my shift, Troy Wade was back at my office demanding to see the security tapes for the whole resort."

"The next morning?"

"Early. The sun was up. I'm not sure if Troy Wade had slept or not. Some of those boys partied all night."

"And did you show Troy Wade the tapes."

"We ran through every security tape we had."

"Did you find out who took the watch?"

"No. But we stumbled upon something bigger than the watch."

"Like what?"

"The morning after the watch went missing, I sat in the security room with Troy Wade for a couple of hours, zipping through surveillance feeds while he drank black coffee and tried to feel better about himself. Right about the time we were finished, we took a look at the video for the pool area…" Reggie said, his voice trailing off.

"And…?"

"Well, first of all, the pool area closed at 11:00 p.m., which meant no one should have been back there. It's just too dangerous with all those people drinking."

"But someone was back there."

"Not someone. Four men. One of whom was the soon-to-be-elected Sheriff Blazer."

"And you saw him on video?"

"That's right. At the time, we had two security cameras out back near the pool. A towel had been thrown over one of the cameras—the one closer to the building. I guess no one noticed the second camera near the gazebo."

"What did the cameras capture?"

"At first it was just four guys sitting on the edge of the hot tub. A couple of them had drinks. There was no audio, so I couldn't hear what was said, but the four men seemed to be in a jovial mood. Four guys sitting around, drinking, talking, laughing."

"Nothing unusual."

"Not until Sheriff Blazer—Detective Blazer at the time—pulled out a little fanny pack and divvied up several lines of cocaine."

"You have the sheriff on video using cocaine?"

"That's what I saw. And the sheriff was generous with his stash. He shared with his friends."

"So all four men engaged in illicit drug usage?"

"They did. And then the video became even more interesting."

"How's that?"

Reggie looked around his yard suspiciously. "Well, after they did a few lines of coke, the four men disrobed and hopped in the hot tub together. From there, you can let your imagination wander."

"You're kidding…"

"Wish I was."

"Who were the other three men?"

"I figure you probably have a good idea who they were."

"I'm going to assume one of them was Detective Will Rafferty."

"That's right."

"Who were the other two?"

"A judge named Vernon Potter. And the fourth was Charlie Sterling."

Edward felt as if he had been kicked in the groin.

"Are you sure that's what you saw?"

"Am I sure? Hell yeah, I'm sure."

"Holy crap," Edward managed to say.

"Not the type of thing that a sheriff who supports God's Law and maintains a strong anti-drug position would like to go public."

"Say again?" Edward choked.

"Everyone knows Sheriff Blazer won his first election largely based on his anti-drug stance. He vowed to clean up Lee County at a time when heroin and meth were booming. He won his second term as sheriff with the help of his public support of God's Law."

"What's God's Law?"

"I can tell you aren't from Mississippi. God's Law allows individuals and businesses to discriminate against gays and lesbians if they are basing their discrimination on their own religious beliefs."

"And Sheriff Blazer supported this law?"

"He did. And between the drugs and the Jacuzzi club for men on the surveillance video, well, that would make Sheriff Blazer one of the biggest hypocrites this state has ever seen."

Edward didn't talk for a full minute and Reggie stared upward, the sun in the blue sky shining down through the tree leaves above.

"Do you think that video was worth killing people over?" Edward asked.

"I'd say the facts speak for themselves."

Another long pause followed. "So you found this cocaine and Jacuzzi video when you were reviewing security tapes with Troy Wade while look-ing for his watch?" Edward confirmed.

"That's right."

"And you gave a copy of this surveillance tape to Troy Wade?"

"I didn't give him anything. He offered to buy a copy of it."

"And you accepted?"

"You would have, too. And he was true to his word. He came back later that day with a brown bag full of hundreds and I gave him a copy. Burned it on a disk."

"And what happened then?"

"Nothing. Troy Wade never mentioned the missing watch again. He never filed a stolen property report. I assume he didn't want the police investigating his lost watch and discovering the video we had stumbled upon. He wanted to keep things quiet."

"What was he going to do with the video? I thought he was friends with Sheriff Blazer and Detective Rafferty."

"I know they went to high school together. I know they had a busi-ness relationship with each other. But I never got the impression they were friends."

"So you sold him the surveillance video?"

"I did. And I did it for the money. Simple as that."

"Everyone's motivated by something. Money is the easiest to understand."

Reggie shrugged his shoulders.

"So, you illegally sold a video that wasn't yours to sell?"

"And it wasn't yours either, so why do you care? Troy Wade offered to buy it and I took him up on it. Hell, if Digger knew about the hot tub video, he would have told me to destroy it. I mean, he wanted me to delete all surveillance videos of strippers with their clothes on. What do you think he'd want me to do with a video of four naked men doing coke and fooling around in his hot tub?"

"So Digger never knew about the four men?"

"I never told him."

Edward shook his head in disbelief. "Did you ever see Troy Wade again after you sold him the surveillance video?"

"A few weeks later Troy Wade died of a heart attack."

"What do you think happened to his copy of the video?"

"I think Troy Wade's son, Pervis, found his father's secret surveillance video after his father passed away. I think Pervis Wade played that DVD and saw what his father and I saw. I think Pervis Wade decided he was going to keep that video and use it."

"Are you speculating?"

"Not entirely. Pervis Wade paid me a visit once out at Cedar Creek. Before I left the job. He wanted to know if I knew anything about any security tapes his father owned."

"What did you say?"

"I played dumb. Said I didn't know what he was talking about or how his father could have gotten his hands on any of Cedar Creek's surveillance tapes."

"Do you think Pervis Wade killed Charlie Sterling because of the security tape?"

"I do, somehow, some way. And for that I feel bad. But it was after the fact. There's no way I could have guessed Troy Wade would have passed away and his son would have found the surveillance tape."

"Any guess on what happened between Charlie Sterling and Pervis?"

"I think Pervis saw Charlie in the surveillance video. I think he set up a meeting with Charlie and blackmailed him. Maybe Charlie didn't like being blackmailed and he threatened to go the police and let them know their escapades had been caught on video. Either way, something pushed Pervis over the edge and he killed Charlie. It's easy to speculate Pervis used that same video to blackmail the police and Judge Potter. Made all the charges against him in the Charlie Sterling case disappear."

"And after Pervis blackmailed the police, the police showed up at Cedar Creek with a search warrant looking for other copies of the compromising security tape."

"That's the way I figure it. The police came out to Cedar Creek saying they were looking for the missing watch, but in reality, they were looking to see if there were any other copies of the hot tub surveillance video."

"What did you tell them?"

"I told them we don't keep our security tapes that long."

"That's what Digger said."

"It's true."

"Is it, Reggie?" Edward asked.

Reggie stared at Edward and raised his hands, leaving the electronic scanner in his lap. "Okay. Okay. You got me. I did keep an extra copy of the video. I kept it for a whole month. But as soon as Charlie Sterling was murdered and Pervis Wade walked, I destroyed the only copy I had."

"You got nervous?"

"Pervis Wade made most people nervous."

"Yes he did. And with good reason."

Reggie nodded.

"And how did you establish your relationship with the Lee County Sheriff's Department? How does that conversation come about?"

"Sheriff Blazer. When he and Rafferty came out to serve their search warrant, it was pretty obvious I knew why they were really there. I'm sure they picked up on it. I mean, Sheriff Blazer was a detective at the time and Rafferty became one. Detective types are pretty good at reading people. Anyhow, after I told them I didn't have the video they were looking for and that Cedar Creek didn't keep their surveillance tapes that long, they seemed relieved. Real relieved."

"Relieved enough to offer you a job?"

"They didn't come right out and offer me a job. But Sheriff Blazer let me know the Lee County Sheriff's Department contracted security work and that someone with my skills could be a good fit."

"Meaning someone with a security background?"

"I believe his exact words were: 'Someone with a security background who knows how to keep his mouth shut about things they've seen.'"

"And what else?"

"What do you mean?"

"I'm just wondering if there wasn't something else in that equation between you and the Lee County Sheriff's Department."

Reggie paused. "What makes you say that?"

"Just the way the Lee County Sheriff's Department operates. I wonder if they didn't threaten you with something. Maybe catch you with a pound of weed in your trunk that wasn't yours. Hold something over your head."

Reggie glanced back at his house. "Who you been talking to?"

"No one."

"There ain't no way you're coming up with that theory on your own."

"The Lee County Sheriff's Department framed my neighbor for my wife's murder. Planted evidence. So I know that's in their repertoire."

"You don't know what you're talking about."

"Maybe I don't. But you also seemed pretty eager to accept the cashier's check I offered you."

Reggie sat stoically for several seconds. "It was crystal meth, and they planted it in my mother's living room sofa."

"Holy shit," Edward whispered.

Reggie's pupils narrowed. "What kind of people threaten to put an old woman out of her house and send her son to jail. Who does that?"

"They've done worse."

"Well, that's what happened. They set me up and then made it all disappear. Told me they could make it happen again anytime they wanted. I was offered work contracts or prison. I took the work."

"I would have, too."

Reggie sighed. "Like I said, if anyone ever asks if you and I spoke, I'll deny it."

"I don't blame you."

Silence fell on Reggie's front lawn.

"And you're sure you don't have another copy of that video? Maybe you kept one just in case? For a rainy day?" Edward asked.

"You think the sheriff would have given me a job if he thought I still had a copy of the video?"

"How would they know?"

"Because they asked me about the video during my polygraph."

"What polygraph?"

"A polygraph was required as part of the background check before I could work as a security consultant for Lee County."

"And they asked if you still had a copy of the video?"

"It was one of the questions."

Edward's head dipped, casting his gaze on the ground in disappointment.

"What would you do with the video if you had a copy?" Reggie asked.

"I could come up with something to do with it."

"Well, like I said, I destroyed the copy I had. Troy Wade had the only other copy I know of."

"Which became Pervis Wade's copy."

Edward reached into his pocket and handed Reggie a business card. "Call me if you think of anything else I need to know."

"What about the rest of the money you're promising?"

"You'll get paid."

"You know, most people like to see something before they pay for it."

Edward paused and his eyebrows rose. "Yes, they do."

"And?"

"Consider yourself on retainer. If I call, make yourself available."

Edward stood and shook hands with Reggie. Over Reggie's shoulder, Edward spotted an old woman in a wheelchair sitting at the front door.

"You just shook hands with your mother watching," Edward said. "So, we have a witness."

CHAPTER 57

ROSE STERLING SAT in the shade of her front porch as Edward's Camry slowed to a halt in front of her house. Edward exited the car and waved his hand. Seconds later, he reached the bottom of the porch steps and looked up at Rose. A book rested on her lap, a long bookmark hanging from the binding. She reached out for her drink on the table next to her and took a sip.

"You're back," Rose said.

"I am."

"Did you leave your questions at home?"

"Unfortunately, no."

Rose took another taste of her drink. "Are you still running down Pervis Wade as your wife's killer?"

"I am."

"Any luck?"

"I've made some progress. Met some people. Paid a visit to Cedar Creek."

"You did?"

"I did. Had a nice chat with Digger. He referred me to a guy named Reggie Taylor who was the head of security when your husband had his last seminar out that way."

A hint of discomfort seemed to wash across Rose's face. "Do you want a drink?" she asked.

"Sure."

"It's iced tea. With Captain Morgan and a twist of lemon."

"I could use a little Captain in my afternoon."

Rose stood without excusing herself and disappeared through her front door. A minute later she was back on the porch, filling Edward's glass.

"You caught me in a good mood," Rose said. "Just sitting here on the porch with a drink and the Good Book."

"An interesting combination."

"Almost as good as Ambien and red wine. Did you have a chance to try it yet?"

"Not yet."

"You'll get there," Rose said with a wink.

Edward raised his glass and took a healthy sip. He puckered his lips and lowered his glass back down to the table.

"So can I ask you a few more questions?"

"I wouldn't have offered you a drink if my answer was no."

"You're probably not going to like them."

"Then I guess you're lucky I've been drinking. It makes me like everything a little better."

Edward took a larger gulp and the ice cubes clinked back towards the bottom of the glass. "I think I know why your husband was killed."

"Is that right?"

"Yes. I think your husband was killed because he was being blackmailed by Pervis Wade. I think he met Pervis Wade in the parking lot of Down Home Cooking and was going to pay Pervis to keep a secret a secret."

"And what was that secret?"

"A disk with a surveillance video on it. From Cedar Creek." Edward didn't elaborate. They both stared straight ahead.

"And just what would've been on this alleged surveillance video?" Rose asked.

"I think you know."

"Why don't you tell me just the same? My house, my porch, my prerogative."

"I think it was a video showing your husband engaged in illicit drug usage followed by sexual relations with two law enforcement officers and a certain judge."

"Oh my," Rose replied, shutting her eyes. "Doesn't that make you the clever one?"

"So, it's true?"

Rose caressed her glass, drips of condensation landing on her white dress.

"And the missing Rolex was all a smoke screen?" Edward added.

Rose nodded. "Everyone knew about the missing watch. It was a fitting misdirect that both a grieving widow and law enforcement could embrace."

"Jesus."

"Careful with blasphemy."

"What happened between your husband and Pervis?"

"They had arranged to meet in a public place and my husband was going to pay Pervis ten thousand dollars to keep quiet about the video. It seemed like a reasonable sum considering the impact that video could have had on my husband's business. He would have lost a lot of clients. *We* would have lost a lot of clients. It's possible the business could have survived the revelation of drug use. But no one in business or politics in this city or state could survive the combination of what was recorded on that surveillance tape."

"So you knew your husband met with Pervis to pay him off?"

"That was the deal. But before they met for the payoff, Pervis decided that ten grand wasn't enough money. He wanted thirty."

"Uh-oh."

"And my husband balked. He could see the writing on the wall. He knew that he was heading down a slippery slope and didn't feel like adding Pervis Wade to his permanent payroll. He decided he would meet with Pervis as previously agreed, and would pay him ten thousand dollars. If Pervis demanded more, my husband would tell the law enforcement officers also on the surveillance tape that Pervis was blackmailing him."

"Which Pervis didn't agree to..."

"Apparently not, because my husband never made it home from the meeting. Pervis decided the video was his get-out-of-jail-free card. And he used it."

"And he walked."

"Pervis Wade killed my Charles. All the other stuff is just details. The tire iron. The physical altercation. Whatever. The cops came in and created the story they wanted everyone to hear."

"I've seen it in person," Edward said. "Did the police ever mention the video?"

"Not directly. Not to me. They took items from my house to aid in their investigation of the incident between Pervis Wade and my husband. They never came out and told me they were looking for a video."

"And if they had?"

"That's a good question."

"The answer is important."

Rose took another sip of her drink. "Just what are you getting at, Mr. Winston?"

"You said your husband was prepared to pay Pervis Wade to keep things quiet. A reasonable man would want to see evidence before handing over a large sum of money."

Rose's knuckles whitened. Then she spoke in a quiet voice. "I saw the video. Found it in the mailbox in a plain manila envelope. Had my husband's name scribbled across the front. It was resting between the electric bill and the weekly coupons for Schnucks Grocery. I'll never forget that trip to the mailbox."

"I'm sure it was hard. Forgive me for asking."

Rose shook her head. "I watched the whole damn thing. Wish I hadn't."

"I'm sorry."

"Me, too," Rose said, voice breaking. "I never saw it coming. It wasn't something this Southern woman was prepared for."

"I don't know if anyone would be prepared for that."

Rose set her glass on the table. "I've never been able to shake the feeling that my husband's proclivities were my fault somehow. Or partially my fault."

"It wasn't your fault," Edward said.

"You know, I've never spoken to anyone outside of the church about what happened. And now I'm spilling my guts to a stranger on my front porch."

"Maybe it was time to talk about it. So you can move on."

Rose didn't respond and Edward waited before speaking again. "I have one last question, if you don't mind."

"You want to know if I have still have a copy of the video," Rose said.

"That's right."

"It's in an old suitcase in the spare bedroom."

"Can I borrow it? Or make a copy of it?"

"On one condition."

"Sure."

"It can never go public."

Edward mulled over the stipulation.

"I can work with that."

*

Reggie sat at the small kitchen table, staring at Edward's business card resting next to his phone. Two dirty spaghetti plates hung on the edge of the kitchen sink, threating to slide off the counter. A black pot stood on the stove, the handle of the ladle protruding from beneath the half-closed lid. He could envision his mother watching television in the next room, sitting on the sofa in her favorite position, her only leg buried under a pile of blankets on the cushions.

Reggie stared at the phone number on the business card and spun his mobile phone on the table like a top. Sighing, he told his mother he was going outside and slipped out the back door into the yard. Lightning bugs danced slowly in the hot summer air, weighed down by the humidity and dulled by the heat.

Reggie punched a number into his cell phone and on the third ring, Sheriff Blazer answered.

"Sheriff, I think we have a problem."

CHAPTER 58

"GOOD EVENING, SHERIFF," Edward said, getting out of his car on a street lined with two-story brick homes.

"What the hell are you doing here, at my home?" the sheriff asked.

"Seemed like the safest place to meet."

"Have you lost your mind?"

"No more than anyone else has."

"Trailing a law enforcement officer to his residence is a good way for an accident to happen."

"That would be a fitting end to our story, wouldn't it?"

"What do you want?"

"I want to meet with you."

The sheriff raised both his arms out to shoulder height. "We're meeting right now."

"Not here. I want to meet someplace more neutral."

"Come down to the office. Make an appointment. Act like a normal citizen."

"I don't think you're going to want to have this conversation at the office. And I want Detective Rafferty to be there."

"Why's that?"

"You're going to have to trust me."

"Hard to trust someone orchestrating a federal investigation against them."

"And it's hard to trust an officer of the law who framed an innocent man for murder."

"I just presented the evidence."

"Evidence you manipulated."

"So you say, Mr. Winston. Is there anything new to this conversation?"

"There is something new. Actually something old, but new. I recently came into possession of an old surveillance video from Cedar Creek. A video that could be called *Law Enforcement Goes Wild*. I'm sure I don't need to elaborate on the contents of that video."

Sheriff Blazer turned a deep shade of red and pursed his lips.

Edward continued. "Not what you expected to hear, I'm guessing. Shocking stuff, really. Especially for a man who won elections based on his anti-drug stance and support of God's Law."

The sheriff looked as if the veins in his neck would pop. "My, my, someone has been busy," he hissed.

"It makes you wonder what someone would be willing to do to keep that video quiet."

"And just how did you come into possession of this alleged video?"

"What does it matter?"

Sheriff Blazer's eyes darted up and down his street. "Because maybe the person who killed Pervis Wade stole a copy of that video. Possession of that video would make for a curious chain of ownership."

"Videos can be copied and uploaded in seconds. Who knows how many copies of the video are out there? But, it's not the number of copies that should worry you. You need to worry about how many people have seen the copies that do exist. Right now, that's a very select audience."

"You have no idea what you're dealing with."

"A dead wife and unborn child. I think I have a good idea. And with that in mind, this is how it's going to work. For the last several weeks I've been going through all of my worldly possessions. Item by item. And there are a couple of things I believe were taken by the Lee County Sheriff's Department when you exercised your search warrant for my wife's disappearance. I would like those items back."

"Such as?"

"My favorite Chicago Cubs T-shirt. I realized it was missing a few weeks ago when the Cubbies won five in a row. The missing T-shirt got me looking for other things."

"What else?"

"A pair of winter gloves that I haven't used since moving to Mississippi. A four-iron from my golf bag."

"Were all the items on the list taken when the search warrant was executed on your home?"

"I think we both know they weren't."

"Then there's no evidence to support your claim that the Lee County Sheriff's Department has ever been in possession of these items."

"Fine. Don't give me my things back. You'll be able to watch your surveillance video on YouTube over tomorrow's breakfast."

"You really are a little shit."

"I'll take that to mean we have an agreement."

"Where do you suggest we meet?"

"At the pond where my wife was killed. Near the picnic pavilion. Early. Six a.m. Before it opens. The day after tomorrow. That gives you one day to gather your misplaced evidence."

"According to your claim."

"That's right."

"Anything else?"

"Nope. Day after tomorrow. At the pond. Early."

"I understand your request," the sheriff replied.

"Good," Edward said, turning back towards his car.

"You know, we've identified a suspect in Pervis Wade's death," the sheriff said.

"It wasn't me. I was in Biloxi."

"Yes, you were."

"So why would I care?"

"Because sooner or later we're going to prove you hired someone to kill Pervis. A Japanese guy with tattoos. We have a name. We have a passport photo. We have witnesses. It's only a matter of time."

"Your investigation has nothing to do with me."

"We'll get there."

"I doubt it. Don't forget to show up at the pond the day after tomorrow. In the morning."

"Be careful on the roads out there," the sheriff said.

"I will be. I'm heading straight to Oxford from here. It's an hour away, but I feel safe there. I just don't feel secure in Lee County anymore."

*

Sheriff Blazer called Detective Rafferty as he stepped through his front door. He walked across the beige carpet to the small wet bar near the kitchen and poured three fingers of bourbon in a glass.

"We have a serious fucking problem," the sheriff said, dropping ice into his drink.

"What is it?"

"Our boy knows about the Cedar Creek video. Claims he has a copy."

"How did that happen?"

"How the hell should I know?"

"Do you think Reggie kept a copy all these years?"

"I don't think so. Reggie wouldn't dare. Besides, we ran him through a polygraph back in the day."

"We both know that's not foolproof."

"Any chance Edward could have found the video at Pervis Wade's house?"

"It's possible. What does he want?"

"He says he wants to exchange the video for some of his belongings he thinks we still possess."

"How does he know what we have?"

"He says he went through every item in his house and he has a detailed list of missing articles."

"Do you believe him?"

"I think we're only getting half the story. I don't think he's after his missing belongings."

"Sounds like a trap to me."

"I have no doubt it's a trap."

"What do you want to do?"

"We end this once and for all. All of it."

CHAPTER 59

EDWARD DROVE HIS car up the country road and stopped at the edge of the gate. A white van was parked on the opposite side of the street, facing towards the exit. Just inside the park entrance, the sheriff's SUV was sitting in the middle of the road, ignition off.

Edward got out of his car, pulse elevated. He reached back into his vehicle and plucked an open Mountain Dew can from the cup holder. He shut the door to his car and walked past the sheriff's vehicle, peering through the tinted windows. At the hood of the car, he squinted to see light illuminating the picnic area under the pavilion fifty yards away. Beyond the pavilion, the top edge of the sun was threatening to punch its way over the eastern horizon.

Edward approached the pavilion slowly, the silhouette of the sheriff coming into focus as he closed the distance. Sheriff Blazer diverted his attention from the screen of his mobile phone as Edward came near.

"Good morning, Mr. Winston," the sheriff stated. He extended his hand and Edward ignored him.

"You can never be beyond good manners," the sheriff said. "That's standard Southern hospitality."

"I'm from Chicago," Edward replied. "We don't shake hands with people who let killers run free. Where's Detective Rafferty?"

"He's not going to make it. He has work to do. But rest easy, I'm the sheriff. I can do anything you need the detective for."

The sheriff turned in the direction of snapping twigs where the clearing for the picnic area met the surrounding trees. Reggie Taylor emerged from the woods, his arms cradling a nest of wires and cameras. A large backpack hugged his shoulders. Edward eyed the same yellow, brick-sized frequency detector he had been subjected to at Reggie's home.

"We'll I'll be damned," the sheriff said, marveling at Reggie Taylor's electronics haul.

Edward ran his free hand through his hair and scowled.

"Are you sure you found everything?" the sheriff asked.

Reggie replied. "There's nothing within a hundred yards of this pavilion. I've been here for two hours. I've run multiple sweeps. Covered all the frequencies."

"And what exactly do we have here?"

"Three cameras. Five bugs."

Sheriff Blazer whistled.

"Well, well, well. Looks like someone was trying to save this conversation for posterity's sake."

"It does," Reggie agreed.

The sheriff pointed at Edward with an upward flick of his nose. "Give Edward here a sweep and then head out."

"Will do."

Reggie ran his counter-surveillance scanner over his subject from head to toe. A single beep emanated from the device.

"Cell phone," Reggie suggested.

Edward reached into his pocket and removed his phone.

The sheriff nodded and Reggie swiped the phone from Edward's grip before running a second scan.

"He's clean."

"You can go," the sheriff responded.

"What do you want me to do with this?" Reggie asked, raising Edward's phone.

"Make sure it's not recording and leave it on the hood of Edward's car on your way out. That should be a safe distance from here. But don't turn it off."

"Yes, sir," Reggie replied.

"And take all of this other equipment with you."

Reggie removed his backpack and slipped the mound of electronics into the bag. He pulled the zipper closed and slapped Edward on the back. "No hard feelings."

Edward sneered and raised his Mountain Dew can to his lips. Then he lowered the can and placed it on the table.

Sheriff Blazer waited until he heard the doors on Reggie's van shut and the engine come to life. "Don't be angry with Reggie. You can't fault him for his loyalty. He knows where his bread is buttered."

"It isn't butter that motivates him."

"Reggie has his priorities straight. He's taking care of his family first."

"Fuck you, Sheriff."

"Easy, now. No need to lose our decorum."

"What do you know about decorum?"

The sheriff released a one-syllable chuckle. "Ha."

"You'll have to excuse me if I don't see the humor."

"You're excused."

"Did you bring my belongings?"

The sheriff motioned towards a cardboard box on the concrete floor.

"That's not everything," Edward stated.

"How do you know? You didn't even open it."

"Because I don't see a golf club. I told you I was missing a four iron."

"Maybe you lost it the last time you played."

"And maybe you still have it."

Sheriff Blazer pointed at the box a second time. "That's the stuff you're getting back, if you want it."

"I was pretty specific about my demands."

Sheriff Blazer checked his watch. "With all due respect, I don't think you're after a missing Cub's T-shirt, a golf club, or any of your other stuff. Maybe can we get down to the real business at hand, whatever that may be."

Perspiration grew around Edward's neck. "I want you to back off the investigation into who killed Pervis Wade."

The sheriff paused. "Tell me, Edward. Why do you care about the investigation into Pervis Wade's murder? After all, you weren't involved. You were in Biloxi at the time. With multiple alibis."

"You're right. I was in Biloxi. I wasn't involved."

"So why do you care who killed Pervis Wade?"

"Maybe whoever killed Pervis Wade is someone I could theoretically look up to. A hero, if you will. God knows there aren't enough heroes in this world."

"Finally, something we can agree on. I miss the good old days. Superman, Batman, The Flash, Shazam."

"Besides, the way I look at it, whoever killed Pervis Wade did you a favor, too. With Pervis gone, that makes one less person who knows about you and the surveillance video," Edward said.

"True. Pervis is gone. But now you are in the know. That kind of evens things out."

The sheriff checked his watch again.

"Do you have someplace to be?" Edward asked.

"No. No. I apologize for being distracted. Where did we stop?"

"We were making a deal."

"Ah, yes. You were asking for a favor and I was about to refuse your request. The investigation into Pervis Wade's murder will continue."

"Then I'm going to take my copy of the security video from Cedar Creek to the local press. Leak copies to TMZ. Put it up on YouTube."

"That's blackmail, and in the state of Mississippi that's a felony."

"I'll take my chances."

Sheriff Blazer shook his head. "I'll tell you what, give me a few minutes to consider your offer."

"I'll give you exactly one minute. You're on the clock," Edward said.

Sheriff Blazer turned and stared out across the water of the pond. "While I mull over your offer, I'm curious as to why you chose to meet here. So early in the morning, so far away from civilization."

Edward motioned towards the water with his hand. "I thought this was the appropriate place for the ending to our story. Here, where my wife was killed. Killed by Pervis Wade and covered up by the Lee County Sheriff's Department."

"That's not what the evidence shows. The evidence shows your neighbor, Brent Poole, murdered your wife."

"That's how you made it look. I just don't understand why you can't be man enough to admit what you've done."

The sheriff's phone pinged and he read the message on the screen. "Sometimes people have to agree to disagree. Sometimes you have to let things go."

"I can't believe you're a sheriff."

"And I can't believe you had the balls to have two people murdered."

"I think this conversation is over," Edward said, reaching for his soda can. "We'll see you on the evening news."

"Before you go," Sheriff Blazer said, "There's something else you need to consider."

Edward set the can back down on the table with trembling fingers.

"Getting a little nervous, Edward? Can't say I blame you, really."

Edward's mouth went dry.

"No comment?" Sheriff Blazer taunted. "Fair enough."

"What else about this fucked up situation do I need to consider?" Edward asked.

"It's time to share a little secret with you. After all, you're a key part of it. It would seem wrong to leave you out."

"I'm listening," Edward replied.

"There was another murder in Tupelo this morning. A few minutes ago. On the highway heading out of town. The owner of a security company. Shot with a .357 magnum. Your .357 magnum. It appears that a few items were stolen from the man's work van as well."

Edward's head spun. "What the hell are you talking about?"

"Relax, Edward. Relax. I know you didn't do it. I know because I'm right here with you. Out at this park at the crack of dawn. I'm your alibi. Your airtight alibi."

"You piece of shit," Edward said, choking up. He gritted his teeth and his chest tightened.

"What are those, tears?"

Edward didn't respond, his mind racing.

"Detective Rafferty stopped by your house this morning and picked up your gun. Borrowed it. You really should have taken our advice and installed a security system after your wife went missing. Or locked up your firearm. Particularly when you've been leaving your house unoccupied and staying way out in Oxford. But I guess it's all water under the bridge now. Unfortunately for you, Detective Rafferty is not going to return your weapon. We're going to keep it someplace safe. As our insurance policy."

"And someday out of the blue, I'll be charged with Reggie Taylor's murder. My gun, with my fingerprints, tied to a gun used in a murder. Maybe you'll plant some of the equipment you just stole from Reggie on me."

"You have to admit it does sound like it could be a predicament."

"You'll never pull it off."

"Really? I think we can. But don't worry. As I mentioned, I'm your alibi. Lucky for you."

Sheriff Blazer paused and then continued. "And don't think about reporting your gun as stolen. That could inadvertently tip off the authorities to your involvement in an unsolved murder. And if that happens, you could lose your alibi. With no alibi, matching ballistics, and your weapon with your prints on it, heck, I think a conviction would be easy. Not to mention your cell phone is pinging off the same cell tower as Reggie Taylor's phone as we speak."

"You are an evil son of a bitch."

Sheriff Blazer ignored the insult. "Now, I think we have the basis for a new agreement. The new agreement is that all parties involved keep their mouths shut and everyone walks away. You forget about any video you may have seen or possess and you get to stay out of prison."

"I didn't kill anyone."

The sheriff smiled and winked. "Not today. Not with me as your alibi, you didn't."

"You guys are unbelievable. How many people have you killed? And for what?"

The sheriff clicked his cheek twice in rapid succession. "I'd love to sit around and chitchat, but I think we've finished what we needed to say."

Edward shook his head as the sheriff stepped out from under the pavilion.

"We'll see you around, Edward. Or maybe it's better if we don't."

"Fuck you, Sheriff."

"Good luck on your move," the sheriff said, walking away.

*

Edward sat on the bank of the pond until the sun completed its appearance, sending pink streaks across the sky. He let himself cry, his gaze caressing the surface of the water. Confident he was alone, he untwisted the bottom of the faux Mountain Dew can. He removed the small memory card and examined it in the light before wiping his face dry. He stood, walked back to the picnic pavilion, and grabbed the cardboard box of belongings the sheriff had left on the concrete patio. Lifting the box off the ground, its weight told Edward everything he needed to know. He cursed and threw the empty box to the side. Soda can and memory card in hand, he headed towards his car in silence, his pace quickening.

CHAPTER 60

EDWARD DROVE FROM the pond to his house, parked his car in the driveway, and slammed the driver's door closed. He walked briskly up the short sidewalk, found his front door unlocked, and stepped inside. Boxes filled the living room, the clock on the wall, his sofa, side table, and television the only indication anyone lived there. He stepped around his sofa and pulled the drawer open on the small side table.

"Son of a bitch!" he yelled, glaring at the bottom of the empty drawer. He pounded his fist on the top of the table and then pushed it over onto the floor.

Heart thumping, he exited his house and returned to his car. Behind the wheel, he punched the coordinates of the FBI Field Office in Jackson into Google Maps.

*

Three hours later Edward pulled off the highway in Flowood, Mississippi, fifteen miles outside of Jackson. He visited a Bank of America ATM and crossed the road into a sprawling strip mall with Lowes and Best Buy sandwiching several dozen stores between them. Edward parked in a spot near Best Buy and headed for the front entrance of the store.

"I'm looking for an open box deal on a laptop," Edward said to the salesman in a blue company shirt. The young man looked up at Edward through the thick lenses of his wire-framed glasses.

"You're in luck. Follow me," the young employee said, moving one aisle over. "We have four open box laptops on sale right now. Two were returns. Two are older models. What do you need it to do?"

"Not too much," Edward replied.

The sales guy began going through the specs on each laptop as Edward ignored him and read the signs hanging on the shelf beneath each computer.

"I'll take this one," Edward said, interrupting the salesman's spiel.

"Nothing wrong with that. HP. Plenty of memory. And almost four hundred off the sticker price."

"It should be fine."

"Let me unlock it and I'll meet you at the checkout counter."

Edward zoomed down the memory aisle and purchased a pair of additional memory cards on sale as a two-for-one special. Minutes later he was counting out cash on the counter by the register.

"Would you like our warranty plan?" the salesman asked.

"I won't need it."

"You never know."

"Oh, I know," Edward replied.

*

Edward pulled his new computer from the large Best Buy bag and placed it on the passenger seat of his car. He booted up, slipped the memory card from his Mountain Dew stealth recorder into the small slot on the side of the computer, and opened the file with the audio player.

He listened to the recording in its entirety and then edited the file, deleting his attempt to blackmail the sheriff and leaving the recording to begin with the sheriff informing him that Reggie Taylor had just been killed by Detective Rafferty.

He nervously ripped open the packaging on the additional memory cards he had just purchased and copied the shortened, edited file onto each one. He took several minutes to ensure the files had been copied correctly, carefully replaying the recording. When he finished, he put one of the newly minted memory cards in the glove compartment for safekeeping and placed the second in the storage cubby between the front seats.

Confident he had what he needed, he deleted the file from the computer and snapped the original memory card in two. He slipped the pieces of the original memory card, the computer, and all the packaging back into the Best Buy bag. On the far end of the shopping center, he dropped the bag and all of its contents into a Dumpster.

*

Twenty minutes later, Agent Washington met Edward in the lobby of FBI headquarters in Jackson. A plethora of law enforcement officers entered and exited, crossing the waxed floor. A large security entourage manned a metal detector and conveyor belt scanner.

"This better be good, Edward," Agent Washington said, hands on her hips.

"We need to talk."

"Then talk."

"Not here," Edward said, gesturing towards the people in the lobby.

"Step outside," Agent Washington replied.

On the sidewalk near the entrance Agent Washington motioned towards a small bench.

"I'll stand."

"Suit yourself. Now what brings you to Jackson in such a big hurry?"

"I met with the sheriff of Lee County this morning. I recorded the conversation."

"And why did you go and do that?"

"Because I wanted him to admit he was involved in covering up my wife's murder."

"Did he?"

"No. But he admitted to something better, or worse, depending on how you look at it." Edward held up one of the memory cards with the doctored recording in front of Agent Washington. "You won't need any more evidence to put the sheriff and Detective Rafferty away for a very long time. There's also a judge by the name of Vernon Potter that needs to be investigated. It took all of them to pull off what they've done."

"Is that right?"

"Yep. Turns out that Pervis Wade possessed a surveillance video featuring Sheriff Blazer, Detective Rafferty, Charlie Sterling, and Judge Potter. In that video, the four men were engaging in illicit drug use, as well as other behavior that some in Tupelo may find shocking. And that video was used as leverage by Pervis Wade to avoid prosecution."

Agent Washington stared hard into Edward's eyes. Then she raised her hand and Edward passed her the memory card. "This recording took place this morning at the pond where my wife's body was found. It only has two voices on it. Mine and Sheriff Blazer's."

"And what were you discussing, exactly?"

"Murder. My wife's. Then the conversation took an unexpected turn and the sheriff admitted his involvement in a murder that occurred this morning. Reggie Taylor, the owner of a security company. He has several contracts with the Lee County Sheriff's Department. The murder has been on the news in Tupelo. I headed here as fast as I could."

"You have the sheriff of Lee County admitting to murder?"

"With my gun."

"And why would he admit to that?"

"Because he didn't think I was recording the conversation. He had me swept for listening devices." Edward raised his hand to show Agent Washington his Mountain Dew can. "But they missed this one."

Edward took the can into both hands and slowly twisted off the bottom.

Agent Washington stared at the can and then glanced at the memory card. "I'm sure you can understand my skepticism given, shall we say, everything we've been through."

"You really need to listen to it."

Agent Washington pulled out her cell phone. She punched several keys and pressed the phone to her ear. "I need you in conference room D. Fourth floor. Bring the gang."

"Who was that?" Edward asked.

"One of our technology support specialists. I want this file copied and need to establish a chain of custody from this second forward."

*

Edward sat on an empty chair outside the glass wall of an office while Agent Washington and three other special agents listened to his audio recording.

A half hour later, Edward was escorted into the room.

"Please have a seat," Agent Washington said. She introduced the three men seated at the table around her. The Mountain Dew can sat on the tabletop by itself, as if on display.

"That's one incredible recording," Agent Washington stated.

"These guys are brazen," Edward replied.

"It seems so. Of course, we do have a couple of questions about the validity of this recording."

"That's understandable."

"You claim you made this audio file this morning?"

"I did."

"And you obtained it using the Mountain Dew can on the table?"

"That's right. Mississippi is a one-party consent state. Recording the conversation did not break any laws."

"That's correct. Can you show everyone here how the Mountain Dew can works?"

Edward stood and leaned across the table for his stealth recorder. He unscrewed the bottom of the can and showed the audience the inside. "The memory card goes into this slot," Edward said, pointing with his finger. He screwed the bottom of the can back on and then grabbed the can with two hands. He twisted the top and said. "It comes with a small remote control to turn it on. Or you can give the top lip of the can a little twist."

"And where did you get this?"

"You can order one on the Internet. They have all kinds of drink cans. Shaving cream. Foot spray."

The four agents at the table remained stoic.

"I'm confident whatever I captured is more than enough to put the Lee County sheriff out of business," Edward added unapologetically.

Agent Washington took a deep breath.

"And what exactly did you say to get the sheriff to agree to meet you out at the lake?" the man next to Agent Washington asked.

"I wanted to retrieve the belongings I believe the Lee County Sheriff's Department took from my house when they served a search warrant in my wife's disappearance. Prior to her body being found. I was also hoping the detective would admit to covering up my wife's murder."

"And where is the part of the conversation where you discuss your belongings?"

"I didn't turn the recorder on in time. But I think I caught most of the important parts."

Several of the agents around the table seemed to exchange suspicious expressions.

"And did the sheriff want anything in return? We're trying to understand why the sheriff would admit to murder; tape or no tape."

"He obviously felt safe. And I think he wanted to show me he could do whatever he wanted."

"And you said the sheriff checked you for a wire before he started talking?"

"He did. Actually, Reggie Taylor did."

"The same person you claim Sheriff Blazer murdered with your gun? The same man found shot on a rural road outside of Tupelo this morning?"

"It is. Detective Rafferty actually pulled the trigger, but they both planned it."

"And the sheriff and detective killed this Reggie Taylor in order to frame you?"

"Yes and no. I approached Reggie Taylor last week. I hired his security firm and paid him for information he was privy to. I told him the Lee County Sheriff's Department was under federal investigation and that it was a good time for him to consider cutting ties with the sheriff. It was a business transaction."

"How much did you pay him?"

"Fifty grand, up front. Another fifty thousand due after I moved out of Tupelo."

"That is an awful lot of money."

"It is. But I received a very substantial life insurance check for my wife's death. As I told Reggie, I couldn't think of a better way to spend it than to help put her killers behind bars."

"So you hired Reggie Taylor to scan you for listening devices at your meeting with the sheriff?"

"I think both the sheriff and I hired Reggie for the same thing. But the sheriff didn't know Reggie and I had a prior agreement. At the pond, Reggie scanned me once and allowed the device to identify my phone. In reality the scanner identified the presence of both my phone and the soda can. Reggie Taylor took my phone and then turned off the scanner before he scanned me a second time. Reggie also planted various other listening devices in the woods near the lake and gave the impression that he found them in a search."

"And that got him killed?"

"I don't think so. Sheriff Blazer didn't know I had hired Reggie Taylor. The sheriff didn't know I wasn't properly scanned. The sheriff murdered Reggie Taylor because of what Reggie knew about a surveillance tape that could ruin careers. The sheriff had decided on killing him before the meeting at the pond. It was premeditated. Look no further than the fact that the sheriff and detective stole my gun from my home to commit the murder."

The agents seated around the table took turns locking stares with one another before Agent Washington finished the meeting.

"Edward. Obviously we have a lot of things to discuss and to verify. This conversation is not over."

"I'm planning to move to Lexington, Kentucky, next week."

"Make sure we have all of your contact information."

Edward nodded.

"And before you leave, we are going to need you to make official statements and sign the appropriate documentation," Agent Washington said.

"Of course, anything you need."

CHAPTER 61

AT PRECISELY ELEVEN a.m., the Peabody Duck March began with a line of live ducks exiting the elevator and crossing the lobby of the finest hotel in Memphis. An eighty-year-old tradition that began as a hoax, the ducks now lived in a quarter-million dollar penthouse on the roof of the hotel. Every morning at eleven, the ducks, replete with a human escort, made their way to the large fountain in the middle of the Peabody lobby where they paddled and played until five in the evening, when they retraced their waddle back to the elevator and then upward.

Edward sat in a corner table with his lawyer, Patrick Claiborne, a defense attorney who charged six hundred dollars an hour, duck parade or not. In addition to believing every client was innocent, Patrick Claiborne equally embraced perfectly coiffed white hair and gray business suits from London that cost as much as he made most days between breakfast and lunch.

Edward and his attorney sipped refills of their coffees as the Peabody ducks settled comfortably into their daytime living arrangements. As they finished their drinks, Agent Washington entered the lobby of the hotel. A man in a dark suit, who Edward recognized from the powwow at the FBI field office in Jackson, stood next to her. Both agents' heads and eyes scanned the lobby.

"She's here," Edward said, standing.

Agent Washington and her male counterpart approached Edward's table in the corner.

Edward emceed the introductions. "Agent Washington, this is my attorney, Patrick Claiborne."

Claiborne extended his hand and Agent Washington shook it.

"And this is my colleague, Special Agent Shroud," Agent Washington replied. Both Edward and his attorney shook the man's hand.

"Agent Shroud is now leading the Pervis Wade murder investigation. The FBI has taken over the case, given that we believe the prime suspect has fled the state, and perhaps the country."

With a stern expression masking a twinkle in his eye, Patrick Claiborne set the stage for the meeting. "I have instructed my client not to respond to any questions you may have. Don't take it personally."

"I won't," Agent Washington replied, pulling out her own chair and sit- ting down. Agent Shroud sat to her right.

Patrick Claiborne, attorney-in-charge, motioned for Edward to sit. Then he brushed the lapels of his suit and lowered himself into the chair next to his client.

"How have you been, Edward?" Agent Washington asked, staring across the small table.

"Good."

"Are you getting settled in Kentucky?"

Patrick Claiborne abruptly ended the chitchat. "On behalf of my client and myself, we would like to thank you for being amenable to a meeting here in Memphis, on neutral ground, if you will. As you can imagine, given the behavior of some law enforcement entities, my client doesn't feel safe in Mississippi."

"Let's not throw all law enforcement into the same pot," Washington warned.

"Certainly not. But it doesn't require much imagination to believe the Lee County Sheriff's Department has a long history of friendly relations with other law enforcement jurisdictions."

"Meeting in Memphis was not a problem for us," Agent Washington replied. "Did you receive the list of items we found in the possession of Lee County Sheriff's Department?"

Patrick Claiborne answered. "My client received the list."

"Is that everything that was missing?"

"We believe it is most of the items."

"Unfortunately, it's all evidence at this point. I don't imagine you'll get it back anytime soon."

"We understand."

"And if we find anything else, we will let you know." Agent Washington looked at Special Agent Shroud for verification, which came in the form of a nod.

Washington removed a legal pad and several folders from the leather bag next to her chair and placed them on the table. "First, let me say that the FBI would like to formally thank you for your assistance in providing evidence against the Lee County Sheriff's Department. In addition to murder charges, we have discovered a number of infractions and improprieties."

"I need to see some people behind bars before I applaud," Edward said. His attorney grabbed his arm and squeezed.

"Rest assured, justice will be served. And our appreciation aside, the FBI has several outstanding questions we were hoping you could clarify," Agent Washington said.

"You can ask, but I have been advised not to answer," Edward responded. His attorney shook his head as a sign of caution.

"As you know, our prime suspect in a double murder in Tupelo has still not been identified. We have reason to believe our suspect is a Japanese male. We have reason to believe he may have had an accomplice. We have reason to believe he received help leaving the state. At this juncture, we believe our suspect has fled the country. We believe it is likely he returned to Japan."

"'A reason to believe' isn't suitable for a court of law," Patrick Claiborne responded.

"I hope you find him," Edward added.

"We will. We know that he traveled within the US using the name Taro Ishida. That was not his real name. The real Taro Ishida was enjoying a spa holiday while the man we are looking for was using Taro Ishida's passport and credit cards."

"My client is not aware of this suspect and refutes any implication that he does," Claiborne replied.

"Very well," Agent Washington said. "Be aware that we have located several witnesses in Tupelo who may remember seeing the suspect. A cashier at a grocery store. A food vendor from the Elvis Festival. A couple of guests from the motel where the suspect was staying. However, it seems only two people engaged with our suspect in any meaningful way while he was in Tupelo. One of them is the manager of the hotel where the suspect was staying. The second is a woman who resided in the motel room next to our suspect's. This woman claims to have seen our suspect on several occasions. She has obtained legal representation but has agreed to help the FBI identify our suspect based on passport photographs of Japanese men who have entered the country. Unfortunately, it is a large number of photos to look through."

Agent Washington motioned towards Agent Shroud, who provided further details.

"Over three million Japanese nationals visit the US every year. That breaks down to about 250,000 a month. If you limit that to men, we are talking about half that number. A large number, as my colleague indicated. If we consider the possibility the suspect lives in the US, it becomes a very large number. But we're confident that at least one of the witnesses will allow us to identify our suspect from passport photos. Once the suspect is identified, we will engage Japanese law enforcement to confirm identification. And then the dominos should fall into place."

"My client has no comment," Mr. Claiborne replied, feigning boredom. "With all due respect, I'm not interested in who you cajole to look through photographs. What I want to know is does anyone have any evidence implicating my client in any way in any crime?"

Agent Washington ignored the tongue-lashing and moved to her next question. "The FBI is aware that in the days following the murder of Pervis Wade, your client took a road trip to California. We would like to know the purpose of this trip."

"My client wanted to say hi to his brother and to see his nephew."

"Did he stay with his brother?"

"He just dropped by to say hi."

"So you would like me to believe that your client took a drive to California in his wife's car just to pop in and say hi to a brother who, by all accounts, your client has very little contact with?"

"Is there a crime somewhere in that chain of events?" the attorney asked.

"And where did your client stay when he was in California?"

"He stayed at the New Daimaru Hotel, as already provided."

"We spoke with the manager of the New Daimaru Hotel. They don't have any record of your client staying at the hotel."

"That is not my client's fault."

"Was he with anyone?"

"He was not."

"We also know that your client sold his car while he was in California. The same car he drove to California. Can your client provide an explanation as to why someone would drive a car to California, sell that car, and return via airplane?"

Edward offered another whisper and his attorney responded.

"My client was interested in getting rid of his wife's car and he realized that he could receive a better offer if he sold it in California."

"Seems suspicious."

"Certainly you're not implying that getting the best deal possible on the sale of a vehicle is suspicious," Patrick Claiborne said.

"It is if the sale of the vehicle was executed to hide evidence."

"What evidence is that?"

"Evidence the car was used to smuggle a murder suspect across country."

"Those are strong allegations and my client is not going to respond to conjecture. Perhaps my client wanted to sell the car because the memory of his wife's murder is just too painful and every time he saw that car, he thought of his dead wife."

Agent Washington stared directly at Edward. "Would you like to hear what happened to your car, Edward?"

"I can tell you what happened to my client's car. He took it to CarMax and sold it for a few hundred dollars below Blue Book."

"And within forty-eight hours that car was resold," Agent Washington added.

"Good for CarMax. Capitalism at work."

"Would you like to know who bought your car, Edward?"

"I'm sure my client does not care."

"Your car was bought by a man named Sowaka Ide. A Japanese man, if you can imagine that. We contacted Mr. Ide in the hope of processing the vehicle for evidence. The day after Mr. Ide bought the car it was reported stolen. It has never been found."

"You aren't implying that my client had something do with a stolen car owned by a third party he never met? My client left Los Angeles the day he sold his car. Whatever happened to the vehicle after it was sold had nothing to do with my client. It is inconsequential."

Agent Washington sat motionless, the muscles in her jaws visibly tightening.

Claiborne asked, "I would like to know if there's any evidence in this case that's relevant to my client. Conjecture, misdirection, assumptions, and the hopes and wishes of the FBI are not going to court."

Agent Washington motioned towards Agent Shroud.

"As Agent Washington mentioned, I have taken over the investigation into the murder of Pervis Wade and Barry Lawson."

Agent Washington removed another folder from her bag and spread several large photographs across the table.

"And what are these?" Mr. Claiborne asked.

"Evidence."

"Evidence of what?" the attorney replied, leaning in to look at the photographs of the burned prosthetic finger from various angles.

"This is the single most important piece of evidence we have in the Pervis Wade murder investigation. It was found at the crime scene. It was recovered by the Lee County Sheriff's Department, tagged, bagged, and entered as evidence. It's a prosthetic finger," Agent Washington replied.

"So says you," the attorney scoffed. He selected one of the photos and lifted it for closer examination. Edward joined his attorney in an inspection of the evidence.

"It appears to be severely damaged," the attorney replied after a cursory observation.

"It is."

"I don't imagine the fingerprint on that prosthetic is readable at all."

Agent Washington shrugged her shoulders.

"Furthermore, I imagine if that prosthetic had any physical evidence on it related to my client, we would be having this conversation in a room with a two-way mirror. But seeing that we're having a civil meeting in the nicest hotel in Memphis, I'll assume nothing was obtained that links that finger to my client."

Agent Washington didn't reply.

"Your silence is noted," Claiborne stated. "It seems you're in a bit of a pickle to identify whose finger that is. More importantly, you have nothing to indicate that finger has anything to do with my client."

"We wanted to ask your client if he had ever seen this finger before, or if he has ever known someone who has had a similar prosthetic."

"I assure you my client has nothing to do with evidence left behind at a murder scene. Need I remind everyone that my client was four hours away at the time of the murder with a dozen witness to corroborate his alibi?"

Edward stared at the photographs of the damaged finger as his attorney went back and forth with the FBI Agents. He could feel Agent Washington glaring at him as the banter became heated.

Then Edward silenced the table. "I think I can help you with that finger. I think it came from my house."

*

Patrick Claiborne Esquire stood from his chair as if a fire ant hive had been disturbed in the seat of his fine wool slacks.

"Give us a second," he bellowed, yanking Edward by his armpit and dragging him away from the table in the direction of the ducks in the fountain.

"What the hell are you doing? You're not to offer any response to any question without conferring with me first."

"Sorry. It just came out."

Mr. Claiborne ran his hands through his hair and looked around as if he were suddenly under surveillance. "What can you tell me about that finger or whatever it is? And what the hell do you mean it came from your house? You don't claim evidence that puts you at a crime scene."

"I owned a fake finger very similar to that. I used it for magic. It's a prop for the hidden scarf trick. My wife gave it to me."

"Are you sure it's the same finger?"

"Well, it's hard to be sure with all the damage, but it totally makes sense."

"Why's that?"

"Because the Lee County Sheriff's Department was trying to frame me for murder. I think that finger was just another example of a failed attempt to put me at the scene of a crime. The murder of Pervis Wade."

Patrick Claiborne started nodding, his head thrusting in and out, first slowly and then with vigor. "Let's finish this conversation," he said. "And by that, I mean, I will end this meeting."

"I won't say a word."

Patrick Claiborne and his client sat and Agent Washington and her colleagues waited for one of them to speak. The large photographs of the finger sat in the middle of the table, taunting them.

"My client believes that finger resembles one he used to possess. My client claims it is similar to a finger he owned that was used as a magician's prop. Given the condition of the finger, my client cannot be absolutely certain that is the same finger, but it looks very similar. We believe that if it is the same finger, there's a simple explanation for its existence and its submission as evidence from a crime scene. We believe the Lee County Sheriff's Department placed that finger at the scene of a double murder to implicate my client as a suspect. It is their proven MO."

Agent Washington stared down at the photographs. The silence at the table lasted for a full uncomfortable minute.

"Agent Washington?" Patrick Claiborne said.

"Yes."

"Is there anything else?"

"Let me confer with my colleague for a moment."

"Please," Patrick Claiborne said, leaning back in his chair, gloating.

Agent Washington and her colleague took their conversation to the far side of the lobby and returned several minutes later.

"At this juncture we feel it is in everyone's best interest if we take some time to regroup with our forensic experts. For the sake of thoroughness, the FBI will look into Edward's claim that a key piece of evidence could be his and that it could have been planted by the Lee County Sheriff's Department. Given the current charges against officials from Lee County, it seems both necessary and prudent."

"Yes, it does," Patrick Claiborne said. He reached into his breast pocket and removed a short stack of business cards. He handed each agent a card and shook hands, locking eyes. "If there are any further questions, please contact me first, before reaching out to my client."

*

Edward knocked on room 415 and Mindy opened the door to her fourth-floor room of the Peabody Hotel. Edward stepped in with Patrick Claiborne Esquire in tow.

"Where's your attorney?" Edward asked.

"He'll be back in a few minutes. He said he had an important call to make. How did it go?" she asked.

"We'll see," Edward replied.

"What does that mean?"

"It means that Edward here either did the smartest thing I've ever seen, or the dumbest," Claiborne answered.

"If the law of averages means anything, Edward was due for one of the smartest."

"Thanks."

"You're welcome," Mindy replied. "So what's the plan?"

Patrick Claiborne offered his uncontested legal advice. "The plan is that you make sure you have legal counsel present every time you speak with, or meet with, anyone from any law enforcement agency, especially the Federal Bureau of Investigation."

"And what about their request for me to look at passport photos to identify their prime suspect?"

"What's the harm in looking?" Claiborne said almost mockingly, cocking his head to the side and turning both palms towards the ceiling.

"And if I happen to see who they're searching for?"

Patrick Claiborne twirled his cufflinks as he answered. "I said there's no harm in *looking*. I would strongly suggest against identifying anyone with complete certainty. After all, could you absolutely, positively, without a doubt, identify a person you met only a few times from a passport photo? As a matter of life and death?"

Mindy didn't reply.

"Discuss it with your attorney," Edward said.

Mindy nodded. "I got it."

"Good."

"There's still a chance someone else will be able to identify their suspect from photographs," Mindy added.

"We'll cross that bridge when we get to it," Edward said.

CHAPTER 62

EDWARD ENTERED THE lobby of his corporate apartment in Lexington, Kentucky, and smiled at the concierge. With a deft nod, the concierge drew Edward's attention in the direction of Agent Washington who was sitting on a sofa on the far side of the sliding glass front doors. Edward approached and Agent Washington stood.

"Long time no see, Edward."

"Three months and a week, give or take."

"You're counting? I'm flattered."

"Don't be. I think you were informed to contact my attorney before speaking with me."

"I'm not here on official business."

"I didn't know we had unofficial business."

"We do," Agent Washington said, reaching into her handbag and handing a Japanese newspaper to Edward.

"What's this?" he asked, his eyes running down the page.

"You tell me. You're the one who reads Japanese."

Edward took a second glance at the page and then looked up. "That's a page from the *Yomiuri Shimbun*, one of the largest newspapers in Japan."

Agent Washington pointed to a photograph on the bottom left corner of the page. The photo showed a four-car pileup on an elevated highway that cut through the heart of Tokyo. Fire leapt from the vehicles, the reflection of the flames visible in the windows of the high-rises on either side of the road.

"What's that article about?" she asked.

Edward didn't look down. "It's about a car crash on the freeway in downtown Tokyo. Four cars. Five dead. One survivor. A woman."

"And one Good Samaritan," Agent Washington added.

"Oh, you read Japanese?"

"No, Edward. I don't read Japanese. And it wasn't easy to get my hands on this article. For starters, it took a while to convince a judge we had enough probable cause for a warrant to gain access to your medical records."

"Why would you want to see my medical records?"

"Something a witness said to me in the course of our investigation. Someone I believe you referred to as the local drunk. Can't say I disagree with your assessment of him, by the way."

"What could a local drunk say that was so interesting it compelled you to look at my medical records?"

"He said you and he shared an unspoken brotherhood. He said you both had received serious burns in the past."

"Is that what he said?"

"He did."

"My burns are not a secret. And you can't believe someone who spends every night on the same barstool."

"Well, we did. And a warrant allowed us to access your medical records. Those medical records indicated the initial date and cause of your burns. A car accident in Tokyo. From there we requested assistance from the US Embassy in Tokyo. We had someone from the legal attaché office digging through old newspapers looking for a car accident that could have resulted in your injuries. They found the newspaper article in your hands. It took some effort."

"Sounds like you're expanding your expertise beyond Color of Law."

"I don't like being made a fool of. I called in a lot of favors and stepped on few toes. But it was worth it. We corroborated the information on your medical records in the US with data pulled from the Japanese National Healthcare system. You had a lengthy stay in a hospital in Japan before being transferred to back to the States."

"I did."

"And in an interesting twist, the hospital at the University of Tokyo, where you spent considerable time, shared records indicating your medical bills were paid in cash by an anonymous source."

"I heard it was."

"Do you know what the really intriguing part of this story is?"

Edward tried to remain focused as panic crept in. "Why don't you tell me?"

"The newspaper article mentions a Good Samaritan, a non-Japanese, who pulled a woman from a burning vehicle. And there the story ends. No further mention of the accident. In fact, you are never mentioned by name. Neither is the woman who was saved."

"Sounds like you have questions for the Japanese press."

"Is that all you have to say?

"If you don't like that answer, how about this one? Talk to my lawyer."

"You might want to hear me out. While the article didn't include any names, it did provide Japanese law enforcement with some useful information. The license plate of the vehicle the woman was riding in was visible in one of the photographs taken on the scene, though most of the vehicle was destroyed in the ensuing fire. Our investigation discovered that car was registered to a leasing company. At the time of the accident, that particular vehicle was being leased by a local construction company. According to the Japanese National Police, the construction company leasing the vehicle went out of business."

"Unfortunate."

"All was not lost. According to the Japanese National Police, that defunct construction company was a well-known front for Japanese organized crime. The Japanese mafia. Yakuza."

Edward swallowed as if a hot billiard ball was lodged in his throat.

"With that in mind, we had the legal attaché office in Tokyo coordinate the search of all admission records for all local hospitals for the night of the car accident. Do you know how many other people were admitted on that night with burns received in a car accident?"

"I don't."

"One. A woman named Emiko Fukuzawa. Turns out she is the daughter of a known yakuza crime boss. We then requested the legal attaché office in Tokyo to ask Japanese law enforcement for assistance. We wanted to ask

Ms. Fukuzawa a couple of questions. Do you know where that conversation led, Edward?"

Edward shook his head slowly.

"That conversation ended up nowhere. No one knows anything about the foreign Good Samaritan from the accident. No one has ever heard of you."

Edward remained stoic, his heart racing.

"Do you know what I think, Edward?"

"No."

"I think the woman you saved in that accident was your ticket to committing the perfect crime. I think when your wife died, and you ran into problems with Pervis Wade and the Lee County Sheriff's Department, you decided to call in a favor. A big favor in return for saving a woman with mob connections from a burning car."

"It's an interesting theory."

"It is. And this new theory has allowed the FBI to narrow our search of suspects. We are now going through all known associates of the Fukuzawa criminal enterprise. It's only a matter of time before we match a passport photo with a known yakuza member. Then we'll have one of our witnesses from the motel confirm we have our man. Once he has been identified and taken into custody by Japanese law enforcement, we will confirm that his fingerprints match those scanned by immigration. Then, Edward, with your accomplice implicated, I'm going to cut him the deal of the century. And you will be the trophy."

Edward's mind flashed back to the still-fresh memory of Shiro placing his hands and fingers on a scalding griddle. *Good luck matching fingerprints...*

"You're going to have to send an email and let me know how that goes. I'm moving back to Tokyo at the first of the month."

"I'm aware."

"It's been in the works for a while. So don't accuse me of running from the law."

Agent Washington shook her head. "There's no running from the FBI. Time is on our side. The FBI works cases that are decades old. Decades. And in your case, all we need is to identify one Japanese male. Matching photos. Matching fingerprints. This case will be closed."

"Good luck," Edward said.

"You're the one who got lucky, Edward."

Edward grimaced. "I lost my wife and unborn child. I didn't get lucky at all."

"Maybe you didn't," Agent Washington relented after pausing in what seemed like a moment of empathy. "I assume you heard the news about Sheriff Blazer and Detective Rafferty. They both took plea agreements that will keep them off death row. In addition to plea agreements, Detective Rafferty rolled on the sheriff. It was not unexpected. He's been cooperating with our federal investigation and has provided very important testimony. It looks like additional individuals within the Lee County Sheriff's Department will also face charges."

"I heard there was a plea agreement in the works. My lawyer called me. Personally, I'm hopeful the sheriff and detective get to enjoy some time with the general prison population."

"The plea agreements are better for everyone. They save us all from a lengthy and expensive trial. They also spare you from having to testify."

"And they spare the sheriff and detective from lethal injections."

"Possibly."

"I wouldn't have been sad to find out. To see it through."

"Oh, I'm sure about that. I know how you like your revenge."

"What's that supposed to mean?"

Agent Washington paused for effect. "In addition to providing you with the Japanese newspaper article, I came to Lexington because I wanted to share some information related to Detective Rafferty's testimony against Sheriff Blazer."

"And how does this concern me?"

"You may want to sit down."

"I'll stand."

"Very well. Detective Rafferty has been very forthcoming in the information he has provided to the FBI. He has admitted to involvement in the murder of Reggie Taylor. He also admitted to involvement in the cover-up of Charlie Sterling's death a decade ago. Furthermore, he admitted to assisting in the cover-up in the murder of your neighbor, Brent Poole."

"Among other crimes, I assume."

"Among myriad lesser charges, if that's what you'd call a parade of other felonies. But curiously enough, Detective Rafferty refused to acknowledge any wrongdoing in the investigation of your wife's death. In fact, his steadfast refusal to accept any culpability in clearing Pervis Wade of your wife's murder led us to reexamine your wife's case."

Edward stood at rapt attention.

"We went over your neighbor's original statement given to the police the day after your wife went missing. In that statement, your neighbor, Mr. Brent Poole, claimed to have seen someone fitting Pervis Wade's description leaving your house. The statement indicated that Mr. Poole was standing at the end of the driveway when he saw the last Palmetto Windows truck leave for the day."

"That's what he told me, too."

"And while he was able to give a detailed description of the truck and the driver, he was unable to provide any further information or offer the identity of the driver."

Edward shrugged his shoulders slightly. "Meaning?"

"Well, Brent Poole knew Pervis Wade. They interacted many times on a personal level. He also knew Pervis Wade worked at Palmetto Windows. There's no reason your neighbor would have had any difficulty identifying Pervis Wade on sight."

"Is that right?" Edward mumbled, his mind trying to process Agent Washington's surprise.

"Yes. With Detective Rafferty's guidance, we looked into Brent Poole's history and discovered he ran a successful mechanic's garage in town for over twenty years. Before he retired, his garage was located in a lot not too far from the train tracks. The establishment across the street was, and is, a little place called Palmetto Windows. As it turns out, Brent Poole held the contract to perform maintenance and repairs on all of Palmetto Windows' trucks. He had full access to the premises. He was also on a first name basis with most of the employees. He knew Pervis Wade. He spoke with Pervis Wade on a regular basis. In fact, Pervis Wade once stole a boat that was parked in the back lot of Brent Poole's garage. After Pervis stole the boat, the Lee County Sheriff's Department interceded on Pervis's behalf and all the potential charges related to the grand larceny of a fishing boat vanished. Suffice it to say, the two men had a history."

Edward sat down on the sofa in the waiting area.

"That piqued our curiosity, obviously. We then took a closer look at Brent Poole's background. It took some digging. And while your neighbor had a clean record, he was not without suspicion. As it turns out, Brent Poole was a person of interest in another missing person case. Twenty-six years ago, when Mr. Poole was living outside Meridian. A young mother who lived several hundred yards away from Brent Poole disappeared after leaving to go to the grocery store. She never made it home."

Edward's head swooned.

"Your neighbor was questioned but never charged. At the time, he owned a vehicle that was seen at the grocery store before the woman went missing. That vehicle was later found burned on the outskirts of town."

Edward shook his head. "I don't believe it…"

"I wish it weren't true. But that initial discovery drove us to look even further back in Brent Poole's life. Lo and behold, when he was nineteen, another woman went missing in Brent Poole's neighborhood. He was still living with his parents at the time. He was questioned but, once again, no charges were filed."

"If that's all true, then Mr. Poole tried to frame Pervis Wade for murder."

"That's right. He knew Pervis Wade. And he knew Pervis had a checkered past."

Edward seemed to fade from the conversation.

Agent Washington continued. "Brent Poole was very familiar with the trucks at Palmetto Windows and the lot where the trucks were parked. He could have even still been in possession of keys to the gate and the vehicles."

Edward shook his head.

"Based on that information, we requested your neighbor's cell phone records. On the night your wife disappeared, in the wee hours of the morning, Brent Poole's mobile phone pinged off a cell tower in downtown Tupelo, a mile from Palmetto Windows. An hour later, his phone pinged off a cell tower on Highway 278, not far from the field where the burned-out Palmetto Windows truck was later found. The evidence provides a strong indication that your neighbor tried to frame Pervis Wade for your wife's murder. And Pervis wasn't happy about being framed. When Detective Rafferty contacted Pervis Wade and told him that Brent Poole had identified him as a suspect in your wife's disappearance, Pervis claimed his innocence. Then he vowed revenge. Pervis Wade subsequently killed your neighbor and, according to Detective Rafferty, that murder was made to look like an accident. Also, according to Detective Rafferty, Pervis Wade extracted a full confession from your neighbor, including the location of your wife's body, before Mr. Poole was killed."

"You mean Pervis extracted a confession by parking a car on Mr. Poole's chest?"

"That's right. Pervis used his video tape leverage against the detective and sheriff to avoid prosecution for Brent Poole's demise."

"Jesus," Edward replied.

Agent Washington, still standing, looked down at Edward on the sofa. "I can see how a little religion probably wouldn't hurt at this point," she added.

Edward put his head into his hands and then leaned back on the sofa, eyes towards the ceiling.

"Keep in touch, Edward. Give me a call if there's anything you want to discuss."

CHAPTER 63

EDWARD EXITED THROUGH the automated doors of Fujita Automotive Headquarters in downtown Tokyo. He crossed the street, took two quick turns, and stepped into a standing ramen shop built between the steel supports for the elevated train tracks above. He shoved seven hundred yen into the vending machine and took his ticket to an empty spot at the counter. The cook deftly reached onto the counter, snatched the ticket, and yelled the order into the air. A minute later, Edward's lunch arrived in a bowl.

As the lunchtime feeding frenzy hit its peak, a line of businessmen filed into the ramen restaurant, standing shoulder to shoulder. Edward plucked the last bit of ginger floating near the bottom of the bowl and the man standing next to him at the counter reached for a shaker of seasoning. Leaning in close enough for Edward to smell his breath, the man spoke quickly in a whisper.

"Tonight. Be on the last car of the 9:58 Yamanote train heading towards Ueno from Ikebukuro."

Edward placed his chopsticks on the side of his bowl. "Excuse me?"

The man repeated the instructions and then added, "Don't be late. And bring what you need to bring."

Edward digested his orders as the man stuffed a dangling wad of noodles into his mouth and slurped mightily. Turning away, the man placed his largely uneaten lunch on the counter and exited into the midday sun.

Looking around at the faces in the crowd, Edward poured himself a glass of ice water from the plastic pitcher on the counter and took a sip. It was the second time he had been ambushed at lunch, the first coming at a bento restaurant several weeks prior. The first meeting had been slightly longer, as had been the associated details explaining what was required of him. None of it came as a surprise. He had known Fukuzawa would find him. It was only a matter of time. All debts had to be repaid.

*

On weeknights, the crowds thinned on the clockwise, northern section of the circular Yamanote train line departing from Ikebukuro. It was mostly a matter of geography as a large swath of the city was buffeted on the east side by Tokyo Bay, severely limiting real estate options. For the myriad trains heading west, Ikebukuro was the first stop in an endless string of suburbs and bedroom communities that stretched until the tracks disappeared into the mountains an hour west of Tokyo.

Edward stood on the platform and boarded the last car of the 9:58 train. A half-dozen passengers filled the fifty-foot car, bench seating hugging the walls on both sides. A group of high school students huddled near the end of the car. Two drunk businessmen stood facing each other, swaying with the rocking motion of the train, each man keeping a hand on the strap hanging from the ceiling, affixing themselves like inebriated pendulums. A well-dressed woman with a shopping bag at her feet punched a text message into her phone.

The train doors shut and Edward sat down on the soft blue bench, his back against the windows. As the train continued on its circular path, Edward watched the skyline of each station appear and then vanish into a blur of neon lights and high-rises. Over the next three stations, between the strobe of lights, most of the passengers exited the train, leaving Edward alone in the car with two other passengers.

The train's brakes squealed on its approach to Ueno station, and as the doors opened on the opposite side of the car, a man in a dark suit boarded. Edward immediately recognized the man with the long, death-defying scar on his neck as the man who had given him a ride from Fukuzawa's house and had checked him into a suite at the Ritz Carlton.

Edward and the man exchanged nods.

"Long time no see," Nagata said in Japanese.

A young man jumped onto the train as the doors shut and took a position next to Fukuzawa's veteran employee. Nagata glared at the young man and flicked his head in the direction of the empty end of the car. Suddenly aware of his surroundings and Nagata, the young man bowed and shuffled off, not stopping until he reached the next car on the train.

Nagata straightened his suit and sat next to Edward on the bench seat.

"I was expecting someone else," Edward said.

"I was sent because we've met. I know what you look like."

"You're not the only one."

Nagata nodded once. "Did you bring it?"

Edward reached into his pocket and removed a thumb drive. Nagata turned his palm upward as if ready to catch a falling object and Edward placed the thumb drive in the man's hand.

"Where's Shiro?"

"What do you care?"

"I just do."

Nagata laughed in a low rumble. "Fukuzawa said you would ask about him."

"And?"

"He's not around anymore."

"What does that mean?"

"He's gone."

"Alive or missing?"

"What does it matter?"

"It matters to me."

"He's dead," Nagata said.

"What happened?"

"He took his own life."

"How?"

Nagata ran his fist across his stomach as if he were cutting open his midsection.

"I don't believe you. No one disembowels themselves these days."

"You don't have to believe me."

"Did Fukuzawa kill him?"

"No."

"I don't believe you."

"Then it doesn't matter what I say."

"I would like to know the truth."

Edward locked eyes with Nagata, hoping for a reply.

"When it's time to die, it's time to die," Nagata offered.

The two men sat in silence for a long moment before Nagata averted his glance down to the thumb drive in his grasp. "Is everything on it as requested?"

"Yes. The blueprints and components of the entire Toyota lineup for the year after next."

"Good."

"What's your boss going to do with it?"

"Sell it to the competition. To all of the competitors. And maybe to all the parts manufacturers. Business is war. Companies will pay a lot of money to win a war."

The train slowed as it headed towards Tokyo Station.

"Fukuzawa wanted me to ask you a question."

"He did?"

"Yes. He wanted me to ask you if it was worth it?"

"What?"

"All that happened."

"It didn't go exactly as planned."

"Nothing ever does," Nagata said, standing from the bench seat.

"You might be right about that."

"Fukuzawa also has a message for you."

"What's that?"

"He said if the information on this thumb drive is what was agreed to, your debt is paid. You're free."

"Why?"

"He didn't say. But I think he still has a soft spot for you. You could probably even stop by for dinner."

"I don't know about that, but tell him I said thanks."

"I will."

Nagata turned towards the door as the train made its final approach.

"One more thing," Edward said.

"What?"

"The thumb drive is password protected."

"What's the password?"

"Tupelo," Edward replied.

CHAPTER 64

IN THE BLISTERING Alabama heat, Edward pulled the door open and stepped onto the old tile floor. A glass display case ran along the wall to his left, desserts and pies lining its shelves. A diner counter stretched the length of the restaurant. Booths lined the outer edge of the floor under a wall of windows facing the street.

"Welcome to Ted's," a woman in a light blue waitress's outfit said, turning towards the front door. The blonde waitress's complexion turned crimson and Edward forced a smile.

"How many?"

"Just one."

"Counter or booth?"

"Booth."

Edward followed Mindy to a booth away from foot traffic to the register and toilet. She placed a laminated menu on the table and Edward grabbed it with both hands while looking up.

"I thought you were in Japan."

"I am. I'm just visiting. I'm only here for a couple of weeks."

"How did you find me?"

"I asked my lawyer to ask your lawyer. When did you move?"

"The beginning of the year."

"And you've taken up legitimate employment. That's good."

"Ted's Café has been around forever. It's an institution."

"Are you from Alabama?"

"No. But my fiancé is. Ted was my fiancé's great-uncle, apparently. So I'm sort of working in the family business."

"You're engaged?" Edward asked.

"Yes. He proposed a couple months back," Mindy said, dropping her left hand to the table so that Edward could see the gold band with a small pear-shaped diamond.

"Congratulations. I assume I don't know the guy."

"You don't. But you know *of* him."

"How's that?"

"He used to be a client. Owned a couple of tow trucks in Tupelo."

"I'll be damned."

"At least I know I can trust him."

"That's for sure."

"I know it's all happened kind of fast, but we're going to make a run at it."

"That's super."

The conversation lagged, and Mindy eyed her other customers to see if anyone needed service.

"Do you want coffee?"

"Yes. Black, please. And a breakfast platter. Eggs over easy."

"Coming right up."

Mindy scribbled on her order pad, walked across the diner, and slapped the order on the counter near the cook station. She rounded the restaurant floor, filling customers' cups with fresh coffee, and landed back at Edward's table with a mug in hand.

"Any word from our FBI friends in Jackson?" Edward asked.

"I've seen them twice since I moved to Birmingham. They've stayed in touch with my attorney."

"Your attorney said you're paying your own legal fees now."

"That's right."

"Does the FBI have you going through any more photographs?"

"Not for a while now, but they said they'd be back."

"I don't think it matters anymore," Edward muttered.

"What does that mean?"

Edward swallowed hard. "There's no good way to tell you so I'm just going to say it. Taro's dead. He passed away earlier this year."

"How?"

"He may have taken his own life, but it's hard to know if that's what really happened."

"How did you find out?"

"A coworker of his told me."

"A coworker?"

"Yes."

"Someone in the yakuza?"

"Yes."

"Do you think they killed him because of everything that happened?"

"I asked the same question. I don't think so. But they live by a different code. We'll probably never know for sure."

Mindy wiped a tear from her eye. "Well, that sucks."

"It does."

"I need a minute," she said, taking the coffee pot back to the counter.

*

The breakfast special arrived on three separate plates with a side bowl of grits. Mindy arranged the dishes across the table and filled Edward's coffee mug to the top.

"I'm sorry for everything," Edward said.

"Me, too."

"If there's a bright side, you don't have to keep looking over your shoulder. Crimes are hard to prove without a suspect."

"I don't think there's a bright side to any of it," Mindy retorted.

"You found a trustworthy guy."

"I'd like to think I would have found one anyway. It's been a long time coming. I'm in my mid-thirties and I feel like my life is just starting."

"Mid-thirties is still young."

"That depends on how long you plan to live," Mindy replied. "You know, I've been wondering about something."

"Yeah? What's that?"

"Do you remember you almost told me Taro's real name and I didn't want to know it?"

"I remember."

"I changed my mind. I want to know."

"His real name was Shiro."

"Shiro? Does that have any meaning in Japanese?"

"It usually means castle, but it depends on the characters used to write the name."

Mindy rolled the name across her tongue a few times. "I like Taro better."

"We can call him Taro."

"Do me a favor, Edward."

"Anything."

"Don't forget him. Raise a toast to him from time to time."

"I will."

"And make sure he didn't die for nothing."

Edward felt a fresh wave of guilt wash over him.

Mindy watched through the window as a garbage truck rolled down Main Street. Then she wiped a final tear off her cheek. "Don't take this the wrong way, but I think this is goodbye, Edward," she said. She reached down, squeezed Edward's shoulder, and placed the check on the corner of the old table. Before he could reply, Mindy turned, shuffled across the old tile floor, and disappeared into the kitchen.

CHAPTER 65

HAKUSAN, THIRTY MILES south of Kanazawa, was four hours from Tokyo on the opposite coast. Situated near the confluence of two major highways, the seaside location offered a nice balance between fresh air and exhaust fumes, the latter a necessary evil for a successful car repair shop.

Shiro shut the hood of the four-door sedan with a resounding thud and stepped into the small office in the corner of the one-man automotive garage. He calculated the bill for the work he had just completed as his last customer of the day sat in a worn chair in the waiting area, watching the news on a wall-mounted TV. Shiro delivered the bill to the customer, who paid cash, offering payment with both hands and a bow. Shiro returned with the customer's change and the man's car keys. Then he formally presented his customer a business card that identified Shiro's new name as Junichi Sekine, president and owner of Sekine Automotive Repairs.

As the customer pulled out of the shop and into traffic, Shiro yanked downward on a thick metal chain that ran to the ceiling above. The large metal bay door slowly lowered to the ground and Shiro secured the door firmly in place with a massive lock. He peeled off his overalls and hung them on a hook near a sink on the side of the shop. Standing in an old pair of shorts and a sweaty T-shirt, he thoroughly washed his hands, the cold water running over his scars.

Minutes later, Shiro turned off the lights, stepped onto the sidewalk, and locked the office door. He rattled the handle to confirm the office was secure and looked up at the sign on the building that matched the name on his business card. Several paces from his office, Shiro turned the corner of the building and began climbing the stairs that led upward to an apartment over the garage. He could smell salmon grilling, his mouth watering at the prospect of dinner. Pulling open the door to the apartment, he removed his shoes in the foyer.

He heard his daughter's footsteps before she appeared in the short hall and burst into a run directly into his arms. Shiro picked his daughter up in his hands, spun her around once, and returned her to the floor.

"I need to change," he said, walking towards the kitchen.

His wife welcomed him home with a standard Japanese greeting and informed him dinner was almost ready. He passed through the living room and paused in front of the sliding glass doors leading to the balcony on the back of the building. In the narrow gap between two neighboring build-ings, he eyed a sliver of the ocean in the distance, the water sparking in the dipping sun. He changed his shirt in his bedroom and headed back to the kitchen at his wife's beckoning.

*

Shiro followed dinner with a cold glass of sake in the living room while his wife ran their seven-year-old daughter through her bedtime routine. An hour later, his wife appeared in the living room in a matching pajama top and bottoms.

"Do you need anything else?" she asked.

"No."

"Okay. I'm tired. I'm going to bed."

"I may go for a drive," Shiro said, turning his eyes towards the clock on the wall.

"Don't stay out too late."

"I won't," Shiro replied.

With his wife snoring quietly in the bedroom, Shiro turned off the TV and removed his car keys from a hook on the wall near the front door. He quietly descended the staircase to the street and walked around the corner of the property to the small parking space at the rear of the garage. Behind the wheel, he drove through a maze of residential streets, crossed under the elevated highway, and turned into a fenced property with several warehouses lined end to end.

He pulled his car into the last parking spot, next to a lineup of familiar cars. He exited the vehicle, rounded the front of the car, and knocked on a gray door under a rusting exterior staircase. Seconds later the door opened and Shiro bowed. A man in a suit returned the bow and led Shiro into a smoke-filled room. A half-dozen poker regulars sat around a large table, pushing chips and peeking under the corner of their cards. Hands with missing fingers caressed glasses of expensive whiskey.

"What are you drinking?" the man-in-charge asked.

"Sake. Cold."

"Not a problem."

"What's the game tonight?" Shiro asked as the man opened a refrigerator in the corner and removed a chilled bottle of sake.

"Texas Hold 'Em. But we were thinking about doing a Cho-han game. Word is that you know something about it."

"I may."

"You want to give it a try?"

"I can, but tradition dictates the proctor of the Cho-han game gets a cut of the action."

"Just this once," the man replied, delivering his customer's drink.

"Kanpai," Shiro said, raising the glass and swallowing half the contents in one gulp. "Let's play."

AUTHOR'S NOTE

SPOILER ALERT!!!

The passage below contains spoilers for *Out of Tupelo*:

When someone asks where I get an idea for a book, my usual honest answer is, "I don't know." With *Out of Tupelo*, however, this isn't the case. Unlike most of my other books, the general concept for *Out of Tupelo* was derived from a combination of real-world experiences.

The first influence for the book pertains to the main character, Edward Winston, who was loosely based on a good friend of mine. Much like Edward, my friend is an American who previously lived in Japan, speaks fluent Japanese, and once worked for a Japanese automobile parts manufacturer in the US.

The second relevant component for the *Out of Tupelo* storyline was triggered by an article I saw in *The Guardian* about a Japanese woman who makes artificial fingers for Japanese mafia members who are hoping to change careers. I have a vague recollection of other stories covering the same topic, but the article in *The Guardian* was the one I remember most clearly.

The final piece of the puzzle for *Out of Tupelo* fell into place as a result of a personal experience. During the 1990s, I lived in Japan on three separate occasions for nearly six years in total. I spent much of my time in Western Japan, some of it in a former coal-mining region well known for its large mafia population. It was during this period that I became acquainted with a senior Japanese mafia member who frequented the same *izakaya* that I did. One night, after several rounds of drinks, a conversation with the man turned into an interesting multicultural Q&A about drugs, gambling, and prostitution. At the end of the conversation, the man asked for his check and then nonchalantly informed me that if I ever needed anyone killed, he could do it for 200,000 yen. The man has since passed away, but at that moment a story was born. It just took me twenty years to write it.

www.ingramcontent.com/pod-product-compliance
Lightning Source LLC
Chambersburg PA
CBHW030649120726
47905CB00001B/135